SHREWD OPERATOR

■

Though most people didn't realize it, Evelyn Wade was an old lady, three months shy of seventy-three. Evelyn could feel the age. But her mind — that was what counted. Her mind was as sharp as ever.

What had she really heard? The relaxed voice of a young boy, relaxed until he said "body shop." Why would that make him nervous? Because he said something he didn't mean to say. He could have been someplace he shouldn't have been. Or he could have been revealing something he shouldn't. Evelyn pushed the blanket to her feet and slid up a little in the chair. At first, the boy sounded as if he were alone, she thought. Then something changed.

Something was wrong, definitely wrong.

■ ■ ■ ■

LONG LINES

LONG LINES

A Novel of Suspense

REMAR SUTTON

THE MYSTERIOUS PRESS

New York • London • Tokyo • Sweden

MYSTERIOUS PRESS EDITION

This Mysterious Press Edition is published by arrangement with
Weidenfeld & Nicolson, 10 East 53rd Street, New York, NY 10022

Cover design by Barbara Buck
Cover illustration by Doug Henry

Mysterious Press books are published in association with
Warner Books, Inc.
666 Fifth Avenue
New York, N.Y. 10103
A Warner Communications Company

Printed in the United States of America

First Mysterious Press Printing: May, 1989

10 9 8 7 6 5 4 3 2 1

To 603, *and the Evelyn there*

Kristy, may you
never dial into
disaster...

Susan Suits
10-24-89

LONG LINES

1

I

EXCEPT for the "panic mode" at American Opinion Research, Evelyn Wade wouldn't have worked that night. She seldom worked nights because after ten P.M. the crosstown bus didn't run again until midnight. It wasn't fear that prevented her from walking the three blocks from Peachtree Street down Tenth to Myrtle. Though midtown Atlanta—and in particular the blocks westward from Myrtle to Peachtree—no longer housed what Evelyn called "my kind of people," it was certainly more stable and respectable than its previous incarnation as Haight East.

It wasn't the neighborhood, then, but rather her hip that kept Evelyn home at night. After she fell, her doctor referred to her right hip as an "eight-year replacement." The average person walking an average distance each day could feel confident that the steel ball that fit in the Teflon-lined hip socket would allow customary walking for eight years before the ball wore the socket thin. Then the socket would need replacing. Evelyn thought of that often in this seventh year, steps adding up like the meter of a cab. She thought of it that night too, but she said yes anyway when the supervisor at American Opinion Research asked her to work. "Evelyn, we really need you tonight," she'd said. "Coke presented Pete with a panic mode this morning, and even Dallas and Chicago are going on line with the study."

Now Evelyn was sitting at a small partitioned booth made of pegboard-type material, one of perhaps twenty such booths in a large bay. Like the other operators, she was dialing the numbers that appeared on the computer screen in front of her. The random numbers were fed from "Martha," AOR's main computer in Dallas.

Evelyn Wade had called thousands of strangers around the country during the past four years. She had asked their opinions on everything from soft drinks to girdles, carefully typing their responses on the Hazeltine keyboard that fed them to her screen and simultaneously to Martha in Dallas.

It was ten o'clock. Evelyn massaged the skin on her neck, then pressed "/1" on the keyboard. Martha's electronic finger drew a short line of numbers from left to right across the screen, 312-211-6801, skipped a space and dropped a respondent number, 267, to identify the questionnaire.

She dialed and began to count the rings. Long-distance telepathy, she called it. The number of rings would determine the productiveness of the call. If someone answered on the first ring, it would be a bad call, someone asleep by the phone and not the least interested in anonymous older voices. If someone answered on the second or third ring, especially if that person answered with a bright "hello" rather than a "yes," it would be a good call. Five rings and she would hang up. Five rings meant no one was at home, or it could mean that people were home but busy. Every operator had funny stories about those calls. "You would be surprised what you can see over a phone after the fifth ring," Evelyn would tell friends.

At the very beginning of the fifth ring, before Evelyn could hang up, 312-211-6801 answered. A young boy spoke with a strong, determined voice. Without waiting for more than a hello, Evelyn lightly touched "/2" and began to recite the words of question 1, her eyes on the screen but the words coming from memory.

"Hello, I'm Evelyn with American Opinion Research, an independent consumer research company, calling long distance from Dallas, Texas. . . ."

Dallas, Texas, was, of course, a falsehood. The headquarters of AOR *was* located in Dallas, and the Chicago and Atlanta offices had always instructed their operators to locate their calls there, too, when doing soft-drink studies. The Atlanta office believed this had something to do with Coca-Cola's being in Atlanta; no one knew for sure.

Evelyn continued to recite, "We are making a survey on carbonated soft drinks and would like to include you or someone in your home among the people across the country who get to express their views on carbonated soft drinks. May I speak to a person in your family who drinks carbonated soft drinks?"

The first words from the other end were always the most important. Evelyn took them like pieces of a puzzle and shoved them together quickly to make a picture. She looked at the screen, listening to silence for a moment and then a laugh.

"Lady, you don't have no home, but you do have the number-one pop junkie in Chicago—I'm working on my sixth root beer right now! This is a body shop. . . ." The boy's voice paused, then added quickly, ". . . of sorts." The words trailed off tentatively, as if they should be drawn back. He laughed again, forcing a little to cover up the hesitation.

Evelyn made a judgment call. The boy wasn't at home, as AOR policy required, but he had a home somewhere. She could get that number at the end of the survey. And she liked talking to kids.

"Are you or any member of your immediate family employed by any of the following companies: advertising agency, market research company, food processor, or soft-drink bottler/manufacturer?"

"Nope."

Evelyn wanted to bend the rules. Every question was always to be asked verbatim, every answer taken down verbatim. But the next question—"Are you thirteen years of age or older?"—always caused problems for young men, a taunt at their manhood. She asked it anyway. His feathers rose.

"Lady—just ask my girl that!"

His answer had brought a slight smile. "Generally, how many times a day or week would you say you drink a carbonated soft drink around this time of year?"

"Well . . . let me see, I think abou—"

Until that moment Evelyn's eyes had been softly unfocused, the natural habit of someone who must concentrate on hearing an unseen speaker. But at the abrupt break in the young man's voice she looked at the screen, not at any words there but at the screen itself, as if concentration would make it show the uncomfortable images that formed in her mind. Silence, a millisecond of silence, was followed by a brittle "*No!*" It was not an order but a plea. She heard a single, hard pop, and then the hollow sound of the receiver banging.

"Hello? Hello?" Evelyn heard the banging of the phone again, and then she heard fast and deep breathing. Someone had picked up the phone.

"Hello? Young man, are you all right?"

"Yes."

It wasn't the voice of the boy. Evelyn hesitated. Then the voice, a man's, continued.

"What do you want?"

Her response was an involuntary one, company policy, words evoked again and again on soft-drink surveys.

"This is Evelyn with American Opinion Research in Dallas, Texas. I was speaking with a young man. Could I speak to him again, please?"

The man said nothing. And then she heard a strange sound, something at a distance from the phone, something solid tapping insistently against something solid.

"Is everything okay there?"

" . . . Lady, we had a shelf fall. Now who are you?" The voice was rushed, distracted, nearly as staccato as the tapping. Evelyn leaned

6

forward in her chair as she repeated the words. "This is Evelyn with American Opinion Research in Dallas. May I speak to the boy again, please?"

In the silence following her words other sounds took command, pulling her consciousness back to her surroundings. All the voices had abruptly stopped their long-distance droning. Chairs pushed back from cubicles, people stood up.

Martha had crashed. Something down the lines, deep inside the computer, had turned off. The screens of the Hazeltines were blank. The WATS lines tying each operator to an interview were dead. Evelyn sat still, watching.

"Okay, everybody, be quiet for a minute and listen to me," Teresa Whitmore yelled, raising one hand in a shushing sign as she lifted the telephone handset that tied Atlanta AOR to Dallas AOR.

"Okay, now . . . everyone get a problem report and fill it out. I'm trying to find out what happened."

Evelyn remained still for a moment, then took the sheet titled "Exception and Problem Report" from the shelf above the screen. She listed the time and her employee number, then put a "3" at the question that asked, "At what number did the problem occur?" She thought for a moment before answering the next question, "What was the nature of your problem?" Then wrote, "Computer and phone lines went dead during a physical disturbance at the responding number." As she wrote, the supervisor came up beside her chair.

"Evelyn?"

She looked up, her pale blue eyes instantly meeting those of the young woman. "Teresa? I'm finished with the form. Do you know what we're doing yet?"

Teresa smiled and shrugged her shoulders. "Nothing more tonight." Teresa leaned in and took Evelyn's sheet. "I'll take this up for you. Then we're going home, and I'm going close to your place. Do you want a ride?"

Evelyn pushed herself up from the chair, her right hand going to a cane after she rose. "Teresa, I just had the oddest phone call. Why does Martha always go ga-ga during the interesting ones?" She paused. "I think something was wrong there."

"Like what?"

"I don't know. It was a young boy, a spunky but nice one. He fell." She looked away, the feeling of the phone call pulling her away from the bay. "He fell. Or something. A man said the shelf fell."

"Maybe *that's* what happened to Martha. Someone knocked a shelf on it!" Teresa said. "Evelyn, let's get out of here. Louise is going to close the place up."

Forty minutes later, Evelyn was sitting in the living room at 91 Myrtle watching the late news and sipping a cup of tea. Her cane was resting on the side of her chair, one of two matching light tan chairs. The other chair had been Grady Wade's. Though he had died four years before, the living room still contained his presence. He had designed and built the fieldstone fireplace from stones brought in many trips from the Wades' old farm in Marietta. Grady had also paneled the white pine walls, long covered with pictures of trips, children, and friends. Even the old clock on the mantel was a reminder of him. It said 6:25, as it had since his death.

Evelyn was wearing a dark green night robe, her feet in furry slippers and a light plaid blanket over her knees. She was looking at the television screen, but her attention kept drifting back to the call. You don't yell "No!" like that when a shelf falls, she thought as she turned the sound over again in her mind.

Though most people didn't realize it, Evelyn Wade was an old lady, three months shy of seventy-three. Her hair was still jet-black, but her skin had lost its tone, thin layers of flesh gathering around the base of her neck and settling slightly along the jawbone. She was shorter, too, five foot four, old bone compacting onto old cartilage in her spinal column. Evelyn could feel the age. But her mind—that was what counted. Her mind was as sharp as ever.

What had she really heard? The relaxed voice of a young boy, relaxed until he said "body shop." Why would that make him nervous? Because he said something he didn't mean to say. He could have been someplace he shouldn't have been. Or he could have been revealing something he shouldn't. Evelyn pushed the blanket to her feet and slid up a little in the chair. At first, the boy sounded as if he were alone, she thought. Then something changed.

She shook her head as she used both hands to push up from the chair, then steadied herself by touching the wall. You just don't yell like that when a shelf falls. She walked from the room, her hand turning off the light switch with a casual brush against the wall. And then there were the noises—the phone banging and the other sound, the tapping. And what was the sound before the tapping? A pop, nearly; flat surfaces coming together abruptly, but soft surfaces, not hard.

Evelyn settled into bed on her left side, on her good hip, on Grady's side of the bed. She thought of the man's voice. He was distracted, short of breath. She had heard no exchange with the boy. If the man had said anything to the boy, she would have heard it.

She shifted slightly, then reached to the nightstand and picked up a satin cap, placing it carefully over her hair. Evelyn turned off the light. Something was wrong, definitely wrong.

II

The loudness of the ringing startled him—Bobby Medlock usually answered the phone on the wall outside the office. But tonight he was in the private office itself, where he really shouldn't be. He had entered the office on a dare, like a challenge any kid might take to enter an old deserted house or a graveyard. "You ain't got the balls, Medlock," the other mules had said. As the most trusted "mule" of the Anton Vicovari outfit, Bobby had dropped just-stolen cars at Central Body Shop many times, usually pulling them quickly into the bays where mechanics waited to chop them into parts.

But occasionally, like tonight, he had brought special cars there when the building was empty, opening the gate and large back bay doors by himself. All mules stole cars—the outfit employed dozens of kids—but only Bobby got to do the special work. He was proud of the trust. So proud that until the dare he had never entered the private office. Opening the file cabinet and sneaking a look was an afterthought—innocent curiosity. He had just tugged a bulky printout from the drawer when the phone rang. He figured it was Angie Weiner. After most special pickups, he would wait for a call from his friend and boss. Now Bobby was sitting in a green metal chair next to the desk, the printout on his lap. He was enjoying the conversation with the old lady. Bobby Medlock had never had anyone pay much attention to his opinions. An empty can of Hires root beer was sitting on the desk. Bobby's heels rested on the floor, legs stretched out in front of him.

As he entered the room, Rick Kanell did not notice the legs, however. It was the sight of the printout that set off the explosion. Bobby Medlock saw the violence before feeling it, a fist arching upward, the knuckles colliding with the chin, pushing the head back and to the side. Bobby's hands dropped limp. The phone dropped against the side of the desk.

Kanell stood rigid for a moment, his gaze fixed on the boy. What had they taught him in the service? "They don't stay alive if you hit them between three and five." The kid was dead. He had died the moment he was hit. All voluntary movement ceased but the traumatic reaction of still-living muscles began instantly—arms and legs went rigid, toes awkwardly turned inward, backs of hands pushed against legs, slapping them.

Kanell began to sweat as he watched the seizures. *Why the hell was the kid there?* Was he the mole? The goddamn kid had to be the mole. Kanell lifted his eyes to the phone receiver. Who the hell was the kid talking to? The receiver dangled by the side of the desk. He hesitated, then picked it up quickly. He was breathing hard as he listened.

"Hello? Young man, are you all right?" The voice of an old lady. Why the hell was he talking to an old lady? Kanell's eyes darted to Bobby Medlock's body as it began to shake violently, the mouth open, eyes staring.

"Yes. What do you want?"

"This is Evelyn with American Opinion Research in Dallas, Texas. I was speaking with a young man. Could I speak to him again, please?"

As she spoke, Medlock's chair began to vibrate a rat-tat-tat. His body tumbled to the floor, quivering. Rick Kanell looked at it. How old was the memory? He was standing, looking up at his mother; her hand was wrapped around the head of a flailing chicken. The head popped off with a swing of her arm and a flick of her wrist, like the casting of a fishing rod. The chicken's body was quieter, Kanell thought, only raising dust from the flapping of wings against the soil.

"Is everything okay there?"

Kanell's mind went back to the phone. Who was the kid talking to? "Lady, we had a shelf fall. Now who are you?"

"This is Evelyn with American Opinion Research in Dallas. May I speak to the boy again, please?"

The phone went dead.

Without looking down Kanell stepped over the body and sat at the desk. He needed to be calm, to think. He took a small, dark brown bottle from his right pocket, opened it, and grasped the small spoon attached to the cap. His hands shook slightly as he sucked in a spoonful of fine white powder in each nostril. The Vicovari outfit of Chicago did not deal in cocaine. Anton Vicovari preferred activities that elicited minimum interest from the general population and from law enforcers who took their cues from the public. Like car theft and pornography.

But Rick Kanell loved the fine white powder, and he used his position in the Vicovari outfit to acquire the purest cocaine for the lowest price.

Kanell was the most important "front" for many of the outfit's illegal business operations and all of their legitimate enterprises. His business acumen and relationships with the Chicago business community gave him a special—and distanced—role with Anton Vicovari. Very few people, including the police, knew Rick Kanell was one of Vicovari's key men.

Women thought Kanell had to be a model. He was thirty-two. A permanent tan, the product of sun lamps in the sauna next to his bedroom, jet-black hair cut to display a muscular neck and smooth, angled face, and tailored clothes that set off his well-proportioned six-foot frame confirmed Kanell's image as a self-assured hunk, and he liked to hear any woman say so.

The toot was his only friend, though.

He put the bottle in his pocket. He looked at the body. It smelled of urine. For a moment, Rick Kanell thought of calling someone to dispose of the body. The death would be easy to explain: "I caught the kid in the private office reading the printout. . . . " For many months, the outfit had been plagued with unexplained raids and information leaks, which seemed to point to an informant in the organization. The printout, prepared by Kanell, was one of the few documents that might tie Kanell to the outfit.

It was the only reason he had come to Central Body Shop. Kanell was invisible and he wanted to remain that way, more for his sake than the sake of the outfit. Removing the first three pages of the printout, the coding pages, would make it virtually impossible for anyone to tie him to criminal activity.

Kanell began to breathe through his mouth. The smell reminded him unpleasantly of bus stations and of outhouses behind wood shacks on dirt roads; things far in the past.

His eyes went to the printout. It was on the floor, pages pushed out like the bellows of an accordion. As he looked at it, glancing once more to the kid's smooth-skinned, muscular body, the most likely explanation for the kid's presence in the office came to mind: the kid could have been there for Angie Weiner. The thought made him flush slightly. Goddamn Weiner. Angie Weiner ran the mules for the outfit, all of them pretty boys to fit his fancy. He was the one person in the Vicovari outfit who would love to have something on *me*, Kanell thought, and Weiner knows what the printouts could do.

Rick Kanell closed his eyes. He would dispose of Bobby Medlock's body himself. If the kid were there for Weiner—to get something to hurt Kanell—so what? If the kid *weren't* there for Weiner, it didn't matter, either. Whatever the reason for his death, asking the outfit to dispose of a punk kid's body might be a small favor, forgotten except for the favor. But Weiner would know. And Vicovari would know. Favors were never forgotten. The thought made Kanell's flesh hot. Favors bound you to the outfit.

Kanell walked from the small office, walked through the large bay, opened the metal door next to the far wall, then unlocked the back gate. His car was sitting next to the car driven by the kid. *There would be no favors.* He sat in the driver's seat, reached in his pocket and retrieved a silver pen, then paused, rubbing a finger under his nose, the knuckle blocking first one nostril, then the other, as he sucked in. Kanell wrote "American Opinion Research, Dallas, Evelyn" on the back of an envelope and slipped it into his shirt pocket. He pulled his car through the back gate up to the large bay next to the steel door. The security light by the door was too bright, and he turned it off. He walked back to Bobby Medlock's car. The lock on the passenger's door was no longer there, pulled out with a "slammer." The lock on the steering mechanism was no longer there, either, but lay on the seat next to four empty root beer cans. Kanell cursed. Only mules knew how to pull locks like that. The guy *was* here for Angie. He parked the car to the right of his.

An obsessive attention to detail began to rule his movements. He returned to his car and pulled on a pair of leather driving gloves lying on the seat, then walked through the steel door again to a pile of worn, dirty work clothes, which he eyed with distaste. Kanell seldom wore anything dirty. He tugged the paint-splattered rubber boots over his shoes. The canvas overalls hung loosely when Kanell put them on. He walked back to the car. From the trunk he removed a wool cap and pulled it carefully over his hair.

He whistled softly as he carefully straightened the room. Stepping over Bobby Medlock's body, he placed the chair in its normal resting place, then picked up the printout. The pages that had touched the floor had a faint patina of dirt. He blew on them, then removed the first three pages before placing the printout in the top drawer of the file cabinet.

Bobby Medlock's body now lay totally still, and a small pool of urine had formed next to him. Before placing the body in a large, thick paper bag with "Clupak" printed on both sides, used ordinarily for metal filings, Kanell looked at Medlock's chin and neck. He avoided the open eyes. Although he could see no marks on the face, he imagined them. He walked to the paint room and found a coarse steel-wool pad. Kanell rubbed the neck and chin briskly and placed the pad, along with the body, two empty Hires root beer cans, and a urine-stained cloth, in the Clupak bag.

He spent thirty minutes rubbing every surface that might contain a fingerprint, including, finally, the phone. The goddamn phone. Kanell placed the Clupak bag in the trunk of the car Medlock had been driving, a Jensen Esprit, then drove the car a block from Central Body Shop. He then drove his own car several blocks, parked it in the lot of cars next to a sign that said "All-Night Bowling," and walked back to the Jensen. At ten twenty at night Central Time, he turned the Jensen north on U.S. 41 until he picked up Interstate 94 for the drive across Wisconsin to Minnesota.

III

Angie Weiner was sitting in the end booth of Keegan's restaurant less than two hundred feet from the corner of Chicago's Linton Avenue. A pitcher of iced tea, beads of condensation slipping down the side, was in front of him. Weiner was a fat man, too fat, but he was also a quiet, neat dresser. Normally a person wouldn't be aware of how thick he was. But when he pulled in his neck to swallow the tea, almost a reflex action like that of a snapping turtle, the rolls of fat wrapped around his midsection and upper body seemed to climb up, edge out the shirt collar, then fall back on themselves, slabs of skin over fat.

Weiner placed the glass on the table and looked around the room, his face expressionless, eyes stopping first at the red counter stools, two patched with silver tape, then at the calendars that lined the wall behind the counter. All of the calendars, except for the one for the current year, were turned to January and displayed in color the sexiest Chevrolets from the past sixteen years. Along the center of the wall below the calendars, on a narrow unpainted shelf, rolled a parade of Corvettes from those same years.

Weiner looked at his watch. It was after eleven. A cleanup boy glanced in his direction, his glance fleeting and, he hoped, unnoticed. Not many people in the neighborhood of Keegan's knew for sure what Angie Weiner did for a living, but virtually all of them knew not to ask. Weiner looked at his watch again. Bobby Medlock had not answered the phone at Central Body Shop. He was now very late at their backup meeting place. Where was the damned kid? Weiner had been waiting for Medlock to deliver a steamer to him, an exotic sports car. Most steamers were stolen on order and shipped to other countries, since their rarity made them very hard to resell in the States. But this car, a Jensen Esprit, was to be a special gift from Weiner's boss, Anton Vicovari, to the head of an outfit in Mexico City.

Angie Weiner was the personnel manager, of sorts, for two of Anton Vicovari's enterprises in the Chicago area and in Texas. He was responsible for the kids who muled, supplied the stolen cars that made the Vicovari outfit a power in Chicago's professional car-theft hierarchy. Weiner oversaw all the Vicovari automobile enterprises. He also supervised the outfit's pornographic film and bookstore operations. Part of the Vicovari outfit for nearly twenty-four years, Weiner had seen it change from a small-time operation concerned with block control to the most powerful and sophisticated outfit in Chicago.

He had seen Anton Vicovari grow from an insignificant person to a man whose friends included legitimate powerbrokers across the country. Angie Weiner was the oldest link to the beginnings of the outfit. He believed Anton appreciated that. Seniority, even in the organized-crime families of Chicago, had its benefits. For Angie Weiner that meant direct access to power.

He looked at his watch for the third time and poured another glass of tea. He pulled a pen from his pocket and began to doodle, eventually printing the letters "RK," then crossing them out with hard-pressed black lines. Angie Weiner had never liked Rick Kanell. One of the reasons was the normal jealousy felt in any organization by the senior man when the junior seems to have the boss's ear more intimately. Another reason was Kanell's independence. It did not matter to Angie Weiner that Kanell's position as business manager of the outfit's legitimate enterprises dictated some degree of independence. To Weiner, and now even Vicovari himself, that independence was becoming a threat.

It did not matter either that Kanell's seemingly magical ability to launder money was critical to the outfit. In Weiner's eyes, Rick Kanell was a simple number pusher, a punk southern hick who thought he was in the big time just because Vicovari took an interest in him. No, what disgusted Weiner was Kanell's relationship with the man. Paradoxically, it gave him pleasure too. Angie Weiner looked for opportunities to remind Anton Vicovari that outsiders always betrayed. He collected examples that confirmed this the way others collected rare coins, always on the lookout for the one coin that could complete the collection.

Again he looked at his watch, then stood up and walked to the old black telephone on the far end of the counter. He dialed Bobby Medlock's number. The cleanup boy glanced once again at Weiner, pulled out a cigarette, waved it at him, then stepped out the restaurant door. Weiner was alone in the restaurant when the phone call was answered.

"Yeah?" answered Tony Medlock.

"Tony, where the hell's your goddamn brother?"

"Angie! I don't know where he is, he went out about five. Was he doin' somethin' for you? I coulda done better, you know."

Tony Medlock was a cocky kid. Weiner smiled. The younger kids always made the best mules. They would steal cars for the excitement as much as for the thirty dollars. Virtually all of those cars were brought to Central Body Shop, too. Within two hours of their delivery, cars would be completely disassembled, their numbered parts abandoned in "dumps," deserted buildings located in Chicago's seamier neighborhoods. Some of the unnumbered parts were sold or bartered to other outfits. Many others were sold to legitimate shops around the country. But the most popular parts remained at

Central Body Shop. Central Body Shop *was* a legitimate body shop, one of the largest in Illinois, but it was also the nerve center for the outfit's operations. Few people complained about the quality of their body work, and none suspected that their shiny new fenders, shocks, or windshields were stolen.

But only the Jensen Esprit occupied Angie Weiner's thoughts at the moment. He glanced at the door.

"Tony, your damn brother was making a special pickup. He's a couple of hours late. Tell that sweet ass I'm pissed, and he'd better call me tonight."

"Angie—was he getting a steamer?"

"So?"

"I'll bet he's driving around, Angie; I bet Bobby's a hot rooster tonight!"

Weiner hung up the phone and walked out the door of the diner to his car. He began to drive, watching for an exotic sports car, a Jensen parked along the street or in the alleys of the Medlocks' neighborhood. The car was not there. At twelve fifteen Angie Weiner parked his car in a space less than a block from his own apartment and walked up the single flight of stairs that led to 2E. He entered and walked to the bedroom closet and hung his coat next to three other coats, making sure that the distance between hangers was equal. He placed his shoes, shoe trees in each, in the front row of shoes in the closet. The line of shoes looked as straight as the best platoon's line during inspection at Camp Lejeune.

Weiner went to the refrigerator. The shelves were clean, spotless, and the packages in the freezer were labeled with the date each package had been frozen, older packages in the front. He took out a pack of frozen strawberries and set it to defrost in the microwave for a few minutes. During that time he thought little about Bobby; he was more concerned with watering the thicket of plants that contrasted pleasantly with the very neat, regimented apartment. At the worst, Bobby Medlock had been picked up by the police—an easy problem to solve. More likely, Bobby Medlock was pumping some young chicken. There was no reason to worry.

2

TO the right of Dean Buettner's bed was a small square wooden table, purchased at a junk shop and carefully refinished. Sitting on the table was a snooze alarm radio, last week's *Business Week*, an old issue of the *Paris Review*, purchased at the same junk store where he had bought the small table, and November's *Reader's Digest*. *Reader's Digest* always opened Dean Buettner's day.

As the DJ's babble was interrupted for the second time by the alarm, Buettner's hand went to the off button and in the same sweep picked up the *Reader's Digest*. Without sitting up, he rubbed the bridge of his nose, then held the *Digest* at eye level, shuffling through it as through a deck of cards. He stopped the shuffle on page 61, running his finger down the page to word 4. "4. Tendentious (ten DEN shus)=A: biased. B: righteous. C: long. D: boring."

"Shit!"

None of the definitions gave him the slightest idea of what the word meant; it would be an impossible word to use for the day. He threw the covers back and rolled out of bed, still holding the magazine. Buettner walked to the bathroom. His long sculpted body was marvelous proof of the virtues of exercise. He stood at the toilet and looked at the word again.

"Tendentious=A: Biased; promoting a particular cause, as a *tendentious* article pretending to be objective." Buettner left the magazine on the commode top, and took a three-sentence shower.

"Well, Detective Rosenbloom, I'd say you certainly are a *tendentious* son of a bitch, sir! T . . . E . . . N . . D . . . E . . . N . . . T . . . I . . . O . . . U . . . S: Detective Rosenbloom is a tendentious son of a bitch!" He opened his mouth and gargled the word again, rubbing his tongue hard over the inside of his teeth, and spit.

"Well, Mona, that's a pretty tendentious way to feel about the chief detective's number-one man, especially when he's so good-looking!" Without opening his eyes, he reached down to the bottle of shampoo sitting in the left corner of the shower, opened it, and poured a small silver pool into his hand.

"Well! Some people may be tendentious when it comes to their shampoo, but *I* always use Pantene because it smells so sweet!"

Buettner's body wiggled in a parody of the flapper he'd seen on television the night before. He rubbed the Pantene on his head and dug in with his fingernails, a rough and rapid massage, then turned off the hot water and stood there. He believed cold water after hot tightened the skin.

The word had by then settled tentatively in his mind, a tentative placement because none of his attempts to use it seemed quite right. He thought about that as he dressed and walked from his apartment building on this fresh but cold Friday, lifting the hood of the red MG and pouring in about a pint of oil before cranking it.

By seven thirty he was in the office. For his age, twenty-eight, Dean Buettner held a reasonably important job as assistant to Albert Rosenbloom, chief of detectives in Chicago's Auto Theft Division.

Buettner's office was the first door to the left off the small clerk's area, in a five-foot-narrow hall, directly across from his boss's office. His door was stippled by hundreds of small pinpricks where messages had been tacked in, mostly at eye level; the door was seldom closed, though. The small size of Auto Theft's space made a slightly raised voice the best intercom system. Positioned in the top frame of the door, inside just enough to allow the door to close, was a chinning bar. Buettner used it each morning and, at times, during the daily moments of frustration: case loads were always too heavy; budgets were short; judges never seemed to realize that the goddamn auto-theft situation in Chicago kept getting worse, a cesspool of amateurs and professionals and organized-crime families all having a picnic, thanks to cops on the take and weak judges, many of them on the take, too, as just about everyone knew and few cared.

Dean Buettner did a set of thirty chin-ups on the bar and then settled into his chair, his breath less labored than that of a person who has walked up a short flight of stairs. From the center drawer he took a legal pad and began to scan his notes from the previous evening's meeting with Rosenbloom and a detective who had spent many nights during October observing the late-night comings and goings at the largest automotive body shop and wholesale parts operation in Chicago, Central Body Shop.

Only recently had Auto Theft linked Central Body Shop to the Vicovari crime outfit, at least tentatively, and that link depended on the man who would ring the phone in Dean Buettner's office within the next ten minutes—if he called at all. And if he could and would still provide the assistance that would endanger him. The morning for Dean Buettner, then, started with a larger than usual number of ifs.

Buettner read through his notes again, then walked to the clerk's desk and picked up the sealed manila envelope with his name on it. The envelope contained the sixth draft of the department's cause pleading for a warrant to search the premises of Central Body Shop. The warrant was the other big if in the department's efforts to nail something solidly on Anton Vicovari or Angie Weiner, or if not them directly, to throw up a roadblock for the outfit's auto-theft activities. Without the help of the man who was to call, that roadblock wouldn't stand for long—Anton Vicovari's friends in Chicago's law enforcement agencies and courts were too strong.

But the call did come, and it was a good one: as far as the informant could tell, the file cabinet at Central Body Shop still contained an awful lot of paperwork that would interest Chicago Auto Theft. Including a large printout that, the informant said, was the most frequently referred-to document in the office of Central Body Shop.

After the call Buettner returned to his notes, and then at about five of eight began to lay out on his desk the dozen folders that were always stored in the right bottom drawer. When he heard the main office door open, he slipped several sheets out from several folders and began a concentrated effort to look very, very busy, the expression of one completely overloaded with work on his face, as Albert Rosenbloom first entered his own office and then came to stand before Buettner.

When he smiled, Albert Rosenbloom looked like a pleasant man: ruddy cheeks marked with a few thin veins, black hair peppered with gray always cut short (but long on the temples to cover a fast-receding hairline), and a slightly pudgy body that belied the muscles hidden under the middle-aged spread. When he smiled, Albert Rosenbloom looked very amiable, but he didn't smile much, and in the morning about the only thing that could make him do so was the sight of people hard at work. Buettner did not look up as Rosenbloom spoke.

"Where the hell is Trudy? I thought you talked with her about being late?" Trudy Webb, the department clerk, along with Dean usually got the worst of Rosenbloom's morning funks.

Buettner still did not look up, his eyes and hands moving purposefully and with great practice over the folders. It wasn't that Dean Buettner didn't work; he did, and very hard. It was just too difficult to please the unsmiling man at times.

"Albert, it's only eight. Remember, you *told* her eight fifteen today. You know, if she would type that cause again?"

Rosenbloom looked at his watch and growled, unmollified. "Well —it's *nearly* eight fifteen, anyway." As he spoke the main office door opened, and though Buettner smiled inwardly, he did not look up, the point better won with silence. He continued to update a file as Rosenbloom stood there. "Well—Dean, did the damn guy call or not?" Buettner looked up and nodded casually, as if he had never had a doubt.

"Yeah, and we can go on Monday, Tuesday, or Wednesday. Jeez, Albert, I wish I could talk, but I've got all these damn things to get done this morning, you know. I'm pretty *tendentious* about some of these reports." He was looking down again when he spoke. The greatest private game flying around the offices of Chicago Auto Theft when Buettner and Rosenbloom were in residence was that of how long Albert Rosenbloom could ignore the constant and at times deliberately stupid uses of newly found words thrown at him by Mr. Buettner before smiling.

He completely ignored the word for the day, and also ignored Buettner's sanctimonious pleas for a little time to get some work done. That joke was on Buettner: two of the folders that always seemed to appear on his desk early in the mornings, creating the fine illusion of drudgery, now contained notes from Albert Rosenbloom saying: "Smart-ass, when you finally *do* get around to reading this file, let me know." Both of the notes were now four days old. But before Rosenbloom could say a word, Trudy Webb stuck her head in Buettner's office door.

"Excuse me, guys, if you need anything special done this morning, please do get it to me soon, okay, so I can have it done before lunch. I've got a doctor's appointment and Jo's going to cover for me." Jo was a clerk in another department who covered the lunch shift at Auto Theft at least three days a week. Trudy was sure Jo Pinder volunteered for the duty because of her interest in being close to Dean Buettner. He wasn't bad-looking, either. With high, wide cheekbones, even Trudy agreed with Jo that he resembled that English actor Michael York. Trudy was *very* sure that was why Jo had volunteered; it certainly wasn't because of her typing skills. Though that lack of talent was overlooked by the men in the department because of Jo Pinder's looks, it was not overlooked by the forty-five-year-old grandmother now walking from Buettner's office.

Before Trudy Webb could make it back to her desk, the calls began. There would be forty that Friday.

II

On Friday in Atlanta, Evelyn Wade also came in early, at about nine, walking past AOR's receptionist with a "Good morning" that did not change the pace of her movement. Nor did the stairway slow her much. Evelyn's walk made many people nervous. A stranger would think each step was a balancing act. The cane, in her left hand, always moved with the right foot, the left foot following with a barely perceptible pause that lowered her shoulder.

At the top of the stairs Evelyn stopped for a moment and rested. May Montez's voice was always so animated, she thought. She could hear it twenty feet away, floating out the door of the second office on the right.

May was on the phone. Of black and Mexican heritage, she had features some would call Caucasian but skin the deep color of rosewood, polished rosewood. Her office reflected her background, too. Among the photographs on the wall across from her desk was one of May with Jesse Jackson standing with a group of supporters. An angel-wing begonia on the desk was displayed in a brightly colored Mexican pot. Evelyn stopped at the door for a moment, but entered as May waved her in and pointed to a sofa, covered in rusty-brown canvas. Evelyn shifted one of the bold yellow pillows with a quick flip of her cane and sat down.

"Okay, okay, so call me when you know." May dropped the receiver on its base and continued talking as if Evelyn were a part of the phone conversation.

"Evelyn! So, were you here last night? God! Martha can be a bi— bother at times."

"May, I was luckier than most, I'd completed four when Martha went down."

May shook her head. "Ev, sorry, but you worked for naught last night. We lost everything, all of them. You're not going to believe this, but someone in the computer room in Dallas was trying to plug into Martha to pull off tabulations as they came over the lines—I mean this was a *real* rush job—and they *refed* rather than pulled off. Two circuits went, the head crashed and then a fuse melted." Evelyn nodded as if she understood May's description of the problems with Martha, but though she did not understand much of it, she did hear something that bothered her. "Martha's not coming on line till two or two thirty. So you've made the trip in for nothing this morning, I'm afraid. *Tonight*, now . . ."

Evelyn shook her head. "I don't mind about work, but does that mean the respondent numbers are gone, too?"

"Yeah, they're gone. Coke's about to have a stroke, Evelyn. Don't be surprised if someone wants you to work every night next week too. Hey, did you bring me that recipe?"

May was usually good at reading Evelyn's rare moments of worry, but she had not been paying attention. Evelyn fumbled in her pocketbook and pulled out the recipe for boned breast of chicken stuffed with chipped beef. Evelyn looked to the window for a moment, her mind still on the call. "May—if everything is gone, does that mean you can't find a number I called last night?"

May folded the recipe again and placed it in the small pocket of her blouse. "Thanks. No, there's nothing. Why do you want to find a number? A boyfriend?"

Evelyn's chuckle was as deep as her voice. "No boyfriend. He was too young. But it was a funny call. May, now that I've thought about it, it frightened me a little. Have you ever heard the line, 'Golden lads and girls all must, as chimney sweeps, come to dust'? I thought of that line . . ."

"What happened?"

"I don't *know*, that's what bothers me. . . ." She sat forward on the sofa as she recounted the incident, her unusual intensity finally evident to May. "So I *know* something was wrong. And I know it was a Chicago number," she finished.

May looked steadily at her. She said nothing but filled the little pause by pushing her pencil, point to eraser, eraser to point, over and over, as she considered Evelyn's story. She knew Evelyn was not an alarmist.

Evelyn leaned forward a little bit farther, her cane going up like a baton. "Oh, the boy also drank root beer. May, that boy said he was drinking his *fifth* root beer. I'll bet he's got pimples."

"Oh good, honey." May plopped her pencil down. "Then all we have to do is contact all of the body shops in Chicago and ask for the pimpled root-beer drinkers!" They both laughed.

Evelyn loved an infectious laugh. She took the end of her cane and used the tip to push a book on May's desk farther from the edge as she spoke. "May, can you come to dinner on Sunday evening? Asparagus casserole, acorn squash in brandy and brown sugar, London broil, *and* chocolate brownie pie topped with ice cream and *gobs* of chocolate sauce. Dietetic."

"Un-huh. Evelyn, I hate you. Yes."

"Good! Now, how am I going to find out about the boy? May, please don't think I'm silly, but the whole thing bothers me."

"I don't know. . . . Ev! Can I bring someone to dinner?" May's lips parted and pulled up in a smile, a mischievous smile. "He's the guy from Consumer Affairs, the guy who always calls me when someone complains about our phones being bugged. . . . *God*, is he a handsome man! . . . and," she added quickly, "I think the guy is a better detective than I am."

It was legal bugging, of course. American Opinion Research had a permit to monitor all of the telephones in its offices and occasionally some disgruntled caller would learn that. Then May Montez would invariably receive a phone call from a man named Jay Preston, assistant to the director, Department of Consumer Affairs, Secretary of State's Office. On two occasions Preston had visited AOR and May. Very bright and crackling with energy, Jay Preston was a sinewy six feet tall. Before Evelyn could finish her yes, May interrupted.

"Evelyn, he's a black man."

Evelyn didn't mean to hesitate, but she did before repeating the yes, her expression shifting slightly.

"No, I don't have to bring him. . . ."

"But I *want* you to bring him, my dear. *He's* the detective," Evelyn said. She laughed to cover her momentary awkwardness as she pushed upright and started for the door. Evelyn felt a little confused, and a bit startled at her reaction. "Come about six thirty, all right? Both of you."

"Okay, I'll ask him and let you know." From her door, May watched Evelyn as she gripped the handrail tightly and began to negotiate the stairs.

Evelyn tried to brush away her uneasy feeling as quickly as it had come to her. But the short walk out the side door and up the gentle slope to the MARTA bus stop wasn't the right distance. Evelyn thought of May like a grandchild. And her color had never really been important. But Jay Preston was really black. Evelyn chuckled. She had spent most of the adult years of her life teaching her students that color shouldn't determine friendships, had preached it at her church and to her friends too. She had entertained blacks in her home and slept in the same room with them at church retreats.

But she had never thought of a black person as a companion, maybe lover, to someone she really felt close to. Evelyn shook her head as she waved her cane at the bus. Jay Preston was probably the closest person to a real cop she would ever tell her story to. And he obviously was a person May Montez wanted to know. As she pulled herself up the bus steps, Evelyn thought of Katharine Hepburn in *Guess Who's Coming to Dinner?* She admired Hepburn's role. As the bus pulled away, she tried to remember how that movie ended.

By eleven, Evelyn was sitting at a table on the first floor of the Atlanta-Fulton Public Library. Her cane was hanging on the back of the chair. Most of the places at the tables for four were filled, including the other three at hers. To her right, a black kid was reading the *Atlanta Constitution*; directly across from her, two young college students dressed in jeans and wearing loafers without socks hunched together over a notebook, piles of textbooks resting by a knapsack. A middle-aged lady sat at the next table to her left; Evelyn had nodded very briefly to her as she sat down, placing the thick Chicago yellow pages in front of her. The thirteen hundred pages contained somewhere, she was sure, the telephone number of the place she called the night before.

Le Carré's George Smiley had given her the idea. Within the most complex mystery was a single thread that always led to the unraveling. Evelyn was sure that thread in her case was the telephone number. Since the respondent number was lost in Martha's collapse, she had made up her mind on the bus into town to try to find the telephone number herself. If she put down and studied all she knew, perhaps, just perhaps she could find it. Her friends would no doubt think her foolish, but that did not bother Evelyn Wade. She was a very determined lady, and anyway they needn't know, she thought. So she had ridden the bus past her stop to the MARTA station and taken the train downtown. She got off at Peachtree Center and, before walking the two blocks to the library, stopped by Woolworth's to buy the green spiral-ring notebook that now rested by the yellow pages in front of her.

Evelyn looked at the phone book, then flipped through the pages to the heading "Body Shop." A notation there said "See Automobile Body Repairing." She flipped back toward the A's and found the section. It filled over sixteen pages, large and small ads with high-lighted telephone numbers, surrounded by columns of names and numbers in regular print. She began to slide her finger down the listings, looking for numbers that began with 2. "I know the number begins with a 2," she had written on the first page of her notebook, "because it was the same number as the last digit of Chicago's area code, 312. I dial that area code all the time."

Evelyn found the first 2 at the top of the second column of numbers and carefully wrote "A-1 Body Shop," and its address and telephone number on page 2 of her notebook, which she had headed "Potential Telephone Numbers." She listed fourteen more beginning with 2 before finding the number for Central Body Shop,

211-6801. As with each of the numbers before it, and after it, she looked up, her mind trying to reconstruct the movement of fingers over the keyboard the night before, then listed the name, number, and address by the number 15 in her notebook. Evelyn flipped through the remaining pages of body shop listings. She knew it was there, the thread was there. But she hadn't known that there would be so many numbers.

It took an hour and a half to find the last body shop with a phone number beginning with 2, Young Buick, Inc. The information on her last find was dutifully written by number 54. Then Evelyn got up to stretch and get a drink of water, with a very depressing thought on her mind: how in the name of all things that were good would she ever narrow the number down?

The two students were gone when Evelyn returned to the table, replaced by a young mother and her child. The woman placed a Dr. Seuss book before the little girl and said, "Mindy, honey, I'll bet you can't read this whole book while Mommy reads!" Mindy didn't look up or speak, both arms instantly grabbing the book and holding it tightly, as if someone might pull it from her grasp. Evelyn smiled at the mother and turned her attention to the notebook. On the top of a clean page she wrote the words "Other 'Body' Shops" and she began to flip through the telephone book again. "Massage" began on page 513.

Evelyn Wade had never thought much about massage parlors except when they were settings for some spicy passage in a novel. Some very good novels had used them as a vehicle, too, she remembered. But she did know that "body shop" was slang for house of prostitution, and that prostitutes always advertised under "massage" in the yellow pages. Very logical, she thought, as her finger began to slip down the numbers, her eyes occasionally going to the suggestive drawings accompanying many of the ads. Evelyn wondered if the ladies were as good-looking as the drawings.

The first number starting with 2 was for AAA Relaxation. Evelyn looked up, amused at her task. She looked up just in time to catch the young mother's eyes as their glance moved from the yellow pages to her face. Evelyn Wade never spoke to people at the table in the library, etiquette dictated that. But the thought of a young mother imagining a licentious old woman seemed to call for an explanation.

"Uh, you see . . . I'm looking for a young boy . . ."

The mother blushed. Evelyn fought an embarrassed laugh, then quickly turned back to the phone book.

"Mommy?" The child looked up and began to speak.

"Be quiet, honey." The mother sat the Dr. Seuss book on its edges, a barrier to the ads that filled the yellow pages. And the old lady. Evelyn did not look up again.

III

Rick Kanell drove to the back entrance of Mid-West Tool and Supply Company, the loading-ramp side, and parked next to Jimmy Mack's Kawasaki 500. Jimmy Mack was the five-to-midnight guard at Mid-West. He was also a one-man Muzak system. The best view of Mid-West's warehouse interior, he had decided, was right next to the intercom microphone. And the best way to pass the time of day or night was to play a harmonica over that system.

On most evenings Kanell would have stopped and chatted a few minutes with the company musician. But this Friday at six he simply waved his right index finger once and walked down the canyon of shelves to the door that separated warehouse from offices. All of the employees of Mid-West Tool and Supply seemed to like Rick Kanell. Some called him "The Dude" because of his fashion-plate image. Others called him Mr. Kanell because of his position. But most of the forty-one employees called him Rick and respected the friendly demeanor of the company's majority stockholder and president. Jimmy Mack respected Rick more than most. That was why the harmonica tune had shifted to "Hail to the Chief" as Kanell entered the office area.

Today the tune didn't bring a smile, though. Disposing of bodies could take one's mind off lighter things. And there was the note.

That bothered him more than the body. Kanell walked into his office and locked the door. He needed to change his clothes. But first he needed to get his head together. He sat on the edge of the desk and sucked two spoons of cocaine into each nostril, sucked in again, and began to remove his tie and shirt, twisting his neck, hearing it crack as he walked to the restroom. Kanell's office looked like a lawyer's. Though the other offices of Mid-West Tool were furnished sparingly in office modern, his quarters were not. An Oriental carpet covered the floor before the antique desk; the chairs in front of the desk were new, but to the unpracticed eye looked like Chippendale. Old watercolors of mallards in flight hung on the wall next to the bathroom door. The brass lamp sitting on the desk matched the lamp sitting on the marble basin in the bathroom.

At the moment, Kanell took no pleasure in the decor. He looked at his fingers. The nails were still dirty. He began to shave, mechanically, his thoughts carefully reviewing the past hours. The Jensen Esprit was parked in the long-term lot at the Minneapolis airport. Not far from a farm-to-market road in Richfield, Minnesota, Bobby Medlock's body, its arms and legs curled tightly in fetal position, was lying in a shallow indentation, covered with refuse from six large garbage bags Kanell had taken to the site. The spoils of dozens of meals from the previous day at the Richfield Steak and Ale had a stronger odor than those Kanell had imagined were coming from the body.

Medlock's wallet was in Kanell's coat pocket. It was a cheap wallet, a fact that gave Kanell some satisfaction. But one small slip of yellow paper in that wallet bothered him. Kanell splashed hot water on his face, then ran his nails into a bar of soap and scrubbed them. He dried his hands briskly, patted his face with the towel, then folded it and hung it again on the rack. Kanell stopped just outside the bathroom door and mixed himself a bourbon and water.

He sat on the carpet, looking at the contents of the wallet again, carefully placing each of the stray pieces of paper, cards, and one Trojan rubber back in the wallet. He then slipped it into his shirt pocket and sat at the desk. It was the damn note that bothered him.

In a childish hand, part cursive, part printed, were the words "Big A" and the number 211-6801. The number was the private number of Central Body Shop. He looked at the driver's license again. The name Medlock meant nothing to him. But the handsome, smooth-skinned kid on the license definitely looked like someone Angie Weiner would hire. And use for special things. Kanell cursed. Like being one of Angie's playthings. All of Anton Vicovari's people had weaknesses. *Except for me.* Kanell smiled, then, remembering the cocaine, thought it wasn't really a weakness. At least it wasn't like Weiner's thing.

Taking a set of keys from his pocket, he unlocked the center drawer of his desk and slipped out a Mid-West inventory control sheet from the top envelope. The sheet contained mostly numbers. But on the top left corner was a one-sentence notation in Angie Weiner's handwriting: "Rick, here's what we've got new in inventory." The *as* slanted to the left and the *gs* slanted to the right were nearly identical to those on Medlock's note. Kanell shook his head. The goddamn kid *was* probably there for Weiner. He took the last cigarette out of a blue Rothman's box, dropped the box in the square wicker wastebasket, and took a deep drag on the cigarette before lighting it. It would have been better if the kid had been the worm, Kanell thought. Someone in the outfit was a worm, everyone knew that. Too many things were going wrong. Why hadn't the kid been a goddamn worm? Of course, being Angie's mule didn't mean the kid couldn't have been a worm as well, but a worm wouldn't have left a car in the open, he'd already decided that.

So why was the kid looking at the printout? Kanell pushed the papers on the desk as he tried to make sense of the past hours. If Weiner was going to hold the printouts over him, he had failed. Yes, it was a mistake to have kept a copy at Central Body Shop in the first place. And yes, Weiner had said that to Anton Vicovari. But the first three pages, the incriminating pages, were now in his coat pocket. Weiner and his goddamn games. The man was poison.

Kanell sat up in the chair. He was the businessman in the outfit, creating the systems and programs that controlled the flow of product into and out of the centers in response to demand and supply. He had been careful never to ask favors of the family. And, at least in his eyes, he had never dirtied his fingers. He would mention the kid to no one.

He put the small note and Bobby Medlock's driver's license in the folder, then locked it in the center drawer. He needed to think about other things. Like the raid on the dump. On the night Bobby Medlock died, Chicago Auto Theft had raided Anton Vicovari's main dump. The story was on page two of the *Tribune*, along with pictures of the dumpsite. Dumps weren't an integral part of the active side of Division Three, Kanell's innocuous name for car-chopping operations. But they were nevertheless important, as for the chemical manufacturer who had to find sites to dump waste by-products before more chemicals could be produced. The deserted Orion Theatre had been the dumpsite for Division Three for less than a month. Normally such sites were good for at least three months.

There was definitely a worm, Kanell thought as he switched on the IBM System 34. He pushed "PFI" and the menu appeared on the terminal screen. Though all menu titles were visible to anyone who looked, none of the other employees of Mid-West had ever been able to access the information stored in items 37 to 91.

"It's where I play games," Kanell would always say with a smile when questions came up about those items.

It was such a beautiful system. Mid-West Tool and Supply was considered a most successful company in the legitimate business world, and it was. But it was the activities minutely detailed in menu areas 37 through 91 of the Mid-West computer that in reality made Mid-West one of the most unusual companies in the eastern United States. Those menu areas catalogued and directed the five organized-crime operations of Anton Vicovari, the "Car King" of Chicago.

Kanell punched in the access code to line 37 on the menu, "Vacation Days Accrued, Chicago Office," and noted the "601" that popped on the screen instantly. He shook his head. "Vacation Days

Accrued, Chicago Office" represented the number of stolen automobiles whose unsalable parts—those with serial numbers—had been dumped at the Orion Theatre. They'd been busier than he thought. A new dumpsite would be needed that day.

He then accessed line 47 on the menu, "Cash Discounts by Company Account." To the uninformed eye, the numbers and dollar amounts wouldn't mean much. To Kanell they detailed the status of Anton Vicovari's entire "barter system." The system had been conceived and executed by Kanell. Approximately $150,000 worth of pornographic films produced and owned by the Vicovari outfit, for example, were being held for an exchange of a thousand televisions stolen during the past two weeks by a southern outfit close to Vicovari. Kanell planned to trade the televisions, all originally destined for three new Holiday Inns in New Jersey, to a California outfit, for video games and Valium. The video games would be traded to All-Seas Shipping, owned by a Canadian outfit, as payment for the overseas shipment of perhaps seven hundred steamers stolen by Vicovari's Division Two and shipped to friendly customers in the Mideast and Asia. "Cash Discounts by Company Account" summarized the entire operations of Division Four.

Kanell enjoyed the chess moves of that barter system. He could lose himself in that computer. He fed in and controlled everything there. In turn, the computer gave him crisp, clean responses to each command. But the machine could not pick a new dumpsite. Angie Weiner would need to do that. It could not help Kanell deal with Angie Weiner, either. And it could not take care of the dangling phone by Bobby Medlock's body. The old lady on the phone.

Kanell turned the machine off, then leaned back. He had pushed thoughts of her from his mind, an anonymous old lady's voice. She said she was with a research company. Kanell began to rethink her words, then turned his eyes to the screen. *Christ!* He sucked in a breath and held it. A research company. They used computers. Every goddamn number they call—they store. What did she hear? Something, because she wanted to know what happened to the kid. Why did she hang up the phone, you don't hang up the phone if you're concerned about someone. Kanell pressed in hard and rubbed his temples. Until that moment, he really believed Bobby Medlock's disappearance would be forgotten in short order. Street punks always disappeared. But the lady. Kanell didn't need to search for the piece of paper with the scribbled notation. "American Opinion Research, Dallas, Evelyn."

He picked up the phone and dialed information in Dallas.

"What city, please?"

"Dallas. I'd like the number for American Opinion Research, please."

The thought brought a metallic taste to his mouth as a recorded voice droned the number: *his tracks might not be covered yet*.

Kanell put the phone down before calling the number. He needed one more pick-me-up. He wanted to leave the outfit, anyway. The thought had been on his mind for some time. He was too good to need the dirty money of the outfit. Kanell was like a bomber pilot. He steered the plane, making sure the direction was right, but he wasn't really responsible for the things the bombs did. He didn't drop them. He had killed a punk kid, but so what? It was the kid's fault for being there. *Shit, I want out*—a strong thought as he dialed the Dallas number for American Opinion Research.

Evelyn Garner had never met Evelyn Wade in Atlanta. She did not know she existed. But Evelyn Garner worked for American Opinion Research, too—in the Dallas office. She was sitting in booth number 12, less than fifteen feet from the supervisor's desk, when the phone rang.

"WATS room."

Kanell paused. He knew the lady worked there. The receptionist had not hesitated when he simply asked for Evelyn. But he wanted to hear her voice.

"Good afternoon, out there in Dallas. So how's the weather?" His voice was a deep one, with touches of a southern accent.

"Just fine, honey. What can I do for you?"

"I hate to bother you, but I was wondering if Evelyn is working today. The receptionist wasn't sure." He wanted her to say she didn't really exist, had gone, left for good.

"Yes, she's here."

Kanell closed his eyes, then opened them when an image of Bobby Medlock's body entered his consciousness. "Do you think I could speak to her a minute? I'm at a pay phone." The supervisor started to say yes. A friendly caller asking for one of the girls by first name could usually make the supervisors break AOR's personal-call rule. She looked at Evelyn Garner. Evelyn Garner looked older than her fifty-six years. She also looked very involved in her survey.

"I'm sorry, but Evelyn is doing a survey right now. Can I have her call you back?"

He smiled, a bitter smile. "No, that's okay. I'll call her next week. Will she be working then?"

The supervisor laughed. "Honey, *everyone* will be working then. This place is like a prison." She put the phone down and began to look over a sheet of instructions for another survey. The phone call was forgotten as quickly as it had occurred.

Kanell sat at his desk without moving. He had a puppy once. He loved that dog. He had found it in the field beyond the house when he was ten years old. He had named it Butterball because its belly was thick and plump as a melon. One day the dog tried to cross the dirt road before a car passed. He did not make it; the front part of his body did but the back part did not. The dog was dragging himself off the road when Kanell saw him. The back legs were flattened, entrails bloodied them. They were so flat. Kanell had taken a large rock, hesitated, then crushed the dog's head. It was the first time he had ever killed on purpose. He thought of the dog as he dialed the number for Eastern Airlines. He needed to go to Dallas.

Kanell pulled into the driveway of his home on Sycamore Street in Bloomington at seven thirty that evening. He parked the car next to a bright red Fiat Spider convertible, smiling his first real smile since the death of Bobby Medlock. He entered the house quickly, walking directly across the living room.

"So where are you?" he yelled as he cut across the corner of the living room, pulling off his shoes and dropping them on the light brown carpet. Kanell was proud of the house. It suited him, he thought, sleek and tasteful, befitting the president of a successful business. He smiled again as he began to pull off his clothes. He dropped his shirt on the bed, on top of a woman's light tan cashmere sweater. He folded his pants, though they were wrinkled and spotted with small dots of dirt and bits of garbage from Bobby Medlock's gravesite, and placed them on the bed, too. He left his underwear where it fell, grabbed a towel and opened the sauna door.

Her long chestnut hair pulled back from her almost angular face, Jo Pinder rested nearly supine on the upper bench, a pitcher of dark rum and Coke sitting beside her. The glass was held lightly in her hand, the arm extended outward and downward. A bendable straw was in the glass. Kanell took the glass from her.

"Lay down."

"Now, let me see, what is your name?" Pinder slid down the bench, lifting her body occasionally as flesh touched dry, hot wood. Her slightly arched back displayed her full breasts and her slender waist to advantage. Kanell gazed appreciatively at the seamlessly tanned body.

"I tried to call you at work this morning, but they said you were out," Kanell said. "Sorry about last night. Something came up." He took the straw from the glass and sucked in just enough liquid to fill the straw.

"I heard," Jo said. "One of the detectives came in to see Buettner about the raid on the dump last night while I was in the office, and boy, were they in a good mood. Did the raid hurt things?" Pinder asked tentatively. Her job in the outfit was not to ask questions, but to listen. Kanell did not respond, but shrugged. She continued. "Were you out with Angie last night?"

Kanell was sitting on the lower bench. He leaned over her face just enough to release a couple of drops from the straw into her mouth, then moved the straw over her left nipple. The coldness of the drops made Jo's body arch again. It also made the nipple hard. Kanell lifted the drops with his tongue, a circling motion, then held the straw over her navel, releasing the remaining liquid slowly there until it formed a small pool.

"Yeah," he said, "Angie and I had things to talk about." Jo's assumption seemed the best excuse for his absence the previous night. He continued. "Weiner's trying to find a new dump tonight." He set the glass down, his eyes roaming over her body carefully. A tiny stream of liquid slowly began to wander down Jo's left hip. Kanell caught it with his tongue. It tasted slightly salty. He held his tongue still, moving his head upward and around her navel. Jo's belly was flat and smooth. As his tongue carefully lifted the liquid from her navel, she began to breathe more deeply. He placed his lips on her and gently sucked the last drops from the pool.

For two years Jo Pinder had helped him lose himself. Kanell was proud of the fact that he had found her. The red convertible was just one of the rewards he had given her, ostensibly for her efforts in gathering information on the activities of Chicago Auto Theft. But the red Spider convertible had really been a personal gift. Not given with special words, but a special gift nevertheless. Rick Kanell was comfortable with Jo Pinder, and in the narrow range of his emotions, that was unusual.

Jo's hand slipped down the nape of Kanell's neck and back. Droplets of sweat followed the movement of her fingers, forming small lines. She slipped her hand to his chest, palm touching flesh, thumb flicking his nipple, then slid her fingers down the center of his chest. Her fingers barely touched skin; she could feel the tiny hairs that formed a thin path to his navel, then joined the curly hair of his crotch.

"Get on your knees."

Jo didn't open her eyes as he spoke, but slowly turned over. She was still for a moment, then pulled her body up in a kneeling position, elbows supporting her upper weight. Jo sucked in a soft stream of air as he entered her.

* * *

They were sitting in the breakfast nook, still naked. Kanell had a platinum American Express card in his right hand; with it he was carefully chopping the small pile of white dust into finer dust, sliding the chopped portion to the side, slowly forming two piles, which he divided again. The powder was resting on a glass-framed picture of Kanell in scuba gear.

Four inches of a dry straw lay beside the picture. He picked up the straw and carefully cleaned the picture of the left two lines, then bent his head back and sucked in through his nose.

"Why are you so quiet?" Jo pulled the picture to her.

"I don't know. Hell, I think I'm just getting tired of all the crap. You know, I could make it alone." He paused as Jo put the straw to her left nostril, pushing it slowly up the line of cocaine. She rubbed a finger over the specks of powder that remained, then rubbed the finger on her gums.

"Do you think they'll let you out? Who *ever* gets out. You really run your own business now, Rick. They've never asked you to do anything but run Mid-West, have they?"

"Yeah, but . . ." Kanell started to speak, then caught himself. Rick Kanell did not love Jo Pinder. He didn't love anyone, didn't want to, either. But lately he found himself telling Jo more of his thoughts. At times, more than he intended to tell. He changed the subject.

"I'm seeing Anton tonight."

"Oh? Isn't that a little unusual?"

"No. He's just concerned about a lot of things. You know, your prick friends at work are trying to get on him a lot."

She shook her head. "Yeah, and they write about him, too."

"What are you talking about?"

"*Spotlight*. There's going to be an article on him in the next issue. I found out yesterday."

Kanell lifted a cigarette from the pack on the table and lit it quickly. "Have you seen it?"

"No. Everybody's hush-hush about it."

"God, I'm glad you told me. I'll tell Anton tonight."

Jo got up and slipped on a bright blue robe that was hanging across the corner of the kitchen island. She was not looking at Rick as she spoke, but at the tiled counters and white cabinets. It looked like a picture in a magazine, she thought. She would have one like it one day. "Well . . . if you're going out, I think I'll catch a show or something. I'm restless tonight. Do you want me to come back?"

Kanell smiled as he walked to the bedroom. "Yeah, come back. I'm still horny."

Jo Pinder left the house at nine, fifteen minutes after Kanell. She liked to speed, the red Spider taking corners at times fast enough for the back tires to slip with the momentum. She really liked Rick. At first she had provided him information about the activities of Chicago Auto Theft because she was supposed to. But in time she had given him interesting tidbits because she wanted to help him. The gifts were nice too.

She parked on the street less than a block from the White Castle and began to walk. She liked him, but he wasn't the real reason the gifts came. She had to remember that. Jo entered the restaurant and gave a small wave to Angie Weiner, who was sitting in the corner booth, six empty hamburger boxes in front of him. Jo never enjoyed the meetings with Weiner. Even though he smiled and at times laughed, she was never comfortable with him. His look was scary; she noticed it again as she sat down.

"So, how's the beautiful lady?" Weiner wiped his mouth carefully with a napkin.

"I'm fine, Angie. I didn't know if I'd get out. You know how Rick is when he gets home."

There was a moment of silence. Angie very seldom asked questions or reacted to any of their infrequent meetings. He was there to listen. But that's okay, Jo thought. It's what Anton said she was supposed to do. Listen at the office and listen to Rick and tell Angie. She looked at the gold bracelet on her left wrist, then began to talk.

"Angie, he didn't say where he'd been. But he did say he was with you last night. Maybe he was with you after we talked." She hesitated. "He's gone to see Anton." She raised her eyebrows. "Angie, I told him about the *Spotlight* article, and he said he would tell Anton. I didn't tell him he already knew. Was that okay?"

Weiner took a drink of tea. In the beginning he had not wanted Jo Pinder to report to Rick Kanell at all, *he* wanted to provide the information. He smiled inwardly. But that's why Anton was the boss, he thought. He was smarter. As Rick Kanell had become more and more independent from the outfit, Pinder's closeness to him had been the best way to keep tabs on him. Weiner was sure the goddamn bastard was planning to branch out, he'd said that carefully to Vicovari on several occasions. But he would listen more now. Vicovari always listened to Jo Pinder's reports.

"Jo, you want to eat something? It's a fancy restaurant, you know," Weiner said with a large smile. Angie was feeling good.

"No, thanks. I'm going to catch a movie. I told Rick I was going to the movies. I don't think he'll be with Anton very long, so I'd better go." Angie shook his head and smiled again. He had an image of Rick Kanell screwing her in the ass hard, hurting her. He liked the image.

"So where are you going? The Cinema Six is down the street. We could go there together." He was teasing her, as he liked to do. He continued before Jo could think of a reason not to go with him. "But that's foolish, isn't it? You'd probably see someone that'd embarrass us. Like the chief or someone."

Jo didn't wait for any more conversation. "God, that would be hard to explain, I guess, so when do I need to see you again? Or can we talk on the phone as usual?" Angie really did like meeting with Jo, squeezing her nerves, watching her. But he nodded yes, then turned his head to the side, cracking his neck. "No hurry, pretty lady, no hurry. I'll be calling you next week. I'll tell Anton you said hi!"

She left the White Castle less than five minutes after entering it and drove east through Bloomington to the Tara Theatre. She didn't pay much attention to the screen, though. Jo Pinder seldom knew when her comments about work or about Rick had any real meaning to the outfit. She didn't want to know, either. In her eyes, the outfit simply stole cars, that's all they did. That didn't matter, she thought; it's what insurance companies were for. No one was hurt, either; that was the important thing. What she did at work wasn't that bad; she believed that. And what she said about Rick wasn't bad, either. She never said anything important. Jo turned her eyes back to the screen. She had never said anything that would hurt Rick. She really hadn't.

3

THOUGH they had been neighbors since before the death of her husband, Evelyn Wade and Lane Englander had really become friends after his death. Their friendship in a way was a formal one—they talked of many things, but never personal things—but they did enjoy and respect each other immensely.

Mr. Englander's presence at the dinner table at 91 Myrtle this night was different, however, though Evelyn wasn't ready to acknowledge that. She sensed that he understood about the overheard phone call. Something *had* happened to a boy in Chicago. From the moment of their conversation the night before, Englander had become an ally—something Evelyn needed right then.

Jay Preston, May's friend from the Department of Consumer Affairs, was sitting to Evelyn's right at the small dining room table. To Evelyn's left sat Englander, and across from her May Montez. Evelyn's eyes went to Jay Preston as she finished retelling the story of the Chicago phone call. May was right: he was a handsome man, slender as a bean pole, but strong-looking.

Jay Preston sat for a moment before commenting on the story. He was used to old people's stories. Seventy percent of the complaints he took at the Department of Consumer Affairs were from old people. Old people always see monsters in the dark, he thought, lonely people needing conversation and attention more than help.

He shook his head. "It seems too little to go on. Your conversation was so short that there's no way, is there really, to be sure?"

"It was short, Jay, but the voices weren't right. I've listened to so many over the phone. The young boy's voice changed *in the middle of a word* from carefree to a voice filled with, with . . . " Evelyn looked away, her mind trying to form words to express what her mind could still feel. " . . . with a terminal fear. I know that sounds theatrical. But it expresses it."

Preston pushed the small dessert plate to the side. He shook his head slowly, then glanced at May. May's eyes tried to cool some of his skepticism.

"Jay, Evelyn thinks something was really wrong there. She wants us to try to find out what happened. I think it'd be fun to do that, sleuthing about, kind of." She kept her eyes on him.

Evelyn watched the exchange of glances and let May's words sink in before speaking. They didn't sit comfortably with her. She did not want to be catered to. "I'm sorry, but that's not the reason I need you to help me. There is a person, a thinking, feeling person, who was terribly afraid and, I believe, hurt. It doesn't matter where he was, and it doesn't matter that we do not know who he is. . . . Does that make any sense?"

Evelyn gave a short smile, pushed herself up, and began to gather the dessert plates, piling one on the other. "You three go sit in the den, I'd rather do this myself," she said as three other sets of hands became busy. She walked to the kitchen. Evelyn felt very isolated there, her hands resting on the lip of the sink, eyes turned toward the window but looking at nothing. Lane Englander walked in behind her, carrying the sugar bowl and creamer. He was six feet tall, and his hair, grayer than Evelyn's, added to his professorial look.

"Evelyn, I'll just sit these down on the counter, if that's okay. Well!

43

I haven't eaten like that in a long time." Englander wasn't sure what else to say. But he knew he needed to say something. "Evelyn . . . I think it's because they're too young. Do you remember how it was? People don't feel vulnerable when they're young."

He looked for something to do in the kitchen as Evelyn smiled but continued her dishwashing routine.

"You know, I've got to paint these kitchen cabinets, Lane. They're looking *awful*; you don't see them wear, then *boom*, they look so worn."

After she had finished the dishes Evelyn turned to face Englander, her hands held up like those of a surgeon before the gloves are put on. She shook them lightly. "Lane, I don't want to be a foolish old lady. But you know, *I'm right*. She shook her head. "*I know what I heard.* Now . . . if I can just convince them." Lane nodded, then looked toward the den. "Well, we won't convince them in here. Let's get to work."

As they entered the den, Jay was leaning forward in a chair, gesturing. May nodded, her attention completely on him. She was not smiling. "Evelyn," Preston said, "I wanted to ask you about what the boy said. Why did that bother you?"

"It didn't, it just didn't ring true. He wanted to withdraw the words, 'a body shop . . . of sorts.' But I'm already looking into that." She reached to the table by her chair and picked up the green notebook, waving it twice. "I can tell you the names of all the body shops, massage parlors, and escort services in the Chicago area." At their startled expressions, she added hastily, "Well, not all, just those exchanges beginning with 'two'. I looked them up at the library on Friday."

"Lord, honey," May said, "what are you doing knowing about massage parlors and escort services? *I've* never even looked at those ads." She paused. "At least not for very long."

Evelyn smiled. "And I'm going to call all of those numbers, too. At least the most likely ones. I've got over eighty. May—I can do that on the WATS lines, can't I? Can't we say I'm just trying to find someone to complete a survey, you know, how we call people back like that? I'll do it on my own time, of course."

May nodded. "That's okay, I'll fix it, but you'll have to wait a few days until this 'panic mode' thing gets over with Coke."

Jay shook his head. Evelyn seemed like an interesting person. And May seemed to like her a lot. That mattered.

"Evelyn, having the numbers is fine. I wish I had people at the office that persistent, but what are you going to ask the people when you call? You don't know enough to ask them. Who are you going to ask for?"

The thought hit May and Evelyn at the same time.

"Why, that's simple, Jay," Evelyn said as she looked at May, "I'm going to ask for . . . a . . ." Montez broke into a smile and said the last three words with Evelyn: "pimpled root-beer drinker!" Lane furrowed his brow, a quizzical expression on his face. Jay simply shook his head, his eyes closing momentarily and a smile creeping on his face.

"Well, that's simple enough, why didn't I think of it?"

"That's right, Jay, *you're* the professional," Evelyn said, serious now, "that's why I need your help."

"Okay, okay, so what are you really going to ask?"

Evelyn pulled in her lower lip. "I'm going to see if anyone was hurt there."

"What if someone says, 'Yes, a shelf fell on someone,' what are you going to say then?"

"Well, if they say that, I'll ask to speak to the boy. I would know his voice, I know that. But Jay, I don't think anyone will say that. Three things were wrong with the phone call. The terror in the boy's voice, the tension in the man's voice—I'm glad I was not there to *see* what had happened; I don't think the man would have let me leave—and, finally, *where* I called. Phones are funny things, they let us enter forbidden places, and *that* place was forbidden." Evelyn paused, "I'm sorry if that sounds melodramatic. . . ." She looked back at Preston.

"Well, Evelyn, how will you know if you've called the right number? What will you do?" It was the first time Jay Preston understood what she feared: she believed the boy was dead. The thought was too farfetched.

"Jay, I want to find the boy. If I can't find him, I want to find the man. And then I want someone to find out *about* the man."

Preston shook his head. "Evelyn, that won't be easy. You know, it's not like it is in the books,"—he gestured to the shelves—"or on television. We don't have time to pay attention to all of our *serious* cases, much less the ones that are so vague. God, I hate to think how overloaded the Chicago police are. . . ."

May was leaning forward in her chair, eyes following the exchange. "But Jay, can't you at least call up there and see if someone was . . . killed or something, at a body shop or someplace that night?"

"You see, that's the problem," he continued. "Unless something very specific happened, something the police already know about, a call from some stranger in Atlanta, even an official stranger like me, isn't going to garner much attention."

"But will you call anyway?" Englander was speaking. "Jay, what can they do, hang up on you? I don't know about the rest of you, but a call is a cheap thing if it will ease Evelyn's mind." That was the crux of it, Preston thought. They were concerned about *her*. He could accept that reasoning.

"Okay, you're right. I'll make a call or two and see what I can find out. God knows, I can find out some things about body shops." He stopped and thought for a minute. "You know, Chicago is the automobile-theft capital of America. They steal the cars and take them to body shops. They do it here, too." He hesitated again. "I'll tell you what, I'll call Consumer Affairs there. If anything's funny, they'll probably know it."

Evelyn shook her head firmly. "Good! Now, enough of that. Who would like some more brownie pie? Or some more ice cream?"

4

JO Pinder was rubbing his back. The thumb and index finger of her right hand spanned his spinal column, fingers pushing in and rubbing in a circular motion. Kanell closed his eyes as Pinder's fingers worked their way down his body.

"How long do you think you'll be gone?" Jo asked as the fingers of both hands began to push in and massage his buttocks. They hadn't made love yet. It was ten o'clock at night, and Kanell had not indicated any desire for sex. He seemed preoccupied.

"I don't know. Jo, work on my neck some. It's stiff."

Pinder was naked too. She moved up slightly toward the head of the bed, her right hip touching the upper part of Kanell's left arm. Kanell's head was facing in the other direction, but he turned it to her while her hands massaged his upper neck. He kept his eyes closed, though, irritating Jo a little; he was missing a lovely view. After a moment, she crawled up on the bed, straddled Kanell's back, and continued to massage his neck.

Jo wanted to ask Rick why he was leaving when so many things were going wrong. Her curiosity wasn't calculated, not part of her job, she thought; but she put the questions away. She didn't really need to know. "Rick, I've got some friends in Miami. If you have any time, you could look them up." She pinched the flesh of his neck. "But if you do, *don't touch.*"

Kanell did not really want to talk about the trip. He had planned it carefully, making sure that all of his tracks were covered from everyone, including Anton Vicovari, Angie Weiner, and Jo.

He thought for a moment before speaking. "No . . . thanks, Jo. This is kind of a special trip for Anton. He'd be real pissed if he knew I talked about it at all with you. I know you won't see him, but if for any reason you talk to him, or to the prick, just say you're glad I'm taking a week off. That's what I told them you knew, okay? It's just a vacation. I'm going bareboating through the Keys, okay?" He pushed her over as he rolled to the right of the bed. Kanell would never expect Jo Pinder to have contact with anyone in the outfit other than himself. To his knowledge, she had never met Angie Weiner, had only talked to him on the phone occasionally, and she had met Vicovari only in his presence. But Kanell was being very careful, covering *all* of the tracks. Just in case, he thought, he wanted her to say what he'd already told them.

Jo was on her side facing him, her hands toying with the light hairs of his chest. "So what am I supposed to do if something happens at work? Something you need to know? Write you a letter or something?"

Kanell's right hand began to flick her nipples absentmindedly. "No, I'll call you every couple of days."

"Rick, call me between eleven thirty and twelve thirty, that's when I'll be in Auto Theft." She gave a short laugh. "That's funny. I'll be there every day except tomorrow. If I don't answer, hang up or something." Jo ran her thumbnail lightly up the back of his hand still fiddling with her breast.

"Make love to me, okay? I don't want to start a week away from you horny."

Kanell seemed at last to notice the growing irritation in her voice. Without a word he reached over and pulled her head to his.

It was cool in Miami, but Kanell didn't feel that coolness. The E corridor was filled with fast-moving people as he exited the flight from Chicago, his eyes searching for an information counter. He turned right and headed toward the D corridor. Good, he thought, as his eyes found a monitor labeled "Delta Arrivals and Departures." Flight 786 for Dallas was the sixth flight down on the monitor. He picked up his pace. The damned flight *would* be on time. Kanell cursed again to himself when a woman stopped him at the entrance to the D corridor. She barely looked at his ticket folder, waving him through without once glancing at his face.

"Here you are, Mr. Black, have a good flight now," the attendant said as the door to the plane closed. Kanell walked down the aisle to the thirteenth row, seat C, in the tourist-class section. He loved first class. But he believed the anonymity of the cattle section would be more appropriate for Mr. J. C. Black.

Flight 786 was in the number-one takeoff position when Angie Weiner answered the phone at his apartment in Chicago. A man with cheap new shoes and a laying-on-hands suit was on the phone, and he was nervous.

"Angie, dammit, he didn't stay in Miami. The little bastard took another plane."

Weiner thought for a second. "Why the hell aren't you on the plane? I gave you enough money to take a flight."

The man shook his head. "Hell, I couldn't get down to the gate. They stopped me at the security check, Angie. I tried to get through there, but some black bitch stopped me. You gotta have tickets to get to the goddamn gates here. Nothin' but spicks and black bitches here, dammit!"

"Where the hell did he fly to?"

"Shit, Angie, there must be ten thousand gates here. He did stop and look at one of those screens for Delta, you know, those overhead screens. What do you want me to do?"

Weiner flexed his fist. "Get the hell back here, Robert," he said, "I got things to do." Weiner hung up the phone and walked toward the bedroom.

"Angie, you looked pissed as hell," a young boy named Leslie said. He had the sheet pulled up just below his navel. "So, ya got a problem or something?"

Weiner sat on the side of the bed. "The world's full of dumb shits, that's what." He looked at the kid. "But you're not that dumb are you?"

"Shit no, man," the kid said as he closed his eyes.

Kanell was sitting in the parking lot of American Opinion Research in Dallas, by ten P.M. At eleven a teenage girl left first, then two older women, then a man with more belly than height—Kanell didn't respect people like that—then another older woman, then a black couple "shaking and jiving," as he called it; he didn't really like blacks. Then a group of ladies of indeterminate age crawled into one car. Kanell cursed. There were too many older women. He drove his car, a stolen one, to DFW Airport, parking it in the long-term lot. After placing the parking ticket carefully in his wallet, he pocketed his gloves, entered the nearest terminal for a drink, then took a limousine back downtown and from there a cab to a motel.

At ten the next morning Kanell was standing in front of a display case containing perhaps a dozen shirts, including his favorites, brightly colored Alexander Julians. The young woman who approached him from behind the counter looked like one of his favorite things too, but he did not want anyone, especially a smooth blonde employee of Saks Fifth Avenue, Dallas, to remember his visit.

"Sir, can I help you with something?"

Kanell did not look up, but pointed to the silk Julian with the ninety-eight-dollar price tag. "Yes, if you have that in a sixteen thirty-five, I'll take it."

The smooth blonde kneeled down behind the counter, then

placed six of the silk Julians on the counter, her finger quickly pushing down the white tab on each collar until she found Kanell's size. The lady had big tits, Kanell thought. She was wearing a bra, though, not a hint of nipple advertising itself. His eyes lifted from the lady's breasts as she straightened up and said, "Now will that be cash or charge?"

"Cash, please, and put it in a Saks box. It's a gift for someone."

He walked a block before coming to a bus stop. Kanell didn't like buses, didn't like the types of people who rode them. He stood during the twenty-minute ride, finally leaving the bus very close to a large Sears sign. He turned the Saks box with its label against his body before entering the store. The lady who waited on him was much older than the smooth blonde at Saks. She probably looked a lot like Evelyn, he thought, old and dumpy. A perfect person to pick a sweater for Evelyn.

At the Eckerd drugstore in the shopping plaza he bought address labels, a gift tag, scissors, some plain wrapping paper, and tape. It was sunny, in the seventies. He sat on a bench in the park across from Sears, oblivious to the people around him who were enjoying the sunshine, and placed the sweater from Sears in the Saks box. With his left hand he wrote "To Evelyn, from a friend" on the gift card and put it on top of the sweater. The package was addressed simply to "Evelyn, American Opinion Research, 1324 Smithfield Place, Dallas, Texas, 75222." Kanell mailed the package at the main Dallas post office sorting center—he wanted the gift to arrive the next day—and took a cab to the Days Inn.

He sunned from one to five, a nautical map of the Florida Keys occupying his thoughts. Kanell paid particular attention to the small marinas normally used by inexperienced bareboaters and seasoned captains alike, committing the marinas and many of the small towns around them to memory. Calling Jo Pinder was an afterthought. He didn't want to call, didn't want to know what was happening in Chicago. It was very easy for Rick Kanell to live his life in compartments. But at six thirty he dialed his house, where Jo was staying while he was gone. When an operator came on the phone and said, "Room number, please," he started to say, "Two seventeen," then changed his mind.

"Operator, make that a credit-card call, please—can you hold on just a second," he said, dropping the phone on the bed as he reached for his wallet. He gave the operator a clean telephone-credit-card number, finishing just as Pinder picked up the phone. The card number was "wild," generated by a friend at the phone company.

"Hello?"

"Jo . . ."

The operator interrupted. "Sir, that calling card is invalid; would you have the new number?"

Kanell hesitated.

"Hello, Rick?"

"Operator, just make the call collect from Mr.—from Rick."

"Hello, ma'am, I have a collect call from Rick in Dallas, Texas. Will you accept the call?"

Damn it! Kanell thought.

"Yes, I will. Rick! So why aren't you in Miami?" Pinder continued, not waiting for his answer. "Rick, something's up at the office. I'm glad you didn't call at lunch, because the place was swarming with people."

"What's so unusual about that?"

"I didn't know many of the people, that's what. Do you want me to do anything?"

"No. I'll call you tomorrow. It's probably nothing."

Jo laughed. "Okay. I miss you."

"Yeah. I'll call you tomorrow." He hung up the phone and cursed again, *goddamn AT&T and their credit cards*.

By seven in the evening Rick Kanell was sitting at a new singles bar in a western Dallas suburb. He looked up as a brunette in designer jeans and a blouse opened just enough to show hints of things to share with the right person sat by him.

"Honey, I've got to compliment you on something," she said. She had even, white teeth. When she spoke, her lips pulled back and up, exposing them, the Cheshire Cat's smile.

"I'm so handsome, right?" Kanell grinned. She laughed.

"Well, you'll do. But I *really* like your taste in shirts. Mine's a Julian, too."

II

Rick Kanell's house on Sycamore was very interesting in many ways, Jo Pinder had always thought. Six large panels of glass rose fourteen feet to the roof, a dark green tile roof. Just to the right of the thick glass front door was a teak stairway leading to the loft area. The furniture in the house was chosen by a decorator, and chrome and teak and the latest in electronic gadgets were everywhere.

An IBM PC sat in the bedroom, tied to the System 34 in Rick Kanell's office via the only phone with a cord in the entire house. Five other units were older cordless models, the type that allows a user to move around while talking but that doesn't allow dialing away from the base unit. The phones were free, of course, part of the barter deal with another family, and they worked perfectly well, as Jo Pinder was finding out as she dialed a number and began to roam the house, snooping and prying into the little personal things that occupy all homes. She was heading up the stairway as Angie Weiner answered.

"All right."

"Angie, it's Jo; I'm at Rick's."

"Has he called?"

"Yeah, but first let me tell you that *something* is up at the office; I don't know what, but even during lunch the doors are closed every time Dean and Rosenbloom start to talk. They got a phone call from some judge's office today too, and Albert closed the door for that as well."

"Can you ask anything that will tell you what it is, or can you look at the files? Is there a file you can look at?"

"Angie, the only way I get close to Buettner is to let him look down my sweater; they don't give me much chance to look in the files or their office usually, because they take so damn many different lunch breaks." Jo Pinder was a much more relaxed person with Angie Weiner on the phone than with him in person, or with just about anyone, for that matter. Like Kanell, she was not very good at looking people in the eye; but unlike Kanell, she was afraid of what *she* might see as much as she was of what might be seen. In her own mind she was a fragile person who needed to be sheltered from too many unpleasant realities.

"If they're closing their doors so much in the office, do you think they suspect something with you?" The question brought a small moment of fright to her. She thought before answering.

"God, I don't think so. Dean's been awfully nice to me." Her voice was a little less confident than it had been.

"What did Rick say when he called?"

"Nothing, really. I told him about all the activity at the office, and he said it was probably nothing. He's in Dallas, you know, not Miami." She said it casually, as if she were talking about the weather. But as she said it, Angie Weiner put down the November issue of *Blue Boy* and stared out the window. Weiner knew Rick Kanell was not in Miami. But he did not know he was in Dallas. The city was a very important business center for the Vicovari outfit. Three of their most profitable porno operatives were there, including a newly remodeled and updated adult film center; but more important, Dallas was the second-largest market for car-chopping activities. Why would Kanell cover up a trip to Dallas by saying he was going to Miami? Weiner smiled. Kanell would lie if he were doing some business for himself, not Vicovari. Weiner rolled the thought in his mind.

"Did he say what he was doing in Dallas?"

"No. And you know, he kind of avoided that subject when I asked him. I only knew the city because I heard the operator say it." The nervousness returned. She did not want to think about the call with Rick; she did not want to think that the insignificant things she said had any real meaning. Anyway, she thought, Angie could just be testing her. He probably already knew why Rick was in Dallas. She began to walk down the staircase, her feet moving slowly as she listened.

"Jo, when is he going to call again? And when he calls, do you think you can get the number?"

"He said every couple of days. But you know how Rick is when he's away: you hear from him when you hear from him." She walked to a teak desk with chrome edges and sat down. Jo Pinder didn't really want Rick Kanell to hurry back. It was very pleasant there in the house alone, as if it were hers. She looked at her fingernails. Two of them were cracked slightly, and all of them were shorter than she would have liked. Work required them to be short. She wouldn't work forever, Jo thought, as her mind drifted away and her answers became distanced and short. About five minutes after her phone call had begun, Jo placed the phone back on its cradle and sat there at the desk, dreaming of things to come.

5

I

ANGIE Weiner was standing by the redwood chair in his living room on Wednesday morning, holding the phone. Plants were positioned around the room. Some were in straw baskets, others sitting in animals woven from palm pine, stained light brown and varnished. Weiner looked at the pig as he waited. It was his favorite animal. Its eyes were clear plastic buttons, the nostrils of the snout steel circles. Weiner's apartment was pleasant, especially considering the address. The corner of Balboa and State Streets was the center of Chicago proper's poorest white neighborhood.

As the voice came on the phone Weiner unconsciously stood a little straighter.

"Good morning, Angie."

"Good morning, Anton. I hate to bother you so early, but our friend has found out that Mr. K. is in Dallas." Angie was speaking carefully. Though the one Vicovari friend who had never disappointed the outfit was the telephone company employee who coordinated all of the legal wiretaps ordered by judges in Chicago, Anton Vicovari still believed in circumspect phone calls.

Weiner hesitated. "Anton, she also said that there's a lot of activity at the office, as if something is about to happen. But I'm really calling you on the other thing."

"I understand that, Angie," Vicovari said. "I'm becoming concerned about our young friend."

Weiner smiled. It was the first time the old man had voiced such an opinion about Kanell.

"You know, Anton, we have, you have many business interests in the Dallas area. I was wondering if he could be doing things for himself down there, not for you. . . ."

Vicovari was silent, thinking. Weiner wanted to say what he really believed: that son of a bitch Kanell was branching out on his own and was probably the reason things were going wrong in the outfit. The bastard should be laid out. But he didn't say it. Anton needed to come to those thoughts himself, he knew that.

"Angie, why don't you go down there for me, would you do that?" Vicovari's voice was pleasant. "I'm sure our friends there could help you understand what's on his mind."

Weiner nodded, a smile on his face again. "Yeah, I think that might be wise. I'll probably go this afternoon."

"And do you feel we need to be concerned about the other information?"

Weiner thought before answering. The raid on the outfit's Orion Theatre dump had caused only a pause in their work schedule. A new dump was operating less than three blocks from the abandoned theater. But Jo Pinder's comments about the activity in the offices of Chicago Auto Theft indicated more than the raid on the dump. "I think there could be a problem, Anton, but it may not have anything to do with us. Maybe someone else."

There was another long pause. "Angie, it might be good for you to be away under any circumstances. I would prefer your absence, should there be any problems. Have a pleasant trip," Vicovari concluded, his last word as soft as his first.

Weiner put the phone down slowly, then ran his hand over his head, rubbing the scalp hard. He was forty-four years old. Rick Kanell had been the one factor he felt kept him from being more important to the outfit. The shit, he thought, was picking the wrong time to feel so damned independent, that little grit with his polished nails and cocky walk and flat belly and cocaine nose and whorey ladies, he always had whorey ladies like Jo, was going to find himself hooked real, real soon. He'd like to hook him himself. Angie Weiner had gigged people with the prod, touching their genitals again and again as they screamed; he got an erection thinking about it. But he had not hooked anyone in a long, long time.

The hook was the beef hook. The person would be tied up, naked, his hands lashed to his sides and his feet bound together at the knees and ankles. Angie had been twenty-four when he hooked the first person. They had lifted the man up between two sides of beef hanging on other hooks, his body shaking like hard Jell-O, had positioned the hook just under his right collarbone, and had pulled him down on the hook. His mouth was taped shut with wide bands of white tape; to Weiner the screams sounded as if they came from his ears, and the body had jumped and wiggled with every scream, especially when they gigged him. "Gig him again, Angie, gig him again and make him wiggle," one of the guys had yelled between laughs. Angie thought about the laugh as he sat down in the redwood chair. He still had an erection.

II

"Buettner! Damn it! You're not going to believe this!"

Dean Buettner looked at his watch. It was almost six thirty, time to get up anyway.

"What's the matter, Albert?" He sat up in bed, still clutching the phone to his ear. It was unusual for Albert Rosenbloom to call him at home.

"Those goddamned wops stole *my car*! The damn thing was in the drive last night, I swear to God, those sons of bitches!"

Buettner held the phone away as he doubled up in laughter, his eyes closed tightly in an effort to compose himself. He pulled the phone back to his ear as Albert continued to rant. "And listen. You tell those goddamned sources of yours if they cut *one fender, one damn fender*, we'll bust every shop in the damn city, and God damn it! Pick me up in forty-five minutes!"

"Now Albert, be calm, be calm. Remember, you told me not to get personally involved in our work. Remember, it's just a car."

"Buettner!"

"Yes, boss, I'll be there." He hung up the phone, sat just long enough on the bed to look at word 7 in *Reader's Digest*, and headed to the bathroom. At six forty he made the first of three phone calls, delivering the same message to each of the listeners: "Look. Someone made a bad pickup last night on 137th Street, a dark blue 1983 Lincoln. The car was the property of Albert Rosenbloom. Lieutenant Albert Rosenbloom, chief of detectives, Chicago Auto Theft Department, Criminal Investigation Division. *Lieutenant* Rosenbloom is very upset by this mistake. . . ." Each listener had responded in virtually the same manner: "Oh shit . . . okay." Buettner's contacts on the street were good, he knew that. But he didn't know if Albert Rosenbloom's car could be salvaged in time. He laughed again anyway as he drove the seventeen miles to the Elmwood section of West Chicago.

Buettner mentioned his phone calls as the two headed toward downtown Chicago. "I called on your car."

Rosenbloom glanced to the left, a chagrined look on his face. "And?"

"Well, you know, the clues aren't exactly profuse." He smiled, trying hard to hold the curve to the barest minimum. Rosenbloom, he thought, might not approve of new words under the circumstances. But the word passed right over his head.

"Dean, don't tell me about clues. This isn't a movie. *I want my damn car!*" Rosenbloom changed the subject instantly. "I wonder how surprised our friends at Central Body Shop will be tonight."

"I think very surprised. The place has followed the same pattern for nearly a month. I'd give my left nut if we actually got Weiner there. Or Vicovari."

Rosenbloom gave out a laugh. "Hell, *I'd* give your left nut too, and your right. But I doubt if Weiner or Vicovari has been in that place. I don't think we'll even pin anything on them, but at least we'll knock a hole in them." He smiled again, a wry smile. "Shit, I hope Vicovari sees *Spotlight* before the raid. The bastard will think we're picking on him."

Buettner pulled into the underground entrance to the building. He had forgotten about the *Spotlight* article. "Albert, I'm going by Supplies to pick up some copies, okay? That is funny. A one-two punch at Vicovari."

Spotlight was the second publication Dean Buettner usually looked at on any given Wednesday. It was a flimsy thing printed on stock, which reminded him more of comic books than an official publication by the Chicago Crime Commission. With its Dick Tracy–style drawings on the cover, *Spotlight* was designed to high-light individuals who participated in the organized-crime activities of Chicago but were seemingly above any form of prosecution. The publication had been Rosenbloom's idea, but the story on Vicovari was the result of Buettner's work. For the first time in print, Anton Vicovari's role in organized crime was detailed. Buettner was proud of that story. He waved a copy as he entered the office. "Hey, Albert, are we going to send a copy to Vicovari?"

Rosenbloom barely smiled. "No need to. He probably got a copy before you did." Rosenbloom was sitting on the clerk's desk, his eyes following the wall up to the light fixture. "Dean, why the hell can't you get a strong light in here? Do *I* need to change it myself or something?" He shook his head. "So when do you think you'll hear something on the car?"

Buettner gave an exasperated laugh. "Albert, why the hell are you so worried about the car? I mean, the thing's insured, for God's sake." He watched Rosenbloom's expression. "Albert . . . don't tell me . . ."

"Dean, shut up!" Rosenbloom started walking to his office.

Buettner followed closely, stifling another grin. Rosenbloom turned to face him.

"Dean, I swear to God, if you tell anyone, if you so much as giggle one giggle, I'm gonna have you transferred to Traffic. I didn't have the goddamned money." He shrugged. "And anyway, I was going to pay it this week."

Buettner turned without saying a word and walked to his office. As he shut the door, he let out one deliberate, short, loud laugh, then muffled it. It was going to be a very interesting day, he was sure of it.

He went to lunch at eleven thirty and walked back into the office before twelve, a short lunch. Jo Pinder was just hanging up the phone.

"Dean, that was an odd phone call. Some man, he wouldn't give his name, said the car was in front of 1551 137th Street." She looked at him. Buettner was grinning.

"Bingo! Jo, call over to Lieutenant Nolan's office and see if Albert's still there, I want to talk to him." She nodded, looking up the department telephone listing. "Nolan, Thomas, Chief, Uniformed Police." Why would Rosenbloom be there? She did not voice her question. She dialed the extension, but before anybody could answer, Rosenbloom walked in the door. Buettner was standing by him in an instant.

"Hey! So are things all set?"

"Yeah. Aren't you glad I do your job for you? We're meeting here at eight."

"Good. So that means you can go take a drive with me now."

Rosenbloom didn't appear to be in any mood for games. "What the hell, don't we have a few things that need doing around here maybe, Dean. . . ."

"Albert, come on. It's about the car." Buettner took him by the left shoulder and started heading toward the door.

The car was sitting about six hundred feet from Albert Rosenbloom's driveway. A new door lock had been put in the driver's door. The ignition lock had been replaced too. The old lock was on the passenger floor. Two new sets of keys to match the new locks were in an envelope on the seat. Albert Rosenbloom said nothing as he walked around the car looking for damage. There was none. But as he sat in the driver's seat and tried out the new keys, he grinned.

"Well," he said, cutting his eyes to meet Buettner's, "at least they could have washed the damn thing."

At eight forty, two black-and-whites, one police van, and one unmarked car pulled up to the gate of Central Body Shop. The shop was located on Conservation Avenue, in an area of Chicago's West Side filled with garages, warehouses, a bowling alley, and small pockets of tenement housing and rickety shacks that served as home for poor blacks who had moved north to escape poverty, only to find it there.

The shack that sat less than a hundred yards from the entrance to Central Body Shop had working plumbing and a telephone, both of these luxuries paid for by some man who had visited the older black man who lived there and had "retained" him to serve as a night watchman. The old man had no teeth, a fact that made him hesitant to talk on the phone. But as the cars pulled up to the gate of Central Body Shop, the old man picked up the phone and dialed the only number he knew from memory. He was working his gums as the phone answered.

"Yes?" the voice said. The old man sat there a moment before speaking.

"There's some po-lice cars at the gate. I called to tell ya."

As two uniformed men pushed back the gates, the young mule named Danny dropped the phone, then turned from it, moving fast.

"Close it down! Close it down!" he yelled as he entered the large enclosed bay area. The four men in overalls and protective helmets didn't need to hear any more. One dropped his acetylene torch without stopping to turn it off, threw off his helmet, and headed to the back door. A Puerto Rican man in his fifties cursed in language unintelligible to Danny, turned off his torch, and simply sat on the left front fender of the new Buick beside him. He looked around the bay, his lips moving constantly in a mixture of curses and prayers.

Danny was heading to the office as Buettner, Rosenbloom, and a uniformed officer stood at the door. It was a heavy steel door locked tightly. They cut to the side of the building as Buettner yelled, "Damn it! They know! Albert, get back!" Buettner wanted to get in the office before the filing cabinet was touched. The cabinet was what mattered. He took the butt of his gun and broke two panels in a high window, reached to the side of the window and turned the lock. It wasn't going right. Damn it, he thought as he pulled up, turned his body, and climbed through the window.

A rookie detective, John Rawls, turned the corner of the building to the back door when it flew open. The man running out the door was silhouetted against strong lights as he began to run toward the back fence. He was carrying something in his hand.

"Hold it! Chicago police! Hold it *now!*" Rawls yelled, grasping his gun with both hands in front of him, legs slightly bent. The man started to turn, momentum keeping him from stopping, and raise his hands. Rawls could not see what was in the right one. But when he saw the outline of something in the hand, he acted on instinct and fear. He fired one shot, aiming just as he had been taught. The bullet went nearly to the center of the man's outline, just an inch or so off dead center, entered the ventricle, and doubled him over as he fell. The man hit the asphalt hard. He did not move.

Rosenbloom turned the corner as the body hit, then froze as Rawls pivoted at the sound of footsteps, his stance and the gun in almost the same posture as before the shot.

"Hold it! John, it's me—Rosenbloom." Rosenbloom's eyes moved to the still body. He walked to it as he pulled a flashlight from the holster on his left side. There was a large pool of blood by the man. His arms were pulled up tightly to his body, a stream of blood dripping through his hands. Rosenbloom put two fingers to the man's neck, closed his eyes for an instant, then looked at the man's right hand. Two other men and the rookie were walking up behind Rosenbloom.

He lifted the man's right hand. Grasped tightly in it was a slender leather kit containing two wrenches. The wrench set was a gift; it had been the man's last thought.

"Oh Jesus, the man turned and I couldn't see what he had. Oh Jesus," Rawls said as he looked at the hand.

Buettner hadn't stopped when he heard the shot. He too was standing with his weight equally on both feet, his pistol pointed at Danny's midsection. Danny's right hand was on the open drawer to the filing cabinet. His eyes were focused on Buettner's gun. "Okay! Okay!" he yelled. Danny's fingers were jumping up and down as if they were playing the keys of a typewriter.

"Jackie!" Buettner held his position until Jackie Bell, an Auto Theft detective, arrived to take over, and then ran quickly from the office. John Rawls was standing next to the man's body as Buettner approached. His hand was hanging limp at his side. "Damn it, Dean! I thought the bastard had a gun, honest to God, I thought he had a gun!" Rawls turned and walked toward the gate.

"Someone call Internal Affairs," Rosenbloom said as he walked back toward the bays, his glance momentarily meeting Buettner's. Buettner followed. When they entered the first bay, Rosenbloom turned around, shaking his head gently as if it were sore to move.

"The son of a bitch was carrying a tool kit," Rosenbloom said as he looked back toward the office. "Did we get here in time?"

"Yeah, I think so. The files look intact. Now if we have any luck, maybe this'll all be worth it."

Rosenbloom waited at Central Body Shop for an ambulance and a team of investigators from Internal Affairs. Buettner rode in the lead black-and-white back to Central Booking. Danny, the mule, was sitting in the backseat. He was quiet as the car drove from the outskirts of Chicago to the central district. But as they approached Eaton Avenue, he sat up, his head nearly touching the wire cage that separated the backseat from the front.

"You think you're big shits, don't you?" Neither Buettner nor the driver answered him. "You goddamn cops think you're big shits. You shoot a goddamn man who's doing nothing but trying to make some money without hurting anyone, and it makes you feel good." Buettner was trying to block out the words as Danny spoke. Like the rookie detective, he had never shot anyone. But as Danny continued, Dean's chest constricted, breathing seemed hard.

"He wasn't no crook, no sir," Danny continued. "That man busted his ass all day. . . ." Danny's voice began to break; none of it had seemed that serious. He had *liked* working at Central Body Shop. He liked scheduling the mules, liked the thrill he felt when Angie Weiner called him with a compliment. He closed his eyes when he spoke: "I'm the one who told him about the work." He was quiet for a moment. "That was my uncle."

III

Thursday morning was one of the few mornings during the past five years that Dean Buettner did not learn a new word. He meant to, but his mind was on other things. The raid was bothering him. A man was dead. The rookie detective who killed him, John Rawls, would be transferred to a desk job until the Internal Affairs investigation was completed.

And then there were the files. The office had yielded a book of shipping orders that could be of value; each of those orders would be traced during the next weeks. But the computer printout, the one document Auto Theft hoped would lead to Anton Vicovari, was meaningless. The first three pages were missing; the pages that might translate twenty pages of numbers and letters into a pointing finger were gone.

Buettner was sitting at his desk. Between bites of a ham sandwich without mayonnaise he wrote his report on the previous evening's work in preparation for the interview he knew Internal Affairs would request that afternoon. He did not hear Jo Pinder answer the phone. In fact, he had hardly paid any attention to her during the last twenty minutes. The change in his usually ebullient personality made

Pinder very nervous, too. She knew about the night's activities, had learned about the raid the moment she entered the building. Buettner's quietness, she was sure, harbored suspicion.

Buettner pushed down the intercom button and picked up the phone.

"Dean, there's a call from Minneapolis Homicide, an Earl Brown."

"Thanks, I'll take it." He pushed the button on line 1.

"Buettner."

"Buettner, this is Earl Brown, Minneapolis Homicide. How are things in the Windy City today?" Buettner could tell the guy was going to be talkative. A motormouth he didn't need today.

"They're fine, what can I do for you?"

"We need a little help. We're investigating a homicide, and son of a bitch if the guy isn't from Chicago. Thanks for sharing the fun things in life with us."

"We try, Brown, but you've got Auto Theft here. You want me to switch you to Homicide?"

"No, you sound like such a nice man, and anyway, the guy's one of your friends."

The man's words brought Buettner's thoughts from their wandering. "How so?"

"Well, you see, the guy was eaten to shit by maggots and worms and his eyes were gone, ant eyes, man, according to the reports— you know how those spooks in Autopsy love to describe things. But his remaining two fingers gave us good enough prints to make an ID. He was busted by you guys for auto theft last year, fifteen years old, and the punk was let off, lack of evidence. The dumb fuck got himself killed by someone who was very, very mad. Broke his fuckin' neck and left him in a garbage pile."

"What's the name?"

"Medlock. Robert, no middle name, Medlock. We show an address of 2987 Coyne Street, apartment 6D. A long way up. Buettner, I was wondering if you might know off the top of your head what nice man accidentally killed Robert No Middle Name Medlock, put his little body in a paper bag named Clupak, along with a bloody piece of steel wool embedded with bits of the victim's outer epidermal tissue, that's bloody skin, a hundred-percent cotton rag with traces of ureal fluid, that's piss, and an empty Hires root beer can, two of them, as a matter of fact."

Buettner shook his head. A fucking ghoul. "Brown, I know the guy's name, but that's about it. Give me your number and I'll call you back when I get his file." He wrote the number on the corner of his notes.

Bobby Medlock had run with the crowd near Balboa Street, Buettner knew that. He was a good basketball player too. And he had a brother. Both Medlocks had resented Buettner's intrusion on their turf. They considered him a spoiler, a feeling each of them passed on to Buettner and the other kids. Like Lennie, the one kid who talked straight with Buettner about mules. Buettner made a mental note to talk with Lennie.

Jo Pinder looked up when Buettner walked out of the office, trying to judge from his expression the proper reaction. He looked very distracted. "So what was that about?"

Buettner was headed to the door when he stopped to answer, "Minneapolis found the body of a mule from here; he was murdered. Jo, will you call down and have them send up the kid's file? His name is Robert N.M.I. Medlock; we picked him up a year or so ago."

Pinder nodded. "Boy, everyone is sure down around here. Why isn't everybody feeling up after last night?" Jo hoped her smile wasn't as transparent as it felt. Before he answered she continued. "Is it because of John? He did the right thing, didn't he? The people downstairs said the guy didn't have a gun, but that John thought he did."

Buettner rubbed his fingers just above the brow. "Yeah, he reacted the way we are taught. Get that file for me, okay?"

"I'll call down now." She hesitated. "Was the kid important?"

"Not really . . . except for the fact he was a kid who was killed because he started running with very dangerous people." Buettner looked away. Who was he running with? Lennie's crowd. And that crowd mostly muled for Angie Weiner. And Central Body Shop. He looked at Jo with a more pleased expression.

"Hey, you just helped me."

Jo looked puzzled. Christ, she didn't need to be helping him. "What do you mean? What did I say?"

"It's nothing, you just made me think who the kid probably muled for. He was probably involved with Central Body Shop." Buettner shook his head. "Christ, all the wrong people at that place get killed. . . ." He turned and headed out the door.

"Dean, when will you be back?"

Buettner kept walking, turning his head to yell, "In thirty minutes or so. See ya tomorrow."

Pinder felt better. The mood around the place didn't seem to have anything to do with her, that was the important thing. She needed to talk to Angie. But that was impossible, she thought. He was out of town. Jo did not know for sure where. She needed to talk to Rick Kanell too, and she did not want to wait until evening, when he would call, if he would call. Jo picked up the phone to call Central Files. She should tell someone about the kid too, though it probably wasn't that important.

6

FRIDAY was cool and bright in Atlanta. Myrtle Street was covered in leaves from the tall oaks bordering it on both sides, leaves filling the gutters and covering bits of garbage and empty bottles along the sidewalk. Evelyn Wade muttered slightly as she walked toward Tenth Street, looking down to gauge her steps over the octagonal cement tiles forming the sidewalk, many of the tiles pushed up by the roots of trees. But her eyes kept focusing on the garbage. It had to be the strangers. Residents didn't drop refuse.

Evelyn stopped as she saw an open empty Tampax box. That was too much. In one quick movement she upended her cane and swung it lightly, like the short swing of a croquet mallet, catching the open end of the box with the crook of the cane. That would have been a good shot, she thought, as she took nine careful steps to the dozens of green garbage cans with wheels that sat in front of the houses on Myrtle Street as if they were waiting for a ride. Evelyn's canes were often used for practicing croquet shots, even one-handed shots like this. She lowered the cane and dropped the box into the can belong-

69

ing to 79 Myrtle, then continued to Lane Englander's house, knocking on his door with three firm raps of the cane. He opened it before the cane made it back to Evelyn's side.

"Are you always that eager to have a lady visitor?" Evelyn said with a chuckle.

"They're just so few," Englander said as he led Evelyn into the living room. At sixty-nine, standing six feet tall and weighing in just under a hundred seventy pounds, Englander was still an athletic, muscular-looking man, a weathered face and a thick head of nearly white hair adding to his pleasant and strong appearance.

"Well, did you find out anything?" he said as they sat at opposite ends of a long sofa. The purpose of Evelyn's visit was to report on her phone calls, over thirty of them, to Chicago.

"No. Well, I don't think I did. I called one place, a body shop, and a man there was nearly rude to me; he asked a lot of questions, then asked me for my phone number. I gave it to him after we talked a while. I think he thought I was a regular customer or something like that."

Englander shook his head no. "Evelyn, why would a body shop take your phone number? Are they going to call you when they have an extra fender or something?"

"You know, the man asked me to speak up, too. And we had a perfectly good line." Evelyn paused. "And he asked me twice for my name. I wonder if they were recording the call."

Englander shook his head again. "Something was out of the ordinary there, I think. Do you still have the number?"

"Of course I do."

Englander pulled his upper body straight. "Evelyn, *that* number might be *the* number. I think you should call them back. And don't be so nice when you call." He paused. "Do you want me to call?"

Englander's easy acceptance of her search brought a feeling of vindication to Evelyn. "Then you don't think I'm being silly?"

"Evelyn, what's there to be silly about?" He waved his finger. "If you are telling me that you think a young boy is hurt or dead, that's nothing to be silly about, and it's not that farfetched, either." Englander looked away for a moment, forming his thoughts carefully. "Evelyn, do you ever read about those people who win millions in lotteries? People forget that though the odds may be millions to one, some person's odds were one to one." Evelyn nodded. "And have you ever looked at a phone just as it rang and thought, 'What an odd coincidence,' as if it were mental telepathy or something? Well, how many times have you looked at a phone when it *didn't* ring? That's what counts. It's the odds." Englander shook his head sympathetically. "Chance is the surest thing in the world. And the chances are that phones do interrupt things, like your call did."

Evelyn looked relieved. "Lane, you know, I needed you to believe in me today."

"I know that. Now, who's going to call? Me or you?"

"I'll call, and you listen in," Evelyn said as she went directly to the phone, "and I'll pay you in dinners when the bill comes in."

On the second ring, a man's voice answered, repeating the name of the place. It sounded like a different man.

"Yes, I called the other day. Could you please tell me what you are doing there?" Evelyn was trying to sound as firm as she could, her thoughts going back to the tone of voice she once used to quiet an unruly study hall. The man hesitated before answering.

"Uh . . . lady, this is a body shop. Can I help you?"

"Yes. I want to know why the man I talked to yesterday took down my phone number and name. No one called me."

The man hesitated again. "Ma'am, can I ask where you are calling from?"

"From Atlanta, I . . ."

"Are you with a body shop there?"

Evelyn was irritated. "Young man, in the South we think it's rude to interrupt people. I assume that some people still have manners in Chicago too." Evelyn shook her head firmly.

The man in Chicago started to turn off the recorder. He didn't understand at all what the lady was talking about. But he moved his hand from the "off" button as he glanced at the uniformed officer standing by the filing cabinet. The officer was listening to the conversation with an earpiece, a large grin on his face.

"Ma'am, I'm awfully sorry about that. But could you please tell me once more why you are calling?"

"I was calling to see if anyone had found out anything about the boy. I told the other man that I had overheard a conversation in which a young boy was hurt."

None of Evelyn's words made any sense to the man, but he continued. "Ma'am, when did you call the boy?"

"A week ago yesterday. Do you mean no one told you about *my* call?"

"No, but if you'd like to give me your name and number again, I promise you I'll check into it."

Evelyn felt that she was making progress. But she wanted to know more. "I appreciate that. Now could you tell me if you are with the police?"

Her question stunned him. The monitoring of Central Body Shop's phones had been going on less than two full days, and each of the officers who had monitored and recorded the phone calls during that time had been careful not to betray his function. Excerpted portions of virtually all the calls, with notations indicating whether they appeared legitimate or suspicious, were listed at the end of the day in a typed report. Excerpts of the previous day's calls were already sitting on Dean Buettner's desk, with a notation concerning Evelyn's first call: "N.F.A.," no further attention.

The man looked again at the uniformed officer. The officer shrugged.

"Ma'am, why would you think I'm with the police?"

Evelyn hesitated. The man was probing her as if he didn't want to say yes, but was saying yes. Evelyn was not a good liar. But she did know how to bluff.

"Because you are."

The man did not respond for a moment. Evelyn waited too, and then continued to speak. "Now, young man, how do I find out about the boy?"

"You can be sure I'm going to pass your message on. Could you please give me your name and number again? It might speed things up."

Even after she'd hung up, Evelyn continued standing by the phone. When Englander came back to the room from the kitchen, she turned, then unconsciously took a step toward him.

"How did I do?" she said, forcing a smile.

Englander nodded. "Good. You're very strong, you know that?"

She looked at the door. "I think you need to keep saying that, and I hope you won't mind walking me home."

There she went directly to her bedroom and sat on the edge of the bed, her right foot pushing off her left shoe. She could not reach that foot very well. She stretched to touch the clasp on her right shoe and winced at the effort the stretching took. Evelyn lay on the bed for nearly fifteen minutes before she drifted to sleep. Something was happening. She knew that. But she could not decide what.

II

Though he didn't know it, Rick Kanell's septum, the tissue dividing his nostrils, was slowly being eaten away by the fine white powder he loved so much. The interior veins of his nose were deteriorating, too. But the use of eighty-percent pure did contribute to Rick Kanell's attention to detail. At least he thought it did. Kanell was on the eight A.M. flight from Dallas to Miami. He was working on an alibi.

The night before, his "bait," the Sears sweater in a Saks box, had finally drawn the quarry. Kanell leaned back in his seat, pleased with himself. He had thought the plan would work, though Wednesday's drought had made him antsy. That evening he had watched at least ten older women enter the offices of Dallas AOR around five, but when they had straggled out around eleven, none carried a Saks box or wore the sweater.

73

But Thursday night the plan had worked. Evelyn Garner left the office at 10:55. Kanell did not smile when he saw the box under her arm. He was angry at the woman who had made him wait. She looked very frumpy. She looked like the nosy type, too, probably a gossip.

Kanell had followed the dirty green Comet at a distance through fifteen minutes of thoroughfares and residential streets. As the car made a final turn before pulling into the third driveway on the left, he thought of his aunt. She too had been short and thick. She used to sit on the top step of the house, wearing a shapeless dress, and spit next to the day lilies. The brown-stained flowers and a couple of scrawny privet bushes had been the only plants around the small frame structure. In the dry summer months, the tobacco and juices would slowly pile up just to the left of the lilies, forming a small mound. Rick Kanell had always felt trapped in that house, trapped by the people who surrounded him. He had always hated his aunt, too.

Evelyn Garner's car had pulled behind the house, a dark house, as he slowly surveyed the neighboring houses. But as he drove to the end of the street and turned, his thoughts were of his aunt. She had died when he was eleven, tumbled from the steps, her head landing in the mound of filth by the lilies, her eyes open. They sang "Amazing Grace" at the funeral, he remembered that. After the song, Kanell had stood looking at her, carefully searching for tobacco stains on her face.

Recalling his reflections of the night before, Rick Kanell watched the plane attendants go through their safety routine. He thought how far he had come from that dilapidated and barren house. Evelyn, he was sure, had hurt him. The thought made him feel angry, trapped, as if a box were placed around him, so close that movement would bruise him. Kanell didn't like the feeling that strangers could affect him. Soon, though, the problem would be over.

At one o'clock he entered the lobby of the Fontainebleau Hilton in Miami and walked up to the young man standing at the second registration area.

"Can I help you, sir?"

"Yes, I'd like a room, a good one, for two nights, please." The man turned a card to face Kanell and put a blue Fontainebleau Hilton pen by it.

"Are you here with the Kiwanis group, sir?"

Kanell looked at him. The guy was very swishy. "No, I'm just taking a vacation from my vacation. A couple of guys and I've been bareboating in the Keys. We had a *real* good time, and I'm kinda tired."

The young man looked at Kanell's tan and at the tight muscles of his arms and smiled. "Yeah, I know what you mean." He glanced around the room to make sure that other ears weren't listening. "Planning to do any partying while you're with us? . . . I might be able to help you with that."

Kanell looked him dead center in the eyes. Then he smiled. He wanted the guy to remember him. "Maybe. But right now, I need some rest . . . to store up some juices."

Kanell put his bag, a light one, in room 2323, a corner room overlooking the tropical gardens and very large pool. He went to the bathroom, mussed the bed just in case, then flipped the "Do Not Disturb" sign to the outside of the door and took the elevator to the main floor, walking quickly by the registration desk, then down a long corridor to the Budget Rent A Car desk in the north lobby. He rented the only car available without a reservation and drove the Plymouth Reliant across the Venetian Causeway, pulling onto the northbound lane of I-95.

At the Palmetto Parkway exit in Boca Raton, Kanell turned right and headed toward the ocean. He'd put enough miles on the car. It would be a good alibi, too. He stopped at a 7-Eleven just before the Palmetto Grand Canal bridge, bought a sandwich and a tall Budweiser Light, then turned the car back to the interstate. After parking the car in the All-Right parking lot at the Regency Hotel in downtown Miami, Kanell caught the four-o'clock airport bus in front of the hotel and was standing at the Texas Air counter at Miami airport at 4:35. At his side was a new briefcase, a cheap one. He bought a

75

tourist-class ticket to Dallas in the name of Robert Smithfield, then walked to gate 9E, the farthest gate on the E corridor.

III

Angie Weiner blew his nose and pushed the button on the wall again. He looked at his watch as the picture on the television screen went blank for a moment, then began to display a very thin and elegant woman sunbathing on the deck of a large yacht. The woman was topless. Weiner watched for less than a minute, then pushed the button three times, each time pulling up a different video film. The last picture was of two young men making love. He took his hand from the button and watched. The videotape was much more professional than his own productions, he thought.

When someone knocked on the door, Weiner quickly pushed the button one more time and pulled his coat over his lap. He opened the door when he heard the man's voice.

"Well, Angie, what do you think?" The man walked in the booth as he began to talk. Weiner was in the newest version of the quarter porno flick, the creation of the man standing before him, and he was impressed. The building was new and tasteful, the walls covered in redwood. The individual booths were like a doctor's examining room. They were twice as large as the booths Weiner knew well in Chicago, but more important, they provided a much wider variety of flicks without requiring a person to move from booth to booth. At any time a patron could simply push the button on the wall and watch portions of eight movies, all of them on videotape, all of them with sound.

Angie laughed as he looked at the man. "Hell, David, this is like HBO. I'm gonna see that you get the best flicks first from now on. You got our best operation, you know." David liked that. He was a partner in this particular Vicovari film enterprise, though he had never heard of Anton Vicovari. The man knew only Weiner, and Weiner was the person who had provided him with the money for this pilot film operation.

He led Weiner back to a small room behind the magazine display, waving his hands at the ten video machines that fed the booths.

"You see, everything feeds out of here. *And* we know what any booth is watching, too." The man smiled. "If we have someone important in here, we make a note of their favorite film." Weiner shook his head, but felt a slight twinge of nervousness at the words. He wondered if the man had kept a record of what interested him.

Weiner glanced again at his watch, then turned to the man. "David, I've got to go. I'm flying out at two." The man looked relieved. He had never really known where the money came from, but he did know that being with Angie Weiner was like watching a very bad movie. He walked Weiner to the door, nodding at an older man as he came in, then returned to his position behind the cash register.

Weiner was driving a red Lincoln Town Car. He had rented it in his own name at the Dallas airport, and put over four hundred miles on the car in less than two full days, looking for traces of Rick Kanell. He had found none, though he had talked to Vicovari's largest customers in the Dallas area. "Roadrunners," trucks laden with caps, cowl-roof clips, and at times entire "doghouses," the complete front end of a vehicle from the windshield forward, traveled the route from Vicovari's warehouses in South Chicago to Dallas at least twice weekly, supplying illicit body shops in the city. Prescription drugs, stolen at times from warehouses, but mainly bartered from other families or outfits, arrived in Dallas at least once a week. And then there were the flicks. Next to Chicago, Dallas was the most important outlet for Vicovari productions. Weiner made a mental note to improve the technical quality of their films. Sound, he thought, added a lot of juice to the emotions the films produced.

But even though he had not physically seen Rick Kanell, Weiner was sure his trip had produced information damaging to Kanell. Two of the body shops he had visited had been approached twice during the past month by an individual who said he represented a source for very cheap automobile parts. The source was located in

Chicago. Weiner had smiled when he heard that. Kanell, of course, would be too smart to visit places himself.

Weiner scratched the tip of his nose as he thought about Kanell, his fingers grabbing a single hair there, pulling it out quickly. He flinched slightly. The bastard was somewhere in the city. Probably laughing about the raid on Central Body Shop, he reflected. That raid was another strike against him. It was just too convenient, a vacation at too convenient a time, especially a vacation that wasn't in Miami. The last hit he'd arranged had been perfect, even down to fingering the wrong man for the cops. But for Kanell, he would do it differently. If Anton Vicovari would now believe that Kanell had become dispensable, he would do something special. Weiner clenched his fist, his mind creating an image of Kanell on the hook. The method would have to be modified, he thought. Vicovari would not approve. But Weiner had many ways to inflict pain, that was what he cared about. He was imagining the expression on Rick Kanell's face as he walked up to the rental counter and smiled at the lady there.

A few minutes after four Weiner was picked up at O'Hare by the same man who had followed Rick Kanell to Miami. The man hesitated nervously for a moment and then spoke.

"Angie?"

Weiner looked steadily at him. It was his favorite game with people who appeared afraid of him; he never said "Yes" or "What do you want," he simply looked at them.

"Angie, did you know they found Bobby Medlock? They found him in the woods of Minnesota. Someone had broken his neck."

Weiner continued to look at the messenger for a moment, but his mind was on the kid. Bobby Medlock had been to bed with him for nearly two years. The memory of that first seduction was very vivid. He shifted on the seat as the man turned on Kasper Street and headed east.

"How do you know he's dead?"

"It's on the street. You know, his brother told some of the kids. They didn't know who did it."

Kanell would think it was funny. The temperature had dropped to the low forties, but Weiner put the window down and sucked in the cold air through his nose, two quick sucking motions. Kanell would think it was a real gas.

And then it hit him. Angie Weiner had forgotten about it, really. But Kanell had never really explained where he had been the night Bobby Medlock had disappeared. Kanell had told Jo Pinder he was with him. Weiner had put that down mentally against Kanell but had nothing to connect it to till now. He rolled the window down further. Why the hell would the bastard kill the kid?

He dropped the driver off at the end of Kasper Street and turned the car toward the Gold Coast, glancing at his watch, then at a black-and-white accelerating past on the left. Kanell would kill the kid only if the kid caught him doing something wrong. Weiner did not know what, but the specifics weren't important to him as the car began to move along the strand of high rises bordering the shore of Lake Michigan. He had enough on Rick Kanell, and that information needed to make sense when he entered Anton Vicovari's apartment.

Vicovari didn't like to have meetings in his apartment. But the *Spotlight* article and the raid on Central Body Shop had made him more cautious than usual. Weiner pulled the car into the underground entrance of the building and slid a key into the mechanism that opened the parking area and the elevator. Vicovari's apartment, a triplex, used the twenty-third floor as the entrance for business guests. The door opened onto a circular stairway to the left, which wound up to Vicovari's working area and down to the main living areas. Weiner was led up the stairway by an old black man in a white tie who nodded but did not speak when he opened the door. In the right upper-level foyer was a portrait of a very thin lady. The portrait reminded Angie of the thirties. The lady held a nearly defiant pose, head high and haughty, a bun sitting on the back of her head, which pulled the hair severely upward from her forehead. The painting presented a bearing only royal blood could bring, Weiner believed, an aura of something substantial he knew money could not buy.

He pulled his coat downward to smooth out the wrinkles and sat on a slender red couch before the painting, a stranger in the gallery. Weiner could remember when Anton had been poor. He didn't regret that memory, either. Weiner had been eighteen years old. He had worked fourteen hours a day, loading and unloading the large trucks that pulled up to the dock at one of the independent slaughterhouses in Chicago. Anton Vicovari had run that slaughterhouse, Star Meat Packing. Each day over a hundred pigs were slaughtered there. The animals were run through a very fast assembly line. In single file they were prodded up a narrow ramp, just wide enough for one animal at a time to climb. At the top, a black man stood with a long, wide-bladed knife. He wore a black rubber apron. The black man would coax each animal forward just enough so that a wooden gate could be dropped behind it. A clasp would be fastened to each of the animal's back legs; the clasps looked like the manacles Angie had seen in horror movies. The black man would grab a pig by its snout, jerk the head up quickly, and slit the throat at the same instant, before the animal could fight. Angie remembered the blood pit. As the pig was hoisted up by its hind legs, its front legs jerking toward the body, the blood would collect in a large pit below it. The blood was saved, along with the animal's entrails. Pet-food manufacturers used them both.

It was in that large, open room that Angie Weiner and Anton Vicovari had become bonded to each other. Vicovari had begun to steal cars as a weekend and evening profession. He stole an average of three cars a week, selling each car for less than a thousand dollars. Vicovari felt safe in that pastime. He was making over $100,000 a year and the police didn't know or didn't care that he was in business. Angie Weiner delivered the cars. On the first day of his job, a Saturday, Weiner had been handed $2,500 by a Chevrolet dealer in Deland. When Vicovari gave him back two hundred dollars for his effort, Weiner laughed. He worked a week to make a *hundred* dollars. Within six months, Weiner was finding other kids to steal cars for Vicovari, and his take from that effort was over a thousand dollars a week. He didn't spend all that money, he still didn't spend what he made. Angie liked to save money. In over thirty separate accounts, Angie Weiner had put away over $700,000. But he would have never made that money, he thought, if it hadn't been for the slaughter room.

In the late fifties, three other outfits had been trying to expand their car-theft operations. Two of them, the Moynahans and the Canellis, decided that the best way to expand was to do away with Anton Vicovari. They had intended to run him down with a car early one Monday morning in front of Star Meat Packing. But the oldest mule for the Moynahans had thought poorly of the plan. He had eaten at the Vicovari table. And on the Saturday night before the Moynahan and Canelli outfits had planned to run over Anton Vicovari, the mule told Angie Weiner of their plan.

At a little after seven A.M. on Sunday morning, Angie Weiner and the mule had gone first to the house of Robert Moynahan. The mule knocked on the door, and when the door opened, he entered the room with Weiner. Weiner shot Moynahan's daughter and wife in the head. He then placed Robert Moynahan and his two sons, trussed, in the back of a Star Meat Packing van.

At eight forty-five, Weiner came up behind Jimmy Canelli on 34th Street as he walked across the street to a corner restaurant for breakfast. They put him in the van, too. At about nine o'clock, Angie Weiner carried each of the men up the loading ramp at Star Meat Packing. Weiner put the Moynahans on their sides just in front of the blood pit—he wanted them to have a good view—and then took Canelli to the top of the ramp, slit his throat, and gutted him. He did the same thing to the Moynahan boys. And then he did it to Robert Moynahan. Weiner left the blood and the guts for the pet-food people, but he took the remains of their bodies and dropped them in sacks right next to where the Sears Building now stands, and then he went to breakfast.

Angie Weiner had no problem with those memories, any of them. It was the first time he had tasted blood, and he liked the visceral excitement killing gave him.

Weiner stood up when the butler returned and led him into Anton Vicovari's office. Vicovari was standing in front of a burgundy leather wing chair.

"Angie! How does it feel to have been out of the city for a while?" Vicovari's greeting smile was even but sincere. Angie thought Vicovari looked like a priest, he had always thought that. He was only five foot nine, but his slender body and thin face made him look taller. Vicovari was fifty-four years old, but his skin was smooth and unblemished. His hair, thinner than Angie's, was jet-black and neatly trimmed along the neck.

He sat down in the burgundy chair and pointed to a matching but smaller chair to his left.

"Anton, our friends send their greetings to you. Bonner said to remind you that you owe them a visit."

Vicovari laughed. "Ken doesn't work for a living like we do, but I appreciate the thought. I suppose you heard about the boy?" Weiner nodded. "That's an unfortunate thing, an untimely death. Was he a friend of yours?"

Weiner inwardly blushed. Vicovari could always remind people how much he knew with the most innocent questions. "He was very reliable. But his brother's going to take his place. I have confidence in him."

Vicovari shifted in his chair. "Angie, what do you think about the incident at Central Body Shop? I understand four people were arrested."

He always probed, Weiner thought. He probably knew more than anyone about the raid. "I've talked to Danny, the mule that was arrested. He believes there was inside information. You know his uncle was killed."

"Yes, I think we should probably help them. I understand the boy said absolutely nothing to the police. What really bothers me about the incident is our lack of warning. Jo is an awfully sweet girl, but I'm afraid her information won't do us much good if there is someone who is trying to hurt us."

Weiner had been waiting for the right time to talk about Kanell. "Anton, two things, I'm sorry to say, point to Rick. Really, three things." Weiner paused just long enough to attempt to gauge Vicovari's reaction. Rick Kanell had always had his affection and trust, Weiner knew that. He had never understood it, but he knew it.

Weiner could read no reaction on Vicovari's face, but he continued. "As you know, Rick lied about his trip to Miami. And, as you know, he really went to Dallas. . . ."

Vicovari interrupted. "Did he see any of our friends there?"

"No, but Anton, two of our biggest outlets for the car operation there had been approached more than once by a man who says he represents a better source for parts . . . and that source, according to the man, is located in Chicago." Vicovari nodded but said nothing. "And then there's the boy who was killed, Medlock. On the night he disappeared, *Kanell* disappeared too. He didn't come back until the next night. And he told Jo he had been with me, which was a lie."

Vicovari smiled slightly. "Those things could be a coincidence, you know that. Rick doesn't look for opportunities to tell us what he's doing at times." Vicovari looked away, then went to the stand-up writing desk next to the window. He took a sheet of paper from the top of the desk and returned to his seat, eyes focused on the paper.

"Angie, what records did we keep at Central Body Shop?"

Weiner looked at him, a confused expression on his face. "Really nothing . . . no, that's not right. Though I've never liked it, Rick had us keep a copy of the inventory printout in the filing cabinet." His brow furrowed as he continued, "Did they find *that*? A lot of pieces might fit together if they got that."

Vicovari looked away, then spoke. "They found the printout." He turned to Weiner. "But the first three pages were missing, those with the user codes. . . . Who would have taken the pages?"

Weiner shook his head slowly twice. "The only people who knew about that were me, maybe Danny . . . and Kanell." Weiner wanted to smile, but he didn't. Vicovari might care for Kanell, he thought, but he wasn't blind. The only person who would have removed the pages was Rick. He would have done it to protect himself. If he knew the place was going to be raided, he would have removed the pages.

"Do you have complete confidence in Danny?"

"Anton, Danny could have been off that night, but he wasn't. I trust him."

"And are you sure no other person . . . ," Vicovari said slowly, "would have removed the pages?" Weiner nodded. Vicovari stood up and walked to a bookshelf, his right hand straightening the books there, then continued. "Well, before we come to any decision, I would like to give Rick a chance to volunteer his reasons for these . . . these coincidences." Vicovari would never force anyone to tell the truth. Forced information was too often worthless. But he would give Kanell an opportunity. He turned to face Angie.

"Have we heard when Rick is returning?"

"I'll try to find out today."

Vicovari smiled. "Good! Make sure that Rick knows I would like to see him." His face turned serious, nearly threatening. Weiner had seen that ruthlessness a few times. "Angie, don't take pleasure in this . . . don't take pleasure. You could be wrong."

Angie Weiner was not a good actor, but he acted then, keeping his face neutral. "I'll just get word to him. Maybe it is all a mistake, maybe Rick will explain things." He shrugged. "I haven't really trusted him, you know that, but I don't dislike him."

Vicovari accepted the lie. "I'm thinking, Angie, that we should calm things down for a while. Too many people seem interested in my business. Why don't you let the boys know this is a time of rest."

Weiner nodded as Vicovari finished, "And why don't you have Jo call me before ten tonight? I'd appreciate that."

Vicovari hesitated for a moment at the stairwell as Weiner left, then walked down. His wife and three other women were playing bridge in the living room, an expansive space with tall windows. He walked through the living room, pausing for a moment to chat with the ladies—his wife was winning—and entered the kitchen for a little stomach balm, about two ounces of Maalox, which always seemed to kill the queasiness there.

IV

Rick Kanell's plane from Miami arrived in Dallas at eight ten. He took absolutely no pleasure in what had to be done this night, and the mere fact that he was taking no pleasure in it seemed to make it all okay: an unpleasant task dictated by necessity.

He parked the car about a mile from Evelyn Garner's house and began to walk slowly toward her street. A shopping bag was in his right hand. At about ten fifteen, he cut through several backyards and one empty but wooded lot and entered Evelyn Garner's yard, waiting in the long shadow of a poplar tree not ten feet from the tracks where she always parked her Comet. He looked at his watch. The crickets were very loud, the noise bothered him, but it was ten thirty, she would be there soon, it would be done, and then everything would be okay. He was feeling the chill of a dry Dallas night, and the four lines of cocaine had done little to warm him. He looked at the house. A light was on in the living room, soft music barely audible through the window. Where the hell was the old lady? He knelt down and picked up a few small pebbles that covered the driveway and began to roll them slowly in his hand. The stones did not feel cold, he thought that odd, and then a jumble of thoughts came to him as he heard the car pull into the driveway, tires crushing pebbles. He first felt anger and then fear; why the hell should he be afraid? He tried to correct that: he was not afraid, he was concerned, regretful that an unwanted task was on him, not minutes away, but on him right then. And then he thought of Bobby Medlock's body and the smell of urine, and then he thought of the old lady's voice, *she started it*, and then she was stepping away from the dirty Comet.

Kanell stepped behind her, sealing his right hand over her mouth. She gagged. Kanell was breathing short, fast breaths. His left hand pushed her spinal column forward in a violent thrust. Evelyn's eyes bulged, unblinking. Her arms bent at the elbow, hands touching her breast, fists clenched. She moaned, a shrill sound, and as the muffled sound came to him, he thought about his first night dive, how at eighty feet down he'd reached out to touch brain coral, and a green moray had locked on his hand, fine teeth piercing flesh. Kanell remembered the sound of his own muffled scream, the shrill sound, as his right hand dug into Evelyn Garner's cheeks, rotating the head to the right an inch or so, then forcing it far to the left, over her shoulder. He could see the bulging eyes. And then the muffled sound stopped. He was sweating when Evelyn Garner's lips parted just enough for her lungs to expel air softly, the sound of someone sleeping. Urine trickled down her legs as he dropped her. He began to shake slightly and for an instant felt very light-headed, as if he would faint. He leaned down just enough for his hand to reach her pocketbook, his eyes avoiding hers, and cut to the left of the Comet back through the other yards. Jerky motions of his hands pulled the jumpsuit off. He placed it, and the gloves and rubber boots, in the Sears shopping bag, which had once contained a woman's sweater, and with great effort forced himself to walk slowly, casually, back to the car, little tremors making his arms jump slightly as he walked.

Kanell drove the car back to the Dallas airport, arriving at eleven forty-five. He watched about four dollars' worth of television until three; tried to snooze, but failed, then simply sat in the television chair until six thirty, eyes fixed, thoughts too jumbled to sort, Sears bag at his side. He took the Dallas early-bird flight to Miami at seven and by eleven thirty tried to sleep again, this time in room 2323 of the Fontainebleau Hilton. Three very tall, neat glasses of scotch made his effort successful this time.

7

ATLANTA. It was a double date, Lane Englander's idea. He and Evelyn would treat May Montez and Jay Preston to a Georgia Tech home football game.

Georgia Tech won, too. The Yellow Jackets kicked a field goal with thirty seconds remaining. Evelyn and Lane had clapped and yelled more than most of the people in the D section; twice Evelyn had pushed herself up to cheer. They were still excited as the four finished their hamburgers in the first room off the hot-dog line at the Varsity. Evelyn and Lane had both noticed the sidelong glances and more somber mood of Montez and Preston, but had chosen to ignore them.

May Montez looked at Jay, then pulled herself upright. "Evelyn, I want to tell you this before you hear it Monday, but Jay and I don't think there's any reason to be worried. I got a call at home this morning from the Dallas office. A lady who worked there was killed outside her house last night. She worked on the WATS. But they don't think it had anything to do with work. Her pocketbook was taken."

Evelyn listened, though she didn't understand what May was getting at. The game had really taken her mind off everything. A group of young Tech students laughed at the next table, their laughter drawing Evelyn's eyes. Then she flushed, the implications coming together too quickly and too brutally.

"What was her name?"

May was looking at Evelyn as she began to speak, then turned her eyes to Jay. "Evelyn, Evelyn Garner." Lane Englander's eyes did not leave Evelyn. It didn't make any sense, he thought.

"Was she an older lady like me?"

"Yes, she was."

Lane turned his attention to May. His voice betrayed both exasperation and confusion. "May, how on earth would that . . . killing in Dallas have anything to do with Evelyn? *Our* Evelyn in Atlanta."

"It's because of what I said, isn't it? May, you know what I'm talking about. That night on the phone. I said I was in Dallas. I told the boy that, and I told the man that."

Preston had been gauging Evelyn as she spoke. She wasn't a hysteric, he thought. "Evelyn, it's okay. If someone killed that lady in Dallas thinking he'd done that to you, then he thinks he's killed you. You don't need to be worried."

That was the most disturbing thought of all to Evelyn Wade. If any of this made sense, horrible, unthinkable sense, a lady was dead, cold, alone, because of her phone call. She did not think about death in a fearful sense for herself: Evelyn was a person of faith. But the thought of a phone call, *her* phone call, killing someone made the flesh on Evelyn Wade's body very, very hot. She rubbed her hands on a napkin. "Well, I don't feel right talking about this here. Why don't we go to my home?" The house would protect her, she thought.

They were quiet in the car, their conversation touching on the game and on the weather, on any subject but the one on their minds. Evelyn was nearly gay in her mood, but her words drifted off at times. Lane Englander brought the subject up again as the four of them settled by the stone fireplace at 91 Myrtle. In front of the fireplace was a large green plant, the leaves brushing against the screen. There had been no fire in over two years.

"May, what happened in Dallas?" Englander said. "I mean, was it something that *couldn't* be connected?"

May wanted to say something to make them all feel better. But she did not want to shade the significance of the event. "The neighbor who found the body said her pocketbook was missing. She found her next to her car in the backyard." May looked at Evelyn. "Evelyn, the lady worked on the phones that night; you know how that goes." May smiled slightly.

The pocketbook story would not do it, Evelyn thought. "Why would a man wait at someone's house to steal her pocketbook? To take a life, wouldn't someone take more than a *pocketbook?* Why didn't they take the car?"

May shook her head. "That's what the girl in the Dallas office said. Maybe the man was crazy or something."

Evelyn pursued her line of thought. "May, did she live alone?" May nodded yes.

"If the lady lived alone, why wouldn't the man have robbed her house?"

Lane responded, "Evelyn, how many times have you seen strangers roaming this neighborhood? Drifters just float in and out of neighborhoods doing harm, then drifting away. Maybe the person didn't know the house was empty."

"Evelyn, that's right, you know," Preston said. "All of this could fit together, but all of it could be unrelated. That doesn't mean we shouldn't check on it, though. I found out a few things on Thursday, and I'll check a lot more closely now."

"*What* did you find out?" Evelyn picked up quickly.

"That body shops in Chicago have a lot to do with automobile theft. I talked with some people in the office who said a type of auto theft, car chopping, is very big there. Chopping is—"

"—when they cut up cars and sell the parts or glue them together and make other cars; I've read about that," Evelyn said, interrupting him.

Preston smiled as Evelyn continued, "That could explain why something was funny when I called up there." Evelyn had not planned to tell May and Preston about her call to Central Body Shop. It didn't seem to have that much significance. But the death of a lady she did not know in Dallas had given importance to many things.

"You mean you actually called all of those numbers you told us about?"

"Yes, and at one of the body shops I got the police."

"You mean they knew about the boy?"

"No, they wouldn't comment on that. But don't you think it's a little unusual for the police to be answering the phone at a body shop, and taking down the number of an old lady in Atlanta?"

"Yes, I do," Preston said, "and if you'll give me that number, I'll call it first thing Monday." Evelyn was glad Jay Preston was calling Chicago, but she had a call of her own to make, to Dallas. No one, she thought, really felt as she did about this.

"I wonder if she had someone who loved her." Evelyn said it not as part of any conversation, but out of the need to say it. "I wonder if she saw him. What do you feel at a time like that?" She shook her head. "I'm sorry, but I need to rest." She smiled. By eight o'clock Evelyn was sitting alone in the living room of 91 Myrtle, reading page 5 in her spiral-ring notebook. As she read her carefully written notes, Evelyn's eyes began to tear. The excitement of her "investigation" showed in many of the paragraphs in the notebook. But now she knew the boy was dead. The man would never have killed the woman, she thought, unless the boy was dead. The man was out there. She did not know how, but she had to try to stop him. Evelyn closed her spiral-ring notebook at eight thirty, after entering her notes from the day's conversations, and went to sleep in the chair.

8

I

WHEN Evelyn Wade walked into the phone bay of American Opinion Research at eleven, there were eighteen empty booths, but she sat down at her booth. As she dialed information for Dallas, she thought about the boy on the phone and the lady in Texas. She did not know what they looked like, but as the operator in Dallas answered, her mind presented a jumbled picture of Grady Wade, his body cold and hard in the coffin. He was so cold; she wanted to hold him, to feel the warm familiarity of his touch, but his flesh was cold and hard. It felt empty. She had never felt that lonely.

"Information for what city, please?"

"Uh, yes. I'd like the number for . . . the Dallas police homicide division, please."

"Is this an emergency?" It was too late, Evelyn thought. They were already dead.

"I'm sorry, but it's not." Evelyn thought that sounded a little odd to the operator, but she did not care. She wrote down the number but paused before dialing it. She was calling about murder. Not the abstract thought, but about someone who was cold and hard and empty.

She was standing next to Grady Wade's bed in the hospital when he died. A nurse had simply looked up as she touched the wrist, then lifted her fingers as if the flesh had stung them. "Is that all?" Evelyn said. She touched him and his flesh still felt familiar. She kissed his lips; they were warm but they did not return any feeling.

Evelyn looked hard at the number in her notebook, wiped the sweat from her upper lip, and dialed. As it rang, she took a deep breath.

"Dallas Police," a woman's voice answered.

Evelyn's eyes were fixed on the blank screen of the Hazeltine. She blinked and then spoke.

"Uh, yes. I would like to talk to someone about a murder."

The tone of the woman's voice didn't change. "Ma'am, do you want to report a murder?"

The word itself seemed to cause a bruise. "No. I want to talk to someone who can tell me about a murder. I think the wrong person was . . . you see, I think the person meant to kill me. . . ."

No. That was not clear. She felt embarrassed as she tried again. "Miss, I just need to talk to someone who can tell me about a lady who was found dead last Saturday morning. Did I call at a bad time?"

"Hold on, please," the woman said in a perfectly neutral voice.

Evelyn had forgotten that she was sitting in the booth when the clerk came on the phone.

"Yes, can I help you?" The voice was level and cool. Evelyn was very determined when she began to speak. She wanted the person to believe her, understand her.

"Good morning. I am trying to find someone who can tell me about the murder of a lady named Evelyn Garner. Can you help me, please?" Evelyn concentrated on the blank screen as she talked, focusing her thoughts.

"Ma'am, can I have your name?"

"My name is Mrs. Grady Wade, *Evelyn* Wade, in Atlanta, Georgia."

"Ma'am, do you have information or evidence to present? Are you calling to claim a reward?"

The thought irritated her. "No, I am *not* calling about a reward. You see, I was doing an interview, and I heard something happen to the boy. . . . "

The woman interrupted her. "Ma'am, just a minute, let's back up. Could I please have your phone number?"

"Well, yes. But I just wanted to talk to someone. You see, I think the person killed the wrong Evelyn; he meant to kill *me*. The man who killed Evelyn Garner, I mean." Evelyn shook her head. Nothing, she realized, was making any sense. "Miss, I'm sorry if I sound a little flustered, but this is . . . new to me."

The clerk began to write on a pad headed "Chrono." "That's perfectly okay, Mrs. Wade. Now, why don't you start at the beginning?"

Evelyn told her story of the phone call and then paused. "Miss, does that make any sense?"

"Yes ma'am, it does. It may be nothing, but I'm going to have the investigator assigned to the Garner case give you a call. That may be tomorrow, but he will call you, okay?"

Evelyn smiled slightly. "Thank you very, very much, miss. I needed someone that would understand."

The woman hesitated. "Mrs. Wade, if you feel in any immediate danger, I'll try to have someone call you right away. Would you like me to do that?"

The thought had never really hit her until then. She said no, then thanked the woman again and hung up. There was a killer out there, she knew that. But she had never really thought that he could threaten *her*. There was a man who would kill her right then, if he could.

Evelyn felt anger more than fright, a deep, black anger, the feeling of a brutal violation. Right then she needed to talk to someone in Dallas who had known Evelyn Garner. She dialed Dallas information again and quickly wrote down the number for the only E. Garner in the Dallas suburb of Brentwood, where May Montez had said she lived. If people loved the dead lady, Evelyn thought, they would be at her house now. Packing things. Visiting.

The number answered on the first ring, the voice a woman's.

"Hello?"

"Uh, yes, this is Evelyn Wade in Atlanta, Georgia. . . ." Evelyn hesitated. "I was a friend of Mrs. Garner." Evelyn believed that. Her life had become inextricably involved with the dead woman's.

"I'm Mabel Barris, her neighbor," the woman said. "Thank you for calling, but Evelyn's family is with the preacher right now. They're leaving for the funeral soon."

Evelyn wrote the name "Mabel Barris" in the spiral-ring notebook. She needed to ask many things, but none of her questions seemed appropriate. She cleared her throat.

"Mrs. Barris, would it be possible for me to call you later? You see, I'm afraid I may know something about what happened and I think you might be able to help me."

The woman in Dallas was silent for a moment. "What do you mean? What do you know? Do you know who killed Evelyn?"

"No, that's not what I mean. . . . Mrs. Barris, could I please call you later?"

"Yes, you can. What did you say your name is?"

"Evelyn Wade. I work for American Opinion Research in Atlanta. Mrs. Barris, are you the person who . . . who found Mrs. Garner?"

"Yes, I am. I'll never forget that as long as I live. I'm sorry, the family is coming out now, I've got to go. Do you want my phone number?"

She wrote the number by Mabel Barris's name and placed the receiver on the hook, her hand continuing to rest there. She felt very alone.

Evelyn pushed herself up from her chair and began to walk to the inside stairway that connected the WATS rooms to the executive floor. She had not seen or talked with May Montez since the previous afternoon, but she needed the comfort of her friend. She stood at May's door for a moment before entering.

"Are you thinking about that handsome man, Jay Preston, May?"

"Evelyn! I was thinking about you," May said as she rose from the desk and walked to Evelyn, placing a light kiss on her forehead. "How are you?" May pointed to a straight-backed chair as she continued to talk.

"Sit down, honey. What did you do yesterday after we talked? Jay swept me away for the afternoon, or I would have called you again. He likes you, Evelyn."

"Honey, I like him too. He's handsome and smart and if he makes you happy, I like him. A lot." Evelyn's hand moved back and forth on the chair's right arm as if she were wiping dust from it. "May—I called Dallas this morning. I talked to Evelyn Garner's neighbor. The funeral is today. She had a family, I'm glad of that."

May was sitting in the chair next to Evelyn. She reached out and touched her hand. "Ev, I wish to God all of this wasn't happening. I worry about you." Evelyn turned her head and looked out the window. "May, calling her house made me feel very lonely, as if I'm the reason she's gone from it. I *know* that's wrong," she said, turning back to face May, "but I feel responsible." Evelyn placed her right hand over the left, touching her ring. "I also feel a little afraid. It's an odd, terrible feeling to believe someone thinks he's killed you. You know, he *would* kill me. He's already killed two people."

"Ev, that scares me. But remember what Jay and Lane said Saturday; if there's someone out there who thinks you are dead, then you don't exist." May shook her head. "I know that's awful consolation, but it makes *me* feel better. And anyway, Jay is going to do some calling today. Do you feel okay staying at the house by yourself? I could stay there, or you could move to my place. Do you want to do that?"

Evelyn gave a short, abrupt laugh. "Lord, I'm not that afraid. I feel like my home protects me, the memories there. But I love you for the thought."

Evelyn began to push up from the chair. "Well, I'm going home.

You will call me if Jay finds out anything, won't you?"

May watched Evelyn as she began to go down the stairs. She needed to think of something to do, something to help Evelyn, to help find this man. She looked at the phone. It all revolved around the phone. She picked it up and dialed 22, the direct-dial access number to AOR's Dallas office.

Evelyn made herself a cup of tea as soon as she got home, and now she sat in her kitchen, drinking it and brooding. She had not recieved a call from anyone at Central Body Shop. The lack of response irritated her. Evelyn walked back to the phone and dialed the number for information in Chicago. She asked for the number of the Auto Theft Division.

"Ma'am, which branch? There are seven numbers for Auto Theft."

"Well, I don't know. Could you please give me the main number, I guess."

Evelyn wrote the number on the bottom of page 6 in the spiral-ring notebook. She took her tea to the living room and sat down for ten minutes before she dialed.

The clerk who took her call was located one floor below the offices of Albert Rosenbloom and Dean Buettner. She logged the phone call on page 51 of the theft-report sheet, writing a notation by Evelyn Wade's name and phone number. It read: "Lady has some information about activities at Central Body Shop; referred to Monitoring." The clerk had noted fifty-two calls before Evelyn's. At four she would turn a copy of her notes over to another clerk who would make six more copies of each sheet and send copies to the various investigation supervisors. The notation concerning Evelyn Wade's call and query would eventually end up on the desk of the detective heading up the surveillance of Central Body Shop's telephones, the same detective Evelyn had talked to on her second call to Central Body Shop. A copy of all the day's calls would also end up on the desks of Albert Rosenbloom and Dean Buettner.

Evelyn napped until nearly two o'clock, a long afternoon nap for her, too long, she thought. Long afternoon naps meant less sleep at night. She walked to the living room slowly. Long afternoon naps also made her stiff.

The notebook was sitting in her lap as she dialed the number for Mabel Barris in Brentwood. Evelyn wanted the call to provide some real information. She had outlined three questions on the top of page 7 in the notebook, hoping those questions would better focus her conversation.

The call was answered on the second ring.

"Hello."

Evelyn cleared her throat. It felt dry. "Mrs. Barris? This is Evelyn Wade in Atlanta. Am I calling you at a bad time?"

The lady hesitated before answering. ". . . No. I was finishing lunch. Mrs. Wade, you know, I've never heard Evelyn Garner mention your name. I thought about that at the funeral. Would you please tell me how you know her, *knew* her?"

Evelyn was not prepared for that question. She stuttered, "Uh, I knew her through work only. We had mutual friends there—Mrs. Barris, how long did you know Evelyn?"

"For over ten years, since her husband left. We visited just about every day. She was sitting on my porch the day she died. . . ." Mabel Barris stopped just long enough to compose herself. "You know, I *told* her not to go into work that day, she'd been working too much. They work you to death at that place. . . . I'm sorry, I didn't mean to say it like that. You work for that place, too, don't you?"

"Yes I do. But I normally work days. I . . ."

Mabel Barris interrupted her. "Mrs. Wade, why did you say you might know what happened? The police said it was probably a mugging."

Evelyn detailed her theory of mistaken identity. Mabel Barris was quiet, thinking, and then she spoke.

"You know, that's an odd story. Do the police know that?"

"I called the Dallas police this morning, they're calling me back. It *is* an odd story, I know. That's why I need you to help me, please. Would you answer some questions for me?"

"Yes, I'll answer some questions. But would you first give me your phone number? I don't mean to sound silly, but your call scares me."

Evelyn gave a very short laugh, a bitter one. "I know. My number is 404-427-1657." Evelyn tilted her head down and looked at the first of her questions.

"Mrs. Barris, did Evelyn Garner receive any strange phone calls at work that you know of? Did she ever tell you about phone calls from strangers?"

Mabel Barris thought for a moment. "No. She talked about work a lot, about the funny things that happened there, but she never said anything about any phone calls."

Evelyn put "no" by the first question, then glanced at question 2.

"On the day she . . . she died . . . did you say you saw her then?"

"We sat on my porch for an hour before she went to work."

"Well, did she say anything, anything at all, that was out of the ordinary?"

Barris was quiet again. What had she talked about? "No. We talked about the things that were important to us; our daughters . . . and the street light in front of the house which was out. It's still out." Barris laughed sadly. "I joked with Evelyn about men wanting to date her. She didn't have one date in all those years. Evelyn was quiet, but she was nice."

Evelyn Wade thought for a moment. "Why did you joke about it *then?* Was there a reason you joked about it then?" It seemed like a meaningless question.

"You know, that *is* strange. . . . I was joking with her because of the sweater."

"What sweater?"

"Someone sent her a sweater at work. It was waiting on her there on Thursday, the day before she died. There was a card, but there wasn't a name on it. Isn't that strange? I kidded her about it before she went to work, said she had a secret . . . admirer."

Evelyn looked down. Why would someone send a package without the sender's name on it?

"Mrs. Barris, do you know how the package was addressed? Was it mailed to her?"

"Yes. It just had her name."

"Her full name?"

Barris hesitated. "You know, that's right. It only said 'Evelyn.' She showed me the outside address and the card inside. The card said, 'To Evelyn, from your friends,' or something like that, but no one sent it to her from work. She thought I might know the handwriting. What are you thinking?"

Why would you write only a first name when you addressed a package? Evelyn thought. You might do that if you knew someone very well—or if you didn't know the person's last name.

"Mrs. Barris, I'm not sure what to think. When did she receive the package?"

"On Thursday, the day before she died. Didn't I say that? She showed me the sweater first thing Friday morning. We had coffee lots of mornings. . . . Does the sweater mean anything?"

"I don't know," Evelyn said as she shifted in the chair. "Did you tell the police about it?"

"No, I didn't think about it. They didn't really ask many questions, and I was so rattled. Should I?"

Evelyn frowned. "They probably won't pay any attention to it, but yes, Mrs. Barris."

Barris was quiet. "You know, I didn't know whether to talk to you or not, at first. But it does make sense. What are you going to do?"

The question frustrated Evelyn. "I'm going to keep trying to find people to *listen* to me. You know, I really didn't know Evelyn Garner, but I feel very close to her." She paused. "She died because of my phone call. I will never be able to accept that. Mrs. Barris, thank you for talking with me."

Evelyn hung up and began to summarize carefully on page 7 her conversation with Mabel Barris. The man was very smart, she thought. He was very detailed in his approach to killing. He was also obviously involved with Central Body Shop. Why else would he have been there? But why did he kill the boy?

The phone rang twice before Evelyn heard it. She answered in a subdued voice, a weaker voice. It was May.

"Ev, I've been trying to call you. I talked to Jay. He called Consumer Affairs in Chicago and they gave him the name of the chief of detectives in Auto Theft up there. But he's out. Jay left word, though."

Evelyn laughed. "Don't hold your breath, I called up there too, and someone's going to call *me* back too. I don't think those people work. May . . . I talked to the dead lady's neighbor."

May could sense the heaviness in Evelyn's voice. "What did she say?"

"She told me about a package which came to the office for the dead lady. It only had her first name, and it had no sender's name. May, that package was used by the killer to identify her."

May was sitting on the corner of her desk, looking down at the pile of papers in the desk's center. She had never seen a dead person, seldom attended a funeral. But an image flashed through her mind—of Evelyn dead and alone in her home. She closed her eyes to push the image away, then looked to the window.

"Ev, I worry about you being there alone. I *know* this guy can't know about you, but it bothers me. Don't . . ."

Evelyn interrupted. "Don't worry about that, just keep talking to me a lot. That makes me feel safe. I promise I'll tell you when I can't be alone."

"Okay, but I'm going to call you until you get tired of answering the phone, okay?"

"Okay, sweet," she said as she hung up the phone. Phone calls would be enough support for now. She was living on an earthquake fault, she felt that worry. But the ground had not started to shake yet.

9

DEAN Buettner's word on Monday was stealth. But the word wasn't on his mind at the moment.

"Here!" Buettner yelled, cutting past the kid on the right, then catching the ball with his right hand. The hand stretched high in the air. He shot. It missed the backboard.

"Shit!"

"Hey, Buettner, so where's the hotshot today?" one of the kids yelled.

"The hotshot is still thinking about his date last night, that's where, bimbos. You won't live to see the day a woman'll treat you that well."

The others laughed and began to walk toward him, occasionally stepping over the trash that covered portions of the makeshift basketball court. Two of the boys put out their hands, palms up, and grinned as Buettner slapped the palms hard. He joined the pickup game of young boys every couple of weeks; mostly white kids, most of them were young enough to enjoy Buettner's skill without resenting the badge.

They walked to the street. It was barely fifty degrees, but the group did not seem to notice the cold. Buettner enjoyed their recklessness, and he enjoyed a pickup game as much as anyone, but he was usually working when he played. He ran his hand over the back of his neck.

"So, what do you hear about Bobby Medlock?" He asked it without any time for the kids to prepare their reactions. They looked at each other.

"He's dead," Lennie, a black kid, said. Fifteen, slightly pudgy, very streetwise, and very good at the arcade games, Lennie was a source, of sorts, for Buettner. Lennie ran with the kids who muled for many outfits in Chicago. But he didn't mule himself. Of the dozens of kids Dean Buettner had come to know during the past four years, Lennie was one of the few who had a chance to climb out of the circle. Lennie also liked to read. Each month, Dean Buettner's copy of *Reader's Digest* eventually made its way to his hands.

Though they were friends, Buettner and the black kid paid little attention to each other when others were around. They had not planned the distance; it was a natural, protective understanding, never spoken.

"I *know* he's dead, schmuck," Buettner said. "What do you hear about what happened?"

"We don't hear *nothing*," a lanky kid with red hair said. "His brother just says his ma's pissed. Bobby made a lot of money. . . ." The kid stopped talking.

"I *know* he made a lot of money," Buettner said. "So, what'd he do to make all that money, dance ballet?"

"He muled," the red-haired kid said.

Buettner shook his head. "Jesus Christ, I *know* that. He got picked up once. But *who* did he mule for?" Buettner thought he already knew the answer to the question. Bobby Medlock ran with all of these kids, and most of them muled for Angie Weiner and Central Body Shop. But he wanted someone to say that.

"Fuck you, Buettner," the kid named Kowakoski said. "You goddamned cops always sticking your nose in, man. Who gives a damn?"

"Kowakoski, your brain is a pimple. Simple as that. A gnat's got more sense. When one mule's light's turned off, some other mules gonna get their brain smashed, too. You want to be next, Kowakoski?"

Kowakoski looked at the others, then spoke up. "Buettner, don't give us no shit, man. Bobby was a *big deal*, man. . . ."

"He *ran* mules," the red-haired kid said, interrupting him.

"And so?"

"You 'spect us to stand here and talk about a guy who *ran mules*? Talk about shit!"

"He sure did have a pretty car that night . . . ," Lennie said quietly.

"Like what?"

"One of them fancy things. He rode me around the block. I didn't know the car was hot, you understand." The other kids laughed, but Lennie's face looked like a little brown cherub's.

"Lennie, *what* night and *what* car? What night did you see Bobby Medlock in his personal fancy car that wasn't stolen?"

"The night he never came back, you dope. And it was a Jensen Esprit. I know, 'cause I got the manual from the pocket. Bobby let me look at it. I'm gonna buy me one of those cars when I become a detective."

"Yeah, Lennie," Buettner said, "and I'm gonna be black soon, too." He wanted to talk to Lennie alone. But that would have to wait. Lennie had already confirmed what he wanted to know. If Bobby Medlock had been driving a stolen car the night he disappeared, and if he had been around Lennie, he was working for Angie Weiner.

The kids began to walk down the street. "Hey, Buettner, you gonna buy us a beer?" They laughed. At times, he would buy them something, but he never bought them beer.

"Kowakoski, how about if I buy you a lollipop? Are you old

enough for a lollipop?" Kowakoski did not smile. He was the most antagonistic of all the kids who hung around Pulaski. He put the fingers of his right hand to his mouth and threw Buettner a kiss, a smirk on his face. When Lennie saw it, he circled around Buettner, arms stretched out like wings, and quietly said, "Isn't that *heart-rending*? Word eleven, September," then continued down the street with his arms outstretched. Buettner looked at his watch, then turned to jog the short block to the car.

Albert Rosenbloom was sitting on the corner of the clerk's desk when Buettner entered the office. Buettner threw him a salute to the side, said, "Hi, boss," then continued to his office. Rosenbloom followed.

"Dean, where you been?"

"Just with the boys. You know the mule Minneapolis Homicide called about? He was muling the night he disappeared, and I'm sure it was for Weiner." Buettner shook his head. "The dumb bastards. They really think it's all fun. Incidentally, one of the kids rode with him in the car he stole. It was a Jensen. I'll pass that on to Minneapolis."

Albert Rosenbloom had a smirk on his face. "Buettner, you and your kids. A damn street kid's word's about as reliable as the weather."

"Right, Albert. I suppose you want me to use stealth rather than contacts, right?" Buettner shook his head in mock despair. "How quickly we forget. Has it slipped your mind that one of those kids got you your car back in one piece last week?"

Rosenbloom turned a pleasant shade of red, then left the office. He was smiling as he walked out.

Buettner spent the next hour reading reports. He was flipping through a computer printout titled "Recoveries" when the word "Jensen" caught his eyes. He broke into a smile as he read the summary by number 188: "1985 Jensen Esprit. Report missing: November 1 by Lake Park Police. Recovery: Minneapolis Police. Location: Minneapolis airport. Disposition of vehicle: to owner, James Greenbaum. File 27787 Lake Park."

It was a very easy confirmation that Bobby Medlock was in a Jensen, Buettner thought. Medlock's body had been found in Minneapolis, too. Buettner tapped his fingers. He wanted to know more. He dialed the number for the Lake Park Police.

"Good afternoon, Lake Park Police. May I help you?" Hell, Buettner thought, the fancy neighborhoods always had the world's sweetest-sounding police. She sounded sexy, too.

"This is Detective Dean Buettner, Chicago Auto Theft. How are things in moneyland today?"

"Green. Now, what can we do for you?"

"I'd like to talk to someone in your records department. Do they work a full week, or are you folks on a vacation schedule out there among the mansions?"

"Well, most of the staff has left for their weekly visit to the tennis club. But I think I can find you someone. Hold on just a sec, Officer Buettner in the ghetto." Buettner laughed.

In a moment a male clerk came on the phone.

"Brisbane. Records."

"Buettner. Auto Theft. Good afternoon."

"What can we do for you, Mr. Buettner?" The guy sounded real dull, Buettner thought.

"Yes, I was wondering if you could give me a quick review of your file number 27787."

The man answered quickly, "Hold on a minute, Mr. Buettner."

"Thank youuu, Mr. Brisbane." Buettner pushed the recovery report to the left side of his desk, over the telephone monitoring report from Central Body Shop.

"Well now, Mr. Buettner, what can we tell you?"

"Could you read me the owner's statement, please?"

"You know, this car has been recovered. Are you sure this is necessary?"

What a yoyo. "Yes, please, if you would. We're implementing a stealth policy around here, you know."

Brisbane started reading without a pause: "The owner discovered the car missing from his driveway. There were no suspicious people seen previously. The door was opened with a key, but the owner said all of the keys were in his possession. The owner reported that he had not left the car in the care of any body shop or garage, but that he had some heavy road tar removed at a shop near his place of employment."

"What was the name of the shop that did the work?"

"Let's see . . . Central Body Shop."

"Bingo," Buettner said quietly.

"Is that all, Mr Buettner?"

"Right. Thanks an awful lot."

Buettner dug through the pile of reports on his desk and walked to Albert Rosenbloom's office with the complete Central Body Shop file, including the telephone monitoring report. Notations of two phone calls from a woman named Evelyn Wade in Atlanta were in the report. He had noticed them, along with fifteen or twenty other notations of what seemed like normal calls from buyers around the country. However promising those leads might be, his mind was on the dead mule, the Jensen, and the increasing evidence against Angie Weiner.

"Albert, you know what you were saying about my street kids?"

Rosenbloom looked up, preoccupied. "Yeah?"

"Well, they're doing okay by me. The mule that was killed definitely worked for Central Body Shop. The guy who owned the stolen Jensen mentioned the place in the theft report."

"So?"

"So who's the guy most associated with Central Body Shop and the mules?"

Rosenbloom shook his head in disgust. "Dean, so what are you, in Homicide these days? I don't have time to think about who killed that mule."

"Even if it's Angie Weiner?"

"What are you talking about? Weiner stays away from stuff like that these days. He may be dumb, but he's not *that* dumb."

Buettner pulled out two pages of notes from a meeting of the Chicago Combined Crime Strike Force. "Albert, let me show you something. It's from the Strike Force meeting, and it touches a lot on Weiner's role with Anton Vicovari. Number one, he likes little boys, kids. Number two, he's suspected of distributing Vicovari's porno flicks. Number three, he sets up kids for starring roles in the flicks shot in Chicago, but he only sets up young guys, like the guy who was killed."

Rosenbloom wasn't enjoying the conversation. "Dean—so you're telling me he's a kinky porno freak. Christ, *I'm* a porno freak, and that doesn't make me a killer." He looked at Buettner's smile. ". . . And that doesn't make me a pervert, either. Why the hell did I ever get you and your damned four-syllable words?"

"It's only one syllable. Today it's only one syllable. If I use only one syllable, can I stay, Albert?"

Rosenbloom closed his eyes and slowly put his head on the desk. He could not stay mad at anyone that crazy.

"Seriously, Albert. The dead kid was a big deal with the other boys. They say he ran mules for his boss, and his boss had to be Weiner, he was probably letting Weiner suck his cock, too. Or maybe Weiner tried and the guy got violent or something. Anyway, I'd like to follow up on it some. Putting Weiner out of commission on *anything*, including bad taste in sex partners, would get to Vicovari, at least a little. Besides, it would make *awfully* good press for the department. You know, one division helps the other in brotherly love, all that shit."

Rosenbloom waved his hands in front of him. "Okay, okay, get out of here." He turned his attention back to the letter on his desk, then looked up just as Buettner stepped from the office.

"Dean, what's happening on the phone monitor at Central Body Shop? Are any suckers calling in?"

"Yeah. The word is getting around, though. The phone doesn't ring much anymore, unless it's a legitimate call. I'm going over the monitoring reports in the morning."

"Okay. And, Dean?"

"Yeah?"

"One syllable only."

II

Rick Kanell was driving slowly, cars honking at times as they passed him. He sucked in the mucus in his nose again and cursed. Kanell was vaguely aware that his cocaine use had increased during the past two weeks, but he wasn't aware how much. He was using nearly two grams a day, enough to provide two thick lines an hour. Enough to kill the occasional user. But even that wasn't providing the up he needed. He felt constantly tired; except for the short burst after downing the lines, the rush of energy seemed harder and harder to achieve. He was drinking more, too, especially at night. But sleep came hard, even with the booze.

He turned the car right on Balboa. When he could, Rick Kanell avoided the seamier parts of Chicago. His contempt for poor people and their life-styles, even their clothes, was strong. He pulled the car over in front of a diner less than a hundred feet from the corner of State Street, then looked at his watch. A bag lady shuffled by the car, her head and eyes down, looking at nothing. Kanell watched her for a minute until she reached State Street. She had absolutely no value, he thought, as worthless as the bits of garbage that littered the gutter and sidewalk. He looked at his watch again. Where the hell was Weiner? Kanell switched the car off, slipped the keys in his right pocket, locked the driver's door, and walked to the diner. He needed something cold to soothe his throat.

Kanell was there to pick up Angie Weiner at the request of Anton Vicovari. Vicovari wanted to meet with them both, but he did not want them to arrive separately. Kanell understood that thinking, that did not bother him. Anton Vicovari was an especially careful man, more so when things seemed to be going wrong. But Kanell did not want to meet with Weiner, much less pick him up. For Kanell, being with Weiner was like being with the bag lady, only worse. Weiner had no value, at least to him. Though Kanell would not admit it, Angie Weiner was one of the reasons he wanted to be gone from the outfit. He did not need to deal with people like the fat queer.

He sat in the diner for ten minutes, oblivious to the old man on his right. As Angie Weiner walked past the window to the door, a mud-caked white van pulled up directly across from Kanell's car and parked. Kanell stood up and walked to the door as Weiner entered.

"Where you been, Angie? We're running late." Kanell glanced quickly from Weiner's shoes to his head. Weiner's shoes gleamed. The suit was dark blue, nearly black. To Kanell, it clashed with the light tan hip-length topcoat. The guy looks like he belongs back in the meat-packing business, he thought.

Weiner smiled before answering. "Sorry, Rick, I was busy. So how was your trip to Miami? Things were really busy while you were gone." Weiner turned and headed out the door in front of Kanell. Rick stopped just long enough on the passenger side of the car to unlock the door, then spoke as he walked around the car. "Yeah, so who do you think's the worm? Anton said we didn't even know about the search warrant." Kanell did not want to talk too much about his absence during the past week. The raid on Central Body Shop had come at a bad time, he knew that, and he hoped Weiner would not pick up on the topic. Neither of the men looked at the muddy white van as they entered the car.

Weiner rubbed his hands together as Kanell started the engine. "Who's the worm? Hell, I don't know. Maybe we're just having bad luck these days." Weiner smiled. He thought the question was amusing and ballsy. If there's a worm it's you, he thought, as his eyes turned to Kanell. "Rick, Anton said to park in the basement. I've got a card to get us in."

"That's okay, I always park there, even for dinner parties. God, Anton can put on a spread when he wants to," Kanell said. He enjoyed reminding Weiner how very different he thought their social standing was with Vicovari. Kanell did not mention that he had not eaten at or even visited the apartment in over a year. In his mind, their relationship was frozen at its peak. But in reality that peak was nearly three years ago.

Weiner was quiet as the car continued eastward to the shore. He was a very patient man. Let Kanell say what he wanted to. Very soon

Kanell would be out of time. Very soon Anton would say something, and he would be out of time. The thought brought a smile to Weiner's face as the car slowed nearly to a stop and turned right into the basement parking lot of the high rise on Lake Shore Drive.

"Ricky! You two come in; I'm sorry you had to wait." Vicovari first shook Kanell's hand, then Weiner's. He was dressed in dark gray slacks and a lighter gray sweater. Kanell walked into the office in front of Weiner, went directly to the chair closest to Vicovari's desk, and sat down.

"Anton, I thought about you when I was in Miami," Kanell said. "I went to eat at the Bayou, that place with the good langoustinos. God, they have good food there." He continued to ignore Weiner.

Vicovari didn't acknowledge the comment immediately, but turned to Angie. "Angie, be comfortable, have a seat. . . . Rick, you know, I haven't been to Miami in a year. So what did you do down there?" Vicovari's smile invited confidence while he observed Kanell steadily. He wanted Rick to tell him the truth, to say, "Anton, I wasn't in Miami. I was in Dallas." Vicovari could accept that. He could have legitimate reasons to be in Dallas. He liked Rick Kanell. He wanted to hear the truth.

"Hell, Anton, I spent four days bareboating in the Keys with a friend; we spent a couple of nights at No Name Key." Kanell gave a short laugh. "Anton, I'd forgotten how much work that was. We came back on Friday, and I checked into the Fontainebleau for some R and R." Vicovari continued to smile. He did not ask Kanell about his call to Jo on Tuesday from Dallas.

"Rick, that's why I like stink pots, I want the engine to do the work. When did you hear about the problem at Central Body Shop?"

Kanell was ready for the question. He had made sure that Jo was ready for it, too, just in case anyone from the outfit had questioned her. "I called Jo from Key West on Thursday." Kanell's expression turned to one of concern. "Anton, I started to come back, but thought it might be better to stay away. That's Angie's area, and Jo said she didn't think they really got anything, is that right?"

"Auto Theft has a shipping book, and a copy of your printout, but part of it was missing. The first three pages. I don't think they can learn much without those pages, can they?"

The three pages? Kanell's eyes cut quickly to Weiner, then back to Vicovari. The three pages. Kanell started to say that he had them, but pushed the thought away. If Weiner had really sent Bobby Medlock to Central Body Shop to get those pages, to use them against him, then Weiner would tie him to the kid's death if he knew he had the pages. Kanell's mind was beginning to slow down and blur a bit. He shook his head.

"No, the printout doesn't mean much without the codes. And not much then, if you don't know what you're doing." He forced a laugh, glancing from Vicovari to Weiner and back to Vicovari. "Hell, Angie's always had trouble reading the damn thing even *with* the codes." He looked at Weiner. There was a thin smile on Weiner's face.

Vicovari turned his attention to Weiner too. He smiled as he spoke. "Hell, Angie, don't let that bother you, I can't do much with it, either. That's why we have Rick, he's the numbers man."

"I know, Anton." Weiner managed a casual tone. He changed the subject. "Rick, did you hear about the mule, about the kid that was killed?"

The conversation was moving too fast, Kanell thought. He was trying to separate the realities from the lies. When *should* he have heard about Medlock? He had killed him nearly two weeks ago, but when would it have made sense to hear about it? When did they find the body? He could not remember. Kanell's face felt hot when he answered. "Yeah . . . yeah, Jo told me. Do they know what happened?"

"Who? Does who know?" Weiner's tone was light.

"Do the police know? I mean, didn't they find him?"

Weiner nodded. "Yeah, they found him in Minneapolis. You know, he was making a special pickup for Anton the night he disappeared." Weiner paused and smiled. "It's the damnedest thing, we know he picked up the car, then he just disappeared."

Kanell was fighting hard to keep his confusion from showing. If the kid *had* been doing something special for Vicovari, what the hell was he doing looking at the printout? But Weiner could be lying, he thought, he could be trying to trap him. But Anton was sitting there, he wouldn't lie in front of Anton. With effort, Kanell swallowed, his throat very dry and raw. Again he forced a smile. "Hell, Angie, some dumb kid takes a fancy sports car and who knows what the hell will happen? Maybe he picked up a hitchhiker or something."

Vicovari pulled his lower lip at the mention of a sports car. How would Kanell know that? The car had not been mentioned. "It doesn't matter, what matters is the attention the police are paying to our car operations. I don't like it for two reasons: money, and embarrassment to me." Vicovari turned to Weiner. "Angie, I want us to slow things down for a while. Let's concentrate on everything but chopping; the chopping is too visible. Leave it for now. Why don't you look into that film enterprise you mentioned? People don't seem to bother us there."

Weiner nodded agreement. "Good. I think there's a lot of money to be made there. What are we going to do about Central Body Shop? Are we going to take it back over?"

Vicovari wasn't smiling when he answered. Over half a million dollars' worth of stolen parts, *his* parts, were still sitting there. Because those parts had no serial numbers, the police had not been able to trace them and identify them as stolen. But he was not exactly anxious to claim them. "My lawyers are looking into that now. I may forget the parts and the building, it depends. Angie, are they still tapping the phone?"

"Yeah, that old nigger who watches the place for us says they're there every day."

"What tap?" Kanell's question was a little sharper in tone than he intended. "When did they start tapping, before or after the raid?" Kanell was thinking about the lady on the phone the night Bobby Medlock died. Had that conversation been monitored?

Weiner looked exasperated. "Why the hell does that matter?

Everyone was careful on that phone. Anyway, they started it the day after the raid."

Vicovari turned his attention back to Kanell. Weiner was right. Rick Kanell could no longer be trusted. He had lied about his trip, and to make that lie worse, he had used an old piece of their friendship to place that lie. The Bayou in Miami was the first nice restaurant Rick Kanell had been to with Vicovari and his wife. He had spent a week with them—like a son, Vicovari thought. And now he had lied about Jo, and about Bobby Medlock. Kanell had done something with that kid. The boy did not matter; the lying was the problem. Vicovari was not sure if Kanell had taken the first three pages of the printout. But he did feel that Kanell's absence during the raid, an absence again covered with lies, was damning enough. To Anton Vicovari, Rick Kanell died right then. He no longer existed. But the matter would have to be dealt with carefully. He smiled again as he spoke to Kanell.

"Rick, how is the barter operation going? You know, I'm going to be a poor man if things keep going wrong, so you're going to have to make up some business in your area. Can you do that?"

Kanell brightened. "Hell, Anton, we've got stuff stored all over the country. You know, I can barter out a million dollars' worth of bonds this week; we got them last month, and they're like money." He paused. Kanell was feeling more relaxed, on comfortable territory, for a change. "Anton, we really need some more barter sources in the South; that's becoming the place to dump things, especially bonds and prescription drugs. There are some bankers down there who seem anxious to do things. I'm going to check that out, if it's okay."

"Good . . . Ricky, you know there might be a lot of expanding we could do in your area; I need to understand it a little better, though." Vicovari snapped his fingers once. "You know, we could go down to Low Notch and go over your whole operation. I like it down there in November, and you can even take Jo. How does that sound? . . ."

As Vicovari continued to talk, Kanell felt his anxiety drain away.

He then looked at Weiner smugly. His role seemed about to expand while Weiner's was shrinking, and Weiner had not been invited to Low Notch, Vicovari's mountain retreat in Virginia. The private club contained nearly two hundred "cottages," long an enclave of the wealthy. Rick Kanell had been there twice.

"Anton, do you remember when you showed me the Hunt Club property? That's the most spectacular piece of land. I'd love to go back there with you. Jo will die when she sees your compound; she likes fine things."

Vicovari made a mental note to call Jo Pinder before Kanell could arrive home. She had already been to Low Notch as *his* guest.

Kanell continued. "Anton, when do you want to go? I'll have to tell Jo to get off."

"Why don't you go Saturday? And Rick, why don't you get me a complete printout of all you're doing before you go? I'll study it this weekend and be down on Monday."

Angie Weiner had not understood what Vicovari was doing until that moment. He had never been to Low Notch and could not know that the Hunt Club Kanell had referred to, 22,000 acres of fenced-in land, had been the scene of at least one accident in the last seven years: two men who knew Anton Vicovari well, like Kanell, misjudged that friendship. Weiner didn't know about the Hunt Club. But he did know Anton Vicovari. Weiner smiled.

"Rick," Vicovari said, "is Jo hearing anything at the office about the wiretap at Central Body Shop? Will you ask her?" He indicated Weiner with a nod. "Angie's done his best to get the word out, but I'm concerned some friend might be trapped on that phone."

Kanell nodded.

Vicovari stood up. "Well, enough of this. I've got a party in an hour, the kickoff for United Appeal. Why don't you both touch base with me tomorrow?" He looked at Kanell. "Rick, you look good, bareboating must be good for you."

Kanell tried to keep his eyes on Vicovari, but he couldn't. He looked down his coat and brushed away an imaginary speck of dust before taking Anton's hand. "Thanks. I'll talk to Jo tonight about

Low Notch." He turned to Weiner. "So, do you want a ride back to the diner?"

Weiner wasn't sure if he was to stay or leave; he looked at Vicovari, but his expression was neutral. "Sure. I'm going to check on that film idea tonight, Anton. Maybe I can tell you something about it first thing in the morning."

Kanell and Weiner drove away from Lake Shore Drive at six forty. Neither of them talked much on the drive back to Balboa and State, and neither of them noticed the brown Volkswagen that now followed their car at a safe distance.

10

I

DEAN Buettner arrived at the office before seven. He always took pride in being the first person to arrive at Chicago Auto Theft. But this morning a light was already on in Albert Rosenbloom's office. The light scared him. Albert never came in early, Buettner thought as he knocked lightly on Rosenbloom's door, then entered.

Rosenbloom was sitting at his desk, looking at the window. He did not acknowledge Buettner.

"Albert, what's wrong?"

Rosenbloom was still for a moment, then he turned, red-eyed, to Buettner. "It's Kati." His daughter, eleven years old. Rosenbloom looked away again, then continued very quietly. "A man pulled her off her bike. And held her. And then he put his hands down her pants. He said, 'Say hi to your father for me, *Kati.*'"

They had put a bomb in Rosenbloom's car once, Buettner remembered. They had fastened it to the left wheel strut, where it stayed for two months, never exploding. Rosenbloom's son had finally found it there, the wires pulled loose by the motion of the left spring. And how many times had they called Rosenbloom's house? Eight or ten times a year, always when he wasn't at home, always when one of his children might answer. "Where's your father, kid? Have you seen your father lately? *Is he okay?*"

"Albert, is she okay?" Buettner said gently.

"How the fuck are you okay after that!" Rosenbloom slammed his hand on the desk. And then he said quietly, "I'm sorry. We took her to the hospital."

Buettner didn't need to ask the next question. Chicago Auto Theft was causing major problems for only one crime family at the moment, and it was a family renowned for their dirty tricks, and for one lieutenant who liked pretty boys and probably liked hurting pretty girls.

"I guess you know who's probably behind this?"

Rosenbloom, his face completely expressionless, eyes unblinking, looked at Buettner. "Goddamn it, you know, and I know, and I'll kill him, Dean. Get me the files on Anton Vicovari."

I I

Evelyn Wade was on the small, glassed-in porch when she heard the ring. She looked at her fingers. They were caked in potting soil. She hesitated for an instant, then dunked them in the red enamel water pitcher. She shook her hands as she walked to the phone and finally dried them on her apron.

"Hello?"

"Mrs. Wade?"

It was an unfamiliar voice, but Evelyn knew it was someone from Dallas or Chicago. "This is Evelyn Wade," she said quite formally. Evelyn was determined to sound like more than an old lady with a crazy story.

"Ma'am, this is Detective Fritz Taylor with Dallas Homicide. I

have a note here that you might have some information about the
death of Evelyn Garner."

"Yes, Mr. Taylor, I do. I'm going to start at the beginning and
hope this makes sense, but do let me know if I go too fast for you."
Fritz Taylor leaned back in his chair, resigned to patience, as she
began to speak.

Evelyn related incidents and times without referring to her notebook, her voice trailing off as she finished the story, "Mr. Taylor, I
hope that makes sense. . . ."

Taylor was leaning forward on his desk, oblivious to the sounds
around him. "Mrs. Wade, that's perfectly logical, I think."

"Good!" Evelyn said. "And there's more. Don't you think it's a
pretty big coincidence that I make a phone call saying I'm in Dallas,
and a woman with my first name is murdered?"

"You know, her pocketbook was missing. We think it's a simple
case of mugging and robbery."

"No, that doesn't make any sense," Evelyn said. "The lady was
found by her car in her yard, which means the man had to be
waiting on her. Do muggers wait in working-class neighborhoods,
kill people for a pocketbook, and neglect to go into empty houses
and steal more valuable things or take their car? It doesn't make any
sense."

This lady knew more about the case than he did, thought Taylor.
"Mrs. Wade, do you have the phone number of the place you called,
the body shop in Chicago?"

"I certainly do. And that's another thing. Mr. Taylor, do you know
what chop shops are?"

Taylor laughed. "Yes, we have those out here, too."

"Well, when I was talking to the boy, he indicated that the place
wasn't a normal body shop. And when I called the number last week,
the *police* answered the phone. Mr. Taylor, I may not know much
about your business, but if I'm right on any of what I say, I'm right
on *it all*. . . ."

Her voice trailed off again. Taylor started to respond, but Evelyn
interrupted him. "Oh Lord, I nearly forgot the most important

thing, how the man knew what Evelyn Garner looked like and where she lived. The day before Evelyn Garner died, she received a large package at work simply addressed to 'Evelyn,' and there was no sender's name on the package. No one would send a package to a large business with just a first name on it. Unless you didn't know the person's name." Evelyn spoke slowly and deliberately. She was silent.

"Mrs. Wade, pardon me for being slow," Taylor said, stopping in mid-sentence. "You mean you think the man watched for someone to come out with the package?"

"Well, wouldn't you do that? Wouldn't it work?"

Taylor shook his head. "Mrs. Garner, I mean, Mrs. Wade, yes, I might do that. Now, would you give me the telephone number of that body shop you called?"

"Of course, it's Central Body Shop, and the number is 312-211-6801." Evelyn paused. "Mr. Taylor, please. If you check on this, will you let me know what you find out? It's important to me."

"I understand that. Mrs. Wade, do you live alone?"

She felt flushed as she answered. "Yes. But I'm okay. You see, this man already thinks I'm dead."

Evelyn hung up the phone and entered Fritz Taylor's name, with an exclamation point after it, in her notebook before walking back to the small porch. Finally, she thought, maybe some of the phoning was going to pay off.

She had worked on the violets and gloxinia for less than ten minutes when the phone rang again. She walked to the kitchen and picked up the phone gingerly. It was May.

"Evelyn, honey, getting you on the phone is like getting the president. How are you this morning?"

"Oh, I'm feeling better. The detective from Dallas called me, that's why the phone was busy. I think he's sincere." Evelyn continued to wipe her hands on her apron as she talked. "He sounded like a boy himself. But he was nice."

"Good. Did he say anything important?"

"It wasn't what he said; it's the fact that he listened to me. Did you ever talk to Jay?"

"That's why I'm calling, and why I tried to call you three times yesterday. Aren't you getting hoarse?"

Evelyn chuckled again. "I can't help it if I'm popular. What about Jay?"

"Chicago Consumer Affairs called him back. Chicago Auto Theft is pursuing the car chopping, and the body shop you called was a big center for car chopping."

Evelyn shook her head. "What did Jay say about that?"

"He wasn't surprised, but he was a little bothered by it, like I am. All of these things keep pointing to a lot of bad people. Are you okay?"

"I've never in all my life had so many people ask how I am. I'm fine. I just want it all to be over. Do you want to help me a little for dinner tomorrow night? Could you bring some wine?"

"We'll bring lots. Maybe we'll all get drunk."

"I may join you! Did you know my husband only got drunk once in his life, and I kicked him out of the bedroom? I wouldn't do that now."

Evelyn checked the time as she replaced the receiver. She began to untie the apron as she walked to her bedroom. She was late. Tuesday mornings were English School mornings. Twelve South American women anxious to practice their English were probably already gathering.

One hour later, in Chicago, a message from Detective Fritz Taylor was sitting on Albert Rosenbloom's desk next to a message from Jay Preston in Atlanta. On Dean Buettner's desk were three things relating to the death of Bobby Medlock: copies of two monitoring reports from Central Body Shop, which listed phone calls from Evelyn Wade in Atlanta, and a fresh copy of Monday's auto-theft summary. The summary contained a notation on another call from Evelyn Wade.

But neither Rosenbloom nor Buettner was in the office. They

were both convinced that the molestation of Albert Rosenbloom's daughter was an act of retaliation by someone in the Vicovari outfit for the raid on Central Body Shop. Dean Buettner spent Tuesday talking with members of the Chicago Strike Force gathering information on Angie Weiner. Albert Rosenbloom spent the morning showing pictures of Weiner and other known members of the Vicovari outfit to his daughter. She could not single out any picture. In the afternoon, Rosenbloom set in motion a series of surprises for Anton Vicovari.

11

JO Pinder was still sleeping, turned on her side facing Rick Kanell. It was six o'clock Wednesday morning. He pushed the sheet off with his feet and looked at Jo's body. Fine golden hairs ran down the center of her stomach, stopping at the navel. Kanell liked morning sex. But the cobwebs were too thick; he needed a pick-me-up first. Two lines.

He lay down again by her, his breath still held in as the powder began to work. Kanell turned on his side and pushed the lower portion of his body against her. She began to stir.

"You're a better wake-up call than a clock, you know," Jo said in a sleepy voice that still sounded sexy. Without saying more, she pulled her body down the bed and buried her head in Kanell's crotch. His eyes were closed, but his hands moved smoothly down her back, then caressed her hair. He sucked in as Jo lifted her head and moved it slowly over his erection, her hair gently caressing it, teasing it. She straddled him, slipping the tips of the fingers on her right hand into his mouth. Kanell was lost. But then she put her hands around his neck, holding on tightly as she pumped, her breasts touching him. At that instant, he lost it. One very rough and fast memory of the bulging eyes of the lady in Dallas, and he lost it. He pushed away, rolled off the bed, and walked to the shower.

Jo followed. Since Rick Kanell had returned from his trip to Dallas she had tried to understand these abrupt mood changes. He had become even more withdrawn than usual. Things were wrong, she felt it. She did not know how the raid on Central Body Shop affected Rick Kanell's relationship with Anton Vicovari or Angie Weiner, if it did at all. She did not know why Kanell had taken a trip to Miami and ended up in Dallas, either. She was surprised that Rick had not invited her to Low Notch yet. Vicovari had called her on Monday to say that invitation would be coming from Kanell, but it had not. Things were wrong, she thought again, as she pulled back the shower curtain just enough to stick her head in.

"Is this a private shower?"

"No, come on in. Find some shampoo, will you?" She opened the sink cabinet and took out a fresh bottle, loosening the cap as she stepped into the shower. Kanell took the bottle and poured the liquid directly from it to his hair. Jo began to rub his back.

"Rick, so why are you so quiet?" She looked at his back. She was uncomfortable with the word "why," it was very dangerous, but the silence in the shower made her more uncomfortable. She had no idea how terminal Kanell's position was in the outfit, but she did feel that he had to like *her*, be close to her, or her position would be jeopardized. She looked at the thin gold bracelet on her left arm as he finally answered.

"No reason, I've just got a lot to do at the office for Anton." He hesitated. Kanell had nearly decided not to invite Jo Pinder to Vicovari's mountain retreat. Kanell wanted that time alone with him. But again, on Tuesday afternoon, Vicovari had mentioned Jo Pinder and Low Notch in the same breath. He continued to massage his hair, his back to her, as he spoke.

"Jo, Anton's invited me to his place in Virginia. He says to bring someone."

Jo looked from Kanell's back to the soap dish as he continued. "He's got a real nice place there. I'm going Saturday."

She looked at his back again, then grasped the flesh of his sides, her fingers massaging in steady strokes. She forced a laugh. "Is that supposed to be an invitation?"

"You want it in writing or something?" Kanell turned around and faced her. His eyes opened just long enough to feel a slight sting from the shampoo, then closed again. "Do you think you can get off? We'll fly down Saturday for a week, maybe. Anton will be down on Monday." He opened his eyes again and kept them open, then ran his hands down her backside, sliding the fingers of his left hand into the soft center flesh of her buttocks.

"So, what am I supposed to tell work? Three days isn't much notice."

"Tell them you won the sweepstakes, or tell them you're having a baby over the weekend, a short pregnancy. What do you think?"

The cobwebs had begun to clear. Though it wasn't a conscious thought, he needed a companion right then. Too many looks from Weiner and too many unspoken words from Vicovari had begun to shake Kanell's confidence just a little.

"Jo, it's really nice there." It was the strongest invitation he could feel. Jo's hand touched his penis. She needed sex right then to lose herself. Jo Pinder wasn't a good liar. She thought about that as she went down on him. She knew how nice Low Notch could be. And her request for five days' paid vacation was already sitting on her supervisor's desk, approved by his supervisor. But Jo did not want to go to Low Notch this time. Too many things were wrong.

Anton Vicovari was in his apartment, overlooking Lake Shore Drive. He was reading. He always read early in the morning, attention seldom leaving the book to take in the gentle curve of lights that bordered the lake. He turned the page and began to read chapter 4 of *To Live and Die in Shanghai*, stopping on the first line as the phone rang.

"Hello?"

"Good morning, Anton."

"Angie, I hope you had a good night."

"Yes, I did. I checked into that thing with Albert Rosenbloom's kid, and none of our people had anything to do with it."

Vicovari nodded. The incident with Albert Rosenbloom's daughter had begun to cause many inconveniences for him. "Do you know yet who did it?"

"I don't know *who*, but I do know that it was an East Side person."

For the first time this morning, Vicovari turned and looked at the early-morning view of Chicago. "I want to know who, Angie; it's very bad timing with all the other problems." Vicovari did not really care that Kati Rosenbloom had been accosted; those matters and tactics had been used by many members of his outfit, too. But the thought of another outfit putting pressure on him indirectly offended his sense of the rules.

"I'll find out," Weiner said.

"Angie—when you find the man who bothered the Rosenbloom girl, let him know I'm not happy. Just talk to him, but let him know, will you do that?"

"Sure. Do you want me to call you later?"

"I'll be out until seven tonight. Why don't you call me then?"

Angie Weiner agreed, hung up, and prepared for the day. He left the apartment just before eight. He had someone to talk to for Anton.

II

"You know, I don't miss driving. Do you still like it?" Evelyn turned slightly to see Lane Englander. Her question was an excuse, really, to look at him. Each week, usually on Wednesday mornings, Englander would offer to share his car for the trip to the Super Kroger off Piedmont. He owned a seven-year-old Peugeot, a white one. The front seats of the car were firm bucket seats that curved up on the side edges, forming little wings, Evelyn thought. Her left hand held onto the left wing as Englander turned on Fourteenth Street.

"It's funny. I didn't used to drive most of the time," Englander said. "I could take the bus to Georgia State. It was quicker. My wife liked to drive. Our last car together was a Gremlin, a lime-green Gremlin XL." Englander dusted off the memory with a smile and a twist of the head, and continued. "Maybe *that's* the reason I didn't drive. Evelyn, it was the *loudest* color! We had lots of fun with that car, but I don't think it qualified as professorial green."

"I remember that car!" Evelyn said as she laughed.

Perhaps once, long ago, she had had a fantasy about Lane Englander. He *was* an attractive man. That was probably why she had kept friendship on a nice but superficial level since Grady Wade's death. But Evelyn Wade's feelings about Englander had shifted in the past weeks. She enjoyed *being* with him, looked forward to talking with him. Though Evelyn didn't want to admit it yet, Lane Englander was beginning to fill a niche beyond friendship.

As the car turned on Tenth, a blond man in his thirties was standing on the corner, waving copies of a magazine called *Swinging Singles* at passing cars and occasionally running up to the window of a car to collect a dollar in exchange for the magazine.

Evelyn reached over and touched Englander's arm. "Lane, you know, that same boy has been selling those things on that corner for at least five years, before Grady died. He's out there every day, even when it's raining and cold. Maybe we should buy a magazine from him. Just to help him. What do you think?"

Englander knew a bluff when he heard one. He pulled the car over to the right.

"Lane! Get us out of here!" Evelyn yelled amid her laughter.

A few minutes later they stood in the kitchen of 91 Myrtle waiting for the water to boil. How many times had they had tea together in the last few months? They both started to speak at once, then laughed, but Evelyn seized the conversation.

"Lane, what bothers me about the whole thing is that everyone keeps calling everyone, but no one seems to *do* anything. It frustrates me terribly."

"That's the nature of far-flung things," he said. "We've got to find someone in Chicago who will listen to us. The detective in Dallas called there yesterday, you called there yesterday, Jay Preston called there Monday, but no one calls back." He nodded at the phone. "Let's have some tea, and then let *me* try getting someone."

They walked to the living room, Englander sitting in the matching chair to Evelyn's right, Grady Wade's chair. For a moment, as Lane talked, Evelyn did not hear his words. Lane Englander was filling that chair in a way that made her more comfortable than at any time since Grady's death. The comforting feeling alone unnerved her a bit. She blinked twice and focused again on Englander as he said her name.

"Evelyn . . . are you there?" Englander stood up. "Let's call. We need to get someone's boss, someone who really knows what's going on. I think we should go to the top, that's the way things get done." Englander was already heading toward the phone. Evelyn followed.

He picked up the phone, grinning as he turned to her. "I assume you know the area code?"

"By heart. It's 312. Who are you going to call?" Englander was dialing the number for information as she spoke.

"Yes, I'd like the number for the chief of detectives in the Auto Theft Department in Chicago, please." He stood for an instant, then turned to Evelyn, making a writing motion with his hand. Evelyn lurched across the room, her hands quickly grabbing a pen. As Englander repeated the number, Evelyn wrote it down. She then flipped through her spiral notebook to page 9 and looked at the number *she* had. She smiled.

"Lane, that's a different number; I called something else. What did you do I didn't do?"

He laughed. "I don't know, Ev. . . . "

Evelyn reached for the phone. "Lane, I'm sorry. I need to make this call. I need to. Why don't you listen on the other phone?" Englander smiled and walked to the kitchen.

The phone rang four times before Jo Pinder answered. Evelyn looked at her watch and wrote down the time, 1:05.

"Yes, this is *Mrs. Grady Wade.* Young lady, I would like to speak to the man in charge, please."

Without pausing, Jo Pinder said, "I'm sorry, Detective Rosenbloom is out. He should be back any minute, though. Can I help you?"

Evelyn did not want to talk to a secretary. "Well, then, I'd like to talk to the next man in charge."

"That would be Detective Buettner. Could you please give me your name?"

"Uh, Mrs. Grady Wade. What did you say the detective's name was?" Evelyn wrote Dean Buettner's name halfway down page 9.

Buettner was eating a sandwich when Pinder buzzed him, his door closed. It had been a hectic day and a half since the incident with Kati Rosenbloom had made the pace at Auto Theft even more frenetic than usual. He picked up the phone, shaking his head as he spoke.

"Yeah?"

"Dean, there's some lady on the phone for Albert. I told her he was out, but she wants to talk to you."

"What does she want?"

"I forgot to ask her . . . sorry. Do you want me to ask her?"

Jo Pinder was very sexy, Buettner thought, but she wasn't worth a damn as a clerk. Buettner tried to conceal the irritation in his voice. "Yeah. But tell her I'm on the phone or something, unless it's important." He placed the phone down and took another bite of the sandwich. As he bit, small drops of mayonnaise hit the desk. "Damn it!" He wiped them with the tip of his finger, then placed the finger in his mouth. The phone buzzed again.

"Yeah?"

"Dean, it's about Central Body Shop and the lady says it's important. Do you still want me to get rid of her?"

"No, I'll take it. What's her name?"

"Mrs. Wade."

"Who's she with?"

Jo Pinder blushed. "I'm sorry, Dean, I didn't ask that. Do you want me to?"

Christ. "No, I've got it."

When he heard the older but formal voice of Evelyn Wade he was sure Mrs. Wade was the secretary for Judge Hames Lyon. Buettner grimaced at the sound of her voice. He had only a day to prepare a request for the judge to allow continued surveillance at Central Body Shop and he had not yet read any of the monitoring reports that would have to provide cause if the tap were to be continued.

"Mrs. Wade, I'm sorry I haven't been back to the judge on the continuation, but I'll do it today for sure."

Evelyn looked toward the kitchen. She didn't have the slightest idea what he was talking about. "Uh, I'm calling concerning Central Body Shop," she said, momentarily stymied.

"That's what I mean. You are calling about the phone tap, aren't you?"

Evelyn blinked. She *knew* they were tapping the phones there. "Mr. Buettner, I'm afraid you have me confused with someone else, but yes, I am calling about the men you have tapping the phones there. I've called them twice and *no one* returned either of my calls. That's not a very good way to run things in my book."

Who the hell was he talking to? "Mrs. Wade, which department are you with?"

Evelyn's respect for law enforcement officers was shrinking. She decided to start again, slowly, looking down at his name before speaking. "Mr. Buettner, my name is Evelyn Wade. I am a widow who lives in Atlanta, Georgia, and I'm not with any department."

Buettner was sitting up now, both elbows resting on the desk. He did not notice that his right elbow was resting on another drop of mayonnaise. The thought crossed his mind quickly that he had discussed a private police matter, a phone tap, with some damned old lady in Atlanta, Georgia. And the lady said she *knew* about the tap. He wrote her name at the top of a legal pad, then drew a dark box around it.

"Ma'am, I'm sorry. Now could you please start at the beginning."

"Mr. Buettner, let me see if I can say this where you will understand it. I work for a telephone opinion research company. Nearly two weeks ago, I reached Central Body Spop at night and talked to a young boy."

Buettner's attention focused on Evelyn's words at the mention of a young boy. His attention did not wander as Evelyn continued with her account, detailing her suspicions. He scribbled notes, but stopped writing momentarily when Evelyn said, "I told the man who came on the phone that my name was Evelyn, that's my first name, and that I was calling from Dallas, Texas. That's what we say. And then on last Friday night, a lady who works for the same company I do, and has my first name, but works in *Dallas*, was murdered. Mr. Buettner, I am calling because I believe the boy on the phone at Central Body Shop was murdered, and the lady in Dallas was murdered by the same man to cover up his tracks." She paused. Evelyn did not know if it was worse to have unreturned phone calls or to have a slow detective. "And I believe the detective in Dallas thinks I'm right, too."

What the hell was this all about? Evelyn's monologue moved around in his thoughts just enough to highlight again the word that smelled of Angie Weiner:—"boy." At Central Body Shop. Bobby Medlock.

"Mrs. Wade, do you know when you talked to the boy?"

"Exactly at ten P.M. on Friday, November one. I wrote the time down."

"I'm sure you did. And what is the detective's name and number?"

Evelyn gave him the information, repeating the phone number twice, and then she gave him her number, repeating it twice as well.

Buettner's thoughts turned back to Bobby Medlock. He did not know if he was forcing an association or not. The incident with Kati Rosenbloom made any opportunity to get close to the Vicovari outfit an important one, but this might be pushing it.

"Mrs. Wade, could you tell me anything about the boy you talked to. How old was he? Did he give his name?"

"Before I answer that, please tell me about the boy. Do you know who killed him?"

Buettner was silent for a few seconds before answering. The silence itself confirmed what Evelyn had known but wanted to disbelieve. "Mrs. Wade, I don't know for sure that a boy was killed at Central Body Shop. I doubt it. But I am going to check on all of this. Now, will you tell me what you know about the boy?"

Evelyn felt a flush of anger. Her life had been changed by the long lines that stretched from her booth at American Opinion Research to a body shop in Chicago, and a lady was dead in Dallas, and this detective wanted to be coy.

"I am going to tell you *nothing* if you don't *talk with me, not around me*, Mr. Buettner. What do you mean, you don't *know for sure*? That means there may be a possibility, and *I want to know*."

He shrugged his shoulders. "Mrs. Wade, I'm not giving you the runaround. A boy that used to work for Central Body Shop was killed some time ago, but he was found in Minnesota, not Chicago. And we have absolutely nothing to tie him to Central Body Shop that night. But what you are saying could be tied in, and I *am* going to do my best to find out if it is. Now, will you please tell me what you know about the boy?"

Evelyn did not hear the question. For two weeks she had lived with the sound and feeling of Bobby Medlock. She had created an image of him in her mind. He looked kind, she felt; she wasn't sure what that meant, but she felt it. She knew he was dead. But Dean Buettner's words seemed to put a heavy weight on her chest.

"Mrs. Wade?"

Evelyn rested her hand on her chest, as if it would relieve rather than add to the pressure. She finally said yes, quietly.

"What exactly did you hear?"

"A scream, and silence, and noises. I did not hear a gun, it was a nearly silent thing, but I did hear enough."

Buettner could tell that the woman in Atlanta was strained. He looked at his watch. "Mrs. Wade, I want to thank you. I appreciate your perseverance. In trying to reach us, I mean."

Evelyn sighed. "I'm not trying to bother people, Mr. Buettner. I believe two people are dead and one of them has my name and died because of my phone call." She hesitated. "Now will you please call me back *regardless* of what you find out?"

Evelyn had begun to put the phone down, when she quickly pulled it to her mouth.

"Mr. Buettner? Mr. Buettner?"

"Yes?"

"I forgot to tell you one thing about the boy. He drank an awful lot of root beer. He said he was drinking his sixth one when I called him. That's why I talked to him, you see, we were doing a soft-drink study."

Her statement struck a faint chord in Buettner, but it faded as he hung up with a thank you.

Evelyn stood by the phone without moving. She did not see or hear Lane Englander when he entered the living room, a smile on his face. But when he touched her shoulder, Evelyn turned to him and began to cry.

III

Buettner hung up the phone as Albert Rosenbloom entered the office. "That call was long enough."

Buettner smiled as he spoke, "Albert, some lady in Atlanta, Georgia, just told me the damnedest story, overhearing a disturbance on a phone call to Central Body Shop, she thinks someone was killed there." He was holding a pencil, playing it like a drumstick. "You know, if what she said makes any sense, it could tie Bobby Medlock to Central Body Shop the night he died." He paused. "I'm sure you wouldn't mind that, would you?"

Rosenbloom shook his head in a slow, deliberate motion. He wouldn't mind that at all.

"I was going to ask you to lunch with Rose and Kati. But I see you've eaten."

"Thanks, but I've got to meet one of the kids," Buettner said as he looked at the time and raised his brow. "Oh shit, I'm late!" He began to move, then stopped. Lennie could wait. He scanned the notes of his conversation with Evelyn Wade and found the name of the detective in Dallas. Rosenbloom gave a short wave and walked out as Buettner dialed. The detective was out. Buettner left his name and number and walked out of his office. Jo Pinder was still sitting there, her hands resting on an old typewriter.

"Jo, do you know where the file is on that mule that was killed, Robert N.M.I. Medlock? I put it out here yesterday," Buettner said, distracted.

"No, but I'll look for it."

"If you can't find it, dig me up the number for Minneapolis Homicide. I think the guy there might want to talk to that lady."

"What lady?"

"The lady I was just talking to, the old lady you didn't ask why she was calling. She may know something about Central Body Shop; anyway, see if you can't find it and put it on my desk," Buettner said as he turned and headed to the door. "I'll be back in an hour or so."

"Yessir." Pinder began to look for the file on Bobby Medlock the moment Buettner headed down the hall. She found it under a dozen other folders on the desk, all relating to ongoing investigations by Chicago Auto Theft. All of the files interested her; with a quick glance at each she noted tidbits for Rick Kanell and Angie Weiner. But the file on Bobby Medlock interested her most of all. Pinder had not been part of any discussions about Medlock with Angie Weiner and certainly not with Anton Vicovari, whom she had not seen in nearly a year. But she had mentioned Medlock's death to Weiner the previous week; the passing comment had not drawn any reaction from him.

Medlock's file told her nothing. In the jargon police departments use, it detailed his arrest the previous year. Pinder looked toward Dean Buettner's office. She seldom entered it when Buettner was gone, afraid of being caught out of place. But Buettner's comments possibly tying Bobby Medlock to Central Body Shop had piqued her interest. And Buettner did say to put the file there. Jo waited another five minutes before going in, then stood there, her eyes searching for something relating to Buettner's phone call with the woman. She saw nothing. Jo walked behind the desk, glanced quickly toward the door, and pulled open the top right drawer.

A yellow pad lay on top of several other pads. The name "Evelyn Wade" was written at the top of the pad, surrounded by a square box. Pinder didn't pick up the pad, but stood there, leaning over slightly, trying to decipher Buettner's scribbled shorthand. A phone number was close to the top. The first line of shorthand said "o'hrd distrb 11/1 C.B.S., thnks wz Mdlck." She could not make out the next two lines, but the fourth, written at a slight angle, said, Jo thought, "Ev Garner Kld Dlls Lst Fri." None of Dean Buettner's scribblings had any real significance to Pinder, but she filed away what she thought they said, wrote Evelyn Wade's name and phone number on a piece of paper, took one more glance at the last line—"Fritz Taylor, Det, Dallas/Garner lady"—and closed the drawer.

Jo walked from Buettner's office and sat again at the clerk's desk. She pulled in her lower lip, then took the piece of paper with Evelyn Wade's name and number on it and wrote: "Evelyn Garner killed in Dallas last Friday." She was sure Buettner's scribblings said that. She looked toward the door, an idle glance masking her thoughts. The lady in Atlanta had called about Bobby Medlock and Central Body Shop and, if Jo's interpretation of Buettner's shorthand was correct, about a killing in Dallas. Rick had been in Dallas last Friday. But he wanted people to think he was in Miami.

It was the first time Jo Pinder really thought about why Kanell had been in Dallas. She turned her mind to other things quickly, trying hard to push away her answer to the question why. Rick Kanell ran Mid-West Tool, that was all he did for the outfit.

Dean Buettner reached Blackie's Video Arcade twenty minutes after leaving Jo Pinder in the office. The arcade was located about three miles from the usual haunts of the mules and other street kids who gathered in the Balboa and Clark Street areas. It was a safe place to meet Lennie, he thought. It was also certainly Lennie's type of place.

Lennie was sitting at the third pinball machine. He had a pile of quarters two inches high on the next machine. But he didn't need the quarters; for over thirty minutes he'd topped his previous score and received one free game after another. Lennie didn't look up as Buettner approached, he simply kept playing the game.

"What *are* you doing, Lennie?"

"Turning white by the minute."

"On a winning streak?"

Lennie's eyes and hands moved together. He gave a quick glance at Buettner, then returned to the game. Lennie was fifteen, but he looked younger. He was very short, barely five feet, but his pudginess made his body seem larger. Though Lennie wasn't the most impressive-looking young man, his eyes were very expressive. He made a quick face at Buettner, an imitation of Groucho Marx's eyebrows and eyes rising and falling in dismay.

"It ain't good us meeting here, I ran into Kowakoski right outside the door. We gotta be more . . . *circumspect*, word fourteen, September. I'm gonna get my nuts cut off one of these days. . . ."

Buettner nodded. "Okay, we'll be more careful, but you'd be cute as a little black girl." Lennie smiled, his eyes and hands still moving together as he did. Buettner continued. "Lennie, Bobby Medlock worked for Central Body Shop, didn't he?"

The game board erupted in color and gave out a raspy, jeering buzz. Lennie slapped his hands on the top of the machine, a look of disgust on his face. "Dean, I just lost. Damn it, you're interfering with my concentration, man. . . . Yeah, he worked for them, I tried to tell you that when we were shooting the hoops." Lennie walked a step to the right and dropped a quarter in Galaxia, an electronic-game version of war in the twenty-second century. Buettner watched for a moment.

"Lennie, you said Bobby Medlock was driving a Jensen the night he disappeared, the one you rode around in?"

Lennie aped a flunky. "That-is-correct-Mr.-Buettner. . . . Is all you gonna do is ax me about Medlock? I thought you had me a magazine? Zing! I got him!"

Buettner snapped his fingers and grimaced. "Damn! Lennie, I forgot. We'll buy you one next door. Lennie . . . I'm trying to find out who killed Bobby."

"Good. He was okay. We got on."

"Well, did he say specifically *who* he was muling for the night he disappeared?"

"Yep. He was doing a trip for Angie. He did a lot of special trips for Angie. I think he was *close* to him, if you know what I mean. Like Kowakoski is close to him. But Bobby wasn't a faggot. Bobby got nice gifts from Angie." He paused. "Kowakoski isn't a faggot, either. He's just mean."

Buettner looked away for a moment. It was the first time Bobby Medlock had been placed with Angie Weiner on the night he disappeared. "Did Bobby say where he was going on that night? Was he going to meet Angie?"

Lennie stopped playing, and for a moment he just looked at the game. He then turned to Buettner. "You're a *gink*, Buettner. That man is *bad business*. You're gonna get me killed talking about him." Lennie turned his attention back to the game. He started bouncing up and down lightly on his toes, as if he were in a boxing match. "There are lots of bad stories about Angie and his boys." Lennie flashed a quick smile. "But I'm lucky. He doesn't like dark meat."

"So why are you shaking in that little black suit of yours, man?"

"'Cause some of his boys don't come back. They just . . . *disappear*. . . ." Lennie said the word in a long, exaggerated whisper, as if he were telling the most frightful part of a ghost story. He said it as he pushed down on the hyperspace button. "Shit! A battleship! Direct hit on the battleship!"

Buettner waited a moment before repeating his question. "Well—was he going to meet Angie or wasn't he, spaceman?"

"He was."

"And where were they going to meet?"

"At the opera."

"Lennie, damn it!" Buettner tried to speak harshly, but his smile gave him away.

"Dean, I am truly perplexed by your question, word twenty-seven, August, since I do not know the co-reck an-ser."

"Did you know Bobby well?"

"Not too. I know his brother better."

"Well, did Bobby drink root beer? Do you know that?"

"Hires."

Buettner did not understand. "What?"

Lennie gave a fast, exasperated glance in Buettner's direction. "How did you ever get to be a detective when you don't know about Hires? It's the best root beer, like champagne. He had a six-pack in that fine machine when he picked me up. Bobby always drank only the best."

Buettner twitched his nose slightly and said, "Bingo." Evelyn Wade's call from Atlanta was beginning, he thought, to point the finger at Angie Weiner. But he needed to know more.

"Lennie. I want you to find out something very important for me. I want you to try to find out where Angie Weiner was last Friday night." Buettner was thinking about the lady in Dallas, Texas. If a lady had died there as Evelyn Wade said, and if Angie Weiner was in Dallas, Buettner would be sure that Weiner was more than a lover of young boys and runner of mules. He would be a murderer.

But Lennie wasn't speaking. "Zing! Zap! Holy shit! The goddamn rocket *got my bases*, Buettner! Did you see that?" He turned to face Buettner. "Thousands of space people have just died and I feel *bereft*." Lennie had a quizzical look on his face. "Did I use that right?"

"Yeah, Lennie. Now, will you check on that for me?"

"Natch. If you'll buy me a magazine." Buettner put his hand out palm up and accepted the slap.

They walked next door. The small shop that operated at the corner had a counter open to the street. Buettner bought Lennie a copy of *Time* and left him standing on the street, his eyes fixed on the first story that caught his attention. Buettner would have recognized the kid named Kowakoski if he had looked a bit more to the right before crossing the street, but he did not see him. Lennie didn't see him, either. But Kowakoski's eyes had not left either of them since they walked from the video games at Blackie's. He watched Lennie until he turned the corner. And then he began to follow him as Lennie returned to State and Balboa.

Buettner arrived back at the office a little before one and walked directly into Albert Rosenbloom's office. Rosenbloom had not returned from lunch yet. When Buettner entered his own office, a telephone message from a Detective Fritz Taylor in Dallas was on his desk. He dialed the number in Dallas, but Taylor was out again. Buettner looked at Bobby Medlock's folder. On the outside flap he had written the name and number of the Minneapolis officer assigned to Bobby Medlock's death. He picked up the phone and dialed the number.

Officer Earl Brown took about two minutes to find the file on Bobby Medlock. He began ticking off the items found with the body, "Okay, let's see. What we found with the body. It was in a Clupak bag, whatever the hell that is. A hundred-percent cotton rag with piss on it, a piece of steel wool, two root beer cans; we've sent them all to the lab, of course."

"Does it say what type of root beer?"

"Yeah. Hires."

At two thirty, Albert Rosenbloom returned. Buettner heard him enter the office and shut the door. He waited a moment, then knocked, his hand opening it just enough to stick his head in.

"Albert, can I see you a minute?" Rosenbloom looked stormy. He didn't look up, but waved Buettner in, then reached to the left of his desk and picked up a telephone message.

"Call this guy, will you? I meant to give it to you yesterday."

Buettner looked at the message, a call from Detective Fritz Taylor in Dallas, then spoke.

"Albert, how are Rose and Kati?"

Rosenbloom shrugged "Like hell."

"Well, I think I've got something that will make you feel better, a *lot* better." Buettner reviewed what he now believed about the death of Bobby Medlock and his certainty that the boy was murdered by Angie Weiner.

By three thirty, Albert Rosenbloom had assigned a team of four junior detectives to man a day-and-night surveillance of the chicken-hawk Angelo Douglas Weiner. Minneapolis Homicide would probably have paid for the cost of the surveillance, the case was really theirs. But Albert Rosenbloom did not want them to. He had his own reasons for this surveillance.

IV

At nine that evening, May, Jay, and Lane were standing with Evelyn at her door. Jay hesitated after saying his good-byes, then leaned over and gave Evelyn a light kiss on her forehead. Englander gave Evelyn a light kiss, too, and was starting to walk out the door when Evelyn stopped him.

"Lane, I forgot. Are you good at changing light bulbs? The bulb over my bathroom sink is out, and I can't reach it easily, I have to stand on a stool." The bulb *was* burned out, but Evelyn really just needed to talk.

When she returned with a bulb, Englander was sitting in the living room, his right hand tossing a red croquet ball in the air, left hand catching it. He threw the ball in the air again. "Ev—where's the mallet? I haven't hit one of these things in a long time." It was a real croquet ball, not the type backyard players are used to; the ball weighed over two pounds.

Evelyn laughed. "Lane, good mallets cost over a hundred dollars these days. I use the one that belongs to our croquet club at Piedmont Park, but let me show you something." She went to the corner and picked up a cane seldom used for walking because of its weight. It was of solid wood, not like the best walking canes of bamboo. A heavy cane, the end shaped like the head of a hammer, but kept in a prominent place for two reasons: It was given to her by her son, and it made a good pickup croquet mallet because of the weight of the head.

"Lane, roll the ball to me." Evelyn turned and in one quick movement—how many times had she practiced it?—upended her cane and let it slip through her hand until the rubber-tipped end was in her grip. She then placed her left hand under her right, leaned over the ball, and said, "To the knot on the board to the left of the door." She swung a steady but strong motion that sent the heavy ball directly to the knot in the pine board. She rolled the ball back and did it again, this time using only her right hand, a very hard shot, one also practiced on most days. Englander clapped.

"You've got to teach me how to do that sometime," he said as Evelyn put the cane back in its place.

"I'm expensive," she said with a smile. They walked to the bathroom, and Evelyn talked while Englander replaced the bulb.

"Lane, you know, I've been thinking about going to Chicago," she said tentatively, "I even called an airline before you all came to dinner." Evelyn straightened a towel, a pink one on the rack to her left. Lane continued to fiddle with the light.

"Oh?"

She looked up at him. "All those people up there don't think this thing is important. But I *do*. . . . Am I being silly?"

Englander tightened the last screw on the globe, then looked at her. "You are the furthest thing from silly I know, Ev. And of course we will go." He said it quietly, but with emphasis, eyes on her. "Just give me time to pack."

"You know, you make me feel good," Evelyn said as she looked away.

"It's my talent with light bulbs," he said as he walked to the door. When they were at the door, Lane Englander gave Evelyn another light kiss, his right hand moving over to touch her hand. Evelyn watched him walk down the six steps of 91 Myrtle before closing the door, then walked to the kitchen. She was feeling better than she thought possible on this night.

12

DEAN Buettner was sitting in Albert Rosenbloom's office
Thursday morning. They had reviewed the status of ongoing
investigations, then started actions on new developments in the
Chicago auto-theft business. As the meeting ended, Rosenbloom
asked for a quick summary of the actions taken on the usual complaints against Auto Theft, complaints from individuals, other
departments, and important political types. As Buettner finished his
review, Rosenbloom smiled wryly.

"Dean, you can add another one to the political file," he said
facetiously. "I got a call at home last night about Vicovari. From a
selectman. The little prick is in Vicovari's pocket like half his goddamn compatriots, but he carries a lot of weight. He's filing an
objection against me, based on harassment."

"So what did you say to the little selectman?"

"I told him to go fuck himself, what did you think?" He paused.
"The little wimp will cause trouble, though. And Vicovari himself

will cause some trouble." Rosenbloom glared. "As we know. . . . Dean, who's supposed to be tailing Weiner today?"

Buettner looked at his watch before answering. "I think Spezzano came on a little while ago. How long are you planning to keep the tail on? I'm having to pull people off other things." Auto Theft had located Angie Weiner at eleven the previous night. Dean Buettner had carefully briefed the officers who eventually found him. They were to look for anything or any person who could cement the department's belief that Angie Weiner had killed Bobby Medlock. To Rosenbloom, removing the man he believed responsible for molesting his daughter would be the nicest blow against the Vicovari outfit.

Rosenbloom shook his head. "Hell, I want to keep it on as long as we can. Then maybe we can give the case to Homicide or something. How badly is it screwing up other things?" It was slowing down many investigations, but Buettner did not want to say so.

"Nothing we can't handle . . . So, I'm going to follow up on some things, okay? Before you know it, there will probably be a queue of people waiting on me to solve problems." As Buettner said the word for the day he turned in the chair and quickly exited the office.

At a few minutes after nine he received a phone call from Jay Preston in Atlanta. Preston avoided small talk and quickly brought the conversation to Evelyn Wade. "Buettner, Evelyn said that some boy was killed who worked at that place. Is that right?"

"Yeah. And it's beginning to look an awful lot like she may be right, the guy probably was killed *at* the place."

"How did he die?"

"A broken neck. Probably hit with a fist, too; nothing was embedded in the contusion."

"*The boy I talked to was hit with that man's fist.*" Preston remembered Evelyn's words the first night they had met.

"Buettner, do you guys have anybody on the murder?" It was the most important question.

"No, but we do have someone under surveillance right now. The guy's a real monster, too."

A small knot began to rise in Jay Preston's throat. Was there any danger for Evelyn Wade? Probably not. But nothing about the whole affair made sense, and he wasn't sure any longer that Evelyn was out of danger.

"Who's the suspect?"

"I can't tell you that. But I will tell you he's very involved in a big auto-theft outfit up here. He also likes little boys. The guy is a real scumbag."

"What's the guy's voice like?"

Why hadn't he asked the lady that? "I don't know, but it's a good thought. Would the lady remember what he sounded like?"

"Dean, this lady forgets *nothing*. She even keeps a notebook with all of the things she knows about what happened."

"Okay, if and when we can, I'll find some way for her to hear what he sounds like." He paused. "How old is that lady anyway?"

"Hell, I don't know. Maybe seventy or so. Why?"

"She sounds awfully together, that's all."

"She is, let me tell you." Jay hung up, and called Evelyn at work to tell her this news.

At eleven, Evelyn's shift was finished. As she began to walk up the gentle hill to the bus stop, she paused and looked back at the office complex that housed AOR. She had never thought before about the people sitting in cars there, but three cars, one parked close to the main entrance, contained people waiting. For the first time, Evelyn became suspicious of the strangers in the space surrounding the building. She could not shake the sense of fear. It was still there when she reached the steps of 91 Myrtle. She looked at the house, consciously alert to how it might strike a stranger, how secure it appeared. The frame house wasn't big, but it was fine-looking, if slightly frayed. The roof was angled sharply, covered in cedar, as were the two dormers. Four large windows, reaching from floor level to the eaves of the roof, made the front look open and inviting. Too inviting. She opened the door, coaxing the lock, then walked directly to the phone and dialed.

"Well, I'm here," she said to Lane Englander. "Give me a few minutes to run to the girls' room."

Englander arrived at five minutes to twelve and began to help in the kitchen.

"Ev, I was thinking. What else do we know about that man? What do we know that can help the fellow in Chicago?"

Evelyn didn't answer for a minute. She was thinking about the voice of the man on the phone.

"Lane, the only thing would be if I could recognize the man's voice. Jay says they may be able to get a recording." She shook her head. "But even if they could do that, what good would that do? They won't arrest him because I say I recognize his voice, will they?"

"I doubt it, but we can't tell what straw will bring down the camel. They must know something, or they wouldn't be following him."

Evelyn pushed her chair out and rose. "Well, then I'm going to call Mr. Buettner and tell him I *definitely* can recognize the man's voice. You know, I am the only living witness to what that man did." She walked first to the double-sided desk and picked up the spiral-ring notebook, then turned and walked to the kitchen. Englander reached for the desk phone. It was 12:45.

Jo Pinder had been in the office less than two minutes when the phone rang. She was late. The regular clerk, Trudy, was ready to leave for lunch and was standing by Pinder. Jo reached beyond her and picked up the phone.

Evelyn cleared her throat. "Yes, this is Mrs. Grady Wade, Evelyn Wade in Atlanta. I'd like to speak to Mr. Buettner, please."

Pinder's pulse quickened at the sound of Evelyn's voice. She turned her head up just enough to see Trudy pick up her pocketbook sitting on the edge of the desk.

"Mrs. Wade, I'm sorry, but Lieutenant Buettner is out."

"Well, is anyone else there?"

"No, ma'am, I'm sorry, but the chief is out to lunch." Pinder hesitated. "Is there anything I could help you with?"

"Well . . . I would like for him to call me. Tell him it's about the man's voice, that I can recognize the man's voice, for sure."

Pinder was conscious of Trudy's presence. She was behind her at the filing cabinet, the drawer closed. "Ma'am, what voice?"

"The voice of the man who killed the boy."

Who killed Bobby Medlock. "Yes," Pinder said, "I'll certainly tell him. Now if you'll give me your phone number again, I'll make sure he calls you." Pinder wrote the number down, trying hard to commit it to memory, and hung up. She turned to Trudy.

"Trudy, this lady called Dean yesterday. She says she can recognize some man's voice who killed a boy, whatever that means." Pinder handed the note to her, her eyes making contact with Trudy's face very briefly. She did not want anyone to read her thoughts.

II

Angie Weiner was walking about twenty steps behind the man, his pace quickening as the man approached an area of deserted storefronts. He wanted to be right behind him when he passed in front of a store less than a quarter block away where the door stood ajar. Weiner was going to talk to the man for Anton. Finally, after two days, of conversations, Patrick Jardine, the man now less than ten steps in front of Weiner, had been identified as the molester of Kati Rosenbloom. A toothpick of a man, short and stringy, Jardine walked with a lounging swagger. Jardine's cute trick with the Rosenbloom girl, Weiner thought, had caused too much trouble for Vicovari. Anton could not leave his house anymore. Unless he wanted the officer in the black-and-white hard on his tail.

As Patrick Jardine approached the storefront, Weiner quickly looked around him. An old man was walking by him, eyes down. Weiner stepped up quickly to Jardine and grabbed his left hand, twisting it hard and bending it behind the man's back, palm out. He dragged him backward, quickly, into the storefront alcove, then into the vacant room. It had been a cloth-remnant shop at one time. Jardine had only a glimpse of Weiner's face as he was dragged backward, and as Weiner hit him the first time, a violent blow to the groin, Jardine screamed, a loud, guttural sound. It was thirty degrees outside the storefront and not much warmer inside, but he was quickly drenched in sweat.

Weiner took a thin nylon cord from the left pocket of his plaid hunting jacket and tied Jardine's wrists together behind his back tightly enough to stop the blood from flowing. He looped the cord around the wrists again, then wrapped the man's ankles together, pulling the wrists back and tying them to the ankles. Twice when Jardine began to yell, Weiner kicked him in the groin. The kicks brought a twitch of pleasure to Weiner.

Taking a pair of pliers from his coat, Weiner knelt down by Jardine, placing his right knee on the man's sweaty cheek. Weiner ground the cheek in the dust and rubble of the floor.

"How are your teeth, prick? Do they feel good?" Weiner lifted his knee and turned the man's head to the far left, pulling the upper lip away from the gums as a veterinarian might inspect a horse's teeth.

"You have too many holes in your teeth, Patrick." Weiner laughed. "What'cha doing with all these holes?" The man clenched his teeth tightly. Weiner hit him with the pliers, a hard blow that only brought one grunt. He then forced his mouth open, holding Jardine's nose tightly shut, forcing him to gasp for breath.

"Patrick, don't bother little cunts and blame it on us," Weiner said as he forced the pliers into the man's mouth. "That's not nice." Weiner then grabbed the man's left front tooth with the pliers, turning it and pulling it out.

Jardine shrieked, then lay still, his breath coming in fast, shallow spurts. Weiner looked at the man's crotch. He swung the pliers full-force directly into the center of it. Jardine screamed again. Weiner hit him there again, harder.

"Patrick, I hope you tell your mother-fucking friends to mind their fucking business, prick." Weiner knelt there for a moment, he had an erection. As it passed, he wiped the pliers off with an old sheet of newspaper lying on the floor, put them in his pocket, and walked out. He had not killed him, Weiner regretted that. But he had talked to him pretty well. That was what Anton said to do.

III

Dean Buettner was sitting in his car, three empty Big Mac containers piled between him and Lennie Ferguson. The two had met in a safer place this time—in a parking lot right next to the 134th Precinct station, an address not frequented too much by Lennie Ferguson's friends. The November issue of *Reader's Digest* was under Lennie's feet. Lennie burped, then took another swig of McDonald's version of a chocolate milk shake. "Dean, when am I gonna drive your car? You *said* I could drive it sometime, and I'm *yearning* to, word twenty-eight, September. I'm yearning to drive it today."

Buettner laughed, pulling his right leg up tightly against his body, his heel resting on a frayed corner of the seat. "I don't have time today, Slicks; it's about work time. But Saturday. I promise we'll do it Saturday." Buettner owed Lennie that.

"Lennie, are you sure about Weiner being in Dallas last Friday?" The day the lady named Evelyn was killed.

Shivering a little from the cold, Buettner cranked up the car again and let it idle. There was a hole in the muffler, but there were several holes in the tan canvas roof. Small drafts through the roof openings cleared out most of the exhaust smell, but not all of it.

Lennie coughed. "This car is a living and breathing *gas chamber*, man. You should rent it out to the state or somethin', you know?" He sucked up the last drop of shake before continuing. "Dallas. My statement is *certifiable*, and that's not one of your words, either. I read it in *Time*. Dean . . .do you really think you can put Bobby's death on Weiner?"

"Yeah, I think Weiner could have done it. Dallas pretty much makes it for sure." He turned the car off. "It's none of my business, Slicks, but how do you *know* he was in Dallas?"

"Dean—am I gonna have to testify or somethin'?"

"Shit no."

"Well . . . you see, there's this pretty young thing by the name of

Gina who runs with the boys who drive Angie on his appointed rounds. She also allows the boys to drive her, too, if you know what I *mean*. Well, this very pretty young thing also takes lessons at a local *arcade* . . . from a handsome and famous black pinball expert, and this famous expert asked her to check it out for him last night. She had to sacrifice her body in order to provide the information, just like they do in the spy stories, Dean."

"Damn, Lennie, you better be careful asking things like that directly. How do you know she didn't tell them who was doing the asking?"

"Buettner! I am handsome and famous, I am not dumb."

Buettner shook his head, "I know; Lennie, we better get out of here."

It was a five-minute drive to the el. Buettner dropped Lennie Ferguson off, one slap of the palm sealing the "See you Saturday," and pulled a U-turn to head east toward the offices of Chicago Auto Theft. His unannounced turn nearly caused the two cars behind him to bump fenders. The kid named Kowakoski was sitting in the second car's passenger seat. He watched Lennie climb the stairs to the platform.

Albert Rosenbloom was walking down the hall with an envelope in his right hand when Buettner came out of the elevator.

"Albert!"

Rosenbloom turned around, then turned again after seeing Buettner, and opened the door to the office. He didn't look too happy, and didn't acknowledge Buettner as he sat in the desk chair and leaned forward, a phone message from Evelyn Wade in his hand. Rosenbloom simply sat there, finally removing six black-and-white glossy prints from the envelope in his left hand.

"So you look like you're having a fine day, boss."

Rosenbloom was looking at the pictures and did not raise his eyes. "Un huh. I told you I'd get my ass chewed."

"By who?"

"The commander, no less." Rosenbloom shifted through the pictures once more, then cast them to Buettner's side of the desk. The pictures were of Angie Weiner and another man outside a diner. Dean Buettner knew Angie Weiner's face, there were many pictures of him in the files, but he did not recognize the other man. He looked at the back for an ID.

"Who took them?"

"Vice. They've been following Weiner, too." Rosenbloom gave out a short snort. "Half the world is following that son of a bitch. I thought the task force was supposed to stop that. You know, why do we have those task-force meetings that take up all of your time?"

"Who's the other guy?"

"Owns a tool company, has no record. That's all we know. Doesn't look like the type to run with Angie, does he?"

Buettner continued to look at the pictures. Weiner didn't look like a fairy, he thought. He looked very mean. How many had the guy killed? More than Bobby Medlock and the lady in Dallas, he suspected. He scrutinized Kanell. The man looked like a lawyer, a rich one. He was very tan; his suit tailored and expensive. At that moment it did not seem important to know who the well-dressed man was. Buettner turned the conversation to Lennie Ferguson, placing the picture of Weiner and Kanell to the side.

"Albert, Weiner was in Dallas last Friday." He waited for a reaction, but there was none.

"So?"

"Oh yeah, you don't know about that yet," Buettner said, glancing down at the message slip from Evelyn Wade, then waving it. "The lady in Atlanta, the one who talked with Bobby Medlock at Central Body Shop the night he died? *Another* lady with her first name who works for the same company, but in Dallas, was killed Friday in Dallas." He paused. "Don't you see?"

"Dean, what have you been drinking?"

"Albert, it all fits together, honest to God, it's another thing that ties Angie to Bobby Medlock's death."

"So what are you going to do with that hot piece of information?"

"Give it to the guy in Dallas, the Homicide guy there, and give it to Homicide in Minneapolis, too. God, this thing's beginning to look like a chess game."

"Well, wake me when something happens. Dean, what did you do with that group of subpoenas? And what did you do on cause for renewing the Central Body Shop wiretap?"

"I'm working on all of that," Buettner said with a touch of guilt in his voice.

"*What* are you doing? Some details, please."

They spent thirty minutes reviewing ongoing activities. When Rosenbloom left the office, Buettner first tried to call Evelyn Wade. Her line was busy. He left the note by the phone. He then tried to reach Detective Fritz Taylor in Dallas, but Taylor was out. Buettner was leaving a message as Rosenbloom walked back into the office, a big smile on his face.

"Get off the phone, Dean."

Buettner looked at him perplexedly, then interrupted his conversation with a very friendly sounding woman at Dallas Homicide. "So, what are you grinning about?"

"I just got a call from Booking, from one of the guys in Vice. I take back whatever bad shit I ever said about them."

"Albert, what are you talking about?"

"They just booked Angie Weiner."

"What! On what charge?"

"Battery and assault with a deadly weapon." Rosenbloom's laugh was almost gleeful. "A pair of pliers."

"What the hell?" Buettner was standing up. He too was smiling.

"He was working over one of the Catuara oldies with a pair of pliers, busted his nuts, too, and left him." Rosenbloom shook his head. "You know, *my* goddamned surveillance lost him for two hours this morning, but Vice just happened to see him drag the guy into a building. When Weiner walked out by himself, they went in and found the guy and took out after Weiner. The guy's at Cook County. He can't talk worth shit, his teeth are busted to hell, and his balls are as big as your damn head, but the guy is pressing charges. God, I never thought I'd owe one to those guys."

Buettner looked back at the phone message concerning Evelyn Wade. "Albert . . . I want to get an audio recording of him."

"What for?"

"I want to play it for the lady in Atlanta. She says she can recognize his voice, the voice of the guy who killed Medlock." He handed the message to Rosenbloom as he continued. "So what did Weiner have to say?"

"Absolutely nothing. Says he's never seen the guy in his life. I guess he always carries a pair of bloody pliers in his pocket to keep him warm or something. . . . Dean, get someone to call our surveillance guys and get them back in. The dumb fucks'll stay out there forever. Put them on something else. And call down to Booking. I want to know when someone comes to get Weiner out. They're going to try to keep him over the weekend, but you know how that goes."

"Yeah," Buettner said in resigned agreement before catching himself. "Albert—we can keep him longer than that." He turned and sat at the desk again, looking for the number of the Minneapolis Homicide detective.

"Dean, what the hell are you talking about?"

"*Albert*, what have I just been talking about? Weiner is a suspect in two damn murders. Maybe we can get some help, a telegram or something saying they are interested in talking with him."

"Okay," Rosenbloom said quietly. "Dean, the damn judge is going to think we've lost our minds when you tell him that cockamamy story, but have at it."

Buettner nodded. "Just let me try to get these guys in Dallas and Minneapolis, and then I'll go down to Booking. I want to find some way to get a recording of Weiner, like I said."

"Okay, but get your ass back *quick*. Your goddamned desk is sinking, like you're gonna be if you don't get some of this mess cleared up."

Before heading to Booking, Buettner placed the pictures of Angie Weiner and the well-dressed stranger back in the folder.

13

I

LENNIE picked up his pace, walking down the two stories of steps that took him from the safety of the Hooper Street station to the street below, where only a few people were out doing their Saturday-morning chores. He did not glance behind him. Another glance would show fear. If they were still behind him, Lennie Ferguson did not want to show fear. But he was afraid. Kowakoski and three other kids he did not recognize had been standing in the same car, less than twenty feet away. Lennie had seen them walk to the door, too, when he used the one glance a street kid can make out of curiosity. What time was it?

Buettner was on time. He was sitting in the red MG less than a block from Richard Daley Park. A frayed copy of *Jaws* lay on the passenger seat. The book was for Lennie, sort of a graduation present for the first driving lesson. Buettner didn't think it would take more than an hour or so, and then the weekend would belong to Mona. He picked up the book and began to read.

Lennie felt them before seeing them again. Kowakoski stepped to his right, hooking his arm through Lennie's right as one of the other kids took his left.

"Hey, Lennie, my man, what'cha doin'!" Kowakoski said as if in hearty greeting, while stepping up the pace. Lennie's heartbeat doubled as they touched him. His first worry was Dean Buettner. They could not see Buettner, and he did not want them to know that he was going for a drive with Buettner; one-to-one meetings with a cop were dangerous for any kid who ran with mules. But as Kowakoski spoke again, tauntingly—"Hey, Lennie, where's your buddy? Are you seeing your cop buddy this morning?"—Lennie began to look down the street, searching for Buettner. They knew.

They cut across the street and into the western corner of the park, just by a large berm topped by several trees and thickety shrubs. Lennie started breathing through his mouth.

"Kowakoski, you Polack, what the hell are you talking about, man?" Lennie forced a smile. An old man looked up at them for a moment, sensed trouble, and quickly looked away. They pulled Lennie behind a group of trees that sheltered a small fountain from wind during the summer.

"You are a lying, mothafuckin' nigger," Kowakoski snarled, a menacing grin on his face, and in the same breath he hit Lennie with a short blow to the stomach, just hard enough to let him know the talk had begun. Lennie faked a faint. As he began to crumble, the two boys loosened their grip to let him fall to his knees, just what he wanted. He curled his fists and gave each a fast blow to the crotch, then sprang up, moving with a speed only fear can bring, and pushed through a small thicket of bushes. The four pushed after him, arms reaching out to close the short distance of the chase. Kowakoski caught Lennie's arm on the back swing and pulled him around, kneeing him so hard that Lennie's moan brought a glance from several people sitting on a bench within hearing range but not able to see. The people moved on, except for an old man who continued to stare ahead, oblivious to the sound.

"I'm gonna kill the son of a bitch," the tallest kid threatened as they dragged Lennie, still fighting, back into the undergrowth just enough to be hidden and flung him down. Surrounded, Lennie curled instantly into a protective position, arms wrapped around his head. But rough hands jerked his arms and legs out, almost spread-eagled.

"Hold him." Kowakoski slid a pint bottle, an old Thunderbird bottle, from his pocket, and as he removed the cap, Lennie's eyes turned up just enough to see it.

"You are a Polack chicken, Kowakoski," Lennie said, still resisting, breathing through his mouth. "You are a goddamn chicken." Lennie did not feel the liquid when it touched his clothes, and he didn't feel it at first, either, when Kowakoski poured it on his hands. It just felt cold, and then it felt hot, and then it felt like flames.

"Angie wanted us to talk to you, prick," Kowakoski's voice grated. "He wanted us to tell you that niggers don't talk to cops." With the tallest boy's hand clamped tightly over his mouth, Lennie couldn't yell yet; but he began to moan, and when the boy removed his hand, he began to scream. When Kowakoski poured the liquid on his face the scream thinned, so high-pitched it seemed to disappear.

"Watch out, damn it! You nearly got it on me!" Kowakoski knocked the tall kid's hand away from his. "Let's get out of here!" The four cut through the bushes and ran by the man who stared at nothing. Lennie tried to run too, but he could not see. He stumbled to the corner of Cassidy Street and collapsed, his shrill scream becoming a moan. People gathered around him slowly, tentatively, and then finally a woman said, "Somebody get this boy some help."

Buettner was less than a block away. He did not see the small crowd, the berm blocked his view. He heard the siren perhaps ten minutes later, but the sound of sirens in the city was no more intrusive than the sound of a low-flying plane. He continued to read. At eleven, after about an hour of waiting for Lennie Ferguson, Buettner folded down the corner of the page, his eyes making one more sweep for the boy, and drove away. Where the hell was the damn kid? Buettner was pissed. Lennie had missed meetings before. But he did think it a little odd that he would miss his first driving lesson.

II

Angie Weiner pulled a small piece of paper from his coat pocket, looked at the number, dropped in a coin and dialed.

"Star Meat Packing."

"Give me Anton."

Weiner remained on hold for nearly two minutes, and then brought his attention back to the phone as the receiver on the other end came alive.

"So, how's the jailbird this morning, Angie?"

"I'm telling you, there are some weird people in that place. Thanks for taking care of things so quickly."

Vicovari did not acknowledge the thank you, but went directly to the matter at hand. "Angie, I thought I might send you down to Virginia."

To Low Notch. To kill Kanell. Weiner began to smile. "When do you want me to go?"

"Probably Monday. I'm waiting to find out when Doug Boldin is going to be available. He works for friends down there."

"Who's Boldin?"

"A good hunter, and a person you can trust. Rick is going hunting with him on Monday or Tuesday morning. I thought you might be on the property, we call it the Hunt Club. There's a very beautiful place there they called Deep Gap, a sheer drop of about twenty-five stories. It's a very dangerous view, though."

Weiner began to smile again. A nice, accidental fall, 250 feet. Angie's first thought was Rick Kanell would have to be conscious. But why have another person involved?

"Anton, you know, I can handle this alone."

"I know. But you don't know the property. You couldn't find Deep Gap. And should something happen, we will need Boldin to go back to the house and tell Jo about the accident."

"How will I meet Boldin?"

"He'll pick you up at the airport."

"And you think it'll be Monday?"

"Probably."

"Okay, then when should I call you?"

"Tomorrow about noon. I'll leave you a number with the service . . . Angie, did you talk to Jo?"

"Yeah, I saw her early this morning. She and Kanell are leaving on the twelve-fifteen flight to Roanoke. Anton, she's very nervous. She doesn't know anything, but she's nervous. I told her just to have a good time and be in touch if she needed to be."

Weiner changed the subject. "Anton, the kid was talked to this morning." Vicovari said nothing. He did not know the name Lennie Ferguson, but he did know that matters like that had to be dealt with quickly. The details were unimportant.

"Very good."

Weiner hung up and, as the receiver touched the cradle, gave a short laugh. He was going to Virginia.

III

There was no sign at the entrance to the Low Notch Club. Most of the people whose cars climbed the mountain, making six sharp turns to reach the quarter mile of level road, saw only the small store directly across from the entrance. Rick Kanell and Jo Pinder pulled their car next to a red Dodge truck with mud-covered wheels and lower body panels. There was a rifle rack in its back window.

Kanell was looking forward to his visit to Low Notch. In particular, he was looking forward to his conversation with Vicovari. During the flight from Chicago, Kanell had thought in detail about his approach to him. He wanted to leave the outfit and buy Mid-West Tool completely, a business proposition. Kanell would offer to finance the purchase at a bank. It was logical, he thought. All of the profits of Mid-West's legitimate operations were already his to take, a gift from Vicovari for services rendered to the outfit. But those services could be taken over by someone else, and Kanell would train him. The money from the sale of Mid-West would more than cover Vicovari's expenses in bringing a new manager aboard. And the financial statements of Mid-West would make a bank loan, especially a loan from a bank friendly with Vicovari, a given. Kanell was optimistic about his chances of convincing Vicovari.

Kanell left the car and entered the Low Notch Gap Country Store. A case of imported snails was sitting by the front door next to the counter. Next to that was a case of Red Man chewing tobacco. The store was clearly an eclectic place. In the winter, it served mostly locals and the passing stranger. In season, its shelves were filled with items usually found in the gourmet sections of finer large grocery stores.

Kanell bought a carton of cigarettes, turned to leave, then bought one more thing. When he entered the car, he handed Jo Pinder a pickled egg wrapped in a napkin. Pinder raised her eyebrows as she took the proffered object with two fingers.

"You expect me to *eat* this?"

"Sure, it's good for you, builds healthy tits and all that stuff," Kanell said as he pulled across the highway and began to drive down the entrance with no signs.

It was a funny gift, Jo liked that. Since deciding that Rick Kanell killed people, Pinder did not know precisely how to handle her feelings about him. People did what Anton said. Jo looked at Kanell. Why was she nervous with him now if she could accept that? Maybe it was the drugs.

She looked at the leaves as they drove. Most of the remaining leaves were red and bright yellow, a few hickories and oaks still hanging on valiantly. And then she noticed something.

"Why aren't there any signs here, Rick?"

"There are. There's the first one." It said simply "Private Road." As the car turned the third bend and passed a lake with large rock houses on the left bank, the second sign appeared. Like the other signs, it was carved in wood. "Low Notch Club." A hundred feet farther down the road another sign said "Members and Guests Only," and around a sharp curve to the right, the final sign said "No Trespassing." As the car wound up the mountain, Rick's eyes followed the houses. He was fascinated with the wonderful things money could buy. All of the houses sat far from the road, and in the summer they were blocked from view by the leaves of trees.

"You know, Jo, if you didn't know any better, you would think there are only ten or twenty houses up here. But there are over two hundred. Lots of them look small, but the back sides drop down the mountain. Tomorrow I'll take you on a walk to see."

Anton Vicovari's compound was nearly at the end of the main Low Notch road. Each of the three "cottages" looked as modest as most of the residences at Low Notch. Only their roofs and first stories were visible from the road. The clapboard structures were painted red, with white roofs and white trim. The back side of each cottage, facing the only private pond on the mountain, was all glass, and the view through that glass went down a deep notch in the mountain, for which the Low Notch Club was named, to an expanse of mountain ridges and valleys.

They stood for a moment, looking out over the range of hills. It was late in the afternoon, and the sun's rays were blocked by some of the taller mountains, turning the valley into a patchwork of light and shadows; the tips of two peaks were lit up in the distance.

"You see the river down there, Jo? And the little church on that second ridge? They're the border for Anton's hunting club. Fewer than a dozen of them, and they own the whole thing, over twenty thousand acres. It's stocked with exotic animals, wild boar and some deer. Jo, the whole damn thing's fenced in, *fifty miles* of fence, at least." It seemed exotic in itself, owning that much fence.

They walked along a patio of fieldstones to the front door of the largest house. Kanell could hear pots being moved in the kitchen as they approached. "Hell, that's Norma Lee, the housekeeper. She's a character; you'll like her." Jo Pinder's nervousness returned. Vicovari had called her especially to say that her previous visit to the mountain should not be mentioned to Rick.

Kanell turned right as they entered, and nearly ran into the robust mountain lady. She was holding a copper pot.

"Lord, Rick!" Norma Lee shook her head, wispy hair flying, "I've got to put some *meat* on those bones! Come in here, I've got hot biscuits and some blueberry cobbler." Before Norma Lee turned to the kitchen, she looked quickly at Jo Pinder and nodded.

"Norma Lee, this is Jo Pinder. She's my houseguest. Can you put her in Anton's old suite?"

"Rick, she can stay any place she wants—where are you going to sleep?" Norma Lee's innocent expression failed to hide the accusation behind the owlish glasses.

An hour later, Norma Lee was standing at the kitchen exit to the house, a heavy gray wool coat over her shoulders. She was looking at the man's watch on her wrist, her head pulling back to focus, when she mentioned the phone call. She had not forgotten it, but Norma Lee liked to tell things in her own time.

"Oh, Rick, Anton called. He's going to be a day or two late, and he wants you to call him." She pulled her coat collar up around her neck and turned to leave. "He's setting you up a hunting trip on the Hunt Club property. With Doug Boldin. You know, he's the new chief. Fire chief, that is." She opened the door and stepped down. "Y'all be good," she said as she closed the door.

The mention of Vicovari made Jo nervous again, but it did not seem to faze Kanell. He declined to call until the morning.

They dined at eight: country-fried steak covered in thick gravy full of fresh green peppers and pimientos, which were finishing the season in the garden under the protective plastic tents; brussels sprouts and okra, both frozen, but also from the garden. Norma Lee had prepared an apple pie for dessert. Of course, the apples were from the trees below the house. Life at Low Notch was deceptively self-sufficient. All it took was money.

14

I

LANE Englander dressed at five twenty, placed a small tray of cheese on a brass table in the living room, then put a new bottle of sherry next to the tray. He would have walked to Evelyn's within the next few minutes, at the scheduled time, but Evelyn Wade was in no mood to wait. The knock came at precisely five thirty.

"Evelyn! I was just leaving to get you." He took the shawl from her shoulders before closing the door.

"I couldn't wait. Lane—I did it. I made reservations for a flight Wednesday morning. One of those Eastern specials. We can't get the cheap fares until then."

"Good! Did you tell May?"

"No, she's out with Jay. They're coming back about eight." May Montez had been staying at Evelyn's since Friday.

Evelyn stood for a moment looking around the room, then sat down as Englander went to the kitchen. Her expression changed from excitement to confusion as he left the room. The trip scared her. The hip was hurting, and the trip meant too much walking, and nights away from 91 Myrtle. She pushed herself up and walked to the kitchen. Englander was slicing fruit. He spoke casually.

"Ev, I'm glad we're going. But what are we going to do up there?"

Evelyn was ready for the question. "Remember what you said? 'Long distance really isn't like being there.' First, we're going to Mr. Buettner's office and *sit on him*. We've got to make him listen. And I want to get the boy's name. Maybe we can talk to his parents, maybe they know something."

She looked at Englander for a response. "And then I thought we'd go to Central Body Shop. Lane, we've got to make a pest of ourselves. What if the man is really insane, what if he's one of those mass murderers?"

Englander looked up with a slightly skeptical expression on his face. "I know, Ev. But what are we going to ask these people? Do you really think they'll talk to us?"

"I don't know. But . . . but at least we'll be *doing* something." Evelyn looked frustrated. "Lane, if we just remind people that two people are dead, and if we're really in the way, don't you think the police will try to help us just to get rid of us? . . . Am I making any sense?"

He waited before answering. "Ev, you are making sense."

They walked to the living room. Englander set the fruit next to the cheese plate, then poured two sherries.

Just before six, Englander removed a cassette tape from its box and inserted it in the tape player. Mabel Mercer singing Cole Porter. As the music began, Evelyn took the last sip from her glass and pushed up as she quietly mouthed the words.

"You know, Grady and I used to dance to Cole Porter's songs a lot. Did you and Barbara ever go to those dances in the park? Lane, we had the *most* fun there. I loved to dance, but those days are gone." She laughed. "I have enough trouble just walking."

Englander rose to adjust the volume. He stood there as Mercer began to sing, "Strange, dear . . ." then turned to face Evelyn, nearly bumping into her. "Do you know Mabel Mercer, Ev? I think she's very special."

"Of course. But you know, in a way her songs make me sad. They're about love, and when I think of love, I think of Grady." She began to hum the tune softly. Evelyn didn't have the best pitch, but she did follow the tune well.

"Ev . . . let's dance." Englander said it abruptly, but his words brought a short laugh from Evelyn.

"Lane, my legs won't move right. And anyway, it's Sunday. Most Baptists don't dance on Sunday."

"I have it on good authority that God does not get mad at old people who dance on Sunday. On Myrtle Street."

Evelyn was slightly flushed. She really wanted to dance, and though she would not admit it, she wanted that excuse to hold Englander gently. She swallowed.

"Lane, I do like this song." Englander had a little smile on his face as she spoke. He put his left arm up in the air, nearly to shoulder level, Evelyn's hand going to that height too, with effort. Their steps did not match the rhythm of the music, but the two moved, really walked, slowly around the floor. Mercer began to sing "Use Your Imagination."

II

The phone started to ring as Dean Buettner unlocked his door. Still immersed in a leisurely weekend with a lady friend, he did not rush to answer but first dropped his bag in the bedroom, then pulled off the sheepskin coat. He picked up the phone on the fifth ring.

"Hello?"

"Jesus, Dean, I've been trying to get you since yesterday morning. Where the hell have you been?" It was Jackie Bell, a detective in Chicago Auto Theft currently assigned to a double shift observing the comings and goings of Angie Weiner. The detectives had begun following Weiner again within hours of his release from jail.

"Off with a friend. What's up?"

"Dean, what's the name of that girl who works in the office at lunch sometimes?"

"Jo Pinder. Why?"

"Is there any reason she would be eating breakfast with Angie Weiner? That's what she did yesterday morning from eight to eight ten." Jackie Bell waited for a reaction, but there was none. Buettner was thinking. After about four seconds he spoke.

"Did you actually *see* them eating together, or what? How could you be that close, you're not supposed to be that close."

"Damn it, Dean, Weiner went in this place, a diner, and then she came in about five minutes later. They sat in a damn booth right by the window. You don't have to be close, *I* don't have to be close to tell who was sitting in the booth."

How long had Jo Pinder worked lunches at Auto Theft? How did she end up *working* in Auto Theft? What did she know? Not much, Buettner thought. She wasn't in the office long enough to know much. But she was alone in the office at times. He turned to the phone.

"Jackie, where did she go?"

"How the hell do I know? I'm following Weiner, you know."

Buettner did not really hear Bell. Anger rose in him as he thought of Jo Pinder. The goddamn bitch was a *mole* and he had wanted to *date* her.

"Where is Weiner now?"

"Fucking around with some kid he picked up. He's in his apartment. Dean, I didn't know whether I should call Rosenbloom on this or not. Is that okay?"

Buettner's eyes were closed, his mind assessing damage. *What did she know?* "You're right, Jackie, don't call Rosenbloom. There's nothing we can do on this until tomorrow, and I can't think of a damn thing she could do to hurt us right now. I'll be a son of a bitch, though. Rosenbloom is going to *blow up.* I think he's the one that started her coming up at lunch. At least she doesn't know about the tail on Weiner, though."

Buettner then remembered that Jo Pinder was out of town. Where had she gone? He did not remember. When was the last time he saw her? Not on Friday at all, he was at the auto auction on Friday.

Thursday. Or Wednesday. The day she fucked up the call from the lady in Atlanta. Atlanta.

"Jackie, hold on a minute." Did Pinder know that the lady in Atlanta overheard the killing of Bobby Medlock? What the hell had Jo said?—"It's about Central Body Shop and the lady says it's important." For the first time Dean Buettner felt fear for Evelyn Wade. If Angie Weiner killed Bobby Medlock and a lady in Dallas, he would kill the lady in Atlanta. If he knew about her. And if he were in Atlanta. *What did Jo Pinder know?* Buettner turned back to the phone.

"Jackie, who's watching Weiner now?"

"Me. Only one of us at night, but we're working double shifts, and two people during the day."

"How the hell are you watching him if you're talking to me? Are you using his phone or something?"

"Jesus Christ, Dean! It's not my fault the damn woman is a damn mole."

"Jackie, I'm sorry, you're right. Now where the hell are you?"

"I'm across from his car in a damn cold phone booth while you are sitting in a warm apartment, that's where."

Buettner closed his eyes again, oblivious to the anger in Jackie Bell's voice. In his mind, he was trying to make sure that the lady in Atlanta was safe.

"Jackie, listen to me. It's very, very important that you *do not lose* Weiner. I don't care what time it is, if you lose him, or if it looks like he's going out of town, I want you to call me. Do you want me to get someone else there with you now?"

"Hell no, Dean; the bastard is fucking some little boy, probably for the night."

"Jackie, if you're away from the phone, if Weiner leaves, *stay with him.*"

"Dean, for Christ's sake, I'm not a damn amateur. I'll stay with him. I'm not tired, anyway. I've only been on this guy for fifteen goddamn hours."

"I know, Jackie, I know. Tell G.O. Bern that I want him to call me from wherever he is in the morning, and tell him to *stay on Weiner*, okay? I'll be at the office before seven."

Buettner hung up the phone and cursed. He at least felt the lady in Atlanta was safe. As long as the tail held on Weiner. Buettner stood by the phone. The goddamn bitch. Rosenbloom was going to croak.

III

Rick Kanell rubbed the sweat on Jo Pinder's back with his palm, pushing down the side of her spinal column in a slow, circular motion. Jo gave out a low, steady moan.

"Do my legs."

Kanell slid his body down the bench until his right buttock just touched her, and began to rub her legs, both hands massaging flesh. He was not aroused by touching or by the proximity of their bodies; many lines of cocaine and tall glasses of tonic with nearly equal amounts of gin had removed that desire. But he was enjoying touching her. Her leg muscles were tight, nearly rigid, the result of a four-hour hike during the warmer midday hours.

Kanell stopped rubbing her legs and walked from the sauna. The cocaine was sitting on a rough-hewn four-drawer pine dresser, the bottle partially hidden in the mouth of a green ceramic frog. Kanell sucked up two spoonfuls and stood for a moment with his eyes closed, his body weaving slightly. He returned to the sauna.

Pinder was sitting up now, her right hand rubbing her neck. Jo, too, was feeling the effects of booze and cocaine, her body being pulled down as her mind raced. Like Kanell, she had enjoyed the distance from reality Sunday at Low Notch had provided. Her role in the outfit was completely harmless, she had decided. Rick Kanell's role was a little harder to understand. He ran Mid-West Tool and Supply, she knew that. And then she had decided that Rick Kanell killed people, too. Pinder was disturbed by that at first. She *slept* with him. It was an odd and selfish worry—one with little concern for the victims, but great concern that Rick might in some way taint her. But worry had faded away at Low Notch. If Kanell was killing for the outfit, Anton must have a very good reason for it. And people did what Anton said. Jo Pinder could accept the closeness of Rick Kanell's body, the hard thrusts that seemed to touch her womb.

Pinder was sitting on the bench above Kanell's, her drink on the bench too, her hand wrapped around it. They were drinking from thick, insulated plastic glasses, but the heat of the sauna had melted the last bit of ice in her glass. She swallowed the tepid liquid, then began to rub Kanell's neck.

"Fuck me. I'm horny, and I want you to fuck me." Her words were slurred, the muscles of her mouth and tongue refusing to work as they should.

Kanell shrugged his shoulders, then pulled them in as Pinder squeezed the muscles of his neck tightly. "It's too damned hot to fuck and I'm too damned tired to fuck and it's Sunday and I don't fuck on Sundays." His words were faster coming than Pinder's and they too were slurred. He continued.

"No one comes to this mountain unless they are special friends of Anton," Kanell said as his thoughts began to ramble, ". . . and I am a special friend and I can bring people here and get drunk and eat Norma Lee's cooking but I don't fuck-on-Sundays. I don't fuck and I want Norma Lee to fix venison, I like her venison. . . ."

"In red wine with mushrooms," Pinder interrupted in her slurred voice. "I like venison in red wine and mushrooms, we *all* like venison in red wine and mushrooms. . . ."

"In red wine and mushrooms," Kanell repeated as his head nodded in cadence with the words, ". . . and I'm going to shoot a deer myself on Anton's property, shoot the damn thing, *bang*, and put it in red wine and mushrooms." Kanell belched. Shoot the damn thing. The words caught Jo Pinder's mind, slowing it down slightly.

"Shoot it and eat it"—she intoned the words as if they were part of a ritualistic chant—"shoot it and eat it on Anton's property, killing is okay if Anton say's it's okay, isn't it Rick, killing is okay if Anton says it's okay. We always do what Anton says do, and that's why *it's okay*, *Rick*." She rubbed her fingers behind his ear lightly. Kanell was very sensitive there. But he did not respond to her words. He opened his eyes and focused them on the wall of the sauna, fixing them there.

"What's okay, Jo?"

She blinked. What had she said? The conversation would have continued as a rambling, insignificant one if Pinder had simply said, "Killing the deer." But the thoughts were not coming in a logical manner, and the tone of Kanell's voice had thrown her further from logic. She stuttered, but her words were not slurred. The tone in Kanell's voice had also momentarily energized her.

"It's okay. Rick, I . . . don't . . . care . . ."

As she said the words, Pinder unconsciously stopped rubbing Kanell's neck, but she left her hands there, stilled. She was trying to sort out quickly what Kanell did and did not know. He did not know that part of her job was to report to him. He did not know that she talked regularly with Angie Weiner, over breakfast at a diner just the morning before, for instance. Pinder was quiet, waiting for Kanell to respond, but he said nothing. She began to rub his neck again and continued. Jo Pinder was not afraid of Rick Kanell then. She wanted him to *understand*. She did not care if he killed people if Anton said it was okay. She could accept that.

"Rick, it's okay. I know Anton said to do it. That's why you killed them, isn't it?"

She said the words in a light, innocent tone, her hands continuing to caress, then rub his neck and the muscles of his back.

Kanell's eyes were still focused on the smooth and slightly stained redwood wall. He had covered his tracks so carefully. What did she know? His voice was calm, very neutral as he spoke.

"How did you know, Jo?"

"I read Dean Buettner's notes. And then the lady called from Atlanta."

Rick Kanell felt nauseous. He did not know if it was the gin or the drugs or her words, or all of them, but he felt nauseous. Dean Buettner was a detective, he knew the name well from Pinder's comments during the past two years. The goddamn police knew. He had covered his tracks so carefully, he remembered the bulging eyes in Dallas, and the goddamn police knew. Who was the lady in

Atlanta? Kanell began to rotate his neck slowly, but stopped when the movement increased the nausea.

"What lady in Atlanta, Jo?"

"Evelyn somebody, the lady who heard the killing." She slid down to the bench next to him. Jo Pinder was beginning to feel very weak as she continued, her eyes fixed on Kanell. But he did not look at her. "But they don't know who did it, Rick, *they don't know*. You see? It's okay. I don't care, Rick."

Rick Kanell did not have the slightest concern for Jo Pinder's feelings then. His mind was racing. He had *killed* the lady who heard the murder of Bobby Medlock. *What lady in Atlanta?*

"Jo, what did the lady in Atlanta say?" He sounded very calm, as if his words concerned the most insignificant thing.

"She heard *it* on the phone. And she can recognize the voice of the man"—Pinder was speaking fast, her eyes wide, lids blinking rapidly—"but Rick, they don't suspect you, I know that."

Kanell's breathing was very shallow but fast, yet not as fast as the thoughts, which brought a metallic taste to his mouth and lips. The goddamn phone. It had started there. Stupid to pick it up. Fucking stupid. *What lady in Atlanta?*

He turned to Jo, his right knee touching her left, and began to run his fingers lightly over her neck and breasts. "Why didn't you tell me before, Jo?"

Pinder looked stunned for an instant. She had told Angie Weiner. Why hadn't she told him? She needed a reason. Her eyes went away as she spoke.

"I was confused. About a lot of things. Rick, I didn't really know what the lady was talking about. And it's hard to read Buettner's writing. I only talked with the lady last Thursday and then his notes made more sense. The police in Minnesota know about it, too."

As she spoke, Kanell had a very strong image of lifting the Clupak bag containing Bobby Medlock's body from the trunk of the Jensen, dropping it in a field in Minnesota, and pouring garbage on it, and then he remembered how the boy's body had flailed, the death throes on the floor of Central Body Shop, and the urine and the steel wool, rubbing his neck with steel wool, and then the memory came back of Kanell's mother, she looked tall then, her hand wrapped around the head of a flailing chicken, the head of the chicken popping off with the swing of her arm and the flick of her wrist, like the casting of a fishing rod. *Who was the lady in Atlanta?* He could not think anymore.

"I want to fuck you now, Jo."

Their walk to the bedroom was an unsteady one. The bed was covered with a down comforter and piled high with shams and bolsters. Pinder lay down on the comforter, her eyes closing as she spoke. "You see it's okay, Rick. Now fuck me." And then she passed out, her mouth dropping open slightly.

Kanell unconsciously stopped breathing for a moment as his eyes moved slowly to the windows. The trees of the apple orchard were dimly lit, as if from moonlight. In the summer the deer ate the apples from those trees: at times their front legs were in the air as their mouths reached for high apples. Deer had the biggest eyes. Eyes that didn't blink. The lady's eyes hadn't blinked, either. *Who was the lady in Atlanta?* What did the boy's eyes look like?

He looked toward the bathroom. The door was open, a white robe with the initials "A. V." bridging the floor between the bathroom and the bedroom. The fixtures in there were black, even the Jacuzzi was black, and the towels were heated on racks, they were very hot and expensive, and everything was tasteful, money made things tasteful. He needed to turn off the lights. Kanell shuddered, his head dropping to his chest. *Who was the lady in Atlanta?* It was his last thought as his body fell to the bed, his head touching Jo Pinder's side.

15

I

RICK Kanell had not moved during the night. He heard a voice calling, but it seemed to be part of a dream, a distanced voice coming only from inside his head. He drifted away and then heard the voice again. This time it sounded as if someone far away down a tunnel were calling him. Then, instantly, his eyes popped open. For a moment, both the voice and the room were foreign. Where was he? He looked at Jo Pinder's naked body. He heard the voice again.

"Okay, you two! I got up at five A.M. to come here and cook for you, I'm putting the eggs on right now. Rick . . . are you down there?"

Kanell felt drugged, his mind and body thick and heavy. But he began to smile. Norma Lee and her goddamn early breakfast, he thought as he yelled, "Okay, Norma Lee, but please give us about fifteen minutes." He looked at the curve of Jo's naked hip and smiled. She had not moved either.

And then the memory of the previous night's conversation began to pound his consciousness. He bolted up, breathing faster but still shallow, as if he had just pulled out of a horrid nightmare. For an instant he decided that the conversation had been a nightmare. Then reality hit him. He began to sweat instantly. Kanell dropped his feet to the floor heavily and sat there, swaying. He was reeling from too many things. The fine white powder that had caused his system to run at such a fast pace had left his body deeply fatigued; the alcohol had further fatigued him, making his tissues and joints sore to the touch; he had slept only five hours. Reeling from too many things.

And then the realities began to hit him again, fast. Kanell walked carefully to the ceramic frog. He could not handle all the things buffeting him without help: two small spoons of powder in each nostril. What day was it? Monday morning. It was a very bright day on the mountain, a clear and bright day with no clouds to add contrast to the sky. But Kanell did not notice the brightness as he turned from the windows. He walked to the bathroom, directly to the shower, and closed his eyes as hot water began to beat down on his face and chest. *Who was the lady in Atlanta?* He leaned against the shower wall to steady himself. The toot was beginning to work and now he finally began to try to focus. Jo Pinder had said a lady in Atlanta had overheard the killing of Bobby Medlock. But the lady who heard him had said *Dallas*. He was sure of that.

He picked up the soap and began to rub it over his body. Why would the lady say Dallas if she were in Atlanta? He did not know. What was the lady's name in Atlanta? Pinder said Evelyn, he remembered that. But Evelyn was dead. He turned his back to the hot stream of water, uneasy thoughts of Jo Pinder gathering quickly in his mind. Why had Jo waited to tell what she knew? She didn't mean to say anything at all. But her job was to report everything. What did she know? She knew about the murder at Central Body Shop. About the police searching for him. Why had she held out on him?

He turned off the shower, shaking his head the way a dog shakes away water after a bath, and walked toward the bedroom, leaning down to pick up the thick white bathrobe from the floor as he walked. Why did the lady say Dallas if she was in Atlanta? It didn't make sense to him. Rick Kanell cast about for easy explanations as he dried himself with the thick robe. He looked at his watch. Eight forty. He slipped on a pair of slacks without bothering to put on underwear, then put on a sweater. Kanell didn't comb his hair, but shook his head again until the wet hair felt comfortable, then combed his fingers through it. He looked at Jo. She could have been dead, she lay so completely still. He did not try to wake her, but walked up the stairs quickly.

He found Norma Lee at the stove stirring eggs with a wooden spoon. Normally Kanell would have looked forward to a Low Notch breakfast, but as he began to breathe harder from his walk up the steps, the mixed aromas of bacon and eggs and coffee and meat cooking brought a wave of nausea. He stifled the feeling.

"Well, honey," Norma Lee said as she spooned the eggs into a bowl, "I hope you two had a good night. Where's Jo?" The very strong smell of the meat in the oven hit Kanell again.

"Norma Lee, she's dead to the world," Kanell said, the word "dead" sticking in his consciousness. He couldn't stand in the kitchen any longer as the nausea hit him again, nearly gagging him. Kanell did not notice Norma Lee's frown as he walked into the dining room. She did not like to fix food for two when only one was eating. Waste offended her mountain sense of frugality. Norma Lee reached down to the oven and glanced in quickly at the meat, then walked into the dining room as if she too were going to eat. Kanell sat at the end of the table, staring at the small portions of food on his plate, not at the view of the apple trees and valley and mountains.

"Rick?"

He looked up, a startled expression on his face. "Yes?" Kanell's thoughts had been on the lady in Dallas.

"Lord, honey, you look *awful* this morning; and look at your plate, a *bird* eats more than that." She took the plate from in front of him and began to fill it with larger helpings from the platters and brightly colored bowls on the sideboard, talking as she spooned. "Rick, I've gotta leave early today, my heart doctor, you know, so I've fried some chicken and made some salads for lunch." The nausea was returning again. ". . . And I'm fixing you a *surprise* for supper. Venison in red wine and mushrooms!"

Rick Kanell had not really been listening to Norma Lee, but at the mention of venison his mind began to run backward to the previous evening. When had he eaten venison? It had not been on this trip; on another one. Kanell's face went blank. But Jo had known about the venison: "We all *like venison in red wine and mushrooms*. . . ." How did Jo know about the venison? She had not been alone with Norma Lee. He had not mentioned it before. Kanell looked up to Norma Lee, a forced smile on his face. She was standing at the end of the sideboard, right hand resting on it and left hand holding his plate piled with food.

"Good, good. Norma Lee, that's one of my favorite things." He paused. "Jo likes it, too."

Norma Lee did not sense the danger in Kanell's leading statement. "I know, honey, she ate *three* helpings in the kitchen before I could . . ." Norma Lee lifted her hand from the sideboard and put the fingers over her mouth, shaking her head and smiling slightly. "I didn't say anything; Rick, don't you tell Anton *I* said it, 'cause I didn't. You did." She quickly put the plate in front of him and turned to walk from the room, saying, "I tell you, there are some strange things going on in this house." The door swung shut behind her, squeaking slightly.

Kanell's jaw slackened. What was Jo Pinder doing at Low Notch with Anton? Kanell did not even know she knew him. But he did know that Vicovari liked beautiful women. When had they been here? What had they talked about? For the first time, Kanell let the thought surface that perhaps he wasn't the only person in the outfit who collected information from Jo Pinder. Or slept with her, either. Why would Vicovari pick Jo? The answer brought a knot to his throat.

Kanell forced six bites of food down, his fork rearranging the other food on the plate as if the movements would hide it. He then yelled a "thank you" toward the kitchen and walked down the narrow stairway. Pinder had not moved. Kanell stood at the end of the bed, staring at her. He had been comfortable with Jo Pinder.

He went to the far side of the bed and took the small brown bottle from the ceramic frog's mouth again, sucking up two spoons in each nostril; less than thirty minutes had passed since his last trip to the ceramic frog. Kanell sucked in abruptly, his chest pulled up, eyes closed.

Opening them, he began to search the room aimlessly until he settled on Jo's purse. It was a large one, of soft tan leather. He looked again at Pinder, a small, slow anger building in his gut. He had been *comfortable* with her, letting her visit beyond the façade just a bit. He never did that. Kanell did not want to believe that venison in red wine and mushrooms, eaten with Vicovari, could violate that comfortable feeling. There had to be another explanation. But he couldn't quite believe that there could be another explanation. Why would Jo be at Low Notch with Anton? He walked to the large tan pocketbook, scooped it up by the strap, then went into the bathroom.

Sitting on the back of the toilet, the cover down, he began to sift through Jo Pinder's incidental belongings. Several lipsticks; a small box of Tampax; a wallet wrapped with a rubber band; keys; a small dictionary and another book, an orange telephone book, the type with pages that can easily be removed or added by pulling together small spring-held clips at the bottom. Kanell began to flip through the pages. His number was in there, the fourth listing under the K, his address written in Pinder's slightly uneven hand below the number. For a minute he found that odd. Jo Pinder practically lived with him.

And then he noticed that the blue ink had faded a lot. She must have put it there when they first met, he thought. He flipped over to V and looked at the names and numbers listed on the right-hand page just after the V tab. Anton Vicovari's name was not listed. His number was not listed under any other name, either.

Kanell's eyes went to the left, to the unlined side of the tabbed page. Jo Pinder had scribbled many numbers and short messages there in different pen-point widths and inks, as was true for the other pages in the book. And then he saw it. Printed in very small, faded numbers, without a name, was Anton Vicovari's private telephone number. He looked at it without blinking, then turned his eyes to the bedroom door. Why? He began to flip through the small orange book again, his eyes this time scanning the tabbed pages as well as the white, lined address pages. None of the names or numbers was familiar.

As he closed the book, the back side of the W-tabbed page caught his attention. Or rather, a faded doodle made him open the book to that page again. The doodle was a W, the lines jagged, like the printing of an EKG. The W was surrounded with a round border just as jagged, and in the border was an old phone number, faded. Rick Kanell remembered that number. It had been Angie Weiner's. How old was that number? Years. He flipped through the small phone book quickly and held the K and V sections open with his fingers, his eyes flicking from his name and number to Vicovari's number, to the jagged W. All three were written in the same goddamn ink. Faded about the same. She had known them from the beginning. The bitter, metallic taste returned to his mouth. How many times had he cursed that scumbag Weiner in her presence? How many times had he been comfortable with her? How many times had he believed her loyal?

Rick Kanell began to walk to the bedroom, anger blotting out nausea. He walked by Pinder's body without glancing at her and took a heavy hunting jacket from a brass coat hook, and began to walk up the stairs. He stopped and turned. Kanell walked to the closet and picked up a pair of shoes. He put them on while sitting on the wide veranda that nearly circled the lower floor of the big house, oblivious to the cold and uncaring that the shoes were slipping over feet without socks. It was nine thirty.

He walked until ten, then entered the kitchen door just as Norma Lee was removing the venison from the oven.

"Rick, you got a call, honey. Doug Boldin. The man you're going hunting with? He says he'll be up about five in the morning, so's you'll have a head start on the animals."

Kanell nodded, a smile on his face. He was feeling energized then, cocaine providing its maximum pleasure. "Thanks, Norma Lee. Do you have the number? I might want to call him later today." Rick Kanell did not want to go hunting with a friend of Anton Vicovari's on the next day or on any day, but he did not say so. *They* were against him, he felt, the word encompassing Weiner first, then Pinder, and perhaps Vicovari himself. The police were after him, too. At least two, maybe three departments, he feared. Minneapolis found the body; Dallas wanted the killer of Evelyn Garner; Chicago wanted a man whose voice could perhaps be recognized by a lady in Atlanta. Kanell was feeling trapped, his carefully covered footprints leading to the body of Bobby Medlock not covered at all. He turned to Norma Lee, but she spoke before he could begin.

"Rick, do you want to taste? I'm really happy with it."

For many reasons he declined, and walked to the card room of the big house. A gun rack of white pine was against the left wall, in it six rifles and a pair of matching .38 pistols. The finely etched pistols were in a mahogany case. Though the case was closed, Kanell's glance went to it. He had shot one of the pistols with Anton.

He sat in a small chair for a moment, gazing at the mountains and the partial view of the Vicovari pond. A previous owner had built the pond by damming the very top of the deep ravine now called Low Notch. Kanell had fished in it on his first visit. That visit seemed to belong to another world as with great effort he focused his thoughts about the lady in Atlanta. If she had been the witness to the murder of Bobby Medlock, why would she have said "This is Evelyn with American Opinion Research in Dallas?"

Kanell looked at the phone on the desk as Norma Lee's voice began to drift from the kitchen, across the living room, into his space. Who was she talking to, who did she call? He started to pick up the phone. If anything ruled Rick Kanell this morning more than cocaine, it was mistrust. Norma Lee had lied to him, too. She had not told him Jo Pinder had been in the mountains before. She was against him, too. What did Norma Lee know? Her laughter calmed the worry. She was talking with a mountain friend. He moved his hand from the phone and took out his wallet, then pulled out a small newspaper clipping. In a few short paragraphs the clipping detailed the killing of Evelyn Garner in Dallas. Kanell had bought the paper in Miami two days after killing her. He reread the article, then placed it on the desk.

In the deepest part of his mind, Kanell knew that the lady in Atlanta, Evelyn, was the real witness to the murder of Bobby Medlock. He had killed the wrong Evelyn. But even though the deepest part of his mind accepted the reality, his conscious mind did not. The conscious mind needed proof. He waited until Norma Lee was silent. He needed a boost. How long had it been? Too long, he thought. But he wanted to know about the lady in Atlanta. Kanell picked up the phone and dialed.

"Information for what city, please?"

"Atlanta."

"Can I help you?"

"The number for American Opinion Research." Kanell wanted the operator to say, "No such number in our listings, sir," but in an instant a recording droned the number. *Damn, Goddamn.* There was an Atlanta office. He dialed the number, his left hand tapping the small desk with his pencil.

As the phone began to ring, Kanell stood up and started to pace the length of the room. All of the phones in the Vicovari compound, save the special phone in the new cottage, had cordless receivers. He paced, then stopped as the phone was answered: "American Opinion Research."

"Yes, this is Detective Dean Buettner with the Chicago Police Department, Auto Theft." How many times had Pinder mentioned Buettner's name? "A lady called my office last week concerning a murder she overheard on the telephone. I'd like to talk to her please."

The receptionist at AOR in Atlanta, like nearly everyone there, knew about Evelyn Wade's phone call and the death of Evelyn Garner in Dallas. The receptionist also knew that a killer was out there. May Montez had not given her many details, but less than an hour ago she had been reminded that something very odd was happening. May had been late to work. She was never late. But this morning she had stopped at the receptionist's desk just long enough to say she was staying with Evelyn Wade "until they find the man."

The receptionist hesitated. The man on the phone had not said Evelyn's name. Wouldn't a police officer do that?

"Can you hold a minute, please?"

"Yes." He began to pace again.

The receptionist rang extension 9233. "May . . . there's a *man* on the phone asking for Evelyn. He says he's with the Chicago Police. What should I do with the call?"

The words sent a small chill through May Montez. Evelyn was spending the morning with Lane Englander, she knew that, she had walked her there.

"Honey, give it to me. Did he say what his name was?"

The receptionist hesitated. "May, he did, but I forgot. I was nervous, you know. But he did say he was with the Chicago Police, Auto Theft."

Auto Theft, Montez thought with a slight smile on her face. For most of the weekend Evelyn had complained that Chicago Auto Theft did not return phone calls. "I don't need his name, I'll get it. Just put the call through to me." She sat up a little straighter, her finger pushing down the receiver button then lifting at the ring.

"This is May Montez, can I help you?"

"Yes, this is Dean Buettner with Chicago Auto Theft. How are you this morning?"

May remembered the name, and as she remembered it, her hesitation about the caller vanished.

"I'm fine, Mr. Buettner. Boy, have we been waiting on a call from you."

Rick Kanell was feeling two things as she spoke. There was another Evelyn. That reality hit him as a wave of nausea surged through him. He pulled himself together with great effort. It wasn't over. The wrong Evelyn was dead.

"Miss, I'm sorry about the wait. But the secretary misplaced my notes on my conversation with Evelyn. Of course, her phone number was on there, too. That's why I called her place of work."

"She's not at home right now, Mr. Buettner, she's at a neighbor's and I'm sorry, I don't know that number. But I can find it and have her call you."

Kanell shook his head. "I'll be out." He said it much too abruptly, his sense of timing was not working well. He checked himself and continued, "I'll be out for the day. But I can call her later, if you could give me her number again."

Evelyn wanted to talk with this man. There was no way, May believed, anyone else would use the name Buettner. The killer could not know that. "Of course," she said, then repeated the number.

Why had she said Dallas?

"Miss, before I go, could you please explain to me why she said she was in Dallas rather than Atlanta? I'm not sure what that has to do with the killing out there."

Montez frowned and shook her head. "Oh, I thought Evelyn explained that to you," she said in a slightly sarcastic voice.

"Well, . . . she did, but honestly, it went by me."

"All of our Atlanta people say Dallas when they're doing soft-drink studies. You see, Coca-Cola is headquartered here, and we don't want people to think all of our studies are for Coke." May paused to give the man time to let her words sink in. "Is that clear?"

"Oh, it's very clear," Kanell said, "very clear. Miss, thank you very much." He cut the words short.

"Wait a minute, before you go." May caught him before he could hang up, "Could you . . . uh . . . tell us whether you are having any luck finding the man? You have a suspect, don't you?"

"I think for sure we've found the man, miss." He was silent again.

"Well, I hope so. *Please* call Evelyn and please tell us anything that develops. Thanks so much for calling, and I hope your day goes well."

"Thanks very much." He hung up the phone.

Norma Lee opened the door to the card room, a dust cloth in her hand. She was startled, first simply by Kanell's presence in the room. She thought the room was empty. But then she was startled by his face.

"Good Lord, Rick," she said, "you look like you've just seen a ghost."

II

Jo Pinder didn't realize it, but the first thing her eyes focused on, the first thing she was conscious of as her body began to awaken and move slowly, tentatively, was an odd thing, a fly. The fly was on a bolster that had fallen from the bed. Completely still at first, it began to walk with very short, quick steps, lurches, really. Pinder watched it for several minutes, her mind climbing from the deep fog of a drugged sleep, as the fly lurched across the side of the bolster, then up the side, like a mountain climber pulling himself up a rope with fast, short efforts. The fly was odd, out of season.

Pinder rolled her feet off the bed, much as Rick Kanell had done earlier, and began to slowly stretch the tissues and tendons sensitive from the effects of the cocaine and the liquor. Her gaze went to the window and she took in the view of the mountains and the sky, then the pond, and finally the small path leading from the pond past the new cottage to the big house.

She looked at the top of the trees on the ridge across the pond again, squinting, trying to bring her eyes into sharper focus. Clear vision might clarify her murky impressions of the previous night. Jo Pinder's body was not used to seemingly endless tall gins and small spoons of coke. As she sat on the bed, her feet barely touching the floor, her body beginning to chill, Jo could remember only a portion of her conversation with Rick Kanell; she could remember telling him, "Rick, it's okay, I know *Anton said to do it*." But her memories of those words did not make Jo apprehensive. It was okay. She felt *closer* to Rick Kanell, because *it was okay*; he knew that now. They did not have to pretend.

She stood and began to walk slowly to the bathroom. It was okay and Rick obviously was glad she knew, for her last memory of the night was Kanell saying "I want to fuck you now, Jo." She could not remember if they made love. As Jo sat on the black toilet, she did not notice that her pocketbook was lying on the floor next to her foot. Even if she had noticed, it would have meant nothing, for Jo just didn't remember all of the night—some of it like erased portions of an audio recording.

Kanell was in the kitchen when she walked up the narrow, steep steps from the suite. He was eating a mushroom still warm from the red wine sauce. Kanell looked very calm.

"So, you finally got up, eh? I thought you were dead or something."

Pinder laughed. "God, I feel like someone's beat me with a stick; I'm sore all over. Where's Norma Lee?"

"At the doctor. She left you some blueberries and cream and toasted biscuits." He placed the foil back over the venison. Kanell was quieter than he had been their first day on the mountain, but Pinder did not notice the change in his disposition. She walked to the refrigerator, her eyes looking for the right liquid to soothe her throat and rehydrate her body. A tall, clear martini pitcher of freshly squeezed orange juice was sitting by Jo's half of a grapefruit, the strawberry in its center now tilted from the pressure of the plastic wrap.

"Rick, can I ask you something about last night?" Pinder's smile was rueful. The question startled Kanell. He had not planned to mention the previous evening's conversation yet. But he masked his uneasiness.

"Sure . . ."

"Did we make love? I remember you asked me, but damn it, I can't remember if we did."

Kanell laughed in relief, cutting it short as the tone started to turn nasty. The lying bitch wanted to know if she got fucked. No, ma'am, you didn't get it, you gave it. He reined the swell of anger in and managed a calm reply. "No, I think we both got a little too wasted last night. Don't you want something to eat?" He did not suggest a taste of the venison.

"Oh, God no, not yet. Maybe just the blueberries, I like that cream stuff Norma Lee makes." She probably had that, too, with Vicovari, Kanell thought. He was enjoying all the unintentional ironies. She continued. "Rick, I hope we're not going to do much today. I really feel like my body's been through a wringer." She began to drink the juice, then walked idly through the swinging door to the dining room. During the middle of the morning, the sun lit virtually all the mountain ranges in view of the large dining room windows, leaving only the notch and the valley far below it in shadow. Pinder took it all in, including the small white church, a dot on the farthest mountain range. Kanell walked into the room.

"You know, Rick, sometimes I wish we could drive over there and see that church. I'll bet it's a pretty thing, real . . . *mountainy*, if you know what I mean."

He nodded. It was a beautiful white mountain church. Kanell had been there with Anton. With Vicovari. He would never see the man again. Too many things were wrong. Jo Pinder was a spy. A traitor. Kanell suddenly felt persecuted, hunted. With great effort he choked down the surging paranoia, and spoke evenly.

"It *is* beautiful. I have been to the church—with Anton." How many times had she made love to *him*? The thought of Vicovari touching her preyed on Kanell.

"We'll go there, Jo; when Anton arrives. Would you like that?" He removed the small brown bottle from his pocket and sucked in two spoons of fine white powder, a new batch mailed to him in Chicago from the islands. Eighty percent pure. He did not offer any to Jo, but looked away, right hand rubbing his throat.

"Jo, I need to talk to you about something—it's *very private.*"

The words did not bother her, but their distanced sound chilled her slightly. She looked at him with a vacant stare as he continued.

"We've got to drive to Atlanta, just for two nights. We'll be back by the time Anton arrives."

At the mention of Atlanta, Pinder instantly thought of Evelyn Wade. The chill returned. It was not brought on by a fear for herself, or for the woman. It was the fear of being involved. She did not want to be a participant or a witness. If Rick Kanell killed because Anton said killing was okay—then it was okay, necessary. But that did not mean she would be involved. She forced a smile.

"But Rick, aren't you supposed to go hunting tomorrow?"

Kanell turned to face her. "I can hunt when we come back." His smile was unusual; it seemed to rise and fall, as if it were a twitch.

"Is it the lady?" Pinder wanted to ask, "Are you going to Atlanta to kill the lady?" but she could not.

"No," he lied, "I'm going to see about a business opportunity for me there. I told you I was thinking about doing something else, didn't I?" He smiled broadly, and the chill bewilderingly came to her again.

"Well, couldn't I stay here and read instead? Or something?" He was lying, she knew it. She did not want to be involved.

"Sure, if you want to," he said, walking to her, his hands pushing her hair back over her shoulder, "but I'm not going to do anything wrong, Jo. You don't have to go with me, but please go with me." Jo did not realize it, but Rick Kanell had never said the gentle word, "please," to her. He had seldom been abrupt or angry or rude with her, but he had always avoided the word because he considered it weak. Jo did not realize it, though; his gesture and the word made her feel better, and then the nervousness returned. Her job was to watch him. And what had Angie said at breakfast two mornings ago? Call if Rick leaves the mountains. Jo nodded slightly, the nod more a reaction to her thoughts than to Kanell's use of the gentle word.

"When are we going?"

"Now."

"*Now?*" Pinder needed to call Angie. And then she thought again of saying no, of staying in the mountains. She would have plenty of time to call if she stayed in the mountains. But her job was to watch Rick Kanell.

"Well, aren't we going to call Anton? Won't he be mad if we're not here? He might come early."

Kanell moved his hand lightly from her neck to her throat, then her breasts. "We'll leave a note for him. But I don't want him to know where we are going . . . you understand. Jo, this trip is for *me*. I don't want him to know." Kanell smiled. "Please?"

Pinder returned the smile, but it was a nervous one. She needed to call Angie. "Well, okay, maybe we can eat at a nice restaurant; that would be fun." *Fun.* He turned to head to the kitchen.

"Jo, I've already packed, except for the stuff in your room. I'm going outside to try and clear my head while you get ready, but let's get out of here quickly, okay?"

Pinder stood there for a moment, her drugged and very tired mind trying to sort out the conflicting loyalties. She then walked rapidly from the dining room down the narrow stairs and over to the large windows. Kanell was sitting below her, a hunting coat pulled tightly around him, at the top of the path to Vicovari's pond. He was listening to a small radio, nodding his head as if it were keeping time. The radio was sitting by him on a low fieldstone wall that bordered a stand of apple trees.

Jo Pinder went to the phone. She dialed the number for Angie Weiner from memory, looking up twice to make sure that Kanell was still in view. As the phone began to ring, Pinder walked with the receiver to the side of the window, standing out of Kanell's view should he look up to the house. Her eyes flicked to the large window and Kanell. She did not want him to see her. She watched Kanell pick up the radio only long enough to adjust the dial, then place it again on the stone wall, his head bobbing slowly up and down.

Kanell's head continued to move as he adjusted the radio dial once more, carefully turning it to just past 55 on the AM band. Just to the frequency that matched that of older-model cordless telephones. The number Pinder dialed rang clearly over the radio. He expected Vicovari to answer. But when he heard Angie Weiner's voice, his head stopped bobbing for an instant. He had decided that Jo Pinder was a spy. He had given her the chance to prove that. But he had not wanted to believe she had betrayed him to the man whose voice was now coming over the small radio.

"All right?" Weiner answered. His small suitcase was sitting by the phone. Weiner was leaving for the airport when the phone rang; he was flying to Low Notch to wait near a thick stand of mountain laurel by a sheer cliff.

"Angie, I'm sorry to bother you, but you said to call if Rick left. He's going to Atlanta *right now*. He says it's on personal stuff." She paused. Pinder did not want to say the rest: "Maybe to kill that lady named Evelyn I told you about."

Weiner was silent for a moment. "Are you going with him?"

"Well—do I need to go?" She wanted him to say no.

"Jo, go with him, and call me when you get there, if you can. If I'm not here, tell my sister. She'll be staying here."

Pinder nodded her head. "Okay. I'll try to call you." She hung up the phone and hurriedly began to pack.

Rick Kanell remained sitting on the fieldstone wall, the radio by his side. Everything was wrong. Jo Pinder was a spy: she talked to Angie; the slut talked to the faggot. Kanell smiled, then began to laugh, an inward laugh with his mouth closed. Here on this beautiful mountain surrounded by tasteful things only money can buy, the slut talks to the faggot. He laughed again. Kanell was beginning to disintegrate. Too many things were battering him; he needed more toot; he had been betrayed; Evelyn was in Atlanta; *Angie, that scumbag, she was close to Angie*. Kanell began to walk to the big house. He left the small radio on the fieldstone wall, and walked up the path past the apple trees.

Kanell was bright, nearly ebullient, when he entered the bedroom. He looked around it quickly, a smile on his face, then turned to Jo.

"Well, have you got everything?"

"Uh, yeah—is it okay if I leave some things here?"

"Sure, we'll be back soon, by mid-Wednesday." His words made her feel more comfortable. She was not sure why, but leaving things there seemed to make the trip less menacing.

"Good." She looked around the room, then at her suitcase. "Well, I'm not going to pack any of my dresses but one, then, and just one pants suit. Damn, I wish I had something smaller to put it in than *this*."

His eyes went to the soft tan pocketbook. "Hell, that thing's nearly big enough to fit a body in, Jo. Put it in there." She gave a short laugh, then walked to the closet. She returned with a small shoe bag.

"Rick, do you think Anton would care if I used this? It was just lying there."

Kanell smiled again. "Jo, he's a very generous man. He wouldn't care at all."

He turned to the door. "I'm going to load my stuff and lock up." Kanell did not mention leaving a note for Anton, but turned back to smile at Jo.

Kanell was closing the trunk as Pinder approached the car. He smiled brightly. "You have everything?"

"I think so. . . . I don't need to change, do I, just for the drive?"

"You look . . . beautiful." That, too, was a word he seldom used when referring to her, though she was very beautiful.

He had changed his shoes, Jo noticed that. Heavy walking boots, new ones, were on his feet. "Let me put this in the trunk, Rick. Why are you wearing walking shoes?"

He opened the right front door of the car, not the trunk. "Just put the bag here. I don't know, I'm wearing them because I want to. Is that okay?" He smiled. The slut wanted to know about his shoes, his goddamn shoes!

The car pulled onto the parkway at one fifteen and for the first twenty minutes of their drive Jo Pinder felt comfortable, lost in the quiet beauty of the mountain ranges and valleys and distant vistas. At one forty-five, Kanell pulled the car into an overlook. Two small spoons of coke in each nostril. Jo noticed for the first time the movements of Kanell's fingers, a slight jumping as if they were dancing to an erratic tune. He drove on. Twenty minutes later, Kanell pulled over again, less than two miles from a small dirt road that led into the tranquil depths of the Meadows of Dan, within eyesight of a sheer cliff known locally as Lover's Leap. No lovers had taken their final steps there, it was believed, but it was a physically appropriate place. Pinder looked at Kanell. His face was drained of all expression, as if all the muscles there had died.

"Rick, are you okay?"

He nodded only slightly, stopping the car completely, then removing the small brown bottle again. He did not speak until two spoonfuls of eighty-percent pure from the islands had again disappeared up his nostrils and he had pulled back on the road. He then quietly said, "No," and continued before Jo could speak. "You know, I like you, Jo." Kanell was driving slowly, his eyes blinking constantly, as if keeping pace with a very fast tune. Pinder was looking out her window as he spoke. But the quiet "no," together with the uncharacteristic compliment, brought a chill to her again. She looked at him. What was going on?

"I like you too, Rick." Kanell held the steering wheel with arms bent, in a relaxed position, but his fists gripped the wheel so tightly that the veins on top of his hands began to distend. Pinder did not notice the veins, though; Kanell's very rapid blinking bothered her. It was quiet in the car.

"Rick, you know . . ."

Kanell interrupted. As he spoke, the blinking stopped.

"How long have you been working for Vicovari, Jo?" The blinking started again. For the first time Pinder became conscious of her heartbeat. Her right hand moved from the window to her lap. She turned slightly to the left, then spoke.

"What do you mean, Rick? I met you two years ago. You know that." She crossed her arms in an unconsciously protective movement.

Kanell stopped blinking, speaking rapidly, as if his words were joined to Pinder's without even a comma. "I mean how long have you been working for *him* against *me*? How long have you slept with him?"

She began to squeeze her crossed arms. He knew. "*Against* you? Rick, I don't do anything *against* you."

Kanell smiled. It was an odd smile, the lips slightly parted, eyes squinting, as if a bright light had been suddenly shined in them. The car was going less than thirty miles an hour, an acceptable speed on the narrow road.

"It's okay, Jo," he said in a high voice, "it's okay; I forget; Anton knows everything. Just like I do. . . . Did he tell you to come to the mountains with me? To *watch* me?" His voice broke as he said the word.

The break, the lack of control brought more fear to Jo Pinder than his words. She tried to swallow, but a knot at the very top of her throat prevented that. "Rick, I don't talk to Anton! What the hell are you talking about? Rick, you're *scaring* me!"

Kanell began to blink again, as if his eyes were opening and closing in cadence with a drill sergeant's "hup-two-three-four." He winced at each closing. "But you talked to Angie, Jo, to *Angie*. Have you slept with the faggot, too?"

Pinder started to protest. "Rick . . . I don't . . . Rick, what do you mean?" His blinking stopped again as the odd smile returned. Kanell's grip on the steering wheel loosened as his fingers began to tap the wheel one by one, as if counting up a very large debt.

"I *listened*, Jo." Jo Pinder's skin felt very hot instantly, the feeling of a person opening the door of a cool, dark room, and walking quickly out to a desert sun. He listened? To what? She started to speak, but Kanell interrupted again.

"I listened on the *goddamn radio*, Jo." He laughed wildly. "It's *so funny*, so funny, it's better than music! AM 55 on your dial!" Kanell began to bounce his hands up and down on the wheel, his shoulders rising and falling like a DJ's, his words spoken into an invisible microphone: "The Rick Kanell Show, brought to you live *and* our guest today, our *slut* is Jo Pinder! Be the sixth caller and get a *free* blow job!" His movements stilled, eyes returning to the cadenced blinking. Kanell began to spit out words as if they were bitter-tasting, as if the violent expectoration would remove the bitter, metallic taste from his mouth.

"*You-fucking-slut. I-liked-you-and-I-was-close-to-you-and-I-wanted. . .*" His voice trailed off.

Pinder's blood was pumping very fast now. But the fear increased as the car pulled into the small dirt road at the Meadow of Dan.

"Rick, what are you doing?" She wanted the car to stop completely; she would jump out if it stopped; or she wanted the car to go very, very fast, it would feel safer. But Kanell did not stop. He continued down the dirt road at twenty miles an hour, the car bouncing hard, springs protesting ruts and holes.

Jo Pinder noticed the oddest thing as the car turned on the road: Rick had not shaved. And then she thought of the fly, its jerky movements up the side of the bolster, walking *straight up* the side of the bolster, a nonsensical thing to remember, and then she thought, *I am going to die and I haven't done anything wrong*, a reality as clear as the final thoughts of one who has slipped accidentally from a sheer cliff, completely conscious, tumbling downward to that one frozen, everlasting second when movement stops.

Kanell did not look at her as he went on talking. "You know, Jo, everything was simple. But the kid fucked it *all up*. I don't know why he was there"—he shook his head—"Jo, why was the kid there?"

He continued down the dirt road. Kanell did not care where the road went, or who might join them on that road. Jo Pinder closed her eyes.

"*Rick! What are you doing on this road?*" He did not acknowledge her question, but placed his right hand quickly on the back of her neck, holding the neck firmly enough to control her movement, but gently enough not to hurt. Jo began to hyperventilate.

"You see, I love to fuck you," he began. "Do you remember that time on the airplane?" He stopped the car nearly a mile down the road and turned to Jo, his left hand going quickly to the front of her neck, fingertips of both hands making contact around her neck. He did not squeeze; the fingers were loose around it.

"You see, I love to fuck you. And talk to you. I felt *comfortable* with you, Jo." Pinder began to cry. Not convulsive movements, but tears seeping from her closed eyes.

"Rick, I did not betray you. *Please* don't hurt me." The gentle word. Kanell released the grip of his left hand just enough to wipe the drops from her cheeks.

"Make love to me, Jo, I want you to make love to me *right now*." Pinder smiled, a brief upward movement of the outer lips, which fell as quickly as they had risen.

Kanell released his left hand for just enough time to unzip his pants, then placed his hand again on her throat, pulling her head to his crotch. Pinder began to fondle him awkwardly, wetness from her cheeks staining his pants. She looked up once, smiling the staccato smile again, but Kanell's eyes were facing ahead, glazed.

Rick Kanell looked down as she touched him again. *She has a pretty neck. She has very pretty hair. How comfortable she's been.*

"I'm sorry, Jo." In one smooth and swift movement he placed his left hand on her forehead, his right hand on her chin, whipping Jo Pinder's head far to the right, far enough to see her eyes. When Kanell heard the crack of her neck, he cried.

16

I

DEAN Buettner's word for Monday was *augury*, and the word intensified the black mood that enveloped him when he entered the office that morning. How ironically appropriate a word it was. Jo Pinder was a traitor, a mole for Anton Vicovari's outfit. After nearly two years of working lunches in Chicago Auto Theft and flirting with Buettner and overhearing conversations and probably taking furtive looks at the files of ongoing investigations—Buettner had tried to remember how often Jo Pinder had been left alone in the office—Pinder had been exposed. He cursed himself for not calling in during the weekend. He would have known *two days ago*—if he hadn't spent the weekend getting laid. The phone rang on the clerk's desk as he walked by. He stopped.

"Dean Buettner," he said tartly.

It was G. O. Bern, the Auto Theft detective who was just completing his seventh hour of observing Angie Weiner's apartment.

"G. O., I'm sorry I'm late. So what's Weiner been up to for the past seven hours?"

"He's still in his apartment with some damn kid, been there all night as I sat here freezing to death. That's *some* news about Jo Pinder, isn't it? She is a pretty bitch. I guess the best moles are pretty, aren't they?" He cleared his throat. It was twenty-nine degrees and snowing lightly in Chicago.

"Who the hell knows," Buettner said, sitting on the edge of the desk as he spoke. "Who's relieving you at eight?"

"Jackie Bell's coming back on and I don't know who else. We'll have two people on him, though. What's all the urgency about?"

Buettner shook his head. His mouth had a dry, musty taste. "I'm afraid Pinder may have told Weiner some stuff that could jeopardize some lady in Atlanta, and I want us to keep him buttoned until we can find out more about that."

"So, who's going to confront Pinder today?" Bern asked.

"No one's going to talk with her this week; she's gone out of town, to Virginia, I think. But I bet she'll have one hell of a welcoming committee when she comes back. Well, anyway, be sure Jackie knows that I want to be kept up on Weiner's movements today, okay?"

"You got it," G.O. said as he hung up. Buettner went to his office, throwing his coat on the one chair across from his desk. He looked at his watch. It was seven thirty—eight thirty in Atlanta. During the fitful sleep of the previous night and for most of the past hour and fifteen minutes, Dean Buettner had had a growing uneasiness about the safety of Evelyn Wade in Atlanta. He believed the lady was in mortal danger, if Jo Pinder knew she existed and had passed that information to the person Buettner suspected of being the killer, Angie Weiner.

Buettner turned his attention to the battered folder containing his notes about Medlock, Evelyn Garner, and Evelyn Wade. He placed a note about a telephone call from Evelyn Wade next to the phone and dialed her number, but before the phone could ring, Albert Rosenbloom arrived, walking directly to his own office. Buettner hung up the phone and walked in behind him before Rosenbloom could sit down.

"Albert, I've got a hell of a shocker for you."

Rosenbloom turned to face him. "Dean, is it going to be one of *those* weeks?"

"Sure as hell is. Albert . . . Jackie Bell was doing surveillance on Angie Weiner Saturday morning. Weiner was eating breakfast at a diner with Jo Pinder."

Rosenbloom looked at Buettner, eyes unblinking, a stunned expression on his face.

"Was Jackie sure it was Jo?"

"Positive."

Rosenbloom hesitated, then looked through the window at the brick wall beyond. Snowflakes were coming down more heavily now. "I'll be a son of a bitch. . . . I wonder how much damage that little slut has done to us anyway."

"I don't know what harm she's done, but I'm worried about that lady in Atlanta who's tied to the killing of the mule, Medlock. Jo took a call from the lady, and I'm afraid she may have made the connection and then told Weiner. We're watching Weiner very carefully, though."

Many pressures had been building inside Albert Rosenbloom. He believed that Angie Weiner and the Vicovari outfit were responsible for the molestation of his daughter. His leaning on Vicovari in response had brought pressure on Rosenbloom from his superiors, many of whom were sympathetic to Vicovari. The strain had not ended there, either. Rosenbloom's wife was drinking too much again. His daughter had withdrawn into a shell. Albert Rosenbloom was a calm man normally. But the news of Jo Pinder's betrayal ended his calm, all of the pressures rising to the surface at once, as if the pressure cooker had burst. He exploded.

"God damn it! I'm going to *kill* that bitch and I'm going to kill that son of a bitch Weiner, too!" He threw an insulated plastic cup across the room. "The goddamned scumbags and that goddamned Vicovari, I'm gonna get him too, that little prick!"

Rosenbloom turned to Buettner. "Dean, what time does that little slut come to work?"

"Albert, she's out of town for the week; in Virginia, she said, but shit, that's probably a lie, too."

Rosenbloom cocked his head slightly, drumming his fingers on the table.

"Have you called that lady in Atlanta yet? If the slut talked to Weiner, she could be in a *shitpile* of trouble."

Buettner shook his head. "I was trying when you walked in. But I think she's okay for now. We've got Weiner buttoned real tight, two people on him."

"Dean, how the hell do you know Weiner's not going to put someone else on her? Just because he killed the lady in Dallas doesn't mean he's going after this Evelyn, too. You need to call that lady and tell her to *get the hell to someplace safe.* And I'm going to go to personnel and find out who recommended Jo Pinder as my damn fill-in clerk."

Rosenbloom left the office at seven forty. Buettner dialed Evelyn Wade's number twice, each time letting the phone ring six times. He did not reach her. Less than ten minutes earlier she had walked the short distance from 91 Myrtle, right arm locked in May Montez's arm, left arm negotiating the sidewalk with her cane, to spend the day with Lane Englander. Buettner then left the office for Central Booking. He needed to pick up an audio cassette.

At nine Chicago time, Albert Rosenbloom returned to the office, stopping first at the clerk's desk to pick up messages, then walking directly to Buettner's office. A tape of Angie Weiner recorded at the time of his release from jail on Thursday was in Buettner's hand, but before Buettner could speak, Rosenbloom broke into a thin smile and said, "Do you know who recommended Jo Pinder for her job?"

Buettner frowned but said nothing.

"Do you know *who* said that he had known Pinder for years and could not recommend her more highly? Shit! *Dean*, she was hired on the personal recommendation of Lucius Vanderkempt, that son of a bitch!" "Loose Lucius," for fifteen years the senior presiding state judge in the Chicago judicial system; the judge who had refused to hold Angie Weiner for the full forty-eight hours he could have held him before releasing him; the judge who had personally called Albert Rosenbloom's boss to bring pressure to stop the alleged harassment of Anton Vicovari.

Buettner dropped his pen on the desk. "God damn it! Albert, that wrinkled worm is part of them! What the hell are you going to do with that little piece of information?"

"I'm gonna savor it, and that's all for right now. This thing's getting a little hot, and I've got to think about the right way to handle it." He paused. "Have you got that lady in Atlanta yet?"

"Tried twice, but no luck."

"Have you called Minneapolis or Dallas and told them about Pinder?"

"I've left word both places," Buettner said. As they talked, Rick Kanell, posing as Dean Buettner, was talking to May Montez at American Opinion Research in Atlanta and writing down Evelyn Wade's telephone number.

Rosenbloom spoke. "Damn it, Dean, get to those damn people. I want to see if *anyone's* got enough to get another warrant on Weiner—including *us*. What judge presides on Mondays?"

"I think it's Hames Lyon."

"Good. He'll help us. Get everything we've got on Weiner together, and let's go over it this morning. *I want a warrant on that man.* And get ahold of Vice. I want to meet with them; let's see if they're ready to let any cats out of the bag, too." At least five jurisdictions or departments were interested in Angie Weiner.

Rosenbloom left the office. Dean Buettner again tried to call Evelyn Wade. He wanted to play the tape of Angie Weiner's distinctive voice to Evelyn Wade, he wanted to know if *that* voice was the one of the man who had killed Bobby Medlock; Buettner was very sure Evelyn Wade could tell him that. It was what her last phone message said. But Evelyn was not at home.

He left the office quickly, with the files on Angie Weiner, pictures of Weiner with Rick Kanell, and a cassette tape of Weiner's conversations in the Booking Office under his arm.

II

The young hustler walked out of Angie Weiner's apartment building. He pulled a light blue jacket tightly around him, snowflakes whirling as he walked past two men sitting in an older Pontiac. The men were roughly dressed, their appearance matching the car and the neighborhood.

"I'll bet that kid's got a sore ass," Jackie Bell said as he turned to the man on his left.

The man glanced casually at the kid. "So that's him? Do you think Weiner will be down, too?"

"God, I hope so; I'm going to be either frozen to death or bored to death if we keep sitting here. Hell! I've been around this damn building since Jesus was born." The two men joked, returning to their card game. Jackie Bell was winning.

In a few minutes, Bell glanced up. "Don't look, but the faggot's on the prowl again, and it looks like he's going for a while, too."

"Why?" The man put down the ten of hearts.

"He's got his suitcase with him."

"Is he going to his car?"

Bell hesitated. "No, he's waiting for someone." The men continued their card game as Weiner stood outside the entrance to his building, then returned to the warmth of the lobby. Just before noon, a bright red Buick pulled up. Bell quickly wrote down the time, then picked up the hand-held radio unit lying between his feet, clearing his throat before speaking.

"Base, this is nine."

"Go ahead, nine."

"Dean wanted to know when we're moving, and we are. Tell him the man has a suitcase with him."

"Roger that, nine. Have fun."

Bell talked about many things as the two cars began their journey. But when he realized that Weiner's car was most definitely heading to Midway Airport, he picked up the hand-held again and called base. "Can you try to reach Dean again? I need to know how far he wants me to follow this guy. Tell him he's about four miles from Midway right now."

"Stand by, nine." Base was quiet for nearly three minutes. The voice of the man at base returned.

"Nine, Buettner is still out of the office with Rosenbloom."

Bell's face went blank. "What do you mean he's *still* out of the office? I thought you gave him my last message?"

"I'm sorry, nine, it's pretty busy around here. So what do you want me to do?"

"Nothing, damn it! Do you think it would be too much to ask that you make sure Dean reaches us the minute he returns?" Bell did not wait for an answer, but sprinted from the car, which was about twenty lengths from Weiner's car. He stood less than fifty feet from Weiner as the man waited to board Eastern flight 341 for Atlanta. Bell walked from the gate to a pay phone just behind the ticket counter as Weiner disappeared from sight, and dialed the direct number for Chicago Auto Theft at twelve forty. The phone rang twice, then an unfamiliar voice said, "Chief detective's office."

"Trudy?"

"I'm sorry, she's out to lunch. Can I help you, please?"

"This is Bell; has Dean gotten back yet?"

The new lunch-shift clerk, a temporary replacement for Jo Pinder, had been on the job little more than an hour, and the phone calls had been coming in rapid order. She was trying hard to get down all of the messages and unfamiliar names, but she had never heard of Jackie Bell. She wrote "Bill" at the top of the message book.

"I'm sorry, he's still out with the chief detective. Could I take a message for him, please?"

Who the hell was this lady? "Yes, tell him the guy's gone to Atlanta on a one-o'clock flight, okay? I'll be in as soon as I can."

She wrote the message down exactly as Jackie Bell said it. The message from "Bill" was the fifth message for Dean Buettner, and the seventh message taken by the new clerk. She separated the top page of the message book, which contained the messages from Jay Preston, the Minneapolis Homicide Department, and the Cook County Hospital. She then turned the page and separated the next three messages: a call from Albert Rosenbloom's wife, the call from base saying "The guy is moving," and a call from the deputy commander of the vice squad.

As the clerk began to tear the message from Jackie Bell, the phone rang again. "Christ," she said as she picked up the phone. It was an irate Chicago resident whose car had been stolen in *broad daylight*, the guy said. He continued to rant as Dean Buettner entered the office. The new clerk quickly handed Buettner five of his six messages. She did not hand him the message saying Angie Weiner was on the way to Atlanta. Her hand was tearing that message from the top of the third page as Buettner walked to his office. Buettner quickly flipped through the messages, prioritizing them. It was five minutes to one. He dialed the number for Jay Preston. The message said "at table nine" and was written by the clerk at 12:45. Preston's phone was busy. He then looked at the call from base. Weiner was on the move, good to know, he thought, then looked to the third message. It was from a Dr. Carty Rodriguez. Dean Buettner did not know a doctor by that name, and he didn't know anyone in Cook County Hospital, either. He dialed the number anyway.

"Yes, I'd like extension 2100, please." The fingers of Buettner's left hand were tapping lightly on his desk as the phone rang. As he sat there, the new clerk entered just long enough to place Buettner's final message on the desk. He glanced cursorily at it, saw the name "Bill," and placed it down as a woman answered the phone. The name Bill meant nothing to him.

"Trauma Center, Burns."

"Yes, this is Detective Dean Buettner. I'm returning Dr. Rodriguez's call."

"Dr. Rodriguez is with a patient," the woman said snappishly.

"Well, would you know why he would be calling me, miss?"

"What was your name again?" she asked with the same curtness. Buettner repeated his name.

"Hold on."

The woman was away from the phone for almost a minute. As he waited, Buettner listened idly to the tape of Angie Weiner.

"Yes, the doctor says it's about Lynwood Ferguson." She said the name as if Buettner would instantly recognize it, but he did not. Dean Buettner was close to Lennie, his young black friend, but he hardly knew his last name or his real first name, a thought that came to him as he remembered Lennie before a pinball machine.

"*What* about Lynwood Ferguson? Is he there?"

"Of *course* he's here, he's been here since Saturday. Dr. Rodriguez is with a patient," she repeated. "He will call you back shortly."

Buettner stood up. "The *hell* he will! God damn it, lady! *What is wrong with Lennie?*"

"Acid."

Buettner instantly felt flushed. "Acid? What do you mean, '*acid*'? *I want to know what happened to the damn kid!*"

"Somebody threw acid on him. Orthophosphoric acid."

Buettner's foot began to tap up and down lightly. "Why the hell are you calling me *today* if Lennie has been there since Saturday?"

"*Mr.* Buettner. The doctor will call you shortly. I've got nine patients in this unit and I don't have time to talk with a rude detective, so . . ."

Buettner interrupted. "So you tell that damn doctor I will be at the hospital in thirty minutes, do you understand me? What ward is Lennie in?"

"Burns ICU, 2124, thank you," the woman said curtly as she hung up.

Leaving his phone messages on the desk, Buettner grabbed his coat and left the office, stopping just long enough by the new clerk to say, "I'll be at Cook County Burns ICU." As he opened the door, the clerk said, "Dean, did you see that message from Bill?" Again the name did not register; Buettner continued out the door.

He arrived at the nurses' station in Cook County's Burn Unit at one thirty and waited, impatiently, for Dr. Carty Rodriguez. Rodriguez was chief resident of the unit, in his mid-thirties and not at all snappish like the head nurse sitting at the station. He shook

Buettner's hand and without looking at the nurse said, "Liz, hand me the chart on the Ferguson boy, please." He began to talk to Buettner before looking at the chart.

"Well, your young friend has certainly been through it since Saturday, I'm afraid."

Before Rodriguez could continue, Buettner spoke. "That's the first thing I want to know, *why* did you *just* call me?"

"The boy has been sedated or in surgery since he was admitted. It's very hard for him to talk even now, but he said your name today." Rodriguez opened Lennie's file and began to read silently as Buettner peppered him with questions. Buettner's foot was tapping up and down again, his head moving up and down in cadence with the foot.

"What happened to him, and where?"

"From what we know, some other kids held him down and poured acid on him," Rodriguez said as he read quickly through the admitting report: ". . . The patient collapsed on Hooper Street by Richard Daley Park at about ten fifteen Saturday morning. An ambulance was called by a man at a laundry; he was admitted with acid burns on the arms and legs and groin, the face and eyes."

His eyes. The words fixed in Buettner's mind. Lennie's eyes had acid in them and he had been sitting right there on Hooper Street reading goddamn *Jaws* waiting for him.

"Do you know who did it or why?"

"Lennie won't say much about who did it, but maybe he'll tell you."

"Can I see him now? Can *he* see?"

"I'm sorry, he can't."

Buettner closed his eyes, feeling the darkness for a moment. "Is it permanent?"

"Probably; but in a way, the boy was lucky. Whoever did this used an unusual type of acid, orthophosphoric acid; it's used in body shops to remove baked-on enamel, and it's slow-burning. We see quite a lot of it."

Body shop. Buettner began to feel a very cold anger as he thought of Central Body Shop and Angie Weiner and the kid named Kowakoski. The rage was first directed at whoever poured the acid on Lennie—he was sure it was Kowakoski—and then at Angie Weiner; and, finally, it was directed inward. Why the hell hadn't he looked for the kid when he was late? Why the hell hadn't he been more careful meeting with that funny kid who liked to play pinball?

"Can I see him now?"

Rodriguez placed the chart back on the counter and turned toward the entrance to ICU. "Detective Buettner, the boy is very hard to understand. We've had to fix his mouth in a partially open position because of the burns on the lips. . . ." Burns on the lips. Buettner felt gut-sick. "And the boy needs all of his energy right now. So please make this a short visit, okay?"

"Can he write something, can he write on a pad or something?"

Rodriguez shook his head. "As you'll see, Lennie is immobile." The doctor led Buettner into a small anteroom and handed him a green paper gown and mask from a shelf.

"You'll have to wear these inside."

Buettner felt stunned as he put on the flimsy paper garment. Shrouded hospital figures were the stuff of nightmares, nightmares made real by the banked machines, beeps, and blinking monitors in the space-age room they entered. Surrounded by a setup worthy of the bridge of a starfighter, Lennie looked pitifully small.

Buettner wanted to put his hand on him, to touch him, but there was no place safe to touch. He closed his eyes as he spoke. "Slicks, so what have you gone and done to yourself?" He opened his eyes as he finished the question and looked at a red dot peaking regularly on a monitor screen.

Lennie's words were slurred, both from the medication and the fixed position of his mouth. He could not say the letters that required the lips to touch.

" 'Uettner, I 'eel 'ad, 'ad." He could not say "bad." Buettner leaned as close to his head as the equipment would allow.

"I know. . . . Lennie, was it Kowakoski?"

Lennie took two short breaths through his mouth before attempting to answer. "Dean, I gotta li', li' wit t'em." He could not say "live," but Buettner understood.

"I know, Slicks, I know." He could do nothing to Kowakoski—yet.

"Dean . . . I can't *uhruse*, uhruse the 'ords any 'ore, 'ord nine, Augus' . . ."

The word was *peruse*. Buettner watched the puffed, distorted lips struggle with the witticism. A sudden sense of guilt tightened his chest and loosened his gut. Lennie was blind because he'd helped. Because he'd helped Dean. Buettner took a deep breath.

"Lennie, they say you are going to be okay." Buettner lied. "Now, I don't want you getting in any trouble till I get back, okay?"

He arrived back at Chicago Auto Theft at ten minutes to three. Rosenbloom was standing by the clerk's desk.

"So who's in the hospital?"

"Lennie, one of my kids. Some of Weiner's scumbags threw acid on him and the kid is blind."

Rosenbloom nodded. He did not know Lennie Ferguson, but he did know that the black kid was special to Buettner. "I'm sorry. Dean—Jackie Bell's been trying to get you. Weiner is on a plane to Atlanta."

Buettner looked surprised. "As of when?"

"He left on a one-o'clock flight from Midway. The plane's supposed to arrive at four their time."

Buettner looked at his watch, his right foot tapping the floor—2:57 in Chicago; 3:57 in Atlanta, nearly four.

"Albert, has anyone tried to get that lady in Atlanta?"

Rosenbloom nodded yes. "I tried. No one is at home. Dean, I've been in court, I'm heading back there at four. We're trying for a cause warrant on Weiner. If I get it, we can have him picked up in Atlanta."

The scumbag's going to kill that lady, Buettner thought as he headed to his office. He dialed the number for Jay Preston at the Department of Consumer Affairs in Atlanta. In a bright cheery voice the receptionist said, "Hold on just a minute, please," then came back on the phone. "I'm sorry, Mr. Preston is in with the director. Could I have him call you back?"

Jesus. "Lady, I've got to speak to him *now*. It's honest to God a matter of life and death."

Preston came on the line. "Well, Mr. Buettner, I'm sorry we've missed each other so much today. But thanks for talking to May Montez, though, that call made us feel better."

"What call? Who is May Montez?"

Preston hesitated. "The supervisor at American Opinion Research, where Evelyn works—didn't you call her this morning?"

Buettner began to feel tightness in the center of his chest as he answered, "Jay, I didn't talk to anyone in Atlanta this morning. What did the guy say?"

"Oh *Christ*, he used your name, that's why May talked with him. May didn't think anyone would know your name. May gave him Evelyn's phone number!"

His name? The scumbag was using Dean's name. He looked at the picture of Angie Weiner and the well-dressed man. "Jay, get to the lady *now*. The guy that killed the other people should be landing in Atlanta right now!"

"*What?* How do you know?"

"We've had him under surveillance. It turns out the guy had a source here in the department."

Preston yelled for his secretary, then turned quickly back to the phone. "Buettner, give me the guy's name and flight number." He looked up at the girl walking in and said, "Gail, get me the airport police on the phone *now*." His attention was back on Buettner.

"Can you give me a description of the guy?"

Buettner looked at the picture of Weiner and Kanell. He carefully described Weiner, then said, "I'll get this wired down to you in case you miss him."

"Jesus, we're running out of time. Hold on a minute." Preston picked up on the blinking line and began to talk to the airport police.

Buettner looked first at his watch and then at the pictures of Weiner and Kanell. Bobby Medlock ran out of time. The lady in

Dallas ran out of time. Lennie? He ran out of time, too. Buettner yanked open his left top drawer and heaved the yellow pages out, then flipped to the heading "Airlines." His eyes were on the number for Delta when Preston came back on the phone.

"We'll never get him, the damn plane's on time for once, but we're going to try; I'll—"

Buettner interrupted. "Preston, I'm getting the hell out of here and heading to the airport. If you don't pick up the guy at the airport, I'm coming down there. I've got a hard-on for this guy, and I'll be damned if he's going to hurt anyone else." He looked at his watch. "Can you call my office when you hear? I'll call here from O'Hare when I get there."

He hung up the phone and dialed the number for Delta Airlines. Buettner made a reservation on the five-o'clock flight, then walked quickly to Rosenbloom's office.

"I'm going for a warrant now, not at four, Dean, and I want you down at court with me. Let's go now," Rosenbloom said, getting out of the chair.

"Albert . . ."

The expression on Buettner's face arrested Rosenbloom's movement.

"So what's wrong now?"

"Albert. *Please.* I want to go to Atlanta. I want to go to the airport right now, and if they don't pick Weiner up at the airport there, I want to be on a plane." He stopped talking as if more words were there to be said and looked at Rosenbloom without blinking. Rosenbloom said nothing, and Buettner continued. "*I* know as much about this guy as anyone, and he used *my* goddamn name to get that lady's phone number, and damn it, I want to get him."

It didn't make any sense, Rosenbloom thought; the department's budget couldn't justify a plane ticket, he was sure of that. But then he thought of his daughter, and of the black kid, and all of the anonymous phone calls to his house saying, "Where's your father, kid, is your father *okay?*" And then he thought of Anton Vicovari. How many people had that man hurt?

Rosenbloom looked up at Buettner. "Have you got any money, Dean? I can't get a ticket that fast."

"No, but I've got a credit card."

"Okay, get the hell out of here and let me try to get that warrant."

Buettner went back to his office and quickly threw his things in an old Samsonite briefcase: his notes concerning Bobby Medlock, the last monitoring report from Central Body Shop, the pictures of Angie Weiner and the well-dressed man, and finally, a red plastic tape recorder containing a cassette tape of Angie Weiner. He walked out the door of Chicago Auto Theft at three twenty-five.

17

I

THE kitchen window at 91 Myrtle Street framed a small garden plot eight feet by twenty. Heavy railway ties enclosed the plot. Since Grady Wade's death only weeds grew there in the warmer months, occasionally attacked by Evelyn with her cane; but at the far end of the plot, the weathered stalk of a single okra plant, grown from seed, remained. The stalk had defied three winters, a thin spire rising above a now flat, grassy base like a tall building rising incongruously in the lowness of the sandy south Georgia flatlands, childhood home to Evelyn and her husband. Evelyn left the stalk there on purpose, a reminder of Grady Wade.

Now it provided a focal point for Evelyn as she looked out the window, the phone in her hand, listening to May Montez: Jay had just called; the man, *the one who killed people*, and would kill her, was landing in Atlanta *right now*. Evelyn did not move her eyes from the stalk as May continued to talk: He knew Evelyn's phone number, probably knew her address, too; Lane was walking back to 91 Myrtle right then, May had called him; May was coming to take her away to a safe place; Jay was contacting the police to get help.

In a curious way, May's words did not seem real, Evelyn thought, and, anyway, it took thirty minutes to come in from the airport. For at least thirty minutes she was safe. Evelyn's mind drifted to the garden. Each morning Grady would walk out and look at the rows, waiting for the okra seeds to pop open and grow. The okra was the hardest thing to grow from seeds. He froze them before planting. Did that help? Evelyn could not remember. She raised her hand to the thumb lock on the kitchen window and pushed it tighter as May finished talking.

Evelyn went to the bedroom closet she used to store out-of-season clothes. In the back, leaning in one corner, was an old, rusted single-shot twenty-gauge shotgun. There was no shell in the gun. Evelyn might not have put a shell in had there been one, but she took the gun and walked to the storeroom. She propped the gun carefully by the door, then entered, her good foot sliding empty cardboard boxes and paper sacks to the side, making a path to Grady Wade's toolbox. Evelyn removed a hammer from the center of the box, and then took the stoutest nail she could find, and began to hammer the tenpenny galvanized nail into the window frame, using both hands, wincing as she swung the hammer. She heard the knock on the door as the nail finally, stubbornly sealed the window shut. Leaning the hammer on the lowest shelf, she walked to the door, using the barrel of the twenty-gauge as her cane.

"Evelyn, it's me," Lane Englander said from the doorstep. She opened the door. Lane walked in quickly, turning for a moment to look up and down the street, then pushed the door shut after him. His eyes went to the twenty-gauge.

"I've got to remember never to get you mad at me," he said with a soft smile. "Can you shoot that thing?" Lane was feeling a heavy sadness as he spoke, and an anger, too. It wasn't right that a madman had chosen Evelyn.

"Well, I don't know, but I think I can try. Come help me." She walked back to the storeroom, handed the hammer to Englander, and began to fish out a large handful of nails from the toolbox. Evelyn waved her hand at the window. "I've already nailed this one, but I want to nail them all."

Lane looked at her with a blank expression. "Aren't you leaving? Isn't May coming for you?"

Evelyn shook her head as she began to walk to the kitchen. "Lane, I'm sorry. If that man's here to kill me, I want them to *catch* him, and the best place to do that is right here." She forced a laugh. "At least we won't have to go to Chicago to find him."

Englander looked at the gun. Chicago would be safer, he thought. But he shook his head affirmatively, regardless of the thought. "Okay. But you are not going to stay here without me."

Evelyn smiled slightly. "I'm going to put on some water."

When they had finished tea and finished nailing the windows tightly shut, they sat in the living room talking of unimportant things. Evelyn's hand rested on the barrel of the gun; Lane, with a blush, had finally removed from his pants pocket a gold-plated single-shot derringer, showed it to Evelyn with a wry smile, then replaced it. The two of them looked like a sophisticated Ma and Pa Kettle waiting for a clan war to begin.

Englander built a roaring fire, started with one match, and for a few moments thoughts of the man seemed to leave them both. But then the phone rang. Evelyn answered it on the first ring.

"Hello?"

"Ev, it's Jay," Preston said hurriedly. "Is May there yet?"

"You didn't get him at the airport, did you?" Evelyn's voice was calm.

"No. And we don't know where he's going, either, so you get out of there the minute May gets there."

Evelyn pulled herself up a little straighter. "I'm sorry, Jay, I'm not leaving. Lane's here, and we have two guns, and I think what we need to try to do is catch the man here. *I'm* the honey for this bear."

"Evelyn, this is *serious*. You've got to leave there, this man is . . ."

"I *know* what he is," Evelyn interrupted, "but Jay, you know the best place to catch him is here." She paused for emphasis. "I think you should set up a stakeout, or something, and Jay, the man is not going to come knock on my door with several people here. No, I'm staying." Her eyes were still on Englander.

"Jesus, Evelyn, I'm coming there right now, but I've got to call back to the office first, my boss is helping me with the police. Let me see what I can do, but turn on all the lights, okay?"

"We're all right, Jay. We've nailed up the windows, Lane's got a fire going"—she said it as if the fire would protect them—"and we'll get the lights on now." Evelyn hung up the phone and turned back to Lane.

"He's here." She closed her eyes for an instant. "You know, this sounds silly, but I have an image of that man violating my home, the structure itself." Evelyn then shook her head and tried to smile, but the smile faltered. "You know, it's a living thing to me," she said as she walked to the window. It was not dark yet, but the twilight neutralized the muted tones of November. Evelyn's glance went to the street light less than thirty feet from the house as she continued. "That light works, and the security light behind the house works too." She turned to face Lane. "That's good, isn't it?"

Englander wanted her out of the house. He shook his head before answering. "It is, it is . . . but Ev . . . I think we should all still go to the show tonight, it might be safer there in the crowds. And I don't think we should change what we are doing just because of that man. Let's keep it normal, don't you think?"

Evelyn nodded yes. It was a special showing at the Fox, *Casablanca*, and the four of them, May, Jay, Evelyn, and Lane, were planning to go there. It had been Lane's idea and had appealed to Evelyn for a special reason.

Evelyn looked back out the window again, her thoughts of a field in south Georgia. She started talking as if her words were not directed at anyone in particular. "When we were married, Lib and Sam, our best friends, they're *still* my best friends, drove us from the reception. They drove us right through a corn field in that old Dodge—to escape, you know—and then Grady and I left for Atlanta. We drove. It took us sixteen hours, and on our second day in Atlanta we went to the Fox. . . . I can't remember the movie now, but I remember the sing-along with the big organ, and the words and notes on the screen, and the bouncing ball to help us keep the rhythm."

Evelyn turned back to Lane. "I haven't been back there but one or two times since the fifties," she said smiling, her eyes going down to the twenty-gauge, "and I never thought I would go back there on a day like this." Her glance went back to the window, face brightening as May Montez began to walk up the six steps of 91, looking up and down the street before knocking on the door. All of Evelyn's friends were alert for demons this night.

Evelyn opened the door before May could knock, startling her. "Evelyn! You scared me," May said as she walked in, glancing again to the street. "Well, have you got everything packed?" May hugged Evelyn and kissed her cheek lightly, then turned to Lane and hugged him too. Danger brought the same naturalness to physical closeness that grief or great happiness could bring.

Lane's eyes were on Evelyn as he spoke for both of them. "May, Evelyn's not leaving, we're going to stay here."

Evelyn began to speak as if her words were part of the same sentence. "And we've already told Jay, nailed up the windows, built a fire, and got some protection!" There was a false ring to Evelyn's tone and manner; her adamance more bravura than bravery. But May did not seem to notice. She was staring slack-jawed at the gun. She then looked at both of them. The look was a confused one.

"That scares me, Ev. *Please*, don't you think you should come to my place?"

Evelyn smiled and hugged May again with her left hand. "I belong here, honey, and if that man comes here, the police will catch him here. . . . Jay's talking to the police now"—she paused—"and if something happens to me here, that's okay, too. This is my home."

The phone rang before May could say anything. Evelyn leaned the gun carefully against the double-sided desk and picked up the phone. Jay Preston was on the phone again, his hurried voice asking for May. Evelyn walked to the kitchen as May took the phone.

"Jay, Ev's planning to stay here."

"I know, but I think it's okay. My boss has helped me and we're going to have some undercover people from CID, at least for the night—they're doing it for him, and because of the warrant."

"What warrant?"

"Buettner? The guy with Auto Theft in Chicago? He was able to get a warrant sent from there for some auto theft–related things. He's on the way down here to help us identify the guy. We've also got a picture of the bastard. His name's Weiner and he's a fat SOB."

"God, all of this scares me. You know, Evelyn has a gun, a shotgun."

Preston laughed. "I know, Lane's got a gun, too. For God's sake, don't stand in front of any of those things."

As Preston spoke, Evelyn walked to May, catching her attention with a tap on her shoulder that caused May to jump slightly.

"May dear, ask Jay if it's okay if we all still go to the Fox tonight."

Shaking her head in resignation, May turned back to the phone. Preston thought before answering, then said yes, they would still go, he would drop them off and then pick up Dean Buettner. "And anyway, that'll keep her out of the house until we find out what the hell we're doing. Hell, maybe they'll get the Weiner guy while everyone's away from the house."

II

Sitting at the upstairs bar of Atlanta's Dynamite! nursing his drink, Benny Longfoot was already thinking about where he was going to spend the night. An eighteen-year-old drifter, Longfoot depended on his looks and personality to find that place, and he thought both were first-rate. His five-foot-six frame, though short, was very muscular and graceful in motion, his face tan and handsome. And he was sure that he had style. This evening, he had dressed entirely in black and white: black jeans, tight ones worn without underwear to display the means of his livelihood better, an equally tight black nylon sweater worn over a white nylon turtleneck, and black shoes, highly polished, worn over white socks. Atlanta was his sixth city for the year; he hoped to stay longer than he had in Miami.

He swirled the melting ice cubes in the last of his Coke and rum and cautioned himself to avoid the weirdos who had driven him away from Miami and the Keys. One had tried to choke him. On another night, two older men who picked him up, two men with small brass rings through their nipples, wanted him to beat them with an honest-to-God whip with honest-to-God metal tips on the end of the leather. A fat man had pulled a knife on him, too. Since then, Foot had carried a knife himself.

He took the last sip of liquid from his glass. For many good reasons besides these, he did not trust people, specifically tricks, anymore. And so Benny Longfoot had been ignoring the advances of the man sitting to his left. The man was fat, just like the man in Key West. Benny looked again at his glass, thought of the solitary five-dollar bill in his pocket, and turned to the man.

"So, you from Atlanta?" he asked with a false smile on his face, the smile of a person who has worked too long and would really rather go home than work an extra shift.

Angie Weiner quickly returned the smile. "No, just in town on a vacation. Can I buy you a drink?" Weiner had cruised the three floors of Dynamite! before settling at the upstairs bar. That bar, he heard from the man who took his money at the front door, was the place to meet the best hustlers in town. Weiner was looking for a date—at least until midnight. Midnight, he had calculated, would be the earliest time a car could arrive from Low Notch. Midnight would be the earliest Jo Pinder could call his apartment in Chicago, waking his sister Flo there, leaving word where she and Rick Kanell were staying in Atlanta.

Angie Weiner already knew the other piece of the puzzle; he was sure Rick Kanell would be found at a house on Myrtle Street at some time during the night, stalking a lady named Evelyn. Weiner did not know why Kanell felt he needed to cover his tracks leading from the lady to the body of Bobby Medlock, but he did know the lady's phone number and address. Pinder had provided the number the previous week. He had used the free services of the Atlanta Public Library's information line to find the street number in the city directory's reverse telephone section. But all of that could wait, he thought, as he turned his attention back to the young boy dressed in black and white. It could wait until at least midnight.

"So how long you been in town?" Weiner leaned over closer to the boy. "Just last night," Longfoot said as he turned the stool to face Weiner, his legs spread apart in enticement, as a window dresser puts the best merchandise on display to draw in the customers. "So, you want a little toot to start the night?" Weiner patted his right coat pocket. The magic powder. Weiner's words quickly caught the drifter's interest.

"Sure," he said with a glance around the room, "we can go to the men's room. Is it good toot?"

"It makes everything just fine." As they walked to the restroom, the boy glanced around the room again, one final look for a better trick.

But when Longfoot returned from the restroom, his mind had changed about the fat man. Angie had already given him two twenty-dollar bills, walking-around money, Angie called it, a sign of more money to come; and Angie had promised a full meal at The Prince's Arms, the fanciest gay restaurant in the city. It was a *professional* decision.

III

As red lights began to flash a 58, signaling the arrival of the baggage of the 5:30 Piedmont flight from Winston-Salem, the luggage carousel jolted to a start with a high screech. It sounded like a shrill and long scream to Rick Kanell. He was sitting in the first vinyl chair outside the South Terminal baggage claim at Atlanta's Hartsfield International Airport. A map of Atlanta lay on his lap, but Kanell was staring at the brown tiles of the floor, overwhelmed by the cacophonous sound.

The footsteps of passers-by, he thought, were very loud and hollow; the voices of others walking past him, occasionally glancing in his direction, were also hollow, and equally loud. Music was echoing through the high space—at first, Kanell thought the music was in his head—and occasionally the sounds of detached, overly polite voices were broadcast over the music: "Will the party meeting Lotus Bersheer from India please come to the Delta information counter in the main lobby. . . . Will Mr. T. J. Ryan please meet his party in the north baggage area. . . ." Mixing with all these sounds was the shrill screech of the luggage mover.

Kanell's very red, dilated eyes returned to the map, three times passing over Myrtle Street on the index before locking on the name. He looked around himself quickly. An old lady caught his glance and kept her eyes on him as she walked past, looking over her shoulder quickly to make sure that the strange-looking man was not following her.

He checked the wrinkled slip of paper again. On it was written the street address that the information librarian had given him for Evelyn Wade's number. He had called from the Winston-Salem airport. 91 Myrtle. *Damn it*. The sounds were intruding too much. He found the street again and quickly flipped the map, looking across and then down, two fingers coming together jerkily until his eyes touched on Myrtle. Kanell looked up again and sucked in. *Toot*. He needed some powder. He marked the street with a red pen, then began to trace the easiest approach to the house at 91. As Kanell focused hard on the map, a policeman first walked by, glancing at the red-eyed man for longer than usual. He did not stop. Then a little boy, about three feet tall, running ahead of his parents, came up to him and stopped, quickly slapping the map, laughing, then running away. Kanell looked up. It was a signal to go, he thought, rising from the seat and heading toward the carousel. In a moment, he bent to pick up a small suitcase, Vicovari's suitcase. In the left side of the bag was the mahogany case from the card room at Low Notch. Both of the target pistols were still there, each gun loaded with six shells. *Boom*. He remembered the sound of the guns. And the large hole, it went right through a four by four. As he began to walk to the exit, all of the sounds of the vast room seemed to follow him. Twice before reaching the glass doors Kanell turned to watch his flanks.

He walked briskly from the building, eyes barely darting to the left before crossing the four lanes of cars pulling up, then cut to a covered walkway that ran the length of the short-term and long-term parking lots.

He left the walkway once to take a ticket from the short-term parking lot's ticketing machine. A woman pushed a cart by him with a sign on the side saying "Rent It for Fifty Cents." The small boy who had startled him in the building ran past, still laughing; he could hear the footsteps of the boy's parents moving fast behind him and for an instant he wondered if in reality they were very clever spies. He laughed out loud at the thought but nevertheless began to cut through the very back of the long-term parking lot to be away from them. And then he saw a woman, her back to him. He froze. She looked like Jo. Kanell watched her until she walked out of sight.

In the very last row of long-term parking, Kanell's mind began to pull together. He needed a car, an unobtrusive one that would not be missed for six hours or so; that would be long enough. A tan Mercedes sports coupe caught his eyes; that fitted him, he thought. But then he remembered the importance of anonymity. Kanell selected a dark blue Buick, about six years old. He opened the door in less than thirty seconds with an improvised jimmy from the toolbox at Low Notch, again glancing quickly around the well-lit parking lot to make sure that his quick stabbing motions with the jimmy had not been noticed. As the door shut, his hand retrieved the brown bottle from his pocket again.

Rick Kanell pulled up to the cashier's window of the short-term parking lot at five forty-five. He was not charged for the short stay the parking ticket indicated. Visits of less than five minutes were free to all. He drove slowly, but for him the drive to the Tenth Street exit of Interstate 85 seemed very short, his mind wandering—the eyes of the lady in Dallas, and the urine down her legs; Medlock's body jerking on the floor. He couldn't remember Bobby Medlock's eyes.

But he did remember the weight of the boy's body; it did not weigh as much as the body of Jo Pinder.

Kanell looked down at his pants. Small bits of dead grass clung to the cuffs of the khakis. How long had he been close to Jo? He turned the car up the Tenth Street exit and turned right without stopping at the red light. He massaged his neck, eyes going to the mirror to make sure that no one familiar was following him.

At Peachtree Street he noticed the blond boy selling copies of *Swinging Singles*. As the light changed, he continued down the slight hill that led to Myrtle Street. Kanell began to blink rapidly again. What the hell was he going to do? Who was going to be there waiting for him? He pulled the car into a parking space just past Piedmont, right across the street from a Super Gyro. He rubbed his chin, but he did not feel the heavy black stubble there, nor could his tongue any longer sense the metallic taste. Kanell looked at his watch. Six fifteen. What did the lady look like? Did she live alone? Would Angie be there? No, Angie wouldn't expect him yet. He looked at his watch again, tapping the dial with his index finger. It was moving too slowly. His mind began to clutter again, and as he sat there the rage began to come again. *What was wrong? Everything was wrong and everything was okay until the lady messed it up, messed it all up.* He grasped the steering wheel tightly until the veins of his upper hand began to bulge again.

Kanell pulled the car from the space and began to drive slowly to Myrtle, stopping the car as soon as he had turned to massage his neck again, pulling down hard on the flesh, trying to think through the thick fog that seemed to come and go at will, blocking his view and his thoughts. He looked to the first house on the left, 67 Myrtle, and then to the large trees that lined the street and the bright street lights, placed there to discourage incidents of nighttime violence.

As the dark blue Buick approached 91, Kanell did not slow its already measured speed. He noticed the car parked in front of the house, and the lights throwing shadows on the shaded windows, shadows of people moving inside. He didn't notice the man standing in the shadows of the house, nor did the man pay particular attention to him. The two detectives from the Atlanta CID, one in the yard facing the street, one in the backyard watching the house, were waiting for a man who fit the description and picture in each man's pocket, a thick man. The movement of the dark blue Buick, its driver silhouetted and partially lit by the street light, was taken as movement of little importance.

Kanell drove two blocks past the house, then turned left, pulling his car behind a large dumpster. *Reconnoiter.* It was like stalking a deer, he thought as he walked to the corner of Myrtle and started along that street toward Tenth. He walked casually, his hands in his pockets, and though Rick Kanell was not aware of it, he was softly whistling a tune, the fingers of his right hand tumbling the dark brown bottle in his pocket.

A block from 91 he slowed his pace, eyes following a small dog moving down the street in front of him. The dog stopped at a small bit of garbage on the sidewalk and swallowed it quickly. The dog. Kanell quickened, quietly calling to the brown and white spotted mutt. The dog stopped for an instant, its head turning to the rear, tail moving like a windshield wiper. It cowered as Kanell approached it and gently placed his hand on its neck, stroking the short fur and loose flesh there. He picked up the dog and continued to talk to it, caress it as he turned and walked slowly back toward the car. He stopped at the dumpster, right hand carefully sorting through the bits of wood and plaster and nails dropped in there until he found a length of rough cord. Kanell fashioned a leash from the cord, then turned and began to walk toward the house at 91 again. At six forty, he passed on foot in front of the house for the first time. He picked up the dog as he passed the six steps, bending down, kneeling for just enough time to check the front of the house. And then he saw the silhouette of the man. The man was sitting on the ground to his right in the shadow of the trunk of a large oak. Kanell walked on. They were watching the house. He did not know who was standing guard in the shadows; at the moment that was not important to him. At the corner he turned left across the street and as he turned the dog licked his hand, then pointed its head in the direction of their movement.

Kanell remembered his dog, half of its body crushed under the tires of a car, crawling toward him. He began to sweat. He placed the dog on the pavement again.

At a small alley less than fifty feet from the corner of Myrtle, he turned left again and headed down the alley, looking between the houses, taking mental pictures of the portions of houses visible across Myrtle. They were watching the house. He laughed quietly. It was so funny. Who was watching the house? Was it the police? He laughed again. Or were they Angie's men? He coughed. About twenty yards farther down the narrow alley, Rick Kanell found a place where by leaning against a tumbling-down garage he had an oblique view of the front door of 91 Myrtle. The dog began to calm as he picked it up and cradled it in his arms as if it were a child.

IV

Five people were now in the house at 91. Jay Preston and a detective from Atlanta CID were sitting at the dining room table eating scrambled eggs and thick sausage. The detective, James Eastman, had never met any of the people in Evelyn Wade's home until about thirty minutes earlier and knew only that he was to help watch an old lady and apprehend a man named Weiner from Chicago.

Lane Englander walked back to the table with a fresh pot of coffee, pouring Eastman a cup. Eastman was about thirty-eight, slightly overweight for his height, the weight showing in his stomach at the moment; he was red-haired, with a military cut, and covered in freckles.

Englander picked up an empty dish and returned to the kitchen. Evelyn was standing at the sink rinsing dishes. It was a confusing time for her. She had seen the man's picture now, a picture of Angie Weiner wired from Chicago. It was odd. Evelyn's mental picture did not fit the reality at all. She turned from the sink as Lane's feet brought a slight vibration to the kitchen floor.

"I wonder where he is now," she said casually as he entered the room.

Englander answered in the same casual tone. "Who knows, but you know, I'm glad he's here; I want it to *end.*"

Evelyn shook her head once, then chuckled. "You know, I really thought I knew what the man looked like from his voice, Lane. I always thought I was good at that, but I was wrong this time."

Evelyn took a pan to the sink and began to wash it. She was drying her hands as the man's voice came to her again. She went to the low breakfast counter and picked up the light sheet of paper just next to a small white radio. It was the picture of Angie Weiner wired by Chicago Auto Theft. Thousands of phone calls at American Opinion Research. Making up faces for voices was something most of the people who called anonymous people did. Young people sounded young, the tone of their voices tighter from vocal cords that had not worn. Old people sounded like their flesh looked—looser, with more edges and more hesitance at times, too.

How do thick people sound? They didn't always have deeper voices, Evelyn knew that. She shook her head. Her image was just wrong, she made herself say inwardly, as much for the safety the words brought her as from a belief in the words. If the picture was the man, then she was safe. For now. Evelyn Wade already knew that the incident had changed her confidence in the safe boundaries she had always believed surrounded most people. But for now, if the picture was right, she was safe. *Where was he?* It crossed her mind that the man might be close, might be driving near Myrtle, might be looking at the house now, and again the odd thought came to her that the man would hurt her house, taint it in some way. She absentmindedly took a kitchen rag and wiped the drops of water from the faucet. Evelyn did not register the presence of May Montez in the kitchen.

"Ev, do you want me to help clean up?"

May's question put Evelyn in motion. She began to move briskly around the kitchen, her hands finding the right shelf or drawer for things without looking at them directly.

"No, thank you, I've got it, and as soon as Lieutenant Eastman is finished, we'll be ready to go." She turned to May. "Did *you* eat enough, honey?"

May answered lightly, but her eyes were watching Evelyn carefully. She could not see the strain she knew must be there. "Ev, I'm turning into a horse, a horse because of your cooking." She paused. "But I didn't see you eat anything at all."

"Fruit. I ate some fruit in the kitchen and a piece of toast. May . . . when is the Buettner man arriving from Chicago?"

"At about eight. Jay's going to drop us at the Fox and then they will pick us up. Lieutenant Eastman is going with us. He's going to be our *bodyguard*, just like in the movies." May smiled and looked toward the living room. "Ev, the fire is going out; don't you want some more logs in the fireplace?" How Evelyn loved that fireplace, and how very much she enjoyed seeing a fire burning there again. Evelyn did not respond, lost in thoughts and feelings. . . .

May asked the question again. "Evelyn, the fire is going out. . . ."

"Oh, honey, I'm sorry. No, we need to let it burn down since we're leaving. A big fire might throw sparks to the living room, right over the screen onto the rug." She wiped her hands on her apron and turned to the living room. "Don't you think we should take something out to the men in the yard? Some coffee or some cookies or something?"

May shook her head no. "I already asked. We don't need to draw any attention to them. If we're lucky, maybe they'll catch him while we're gone." Evelyn cocked her head up. She had not thought of that: to come home, to come to 91 Myrtle and walk up the six steps and walk into the house without fear and have it all over. She prayed about such a possibility as they began to gather at the door, and she prayed about the tenseness that seemed to have come to the group as they gathered. Or was she imagining the tenseness? Did the others feel it, feel the safety of the house? she wondered.

Eastman began to take charge. "Okay, we'll all go in the same car, and please listen to me if I say do something. I don't think there's any way that the man would do anything at the show but let's be careful, anyway." They began to put on their coats. Eastman removed a two-way radio from his pocket and spoke. "Okay, if you don't see anything, we're heading to the show now." There was a pause and then a voice answered clearly, "Everything's quiet out here, only a few people have been by, a lot of dog-walking tonight." As he finished, another voice came through the small speaker, "Roger that, all's calm in the backyard."

They opened the door at six forty-five. Eastman started down the steps first, then May and Jay, and then Evelyn and Englander. They walked slowly, the pace set by the careful steps of Evelyn Wade, her left hand locked tightly in Englander's arm, and her cane, bright red, providing support with the right.

Rick Kanell saw the door open. He stayed crouched, the mutt in his arms, until he saw an older woman. The dog was sleeping, its neck resting on Kanell's elbow, but as he began to rise and run rapidly down the narrow alley, the dog awoke, first licking Kanell's wrist, then turning to watch the swiftly passing parade of shadows. Kanell was breathing hard when he reached the car. He opened the door with his left hand and pushed the dog to the far side of the seat. *That was the lady who started it.* The rage rose in him again as he quickly turned the car in the street, the rear fender hitting against the dumpster. He turned right on Myrtle and slowed as he saw the car turn right. Five people. He cursed. For an instant Kanell thought of ramming the car, ramming it hard, at full speed, with full fury, then shooting everyone in it. If they were with her, they were part of it. The dog looked at him, sensing the anger there, and whined. Kanell began to calm. Be patient. He could wait. He slowed again, keeping the car in sight as he turned left on Peachtree.

At the second light, less than two hundred feet from The Prince's Arms, he switched into the left lane and moved within two car lengths of the other car before dropping behind a small pickup driven by a blond boy, his arm locked around an equally blond young girl as if the girl were trying to escape. Jo. *How many times had he been close to her?* The car passed a clothing store on the left. Kanell's glance, a quick one, took in the image of fine tweed coats, tasteful things, like Anton's mountain, and then he realized that the other car was pulling over. He looked up at the tall sign in front of a Moorish-looking structure. The sign said, "Fox," and Kanell began to laugh. *Fox?* He looked at the dog, rubbing its head gently.

He could have moved around the car containing the old lady as the right front door opened, but he sat there, two car lengths behind Jay Preston's four-door sedan. His jaw slackened as Evelyn Wade exited the car, a brightly colored cane in her right hand. She was a damn cripple. The back door opened, but first he saw the old man climb from the front seat after Evelyn. And then a red-haired man with a slight belly stepped out of the backseat, quickly surveying the people and cars around them. The man looked directly at Kanell, but his eyes kept moving. The fucking guy was blind. And then May Montez stepped from the car. A nigger bitch.

Kanell began to search the street for a parking space. There were none, only moving lanes around him. As Preston's car drove away, he backed up just enough to pull around the car in front of him and stopped in front of the Fox long enough to make sure that the four people were entering the theater. *The theater.* Everything was wrong, and the goddamn lady was going to the show. He turned right at the corner, eyes quickly locking on a Parking sign. "Two dollars, please," said the man at the lot entrance.

Kanell handed him a ten and drove up the ramp without waiting for change. He parked in the first space on the left though it was marked "Handicapped," and did not lock the door or take another look at the mutt before running down the ramp, a car swerving to miss him.

Kanell slowed as he approached the kiosk, conscious of others watching him, conscious for the first time in hours of his appearance. He pulled his sweater straight and shook his head in a violent, short, left-to-right movement as he looked at the woman selling tickets, and smiled oddly. She returned his smile and handed him a ticket to *Casablanca*.

18

I T had opened in 1929, the year of the great crash, a great structure serving two noble purposes: providing a home for the Yaarab Temple of the Ancient Order of the Nobles of the Mystic Shrine and for William Fox's motion picture extravaganzas—a gigantic home of buff and cream brick; of minarets and domes and dozens of four-center arches, lancet arches, ogee arches, and horseshoe arches; with a loggia, an entrance capped and trimmed with caissons and arabesque paintings leading to the enclosed courtyard itself. And what a courtyard it was: the battlements of a vast fortress, minarets and onion domes and giant trefoil arches and burnished metal grills and screens, and above them in the dark blue sky gleamed constellations of stars and silent clusters of white clouds, the clouds slowly drifting across the sky, creating the most perfect illusion of an Arabian night.

From the left of the stage, which swept the length of the vast arch, the great Moller organ would rise: four manuals and hundreds of stops commanded forty-two ranks of pipe, some pipes as small as a finger, others thicker than a large oak branch. The courtyard of the temple would begin to resound with deep and shrill tones: the ceremony, the show had begun, and *everyone* was transported into a mystic night.

Evelyn looked up to the stars and the floating clouds. She was sitting in the second seat, just below and one row back from the balcony. James Eastman was sitting on the aisle, taking in the scene from the stars to the organ. Bob Van Camp began to play the theme from *Exodus*, and as he played a large black grand piano began to rise in the middle of the stage. It too was playing. Lane Englander, to Evelyn's right, nudged her with his arm and pointed at the piano.

"Evelyn!"

She broke into a broad smile. The piano was playing, keys jumping and down, and the pedals moving too, but no one was sitting at the piano. "A *grand* player piano!" Evelyn said with a laugh. And then the great curtain pulled back and in black and white the screen proclaimed: "Sing-Along!" Three thousand people started clapping, and when the words and notes of the first line of "Heart o' My Heart" appeared on the screen and Bob Van Camp's voice boomed, "Follow the bouncing ball!" all of the people in the Fox began to sing.

Lane turned to Evelyn, then placed his palm on her hand. "Are you okay?" he said quietly, his head leaning to her ear.

She did not look at him, but as Englander squeezed her hand tightly, Evelyn closed her eyes for a moment and spoke. "I'm fine." She turned her head to him for an instant. "I really am," she said as her eyes went back to the screen. Bob Van Camp began to play "Moonlight Bay," and as he called over the speakers, "Ladies only," May Montez leaned over Englander and looked at Evelyn.

"Ev! I've never done this before. . . ." She quickly turned again to the screen and joined Evelyn. None of the four people sitting together noticed the slightly wild-eyed man who had entered the row from the far end, stepping quickly over other legs and finally sitting three seats from May. But the man's eyes went to the screen too, after glancing to his left, his mouth ajar. Rick Kanell was breathing hard and feeling weak, he needed toot. As his eyes began to follow the bouncing ball, his head nodded up and down, but to another tune. And then he propped his elbows on the armrests, index fingers stopping his ears just enough to muffle the cacophony battering him. It was an odd mixture, the voices of people singing laid the base of the sound, and then he heard Jo's voice, "Rick, *please!*" and he saw her eyes.

He looked to the left again. Why were they smiling? He moved his fingers from his ears and began to tap them on the arms of the seat. The woman sitting to his left glanced briefly in his direction, then turned her attention again to the screen. The man looked doped, she thought, correctly. Without saying "pardon," she stood up and left the row, moving closer to the screen. Kanell moved to her seat. It was the first time May Montez noticed him, but she spotted nothing of interest in the slightly disheveled man, and she looked forward again as the screen blackened for a moment. As the opening frame of *Buck Rogers in the Twenty-first Century* came to life, a rocket trailing a patchy stream of white smoke behind it, applause filled the great courtyard again.

Evelyn leaned over to Lane, her right hand touching his.

"I wonder if they have him yet?"

Englander laughed. "Ev, we've only been gone forty-five minutes. I don't think they work that fast."

Evelyn shook her head. She lost herself in the screen again as the jerky black-and-white image of Buck Rogers's rocket crossed the screen for the last time and, without a pause, the opening frames of *Casablanca* began.

James Eastman shrugged his shoulders. He looked at the rows to his left and in front of him; nothing there looked unusual to him, only faces in shadows and backs of heads, some bald, some furry, some coiffed so high that people leaned in their seats to see around them. And then he sat forward and looked down the row. Rick Kanell slumped less than twelve feet from him. Kanell's eyes were on the screen, but his expression was so void of any reaction that Eastman wondered if the man were drugged or drunk or simply very tired. He turned back to the screen.

At eight o'clock, Evelyn leaned over Englander and tapped May Montez on the arm lightly.

"May, I've got to go to the powder room," she said in a voice a little louder than a whisper. Kanell's head shifted left quickly, his face still void of expression. He did not hear the words, but he saw the motion. At the instant May began to stand he turned right and started weaving his way past legs to the end of the aisle. He did not see Eastman stand up, wait at the end of the aisle until Evelyn and May were walking, and then follow them.

Eastman escorted the ladies up the aisle, Evelyn holding the bright cane tightly in one hand, the other through the crook of May's arm. She was smiling, but her eyes were downward, looking for safe places to step. None of them noticed the man moving up the far aisle at a faster pace. As Kanell reached the end of the aisle, he turned right and began to walk more slowly. He stood at the side of the aisle, slightly back from view, hidden by a bloodred urn taller than his head. As they walked past him, he followed their movements with the attention of a jeweler's eye close to a magnifying glass, his hand ready to strike the diamond and split it. A crippled old lady and a black whore. Kanell paid no attention to Eastman. He looked at Evelyn's hair. It was soft, curly black, but to his mind it was a witch's nest. He began to follow them as they walked to a broad, red-carpeted stairway leading down to the depths of the structure. He wanted her to fall, to tumble down the steps, and for an instant he thought of pushing her. Kanell shook his head. That would not do. Be patient. With a broad grin on his face, Rick Kanell turned and walked down the aisle again.

He was not aware when Evelyn returned to her seat. Kanell's eyes were on the screen, inward sounds blocking out other sounds, and sight too. As Sam began to play the piano, Ingrid Bergman called Humphrey Bogart "Rick." The name pulled Kanell back suddenly. "Yes?" he yelled, his eyes starting right and left. All eyes in the row turned to him. May's glance was the longest. She could not see his face completely; his left hand covered his cheek as if in thought. The guy was definitely on something.

As Sam continued to play, a smaller piano at The Prince's Arms was playing, too. Angie Weiner was sitting close to it, facing away from the piano. Benny Longfoot was sitting across from him, his head occasionally turning to check his flanks.

II

"Sometime you should see this theater, it's something."

Dean Buettner looked up at the large Fox sign as Jay stopped the car in front of the theater's loggia. Buettner's bag was in the trunk. During the twenty-minute ride from the airport, the two men had talked of little but Angie Weiner. They continued to talk about him as the Fox began to empty. An older man, his white hair and long beard unkempt, walked from the loggia with a tall black-haired woman a third his age on his arm; the woman's eyes were caked in black mascara. Two teenage girls dressed in matching slacks and matching dark green sweaters passed quickly to the rear of Preston's car and climbed into a station wagon. As the wagon pulled away, the car behind Preston's began to blow its horn. Preston looked in the mirror, but did nothing, his glance cutting back to the loggia. James Eastman was walking out in front of the others.

Evelyn's cane was doing double duty as she walked. She used the tip to push the wrapper from a candy bar toward the wall. To Evelyn's right was Englander. Directly behind them was Rick Kanell. He was gauging his pace to match theirs in the crowd. Kanell was staring at the back of Evelyn's head. As the group crossed from the loggia to the sidewalk, he ran into a large, squat woman. "Watch it!" he yelled, pushing the woman away.

At the sound of his voice, Evelyn stopped moving; the sudden stop caused her to sway slightly. *Now who are you?* As the words came back to her, the skin of her arms and legs began to tingle, a hot sensation. The palm of Evelyn's left hand had been resting lightly in the crook of Lane Englander's arm, but as the voice seemed to rush to the center of her, locking firmly to her memory of the man's voice, drawing a knot in her chest, Evelyn tightened her fingers around

Englander's arm, a quick, nearly crushing reflex. She turned her head back, looking for the voice and at the same time not wanting to see it. She saw only the anonymous faces of a crowd, her eyes for a moment following the movements of Rick Kanell as he headed quickly down the crowded sidewalk, his back to her, his hands at times going to the side as if to push away.

Englander looked at her. Evelyn's face brought a chill to him also. "Evelyn?"

She did not respond at first, her mind turning the images of the man, *her* picture of the man, and then the boy's voice came back to her—"No!" For the first time that night Evelyn felt a very tight, nearly suffocating physical presence of fear. She looked quickly to Englander.

"He's here."

"*What?*"

He glanced around them, then led Evelyn quickly to the car, his head motioning to May as she stood at the front door. May hurried to them, her face mirroring the anxiety on Lane Englander's face.

"What's wrong?" Her hand went anxiously to Evelyn's shoulder.

"Honey, *the* man. He was right behind me." Evelyn looked completely calm, the expression of a person who has felt something too deeply to reveal the feeling in expression or word. May pulled Evelyn to the car, the right rear door. James Eastman turned to face the crowd. He had not heard Evelyn's words, but the space around them was filled with the emotions of her words.

Evelyn settled in the seat, and for a moment she did not see Dean Buettner or Jay Preston. Immediately the car was filled, six people, six very quiet people. May spoke. She, too, had not acknowledged Buettner.

"He was behind us."

"How do you know? Did you see him? What did he look like?" Buettner was speaking rapidly. His hand went to the door, a fast motion. *Weiner.* He wanted the man. Preston reached out and grabbed his arm to stop him as Evelyn spoke.

"His voice, he yelled something. I don't know what." Evelyn

shifted her body slightly. "That voice is as real to me as my own body."

"Did you see him? Did you *see* him?" Buettner asked again.

Evelyn shook her head. "Too many people, I couldn't find the man that went with the voice. But he was there."

Preston realized that Dean Buettner was asking questions of people he had never met. "My God . . . people, this is Dean Buettner." The group nodded and spoke, their minds still on the voice. And then Jay noticed the backseat. Four people, none of them small, were crammed together in a space barely large enough for three. The sounds of cars protesting continued, but Preston held the space just long enough for Eastman to come to the front.

Jay turned right at the corner of the Fox, passing the parking lot on the left where a dark blue Buick with a slender man and a dog inside was moving onto the street. The Buick pulled out behind their car, slowed but followed them, dropping back nearly a block as both cars began to cut across town. Preston glanced in the mirror often, but after he turned off Sixth, he did not notice the lights of the Buick again.

They sat in the car for a moment before entering the house. Eastman wanted to talk with both of the detectives standing watch before the first door was opened. At nine thirty or thereabouts, the six people in Jay Preston's car began their walk up the six steps. Evelyn was surrounded as they climbed, and as she opened the door their eyes were not on her but were looking for the fat man, Angie Weiner.

III

The mutt rested at Kanell's side as if he belonged there. A year old, the dog was short and very thick. He didn't look like a dog who had suffered much from hunger. Large brown patches, one encasing his right front leg, gave him a very pleasant, nonthreatening look. Kanell put his right hand on the mutt again as he turned the car left on Peachtree. The dog did not seem hungry, but Kanell pulled the car into the Krystal anyway. He was not hungry himself, except for some toot, but he had decided that the dog needed to eat. He bought a hamburger and fed it to the dog there in the parking lot.

Kanell had not followed Jay Preston's car to Myrtle. He did not know the streets of Atlanta, but he did know the way to Evelyn's house. After feeding the mutt, he drove north on Peachtree. He drove past Myrtle after turning right on Tenth, then turned on Argonne and began to explore the area. In fifteen minutes he had driven all of the short blocks between Penn and Myrtle, the car exploring the farther blocks first, then those closer to 91, circling as a shark circles, coming closer in each pass. He then drove past Evelyn's house, looking left just enough to take in the sedan that had driven the lady away earlier. Rick Kanell did not know if he would kill the people around her or not. His mind was not tracking in patterns that lent themselves to complex thought. But he did not think he would kill the old lady in the house. Or near it. No tracks. Kanell, eyes now dilated and red and tired—as tired as the rest of him— still believed that he would kill the lady and then go away to start again, the thought of a man tumbling from a cliff who believes that maybe the ground will indeed be soft enough to save him. But he would have killed Evelyn even without that hope; all of his hate and rage now centered on her as he drove past 91, then turned left at Tenth, then right onto Piedmont, past the Elks' lodge, past the first entrance to Piedmont Park. Rick Kanell still believed that he would survive. If he could break the trail. If one more killing—or two or three if necessary—would break the trail.

He turned the car around just across from a shopping mall and drove south on Piedmont again. The dog was sleeping now. Kanell turned left at the crest of the hill. The narrow winding street cut to the left just above a steep bank of steps leading down to the main road of Piedmont Park, blocked to all traffic by a large wooden barricade. It then veered to the left by the Atlanta Botanical Gardens, and cut through a hundred acres of tall trees sloping up and down from the road.

Kanell slowed the car as he reached the dark wooded area, then stopped just across from a small dirt road, a service road that disappeared into the depths of the wooded area. *Cocaine.* He sat in the car until the powder had begun to lift him again, then walked down the rutted dirt road, eyes cutting to both sides, then returned to the car. It felt right. He would kill her there. And then he would put her body in the trunk and then he would begin to drive. To another state. He would leave her body where it would not be found, and then he would begin again. Begin again. He could do it.

Kanell drove from the park and made his way back to Tenth. He drove past Myrtle and at about nine fifty, parked the dark blue Buick a block and a half from 91 Myrtle. He put the rope around the dog's neck again, waking him, and began to roam the street, walking slowly down Myrtle, being careful not to look too obviously at 91. He walked quietly up the alley and resumed his earlier observation post.

As Kanell watched, his eyes blinking rapidly again, Angie Weiner was taking his last bite of dessert at The Prince's Arms. Weiner had eaten everything on his plate, including the pieces of parsley garnishing what was left of a thick cut of lamb. He had drunk only iced tea. Weiner looked at his watch again. His mind was on bed first; and then the house at 91 Myrtle and a rendezvous with Rick Kanell.

Weiner looked at Benny Longfoot. The drifter was slightly drunk and slightly high from cocaine, a knife held in his left hand as one would hold the yoke in an airplane. Slightly high and slightly drunk. How many times had he had his way with young studs in that wonderful condition?

Weiner did not drive directly to the hotel, though it was nearly within eyesight. Just five minutes, he thought; five more minutes, a quick detour by the house of the lady named Evelyn, and he would be in bed. Angie Weiner had to check out the house first. He had waited too long to have anything go wrong with his plan for Rick Kanell. Weiner was a very responsible man when it came to pain.

IV

The fire was going again, a roaring fire in a shallow fireplace, throwing enough heat into the living room for most of the men in the room to remove their sweaters or coats. They could not open a window. Eastman was on the phone talking to a captain in Atlanta's Homicide Division. The captain had offered to send a black-and-white down Myrtle frequently during the night. The offer had been declined. The plan was to catch the fly with honey—Evelyn.

Lane Englander was fiddling with the fire, poking it occasionally. May Montez was reading a book called *America*. Or at least her eyes were scanning the pictures and occasionally picking up words. The incident at the Fox had pulled something loose inside of May, the part of us that says that despite everything, everything is still going to be okay. May did not know if she believed that anymore. A madman was out there, a madman had been in voice's reach of Evelyn. How did the man know they were at the Fox? He must have followed them. Where was he now? A sane man wouldn't be close now, May thought. A sane man would know that too many people were sheltering his prey. But then she thought the man could not be sane. He had killed a boy; he had killed another Evelyn too. He could not be sane.

She looked up from the book. Three people were now outside watching the house, including James Eastman; all of the men had guns. Dean Buettner probably had a gun, too, she thought, though no bulge on his body advertised a weapon. The windows were nailed shut and the doors were locked. She had checked the back door again herself to make sure. They *had* to be safe. But then May remembered the stories of dead men who had been much more protected than this on the day of their death, powerful men, not old ladies. And then she thought of the stories of madmen who killed openly, for no reason, with no concern for their own safety. There was no safe place.

In the kitchen, Evelyn was trying to occupy her mind by keeping her hands busy. To keep the voice at bay. She first placed an entire bag of butter cookies on a platter. She toyed with the cookies, arranging them, then rearranging them, then sliding the dark green napkin under them to the left and then a bit upward. But she was distracted again before she could take the platter to the living room. Her hand went unconsciously to a dish towel; she began to rub the counter with it, removing imagined spots. She walked back to the sink and began to dry the faucet and then the sink itself, trying to avoid the thought of the darkness outside the window.

"Mrs. Wade, can I help you?"

Evelyn started, her upper body pulling up quickly. Dean Buettner was standing just behind her as she turned, slightly abashed that he had startled her. Evelyn smiled.

"No, no, I was just getting us some snacks. You can take that platter in for me, if you will."

Buettner walked one step to the left in the narrow kitchen and picked up the platter. "Mrs. Wade, I really do like your house, and I like all of the pictures too. You and your husband must have traveled a lot." Buettner had not really had a conversation with Evelyn Wade, but he wanted to. He did not know many old people and he did not know if they would be interesting or boring, but he wanted to know Evelyn Wade.

She shook her head as they stood there. "Yes, we traveled, at times for a month. I was the navigator." Evelyn paused and laughed. "Grady would get lost and, you know, he wouldn't want to tell me; but I could see it on the map. I wouldn't say a word, though." Evelyn began to walk to the living room, Buettner at her side with the platter. A fresh pot of coffee was already on the table, and as Buettner placed the platter down, she continued.

"Mr. Buettner, are you married?"

"Dean, please call me Dean," he said lightly, "and no, no one will have me."

Evelyn laughed again. "That's what my son always says. Do you have one special friend?"

"No, ma'am." He motioned to a dining room chair and the two sat down. He was leaning forward when Evelyn began to speak of the incident.

"I wonder where the man is now," she said, looking away from Buettner as she spoke.

He shrugged slightly. "We all wish we knew that; but I *do* know that you're okay right now, and that's what matters." He looked toward Jay Preston. "Jay and I are going out in a few minutes, too. I don't really think Weiner's going to come around here tonight; he's too smart for that. But if he does, we'll be ready for him."

Evelyn was quiet for a moment, trying to reconcile *her* image built from the man's voice with the grainy picture of Angie Weiner. "Dean . . . please don't think this is an old lady talking—though it is—but how do you know the man in the picture is the man who . . . who killed those people?"

Buettner's eyes brightened at her question, the look of a man who knows the right answer. "It *has* to be him, the boy worked for him, we know that; and we know he was in Dallas when the lady was killed there . . . and he's *here*."

He had to be right, she thought. But something didn't fit. "I just didn't think he would look like that."

Buettner raised his hand. "I've got some other pictures of him, if you want to see them; they're in Jay's car." Evelyn did not want to see them. She had felt violated when she looked at the picture wired by Dean Buettner to Atlanta. The shots were mug shots taken when Angie Weiner was arrested for pulling teeth with a pair of pliers. The angles of the shots themselves—profile, full front—reminded her that the man committed crimes, that he had been in jail. Evelyn did not want to see them. But she did want to settle in her mind that the voice could fit the man.

"Let's look at them." She pushed up as he started toward the door. Evelyn walked to the fire, then backed away slightly as its heat came to her.

"If that won't warm you, nothing will, Ev," Englander said as he got up from his chair and walked to her, only three steps.

Evelyn nodded, her eyes meeting his. "Mr. Buettner's getting some more pictures of the man, Lane. He's convinced the pictures are of the right man. He doesn't look right to me, though. I'm not sure why, but he doesn't."

As she spoke, Buettner came in the front door. "It's a beautiful night out there," he said as he pulled up a straight chair and opened his case, removing six pictures from a yellow envelope. The pictures were of Rick Kanell and Angie Weiner.

"Boy, I left three inches of snow and twenty-nine degrees, so you don't know how nice it is to be able to walk without a heavy coat."

May looked up from her chair. The man on the phone—how long ago had that been? Twelve hours. The words of the man who said, "This is Dean Buettner," came to her again. A shudder ran through her body. She'd talked to the killer, told him how to reach Evelyn. May walked to Dean Buettner and kneeled down beside him to look at the pictures. She had no strong image of the man. She looked at the man to Angie Weiner's left. Before she could ask the question Evelyn spoke.

"Who is the other man?"

"As far as we can tell, a legitimate businessman. . . . Our vice squad took the pictures last week, so we haven't completely checked him out; but he appears to be okay."

"What is he doing in this picture?" May asked, bothered by something about the unknown man.

"We don't know that for sure. He owns a tool company that sells tools to body shops and the like. He may be simply trying to sell some tools."

Evelyn heard all of the conversation floating around her, but her mind was on the pictures.

"Where is he from?" Her finger pointed to Weiner.

"We don't know. Weiner has never really been in jail long enough for us to find out much about him."

"What does he sound like? Does he have an accent?"

"A northern accent, a *guttural* sound; he doesn't have a particularly deep voice. I've only heard him once, a recording made by a room mike, and the quality wasn't that good." Buettner paused. "Mrs. Wade, I brought it because of your last message when you said you could identify his voice. Would you like to hear it?"

Before Evelyn could respond, the radio in Jay Preston's hand came to life, James Eastman from his position outside.

"There's a very slow-moving car, stopping to check street numbers, coming toward the house now; a kid with a very fat man driving."

A kid. A kid like Kowakoski. Buettner thought of Lennie, and then he thought of Bobby Medlock. He bolted to the back door, grabbing the radio from Preston as he passed.

"Go to that side!" he yelled to the detective now standing by a large oak tree close to the back porch. Buettner cut to the right, dropping to his knees by another detective just to the left of the house. The man was kneeling, gun in hand. They could see the lights of the car from the right.

"Everybody hold your positions," Buettner said quietly as the car came into view. It slowed again just before reaching the house. At first the light hitting the driver's window reflected back, blocking the view of the man. But for an instant, as the car began to pass, the light cut through the glass. The man was looking at 91.

Buettner sucked in a breath and held it when he saw the face. *Weiner.*

"*It's him, let's go!*"

Angie Weiner and Benny Longfoot saw the man at the same time. Dressed in street clothes, he was running toward the front of their car, gun drawn. Longfoot jerked around to look out the back. Two men were sprinting toward the car, one held a gun. *What was the fat queer pulling?* At that moment, Weiner gunned the car. Panicked, trapped, Longfoot whipped out his switchblade and blindly stabbed as hard as he could at the fat man, striking for freedom. Weiner's hand crashed down to block him.

Angie did not feel the knife in his flesh at first, but as his hand hit the drifter's, it pushed the blade downward; the pain, only a sting at first, came to him, and then the full charge of the pain hit him. He screamed, his hand left the steering wheel, crossing his stomach, grabbing the knife still held firmly in the drifter's grasp. The car veered across the street, jumped the curb just in front of 99 Myrtle and rammed the base of an oak tree.

As the car began to crumple and then stopped abruptly, bouncing back slightly, Weiner's body began to move. To him, it moved very slowly; the short distance over the steering wheel became a long distance as his body went up, it seemed very fast, then forward, he could think as he went forward, and as his head crammed against the windshield, he could see the small shards of glass falling on the dash. There was no sound and no pain. He did not hear Benny Longfoot yell. He did not sense him trying to leave the car. Angie's eyes were open, his body leaning forward, head dangling just over the steering wheel. But his stomach began to roil, and as his head hung there, the evening's meal and liquid began to gush from his mouth, choking him. He could not stop it.

Buettner reached the car first. Benny Longfoot was looking at Weiner. His head went to the door as Buettner forced it open.

"Don't hurt me, please don't hurt me, I don't know the guy!" he pleaded as Buettner pulled him out of the car and shoved him to the side. James Eastman held him. Buettner crawled in the car and looked at Angie Weiner. His body was convulsing, chin dripping the regurgitations of a protesting stomach, rolls of fat hanging above his shirt collar. Blood was dripping from Weiner's mouth, too, and from his side.

"Somebody get to the house and call an ambulance *right now.*" Eastman took control. As he spoke, the lights were beginning to come on along Myrtle and the curious were beginning to gather, some running fast to the car then stopping dead still, some walking slowly. Two men who lived across the street were the first to arrive. They had walked quickly from their porch and stood back far enough not to intrude but close enough to see the man's head through the windshield.

"Should we move him?" one of them called in the direction of Buettner.

Buettner shook his head. "I think his neck's broken." Buettner leaned over to Weiner and with his fingers cleared the mucus and partially digested food from his lips, gagging as he touched them.

Weiner did not acknowledge him, but a gurgling sound came inter-
mittently from his mouth, causing drops of mucus to bubble.

"Is he dead?" another voice asked as Buettner looked down
Myrtle.

"Is he dead?" the voice repeated quietly.

"I don't know," Buettner said as he turned toward Eastman.

The questioner took one more look at Weiner's head through the
windshield, then walked away, stopping just long enough to pick up
his dog, a brown spotted one. He was whistling as he walked away.
When his steps had taken him far enough the whistle turned to
laughter, and Rick Kanell, a broad smile on his face, glanced back to
the house at 91 again. He walked on, heading to the narrow alley.

The ambulance came in nine minutes. Weiner's neck was broken.
The lashing forward and back had broken it and severed the spinal
cord. The paramedics administered oxygen to him before trying to
remove his body. A police car had arrived just before the ambulance, drawing more curious eyes, but the laughing man with the
brown spotted dog was not to be seen. His eyes were on the house at
91 Myrtle.

A wrecker arrived just as the two paramedics began to move
Weiner slightly, finally pulling his body up until it touched a back-
brace board and then strapping him to it. But they could not move
him. Two hundred ninety pounds is a hard weight to move at any
time, even with the cooperation of the body, but it is a nearly
impossible weight to move carefully without the help of the victim.

They finally rolled him slowly on his back, one of the men
pulling his legs straight from the other side of the car. At ten forty
they placed him in the ambulance and drove away. From his lookout
near the dilapidated garage, Rick Kanell watched the activity on
Myrtle Street dwindle down.

19

I

EVELYN was standing by the living room window. Lane Englander stood beside her, his hand resting lightly on her shoulder. Evelyn's eyes went to his and then back to the glass of sherry she held tightly in both hands. Her hands were trembling a bit; but she felt the tremor inside, too. The boundaries were out of kilter. She started to speak, but as she formed the first word it left her and she began to heave dry tears, closing her eyes tightly and stiffening her body to stop the shaking. Both of them were quiet for a moment.

"Well, it's certainly not like in the movies," she said with a false laugh. "I don't think I'll ever feel the same again, Lane." She looked around the room. The three remaining people in the house, Jay Preston, May, and Dean Buettner, were talking by the fireplace. Only red coals provided heat now.

Englander squeezed her shoulder slightly, then dropped his hand to the side. "It's okay, it's okay to feel like that." His head was very close to hers, as if they were whispering secrets. "Something would be wrong with you if you felt any other way. But it's all right. I'm not far away at all." She stifled the urge to cry again, and she wanted to hug him at that moment but she could not.

"What are they going to do with the boy who was with him? Are they going to put him in jail? I hope not, if he wasn't involved." Englander guided them toward the living room, holding her hand as they continued to talk.

"Ev!" May said as the two approached the fireplace. "Are you two okay?" May walked to her and touched her arm. "We're all still feeling a little shaky; it's hard to believe that it's over." Evelyn went to the chair and dropped into it. She had not propped with her arms to lessen the impact of the fall, and as her bottom hit the chair she winced, pain running through the right leg.

"I want to thank you all," she said as she looked at Buettner, "and I want to thank you especially, Mr. Buettner . . . I mean Dean. I really didn't think that picture was the man at all." Buettner nodded as Evelyn continued, "And I don't really think I believed all of this was real until now." Evelyn began to choke up. The room was quiet, all there knowing that she needed to talk. "I don't hate him." Did she hate him? Probably she did. Evelyn looked around the room, collecting the safe images there. "I love this house. And I love all of you, too, for caring, and for not letting me be alone. And for *believing me.*"

"Ev, we were talking about that, about you being alone. I want you to let me stay here tonight, and I'll stay here as long as you need me to." Evelyn loved May Montez, she loved her like a daughter. But Evelyn did not want her to stay for the night. Or at least she did not think she did. She wanted to be alone, she needed to be alone in that house. But before she could answer, Englander spoke.

"Evelyn, I can stay here. We're old enough to stay in the same house without chaperons, you know." He smiled as he spoke.

"No—thank you, but I'm going to try to be alone tonight." She looked from May to Englander. "Lane, I promise I'll call you if I become uncomfortable, but you see, I have to face this house alone *sometime*. I've done that once before. And I've got to try to do it now." She forced a smile. "And Lord knows I'll be safe tonight."

May started to protest, but Jay Preston's hand, reaching over and squeezing hers lightly, stilled those words. "Well, okay; but I want you to promise me that you will call me the second you wake up in the morning."

Evelyn looked at her watch. It was eleven twenty. All of her joints felt sore. When she touched them, they felt swollen. She had not been using a cane during the past half hour, but as the people who had protected her began to gather coats and ties, and as May took the last used coffee cup from the living room, she walked stiffly to the corner of the room and picked up the solid wooden cane there, a cane too heavy for walking long distances, better as a pickup croquet mallet. But it had been a gift from her son, and right now Evelyn Wade needed to touch something with very strong memories attached to it.

At eleven thirty, the five of them were standing at the front door. The good-nights to Evelyn seemed to take a long time. Yes, they would all eat breakfast together in the morning; yes, May could gather her things in the morning; no, Evelyn was very sure she did not want to have a drink with the young people.

Lane was standing by her as Buettner, May, and Jay walked down the steps together, taking some of the fullness of the house with them as they left. As she shut the door, Evelyn turned to him and instantly began to cry, holding him. She did not fight the tears and for a full minute they stood there together. As Evelyn calmed, Lane looked at her.

"Evelyn?"

"Lane, I'm sorry. I don't really know how to handle this right now." She paused. "You know, I like buying groceries with you. . . ." Her body stumbled a bit. "No, that's not what I mean. I'm glad I know you. I'm glad you are my friend. Do you understand?"

His nod, a short one accompanied by a smile, was a more appropriate answer than words. "Do you want me to stay awhile? Do you want some wine? Or that good twelve-year-old whiskey?"

"No. Thank you, but I need to try to be alone in this house." She kissed him on the cheek, holding him tightly for a moment, and then she watched him walk down the six steps before closing the door.

Englander walked the short distance to his home without noticing the man sitting in a dark blue Buick less than a block from Evelyn's, too far away. Jay Preston and May Montez had not seen him either. Perhaps they noticed the driver's door of the car open as they drove past and saw the face of the man briefly. But the face did not register. For Preston and Montez, there were no more demons to haunt the night.

Dean Buettner saw the face in profile for an instant, and turned his head as they drove by, his eyes momentarily locking with the man's. The man looked odd. And why did he sit back in the car and close the door when their car approached? Myrtle was a broad street, no reason there. They drove on.

Evelyn was sitting in her chair as Kanell opened the door to the Buick and began to cut through backyards, stealing to 91 Myrtle. In her lap was a book of poems entitled *The Pursuit of God*, by A. J. Tozer. She looked to the clock. It still said 6:25. She picked up the book and began to read the first lines as Kanell stepped close to the window: "Then shall we know, if we follow on to know the Lord: His going forth is prepared like the morning." Kanell watched her for a moment, his face expressionless. But the rage returned. She was the root of all his problems; the crippled old lady was a monster. Kanell put his right hand in his jacket. One of the matching pistols was there, and he fought the manic urge to shoot her right then.

He stepped quietly past the window to the back of the house. The telephone line reached the house across the back of the lot, the line hanging in an arc not more than ten feet from the ground. He started to cut it, *the goddamn telephone started it*, but he did not. Cover your tracks. Rick Kanell wanted the old lady simply to disappear. There would be no crime if she simply disappeared. It did not matter what the police thought. No body, no crime.

Light from the window touched the dust on the windowsill. It touched the thumb latch that held the window shut, too. Kanell pushed up on the window, but it did not give at all. He went to the door on his right. It was in "the new wing," as Evelyn used to call it with a smile when the small porch had been enclosed as a summer room. The door had two keyholes. Kanell first took a pair of gloves from his left pocket. Made of very thin latex, the disposable gloves had been taken from the kitchen at Low Notch. He then removed a short knife, about three inches in length when closed. He slid the blade upward beside each keyhole; the blade touched metal once, the top lock. He put the tip of the knife blade against the doorjamb side of the lock, slowly forcing the knife handle to the right. Kanell repeated the action three times, his left hand pulling the door outward slightly, creating pressure on the cylinder. On the fourth try, the tip of the knife slipped to the right of the bolt. The door was open.

Evelyn felt his movements an instant before she saw him, a very light vibration of the floor. She turned to face him, her hands pulling up to her chest, the left one folding over the right. She did not need to hear his voice to know who he was. The face. The man in the pictures of Angie Weiner. She did not need to hear his voice, but as Rick Kanell said, "Hello, Evelyn," the memory of his voice came to her, emptying her of all hope and filling the void with a pulsing fear; she could hear and feel blood pumping hard in her body. *There had been a mistake. Something was terribly wrong.* Evelyn did not fear death, her life had been built on the goodness of things to follow it, but she did fear dying. The fear nearly had an odor to it, a sound to it; all the times Evelyn had felt fear in the past seemed concentrated, distilled into the present moment. A brief thanks that Lane was not in the house passed through her before she summoned her deepest prayer, *God help me.* Strength comes from many things. With her prayer, Evelyn Wade's thoughts began to shift. She would not die easily. She would fight him, with her mind first.

"You don't look like your voice," she lied. "When I'm calling, I wonder what people look like. You don't look like yours. What did the boy look like?" For an instant she could not control her body. She shook, as if a freezing wind had hit her. Why had she worked that night? Why had that number appeared on the screen? Her thoughts began to churn wildly. Witnesses don't live if they see the killer's face. . . . Killers don't look evil. . . . Keep talking, killers can't act if you keep talking. . . .

"Why did you kill the lady in Dallas?" She looked away from him. "I don't understand. Why are you doing this?" She looked to the fireplace. The single-shot twenty-gauge was leaning against the wall. She looked back to Kanell as he raised his right hand and closed his eyes for a second, both actions seeming to push away thoughts. His red eyes squinted at the old clock on the rock mantelpiece, a perplexed look on his face. He looked at his watch.

"What time is it?"

For the first time Evelyn really looked at the man standing less than three feet from her. His eyes were bloodred. He, too, had a tremble in his hands, and the movements of his arms were erratic. *He was on drugs.* "It's six twenty-five," she said. Kanell did not dispute her, his eyes casting about the room again quickly. He moved toward the chair, stopping inches from Evelyn. She did not look up at him.

"You are going to leave with me."

Evelyn shook her head. "I-am-not-leaving-this-house. I have lived here and, if I have to, I will die here."

Kanell put his hand on Evelyn's neck, fingers slowly tightening, grasping soft flesh. Evelyn's eyes closed. Her fists were tightly clenched and tiny droplets of moisture began to form on her upper lip.

In a calm, almost sad voice Kanell continued. "I am going to make a trade with you." She opened her eyes. "You are an old person. You don't have anyone who will miss you. What are you going to do for anyone if you live?" He loosened his grip, his hand rubbing her neck gently before withdrawing it. He continued. "But there's a kid, a child. She's about this tall"—he held his palm just at his hip—"about five years old, she says." He kneeled down to look directly in Evelyn's eyes. She shuddered. His eyes were the eyes of a madman, but she stared at him without blinking.

"About an hour ago I put the little girl in the ground, about three feet deep, in a box." He smiled. "It looks like a coffin. The box has a hole in the top. I put a piece of drainpipe in the hole so she can breathe. And I'm going to leave her there, Evelyn, you know I will." Kanell looked at the old clock again. What time was it? He was having trouble thinking now. The small brown bottle in his pocket was empty and his body was beginning to protest. He felt very weak. Kanell closed his eyes and tried to focus. He had to continue, he had to get the old lady away from the house quietly.

"I'll leave her there," he said again, "but if you go with me now, I'll let you see me dig her up." He smiled again. "She's worth a lot more than you are, Evelyn, don't you think?"

A child. Evelyn looked at the pictures of children on her wall. And then her thoughts went back to the old trunk that used to sit in the attic when she was a child. It was an adventure to go up there, a musty space, dark and filled with all of the private terrors a child's mind invents. Evelyn hid in that trunk once.

The trunk was just large enough to hold a child, if the child bent down. There were no latches to hold the top shut, but Evelyn could still feel the black tomblike presence of that small space when the top had banged shut. She had pushed against it instantly, and for a second it had resisted. That memory was the single most vivid moment of terror she could remember from her childhood. She looked to Kanell.

"How do I know you will let the child go?" Evelyn was not at all sure there was a child. She would not take that chance, however. She repeated the question.

"I don't hurt children, Weiner hurts children."

She did not speak, but began to push up from the chair. "Where are we going?"

Kanell took her arm. She pushed him away.

"I am going to walk alone," she said harshly as she picked up her cane and began to walk toward the door. Evelyn Wade opened it at eleven fifty, the determination on her face falling away at the sight of Lane Englander as he walked up the six steps of 91 Myrtle.

II

"So, Dean, are you going to stay in the city long enough for May and me to show you the sights?" Jay asked. He, Dean, and May were on their way from Evelyn's.

Buettner turned quickly to Jay, as if he were going to answer. But his face betrayed some other, more urgent thought than a gathering of friends.

"Jay, stop the car. I need to get in the trunk."

"Can't it wait? We'll be at the Plaza in a few minutes."

"Jay! Stop the car!"

Jay pulled over. Buettner took the key out the instant the car was in park, his right hand on the door handle. He rushed to the trunk, returning with the yellow envelope. Dean Buettner had never paid particular attention to the man with Angie Weiner. He had noticed the man's clothes and watch more than he had noticed the face. But as he looked at the face, the profile, he began to sweat. It was the face of the man who had reentered the car less than a block from Evelyn's. *Oh God.* He turned to Preston, his face twisted.

"We got the wrong man. Oh God, the guy was sitting in a car at Evelyn's when we drove away!"

May grabbed the picture. A handsome and neat man, she thought, and then she remembered the man at the Fox. May's voice broke as she spoke, "*Christ,* that man was sitting by us at the show!"

"What's Evelyn's number?" Preston looked at May.

What was the number? She stuttered. "F-four two seven, one six five seven."

Buettner and Preston jumped from the car at the same time. They ran toward a group of pay phones at a MARTA bus shelter.

"Call the police!" Buettner yelled. "Tell them to get Eastman and to get a car there *now.*" He dropped a coin in and began to push buttons, but his fingers would not work. Shit. He dialed again, this time standing completely still as the phone began to ring. He let the phone ring ten times. But at the end of the tenth ring, he slammed the receiver down and turned to Jay as Preston, too, slammed down his receiver.

"She's not there." They ran back to the car, Preston speaking as they ran. "They're sending a black-and-white, calling Eastman too." Neither of them spoke to May as Preston whipped the car in a U-turn, but their silence confirmed all that May could fear. Preston ran the first red light. He was now going sixty miles an hour north on Peachtree, high beams flashing up and down and the horn sending out insistent warning.

The car turned onto Myrtle four minutes later. A police car, its blue light sending faint shadow patterns through trees and across several homes, was parked in front of 91. The policeman, his right hand touching his holster, stood at the front door. He turned and walked back down the stairs at the sight of Preston and Buettner's hurried leaps in his direction. As they reached the officer, May began to run to Lane Englander's house. Maybe Evelyn was there. A second black-and-white pulled to the left of the first, blue lights flashing. For the second time that night neighbors began to gather.

Buettner whipped his identification out for the officer. "I'm Dean Buettner, Chicago Auto Theft." He motioned to Preston. "This is Jay Preston, with the state. Your CID people were here trying to apprehend a killer"—Buettner paused and silently cursed himself—"but we got the wrong goddamn man. We saw the killer right over there, sitting in a dark car, as we drove away, but we didn't recognize him." He looked at Evelyn's house. "He was going to kill the lady who lives here, she was a witness, and now she doesn't answer her phone, so for God's sake, let's get in that house!"

As they moved up the steps, a man ran down the street and yelled, "Hey! Wait a minute!" Buettner turned to him.

"Are you looking for Evelyn?" Buettner nodded quickly.

"We're her neighbors," a young man said as an older man leading a large dog joined him. "She left with Lane Englander. And another man."

He cursed again. Evelyn had tried to tell him Angie was the wrong man.

"Did they drive away in a dark car?"

"Yes, a two-door. We were watching everything that was going on tonight, the wreck and all, and we thought it was kind of funny when she left so late."

"Which way did the car go?"

The neighbor pointed toward Tenth. "He turned the car around in the road. Do you want the tag number?"

Buettner grabbed the man's arm, squeezing tighter than he meant to.

"Yes!"

"Hell, I don't remember it all, but it was a Georgia tag, RMR nine something, a two-door Buick. And it had a funny bumper sticker on it. 'Follow me to Jesus.' "

"She's not at Lane's, and Lane's not there either!" May said as she ran to Buettner's side, eyes on Preston.

As they talked, the uniformed man walked slowly to the driver's side of the second black-and-white and looked at the officer. "I don't really know what's happening here, but I think you better put out a ninety-eight on a dark blue Buick, the tag starts with RMR nine, and you better tell them the guy is armed and dangerous." The man smiled. "Tell 'em it's got a bumper sticker that says 'Follow me to Jesus,' too."

"You know, we just got a call to help these people, a CID detective is involved in this," the other officer said. The man nodded, raising his brow slightly, and walked back to Buettner. At least eight people were now gathered in front of 91.

"We have an all-points out on the car now," the officer said. "Do you still want to get into the house?"

Get into the house? Get into the house? What the hell was the man talking about? Buettner ignored the man's words and turned to Preston.

"Jay, open the trunk." Buettner pulled Preston from the crowd. He removed a gun from his bag. Dean Buettner did not know where he was going or how he planned to find the car, but he wasn't going to stand there like a damn zombie. He turned back to the officer.

"What crystal are you guys monitoring?" The officer answered him.

"Jay, can you get that on your hand-held unit?"

Preston shook his head no rapidly. "Dean, I gave the damn thing back to Eastman; it belongs to them." *Shit.*

Buettner turned back to the officer.

"*Please.* Don't you guys have a hand-held?"

The officer looked at Buettner for a moment and then removed it from his holster. "You lose that damn thing and I'm up shit's creek, you know that?"

Buettner nodded at the officer as he turned to Preston. "Let's get the hell out of here!"

"I'm going," May insisted as she grabbed Buettner's arm. "I'm going, maybe I can think of where they might be." She began to choke up. "*Damn it, I'm going.*"

Buettner did not argue.

III

The length of things now became important, time and distance, and the size of things, too. From the house at 91 Myrtle to the small paved road that entered Piedmont Park at the crest of Piedmont Avenue—just by the tennis courts of the Piedmont Driving Club—was a distance of only 1.3 miles. The length of the winding road itself was barely a mile, and the length of the service road that cut to the right down a steep hill was less than a thousand feet. Distances so close as to invite walking on pleasant nights. The distance from 91 Myrtle to Tenth Street and then to the corner of Piedmont was less than half a mile. At night, a journey of less than ninety seconds by car. The dark blue Buick traveled it in about two minutes, stopped at the light, and then turned right on Piedmont. It was after this turn that a man driving a Burns Security Service car, also traveling north on Piedmont, noticed the sticker on the back bumper of the Buick: "Follow me to Jesus." But the sticker had no significance to him except curiosity. He passed the Buick as it slowed and turned onto the small paved road entering the park.

Evelyn was sitting in the front seat of the Buick, as was Lane Englander. One of her hands was resting on top of his and the other held her cane. The Buick passed the deep steps leading down to the winding main road. The mutt whined in the backseat, a plaintive sound that reminded Evelyn of the madman's words: "I put the little girl in the ground." She shuddered. Evelyn had decided not to let death come easily, not without a fight—if the child were safe. The car passed the botanical gardens on the left as she spoke.

"You know, I don't hate you. I don't understand how people can hurt other people, but I believe in God, and believe that you must know this is wrong. What will it accomplish for you to kill us or the child? Do you do this for a living?"

Kanell laughed softly, his eyes blinking rapidly again. The blinking stopped as they entered the area of tall trees a half mile from the service road, which dropped deeply to the right. A new moon brought a faint light to the tree tops but did not broadcast itself into the depths of the wooded area.

Lane was looking at Evelyn. This man was going to kill them. Englander, too, was thinking of the fight. Evelyn started to speak, but Kanell stopped her, his hand thrown up in a traffic cop's gesture.

"None of it would have happened, you know, without the phone, and the venison, and the radio." He gave a shrill laugh. "You see, I was *close to her*, and I love—God, how I love the mountain. I used to be poor, you know." The car came to a stop and then turned right on the steep service road. It seemed to drop off into a dark void, the lights of the car highlighting deep ruts. Kanell continued. "The boy was Angie's pet, like I had a dog once; I had to kill it, and I don't know why the boy was there, that's when you heard me, and then Jo told me about the venison in red wine and mushrooms and I used Anton's radio and I listened and *damn it* she was talking to Angie, that fat queer."

He laughed again as the car came to a stop five hundred feet down the steep road, the left wheels in a deep rut, tilting the car slightly.

Limbs of trees hung over the car, one branch touching Kanell's door, but the trees themselves seemed to have disappeared in the darkness. The mutt stood up on the backseat, poked its head tentatively toward the front seat, and whined.

The rage hit Kanell again as he reached under the dash, pulling the dangling wires there loose, killing the engine, only his voice now breaking the silence. He slammed his fist down hard on the dash, then in one fast move jerked his head to the right, eyes fixed on Evelyn. "*None* of it would hurt me if you hadn't called. You see? *I don't have any choice.*" He calmed instantly, smiling. "Now come on, you can help me dig up the child." Kanell stepped quickly around the car to the passenger door, leaning toward the glass, his voice exhilarated. "Let's go, let's go! The time bandit's at work, let's *go!*"

Englander spoke quietly, with anguish. "God help us, when the child is free, we've got to do something, we . . . "

"*Open the goddamn door now!*" Kanell screamed. For the first time they saw the gun. In the soft light, the gold barrel looked a dark brown. *God help us.* Evelyn turned her eyes from Englander and began to fumble for the thin handle which would open the door and deliver her to the madman. As she pulled the handle, Kanell yanked the door open and stepped around it, the barrel of the gun pushing into Evelyn's side. She closed her eyes and for an instant started to collapse, all of the strength leaving as quickly as a short breath. She leaned over the cane. Lane put his right arm around her waist and lifted, his eyes trying to meet hers. She was smiling, small tears lining her eyelids. "*I'm okay,* I'm okay," she said rapidly. She looked to the ground, stumbling in the dark.

Kanell walked behind them; two old people, arms around each other, as if they were taking a fine-night's walk in the park. They looked so funny. Old people were funny. Kanell's raucous laugh caused Evelyn to pull tighter to Lane. She looked up a moment, trying to pierce through the darkness, but the tall trees sent shadows over the dirt path, moving shadows, which intensified the blackness.

"Just a little bit more and then we'll dig up the kid. Children are useful, don't you think?" Kanell's tone was light, carefree. They did not answer. "You know, I had to kill my dog; a car squashed it flat as a damn hoecake. *Turn here.*" They paused at a small footpath, but the barrel of the gun, rammed hard in Evelyn's back, made them move again. Evelyn could not see the rough path, her cane tip feeling the way tentatively, as a blind person walks. His voice began to break. "I *loved* that dog." He paused as they came to the end of the small path. "But I had to kill it . . . *Look at me.* . . ." They turned to face him. In the darkness, his body had no depth, only the form of a dark gray cardboard cutout. "I *had* to. You have to do things you don't want to if you're going to be *somebody.*" He dropped his hands to his side. "Well. Here we are."

"Where's the shovel?" Evelyn asked the question. He did not understand.

"What shovel?"

"There isn't a child, is there?"

"Does that matter now?"

"Yes, it does," Evelyn said with conviction, pointing her cane straight up in the air, letting it slip through her hand until the dirt-caked end was in her grip, and then with all of the strength that mortal fear and anger could bring, Evelyn Wade swung the cane. The handle of the cane, hard wood, shaped just like a hammer, rammed between Rick Kanell's legs. His mouth opened, and he doubled over, pitched to his knees, his hands going tightly to his crotch.

Evelyn started to fall, both of her hands gripping Lane's arm, bringing bruises there. The cane dropped to the ground, and bounced lightly as it landed on an oak root.

"*Get the gun!*" Englander fell to his knees, hands moving forward fast, wrapping around Kanell's hands, the gun forced down. Kanell would not release it.

"*Evelyn!*"

You can't bend over to pick things up from the ground when your hip is made of steel and Teflon, but Evelyn tried to reach the cane. Straining forward, she tripped over the root and landed on her right shoulder, rolled to the left, pushed with her right hand on the root, and gripped the cane again. She sat up on the ground, holding the cane as an awkward girl might hold a baseball bat. Evelyn hit Kanell first on the back, tearing flesh there, and then as she steadied herself she hit him on the neck and the very top of the head, as though driving a nail fast into wood. He collapsed, and as his body slumped forward Evelyn hit him again on the neck, with such force that the cane snapped in two. She was crying now.

"*I've got the gun!*" Englander crawled to her, his breathing deep and loud and short.

"Are we okay?" She put her hand on his arm and repeated it. "Are we okay?"

"Yes."

"What are we going to do with him?"

Englander caught his breath for an instant before answering. "We've got to tie him up and walk out of here." He looked at her, seeing only a shadow. "Are you okay? Did you fall?"

"That's all right, all right. What can we tie him with?"

"Evelyn, get his belt!" Englander spoke as he pulled his own belt through the loops. It made a whooshing sound.

"I can't, Lane; I can't get down again." Evelyn began to tremble. The trembling was not from a fear of the moment, but was her body's delayed reaction to the terror of the last three minutes, only a hundred eighty seconds in a crisp November night.

"That's okay"—Englander's words were rushed as he turned Kanell's body. He saw the blood and looked away quickly, pulling Kanell's hands to the front, wrapping them with the belt—*it wasn't going to hold him*—then tied the belt quickly and rose again.

"If he comes to, that won't hold him. Let's get out of here!" Lane put his arm around Evelyn's waist and they began to walk, their eyes downward searching for safe steps, then flicking to the side and back. Englander carried the gun in his left hand, limp at his side, as they walked.

"Evelyn, are you sure you're okay? Are you sure?"

"I may have hurt my shoulder when I fell, but that's okay. Can you start the car? Do you know how to do that thing with the wires?" She stopped, a moment's rest to gather breath. Englander was holding her up slightly now, removing pressure from her feet. They stumbled but continued. In the faint light Evelyn looked pale, but there was no weakness in her eyes.

"I haven't wired a car since I wired my father's, and it was a *lot* easier then, but by God, I can try." His eyes cut to the back again, then forward. The car was in sight.

"We can lock ourselves in the car, if we have to—if you can't walk, and if I can't get it going. We've got the gun."

"No, no, I can walk. If we can't start it, I want to be away from here."

They walked twenty slow steps to the car. Evelyn collapsed on the passenger side, locking the door as it closed, a grimace of pain crossing her face. She lost the next seconds, as if she had stepped away from her body and the terror of that place and the madman, and then she was conscious of Lane leaning forward to the left of the steering wheel, hands fumbling with wires, door open, talking quietly to himself.

The mutt barked. It was standing on the backseat of the car. Evelyn glanced to the right, and as she turned, the madman put his face against the glass of the door, a maniacal grin on his face, blood dripping down his mouth and chin.

"*Lane!*"

He shut the door as Kanell yelled through the glass, "We've got to dig up the child! Don't forget the child!" He began to beat the window with the butt of a knife. "The child, we've got to dig up the child!"

She looked to Englander, the look of fright on her face meeting a bitter expression on his. "Will it start? *Will the car start?*" Kanell cracked the glass of her window with the poundings. "*Lane!*" How had the night started?

"I can't get the thing to work! Evelyn, lean down!"

She did so, covering her ears as Englander's right hand came behind her with the gun. The mutt barked again, and as it did

Englander fired. The cracked glass shattered into small pieces and the sound of the gun brought only silence to Evelyn. She did not hear the shot, and she could not hear Englander's voice anymore. She began to rock forward and back slightly. The madman was gone from sight.

She felt Englander's hands gently brushing away shards of glass. As he pulled her shoulders back, small drops of blood forming on her neck, the right hand of Rick Kanell grasped the lip of the door. The bullet had not touched him.

Follow me to Jesus. Buettner saw the bumper sticker, then he saw Kanell hanging onto the door with one hand. A black-and-white pulled in behind his car, and as May yelled, Buettner ran from the car, Preston behind him. Five police cars were now in Piedmont Park looking for the car that said "Follow me to Jesus." "I saw the damn car turn in less than five minutes ago," the man in the Burns Security car had yelled over his radio, "not five minutes ago."

"Stop! Police!" Buettner yelled. As he yelled, Rick Kanell turned and began to run toward him, knife held high, screaming.

Buettner fired one shot at close range, less than five feet. The bullet first entered the center of the chest, below the neck. It hit the breastbone, splitting it, diverting a now flatter piece of lead up two inches, splitting the bronchial tube and severing the artery touching the heart. Rick Kanell spun around, a pirouette. The force of the blast knocked him backward, literally lifted him from the ground. And then he fell. His head hit first, and then his neck bent backward and his chest touched the ground. He could see. But the air left him, draining out like the slow leak of a tire, never coming back in. His body settled. Rick Kanell thought of his aunt. How final was that memory. *She tumbled from the steps, her head landing in a mound of her own filth, her eyes wide open.*

Epilogue

"THAT'S better!"

Evelyn watched the croquet ball roll to the pin as she walked toward center court. Her cane moved quickly and lightly across the close-cropped grass. "You need to swing your mallet a little more like a pendulum, though," she continued as she held her cane out to Englander, letting go of it just as he handed her the mallet. The exchange was as practiced as two high-wire artists' midair feat. Evelyn's grip as she swung was awkward—her left hand was still in a sling from the events two weeks before—but the mallet hit the ball solidly, sending it straight to the wicket. She rubbed her shoulder gently as the ball rolled to a stop.

"Lane, I'm going to take this thing off when we get home. I don't care what the doctor said."

They walked together to the practice ball, her arm going to his rather than to the cane for support.

"Sure. And I'm going to win my first singles game tomorrow, right?"

She laughed. "Well, maybe I better keep it on a bit longer."

As they began to walk down the macadam path to the parking area, Evelyn's attention was attracted for a minute by an older car moving too fast and too loudly along the road that bordered the croquet court and eventually ran to the deep woods, less than a mile away, where the incident had happened. The car's bumper sticker said, "Jesus Lives." Though Evelyn Wade probably believed that more than ever these days, too many uncomfortable feelings came back to her. Her smile faltered.

"Lane . . ."

"Yes?"

"I don't really think I will ever be comfortable in this park again, you know."

They were at the car before he spoke, his hand going to the passenger door, then moving to her shoulder. "You really are afraid of my croquet potential, aren't you?"

Evelyn's smile was tighter this time, and for a few moments, as they drove toward 91 Myrtle, she was very quiet. Evelyn had been quieter since that night, and more nervous. God knows he was, too, Englander thought, but he was determined not to give in to that.

He cleared his throat. "What time are we supposed to be at the doctor's?"

"Three o'clock."

A psychiatrist specializing in victims of violence. Neither Evelyn nor Lane had wanted to go to him. They didn't see themselves as victims at first. But then the nightmares had started, and then Dean Buettner, on a call from Chicago, had told them how much good people like that could do. The night in Piedmont Park had bonded Evelyn Wade and Lane Englander to Buettner. The phone log at Chicago Auto Theft had many more calls to 91 Myrtle than normal follow-up routine would have required.

The calls at first had been about details that neither Evelyn nor Lane wanted to know and at the same time wanted to know desperately. Angie Weiner—paralyzed permanently because of brain damage caused in the car accident—had been flown to Chicago on a private air ambulance. "Anton—uh, a friend of Weiner's paid for it," Buettner had said. The friend was also paying for a private nursing home. Evelyn was glad the paralyzed man had a friend, she had said to Buettner. He had not responded.

Rick Kanell, his body at first claimed by Chicago Homicide, had finally been buried in a private cemetery near Green Meadow, Chicago. When Buettner had said that, Evelyn wanted very much to know if friends had been at that funeral, but she did not ask. In fact, several hundred people had attended his service, most of them respectable people in the building-supply business who attributed the confusing death and the media stories about Rick Kanell—those things couldn't be about the man they knew—to drug abuse. Wasn't it terrible how drugs could ruin a perfectly good man?

As Englander's car pulled in the drive to 91 Myrtle, Evelyn became lively again.

"Lane, in the spring you have to help me plant tomatoes and okra. That's all we have to plant, but we need to do that."

He parked next to the back door, the new double-action lock on it still shiny. Englander opened the door with his own key and, for an instant, he had to fight a desire to search the house before letting Evelyn in. When would that feeling go away? The doctor had assured them it would.

She turned on the water, and for a few minutes they did separate things. Englander went to the guest room. Most of his personal belongings were there now, including books and family pictures. His exercise mat was on the floor by the bed. The gold-plated derringer was in the dresser drawer.

Several shirts were piled on a chair. He grabbed them and walked back to the kitchen, pointing to the laundry room.

"Do you need to throw anything in?"

Evelyn needed to wash some personal things, but she said no. "Living in sin," as she told her friends with a smile, sounded awfully daring at first, but it was just a temporary arrangement, to keep her comfortable. It had very quickly become so much more than Evelyn would tell them or admit to herself. But that still didn't mean unmentionables were washed in the same load.

At six thirty, Lane opened the door to May Montez and Jay Preston, taking a wrapped plate from May as she entered.

"Lane, this tastes nothing like Evelyn's, but I tried. God knows I tried, and you had better have the poison control center's number right by the table when we eat it."

"You don't need it," he said. "Since I've been cooking some, we have a direct line."

"I have never seen so many nervous cooks in my life," Evelyn said as she moved quickly from her bedroom hall. She was using a new cane—brightly painted, carefully carved with her name on the grip—given to her by the two young people. She kissed them both.

The conversation at dinner centered at first on Dean Buettner, then on croquet. And then on the possibility of a trip together, maybe to a friend's retreat on Grand Bahama island.

"You know, I've been thinking about retiring from telephone research for a while," Evelyn said as she looked around the table. "I think the idea of a place with no phones sounds awfully nice."

No one at the table at 91 Myrtle disagreed with her.

ABOUT THE AUTHOR

REMAR SUTTON'S "Journal" is syndicated in over one hundred newspapers nationwide. George Plimpton called him "a journalist whose perceptions, wit, derring-do, irreverence, downright zaniness, and his skill at presenting all this, make him a very special American commodity." He is the author of the best-selling *Don't Get Taken Every Time* and the recently published *Body Worry. Long Lines* marks Mr. Sutton's debut as a fiction writer, and will be the first of an *Evelyn Wade* series. He divides his time between homes in Atlanta, Georgia, and the Bahamas.

MORE MYSTERIOUS PLEASURES

HAROLD ADAMS
The Carl Wilcox mystery series

MURDER	#501	$3.95
PAINT THE TOWN RED	#601	$3.95
THE MISSING MOON	#602	$3.95
THE NAKED LIAR	#420	$3.95
THE FOURTH WIDOW	#502	$3.50
THE BARBED WIRE NOOSE	#603	$3.95

TED ALLBEURY

THE SEEDS OF TREASON	#604	$3.95

ERIC AMBLER

HERE LIES: AN AUTOBIOGRAPHY	#701	$8.95

ROBERT BARNARD

A TALENT TO DECEIVE: AN APPRECIATION OF AGATHA CHRISTIE	#702	$8.95

EARL DERR BIGGERS
The Charlie Chan mystery series

THE HOUSE WITHOUT A KEY	#421	$3.95
THE CHINESE PARROT	#503	$3.95
BEHIND THAT CURTAIN	#504	$3.95
THE BLACK CAMEL	#505	$3.95
CHARLIE CHAN CARRIES ON	#506	$3.95
KEEPER OF THE KEYS	#605	$3.95

JAMES M. CAIN

THE ENCHANTED ISLE	#415	$3.95
CLOUD NINE	#507	$3.95

ROBERT CAMPBELL

IN LA-LA LAND WE TRUST	#508	$3.95

ANNE FINE
THE KILLJOY   #613 $3.95

DICK FRANCIS
THE SPORT OF QUEENS   #410 $3.95

JOHN GARDNER
THE GARDEN OF WEAPONS   #103 $4.50

BRIAN GARFIELD
DEATH WISH   #301 $3.95
DEATH SENTENCE   #302 $3.95
TRIPWIRE   #303 $3.95
FEAR IN A HANDFUL OF DUST   #304 $3.95

THOMAS GODFREY, ED.
MURDER FOR CHRISTMAS   #614 $3.95
MURDER FOR CHRISTMAS II   #615 $3.95

JOE GORES
COME MORNING   #518 $3.95

JOSEPH HANSEN
The Dave Brandstetter mystery series
EARLY GRAVES   #643 $3.95

NAT HENTOFF
THE MAN FROM INTERNAL AFFAIRS   #409 $3.95

PATRICIA HIGHSMITH
THE ANIMAL-LOVER'S BOOK
  OF BEASTLY MURDER   #706 $8.95
LITTLE TALES OF MISOGYNY   #707 $8.95
SLOWLY, SLOWLY IN THE WIND   #708 $8.95

DOUG HORNIG
WATERMAN   #616 $3.95
The Loren Swift mystery series
THE DARK SIDE   #519 $3.95

JANE HORNING
THE MYSTERY LOVERS' BOOK
  OF QUOTATIONS   #709 $9.95

P.D. JAMES/T.A. CRITCHLEY
THE MAUL AND THE PEAR TREE   #520 $3.95

BILL PRONZINI

GUN IN CHEEK	#714	$8.95
SON OF GUN IN CHEEK	#715	$9.95

BILL PRONZINI AND JOHN LUTZ

THE EYE	#408	$3.95

ROBERT J. RANDISI, ED.

THE EYES HAVE IT: THE FIRST PRIVATE EYE WRITERS OF AMERICA ANTHOLOGY	#716	$8.95
MEAN STREETS: THE SECOND PRIVATE EYE WRITERS OF AMERICA ANTHOLOGY	#717	$8.95

PATRICK RUELL

RED CHRISTMAS	#531	$3.50
DEATH TAKES THE LOW ROAD	#532	$3.50
DEATH OF A DORMOUSE	#636	$3.95

HANK SEARLS

THE ADVENTURES OF MIKE BLAIR	#718	$8.95

DELL SHANNON

The Lt. Luis Mendoza mystery series

CASE PENDING	#211	$3.95
THE ACE OF SPADES	#212	$3.95
EXTRA KILL	#213	$3.95
KNAVE OF HEARTS	#214	$3.95
DEATH OF A BUSYBODY	#315	$3.95
DOUBLE BLUFF	#316	$3.95
MARK OF MURDER	#417	$3.95
ROOT OF ALL EVIL	#418	$3.95

RALPH B. SIPPER, ED.

ROSS MACDONALD'S INWARD JOURNEY	#719	$8.95

JULIE SMITH

The Paul McDonald mystery series

TRUE-LIFE ADVENTURE	#407	$3.95
HUCKLEBERRY FIEND	#637	$3.95

The Rebecca Schwartz mystery series

TOURIST TRAP	#533	$3.95

ROSS H. SPENCER

THE MISSING BISHOP	#416	$3.50
MONASTERY NIGHTMARE	#534	$3.50

VINCENT STARRETT

THE PRIVATE LIFE OF SHERLOCK HOLMES	#720	$8.95

CHRIS WILTZ
The Neal Rafferty mystery series
A DIAMOND BEFORE YOU DIE   #645 $3.95

CORNELL WOOLRICH/LAWRENCE BLOCK
INTO THE NIGHT   #646 $3.95